A COUNTERFEIT HEART

SECRETS & SPIES SERIES

K. C. BATEMAN

978-1-7352313-0-3 –E-book ISBN

978-1-7352313-1-0 –Print ISBN

Cover Art: © Cora Graphics, Italy.

Cover photographs: © Period Images.

❀ Created with Vellum

"Love me or hate me. Both are in my favor . . . If you love me, I'll always be in your heart . . . If you hate me, I'll always be in your mind."

—Anon.

CHAPTER 1

BOIS DE VINCENNES, PARIS, 16TH APRIL 1816

*I*t didn't take long to burn a fortune.

"Don't throw it on like that! Fan the paper out. You need to let the air get to it."

Sabine de la Tour sent her best friend, Anton Carnaud, an exasperated glance and tossed another bundle of banknotes onto the fire. It smoldered, then caught with a bright flare, curling and charring to nothing in an instant. "That's all the francs. Pass me some rubles."

Another fat wad joined the conflagration. Little spurts of green and blue jumped up as the flames consumed the ink. The intensity of the fire heated her cheeks, so she stepped back and tilted her head to watch the glowing embers float up into the night sky. It was a fitting end, really. Almost like a funeral pyre, the most damning evidence of Philippe Lacorte, notorious French counterfeiter, going up in smoke. Sabine quelled the faintest twinge of regret.

She glanced over at Anton. "It feels strange, don't you think? Doing the right thing for once."

He shook his head morosely. "It feels wrong." He poked a pile of Austrian gulden into the fire with a stick. "Who in their right mind burns money? It's like taking a penknife to a Rembrandt."

Sabine nudged his shoulder, well used to his grumbling. "You know I'm right. If we spend it, we'll be no better than Napoleon. This is our chance to turn over a new leaf."

Anton added another sheaf of banknotes to the blaze with a pained expression. "I happen to like being a criminal," he grumbled. "Besides, we made all this money. Seems only fair we should get to spend it. No one would know. Your fakes are so good nobody can tell the difference. What's a few million francs in the grand scheme of things?"

"We'd know." Sabine frowned at him. "'Truth is the highest thing that man may keep.'"

Anton rolled his eyes. "Don't start quoting dead Greeks at me."

"That's a dead Englishman," she smiled wryly. "Geoffrey Chaucer."

Anton sniffed, unimpressed by anything that came from the opposite—and therefore wrong—side of the channel. He sprinkled a handful of assignats onto the flames. "You appreciate the irony of trying to be an honest forger, don't you?"

It was Sabine's turn to roll her eyes.

Anton shot her a teasing, pitying glance. "It's because you're half-*Anglais*. Everyone knows the English are mad. The French half of you knows what fun we could have. Think of it, *chérie*— ball gowns, diamonds, banquets!" His eyes took on a dreamy, faraway glow. "Women, wine, song!" He gave a magnificent Gallic shrug. "*Mais, non.* You listen to the English half. The half that is boring and dull and—"

"—law-abiding?" Sabine suggested tartly. "Sensible? The half that wants to keep my neck firmly attached to my shoulders instead of in a basket in front of the guillotine?"

She bit her lip as a wave of guilt assailed her. Anton was in danger of losing his head because of her. For years he'd protected her identity by acting as Philippe Lacorte's public representative. He'd dealt with all the unsavory characters who'd wanted her forger's skills while she'd remained blissfully anonymous. Even the man who'd overseen the emperor's own counterfeiting operation, General Jean Malet, hadn't known the real name of the elusive forger he'd employed. He'd never seen Sabine as anything more than an attractive assistant at the print shop in Rue du Pélican.

Now, with Napoleon exiled on the island of St. Helena and Savary, his feared head of secret police, also banished, General Malet was the only one who knew about the existence of the fake fortune the emperor had amassed to fill his coffers.

The fortune Sabine had just liberated.

Anton frowned into the flames. The pink glow highlighted his chiseled features and Sabine studied him dispassionately. She knew him too well to harbor any romantic feelings about him, but there was no doubt he had a very handsome profile. Unfortunately, it was a profile that General Malet could recognize all too easily.

As if reading her mind, Anton said, "Speaking of guillotines, Malet would gladly see me in a tumbril. He's out for blood. And I'm his prime suspect."

"Which is why we're getting you out of here," Sabine said. "The boat to England leaves at dawn. We have enough money to get us as far as London."

Anton gave a frustrated huff and pointed at the fire. "In case you hadn't noticed, we have a pile of money right—"

She shot him a warning scowl. "No. We are not using the fakes. It's high time we started doing things legally. This English lord's been trying to engage Lacorte's services for months. One job for him and we'll be able to pay for your passage to Boston. You'll be safe from Malet forever."

"It could be a trap," Anton murmured darkly. "This Lovell says he wants to employ Lacorte, but we've been on opposite sides of the war for the past ten years. The English can't be trusted."

Sabine let out a faint, frustrated sigh. It was a risk, to deliver herself into the arms of the enemy, to seek out the one man she'd spent months avoiding. Her heart beat in her throat at the thought of him. Richard Hampden, Viscount Lovell. She'd seen him only once, weeks ago, but the memory was seared upon her brain.

He, of anyone, had come closest to unmasking her. He'd followed Lacorte's trail to her doorstep, like a bloodhound after a fox. Anton had recognized her pursuer and hissed a warning; Sabine had barely had time to hide behind the backroom door and press her eye to a gap in the wood before the bell above the entrance had tinkled and *he'd* entered the print shop.

It had been almost dark outside; the flickering streetlamps had cast long shadows along Rue du Pélican. Sabine had squinted, trying to make out his features, but all she could see was that he was tall; he ducked to enter the low doorway. She raised her eyebrows. So this was the relentless Lord Lovell.

Not for the first time she cursed her shortsightedness. Too many hours of close work meant that anything over ten feet away was frustratingly blurry. He moved closer, farther into the shop —and into knee-weakening, stomach-flipping focus.

Sabine caught her breath. All the information she'd gleaned about her foe from Anton's vague, typically male attempts at description had in no way prepared her for the heart-stopping, visceral reality.

Technically, Anton had been correct. Richard Hampden was over six feet tall with medium-brown hair. But those basic facts failed to convey the sheer magnetic presence of his lean, broad-shouldered frame. There was no spare fat around his hips, no unhealthy pallor to his skin. He moved like water, with a liquid grace that suggested quietly restrained power, an animal at the very peak of fitness.

Anton had guessed his age as between twenty-eight and thirty-five. Certainly, Hampden was no young puppy; his face held the hard lines and sharp angles of experience rather than the rounded look of boyhood.

Sabine studied the elegant severity of his dark blue coat, the pale knee breeches outlining long, muscular legs. There was nothing remarkable in the clothes themselves to make him stand out in a crowd, and yet there was something about him that commanded attention. That drew the eye and held it.

Her life often hinged on the ability to correctly identify dangerous men. Every sense she possessed told her that the man talking with Anton was very dangerous indeed.

Sabine pressed her forehead to the rough planks and swore softly. The Englishman turned, almost as if he sensed her lurking behind the door, and everything inside her stilled. Something—an instant of awareness, almost of recognition—shot through her as she saw his face in full. Of all the things she'd been prepared for, she hadn't envisaged this: Viscount Lovell was magnificent.

And then he'd turned his attention back to Anton, and she'd let out a shaky breath of relief.

She'd dreamed of him ever since. Disturbing, jumbled dreams in which she was always running, he pursuing. She'd wake the very instant she was caught, her heart pounding in a curious mix of panic and knotted desire.

Sabine shook her head at her own foolishness. It was just her luck to conceive an instant attraction to the least suitable man in Europe. The thought of facing him again made her shiver with equal parts anticipation and dread, but he was the obvious answer to her current dilemma. He had money; she needed funds. *Voilà tout.*

At least now she was prepared. One of the basic tenets of warfare was "know thine enemy," after all.

Sabine drew her cloak more securely around her shoulders

and watched Anton feed the rest of the money to the flames. The embers fluttered upward like a cloud of glowing butterflies.

When this was all over she would be like a phoenix. Philippe Lacorte would disappear and Sabine de la Tour would emerge from the ashes to reclaim the identity she'd abandoned eight years ago. She would live a normal life. But not yet. There was still too much to do.

Sabine brushed off her skirts and picked up the bag she'd packed for traveling. There was something rather pathetic in the fact that her whole life fit into one single valise, but she squared her shoulders and glanced over at Anton. "Come on, let's go. Before someone sees the smoke and decides to investigate."

They couldn't go home, to the print shop on Rue du Pélican. Her heart constricted as she recalled the scene that had greeted them earlier. Malet had already ripped the place apart looking for "his" money. Her stomach had given a sickening lurch as she'd taken in the carnage. Books pulled from the shelves, paintings ripped from the walls, canvases torn. Old maps shredded, drawers pulled out and upended. Their home, her sanctuary for the past eight years, had been utterly ransacked.

But there had been triumph amid the loss. Malet had found neither Anton nor the money. And if Sabine had anything to do with it, he never would.

Anton hefted the two bags of English banknotes that had been spared the flames as Sabine turned her back on Paris. For the first time in eight long years she was free.

It was time to track down Lord Lovell.

CHAPTER 2

THREE DAYS LATER, LONDON, 10:45 P.M

*S*abine pressed her hand to her stomach in a vain attempt to quell her nerves. She couldn't back out now; she'd come to this imposing townhouse for the sole purpose of propositioning the man inside. She straightened her shoulders and took a calming breath. She was Europe's greatest forger. She could fake anything. Even a confidence she was far from feeling.

Number five Upper Brook Street was located in the exclusive, aristocratic enclave of Mayfair. To the east loomed the tree-lined railings of Grosvenor Square. To the west carriages rattled past on Park Lane, and beyond that lay the expansive darkness of Hyde Park.

Even at this late hour the streets were busy. Linkboys, with flaming torches of pitch and tow, ran alongside sedan chairs conveying people to and from their evening's entertainments or followed pedestrians to light their way home in exchange for a farthing.

Sabine mounted the shallow flight of steps in front of the house. The knocker was so shiny she could see her own face reflected in it; the snarling lion's nose distorted her features so she appeared no more than a blur of dark hair and dark eyes. The heavy brass fell against the black wood with a crack that sounded like gunfire.

An elderly male servant answered, dressed in dark livery. If he was surprised to see a lone woman on his master's doorstep at almost eleven o'clock in the evening, he gave no outward sign. Clearly he was both well trained and discreet. Or perhaps it was not such an unusual occurrence, Sabine thought wryly.

He raised bushy gray brows. "May I help you, madam?"

Sabine suppressed a smile. Apparently twenty-four was too ancient to still be addressed as "mademoiselle." She strove to recall her mother's polite, English tones. "You can indeed. I am here to see Viscount Lovell."

"And who might I inform him is calling?" The butler's impassive countenance gave nothing away.

Sabine tilted her head. "Someone whose acquaintance he has been seeking for a very long time. Please give him this." She pulled the letter she'd prepared from her cloak.

The butler took it and she waited to see if he would usher her inside or make her wait upon the doorstep. Perhaps he would send her around the back to the servants' entrance. For some reason the thought made her smile.

Instead he opened the door and indicated for her to step inside. "If you would care to wait here, madam, I will inform his lordship of your visit."

Sabine gave an imperious nod, as if it was no more than she expected. "Please do. I am quite certain he will want to see me."

She glanced around the hallway as the butler strode away. It was suitably grand for the residence of a viscount, with a black-and-white-tiled floor and an imposing staircase curving toward the upper levels. The dark mahogany doors leading off the hallway were all closed. She had not been anywhere so elegant in years, but she would not be overawed. She had lived in a house as grand as this herself, once.

A thin under-footman, emerging from below stairs, regarded

her suspiciously, as if she might be thinking of stealing something. Sabine watched in amusement as he took in her appearance, silently assessing her net worth and social position with one glance.

The dismissive curl of his lip told her his conclusion. No doubt her accent pronounced her as one of the hated French, and he clearly supposed her mistress material, a female of the *canaille*. His eyes flicked insultingly to her stomach and she suppressed another smile. Did he suppose she was enceinte? Come to inform his lordship of her delicate condition? Ha! Sabine caught his eye and returned his insolent glance with one of her own.

He dropped his eyes first.

* * *

"You have a visitor, my lord."

Richard Hampden, Viscount Lovell, glanced at the ornate gilt clock on the mantelpiece and raised one dark eyebrow at his majordomo.

"At this hour?" The clock showed five minutes to eleven. He and Raven had only stopped into the library for a glass of brandy before heading out to White's.

The elderly servant bowed. "A female, my lord."

Richard narrowed his eyes at his butler's studied lack of intonation—and careful choice of noun. "What kind of female? A lady? Or a woman? Because it's an important distinction, as you well know."

The servant drew himself up, his impassive countenance belied by the amused twinkle in his eye. "It's not for me to say, sir. I wouldn't dare to be so bold as to venture an opinion. Suffice to say that she is unaccompanied."

A smile twitched Richard's lips. "Hodges, you are the model of diplomacy. Castlereagh could have done with you at the

9

Congress of Vienna. Say no more. No lady would visit a gentleman's house alone—which makes it all the more interesting."

His best friend, William Ravenwood, Marquis of Ormonde, frowned. "If you're expecting a woman, Richard, I'm off."

"I'm not expecting anyone." Richard took a sip of his excellent brandy. "I ended things with Caro Williams a fortnight ago. And even if I hadn't, I never entertain my mistresses here."

Hodges was still loitering by the door. He cleared his throat and offered forth a folded missive. "She seemed confident that you would see her. She asked me to give you this."

Richard set down his glass and took the paper just as Hodges spoke again. "And though she speaks English, my lord, her accent is decidedly French."

Raven raised his brows at the butler's disapproving tones. "French, eh?" He leaned forward and tried to read over Richard's shoulder. "What does it say? Is it a love letter?"

Richard opened the paper and froze.

"What is it?" Raven asked.

Richard gave a disbelieving chuckle. "It's an invitation. To call here tonight, at eleven o'clock. From myself, apparently."

He turned the paper around so Raven could inspect the perfect copy of Richard's own signature at the bottom of the page.

Raven grinned. "How enterprising. I'll say this, Richard, the lengths to which women will go to get your attention are extraordinary."

Richard half laughed, half groaned. The subject of his popularity with the fair sex was one he found alternately amusing and distasteful.

"I suppose word's got out about you giving Caro her *congé*." Raven chuckled with all the smug satisfaction of a happily married man blissfully un-pursued by a monstrous regiment of women.

Richard scowled at him. "I had to—you know my rules. Three months, no longer. No virgins. No wives. No exceptions."

As a system it had worked exceptionally well for the past few years. None of the women with whom he consorted harbored any false expectation of marriage. Both sides entered into the dalliance knowing it was based on mutual exclusivity and enjoyment, and when it was over they parted ways as friends. He'd never met a woman he couldn't walk away from.

The only problem was, whenever he finished with one woman there was a mad, undignified scramble to be the next in line. It had become even worse since his father inherited the earldom. Richard had been elevated to Viscount Lovell, heir to the Earl of Lindsey, and the women had become even more attentive. The lack of a decent challenge was downright depressing. And despite his very publicly expressed preferences, every last one of them seemed convinced she'd be the exception he'd marry.

He glanced over at Raven. "Is this your idea of a joke?"

Raven held up his hands. "It's nothing to do with me, I swear. I've no idea who she is."

Richard studied the handwriting closely. If he didn't know better he'd have sworn it really was his own signature. Who on earth would have the audacity to present him with what was quite obviously a forged note? And where the hell had they managed to get a copy of his signature in the first place?

His pulse accelerated in anticipation. Nothing like a new challenge to liven things up.

Hodges was still hovering, awaiting instruction.

"Did she say anything else?" Richard asked.

"She did not, sir."

Richard rose to his feet with a smile. He'd been so bored recently. Perhaps his mystery guest could cure his current state of ennui. "Well, then. We'd better see what she wants."

CHAPTER 3

*T*he disapproving servant took Sabine's cloak with every evidence of distaste, as if its shabbiness were offensive. Or contagious. He tried to relieve her of her traveling bag, too, but she retained a firm grip on the handle and scowled at him. He obviously decided a struggle for possession was beneath his dignity and let her keep it.

The door to her right clicked open. Two men stood in the doorway, both equally handsome, but she dismissed the black-haired one almost at once. It was the second face that commanded her attention. The face that had haunted her dreams for weeks.

Richard Hampden's quizzical gaze met hers, and she muttered a phrase more suited to the gutters of Paris than a fashionable London townhouse. Her pulse hammered in her throat, and for the first time she understood what Anton had meant when he'd said that Lord Lovell had "wolf eyes." The unusual amber-brown color was breathtaking. And extremely unnerving.

On the journey from France she'd convinced herself that she'd exaggerated his physical magnetism. He couldn't possibly be as handsome and as intimidating as she recalled. She'd built him up in her mind as some unparalleled demigod and expected the reality would prove utterly disappointing.

She hadn't exaggerated a thing. If anything, she'd forgotten the full effect of that long, lean body, that automatic air of command. Her whole body prickled with alarm.

The dark-haired man sized her up in one long, speculative glance and executed a graceful bow. "Madame." He moved past her and accepted his coat from the insolent servant with a murmur of thanks. "I'll bid you good night, Richard. Enjoy the rest of your evening."

His voice held laughter, but Sabine barely heard him. She was rooted to the spot, unable to look away from the tall man framed in the doorway.

The front door closed with a click. Somewhere, a clock chimed eleven.

Richard Hampden's dark eyebrows lifted. He studied her with a lazy smile and held up the invitation she'd provided between two long fingers.

"Congratulations, madame. You have my undivided attention." He leaned back against the doorjamb and indicated for her to precede him into the room with a sweep of his arm. "Do come in."

Sabine's pulse hammered in her chest, but she squeezed her hands into fists and stepped forward. She was Philippe Lacorte. She thrived on danger. This was nothing.

He didn't move aside as she approached. She brushed past him, determined not to falter, and her right arm made a brief, tingling contact with his own. She ignored the unnerving sensation and strode purposefully into the center of the room. A brief glance at her surroundings—a library, with tall bookshelves and assorted chairs and tables scattered about—was all she managed to note before the door clicked closed.

She turned to face her target, and immediately stepped back. She hadn't heard him move, but he was suddenly right in front of her; his broad chest and shoulders blocked her exit. She had to tilt her head back to see his face. Her stomach fluttered, a queer panicked lightness, and she took another step back, then stopped herself. Retreat was bad. Men like this one, like Savary and Malet, had ruled her life for far too long. She was here to take control of her destiny.

* * *

THE GIRL—NO, woman, Richard amended; she was closer to twenty-five than sixteen—looked up and met his gaze and for one brief, unpleasant moment his brain completely ceased to function.

Thankfully, the sensation only lasted a moment. A sharp stab of familiarity replaced it, like a punch to the gut, and his body heated in pure, visceral recognition. He knew her. And yet he'd never seen her before in his life. He'd never have forgotten that face.

Her features were delicate, gamine. Black brows stood out against the paleness of her skin and sooty lashes made her eyes seem almost navy. Her hair was secured at the nape, but a few strands glistened with a silvery sheen of mist from outside. Her lips made him think of hot, sweaty sheets. Maybe she looked familiar because he'd conjured her in his most erotic fantasies?

Catch her. Keep her. Mine.

Richard suppressed a frown. His instincts had saved him from more hair-raising situations than he cared to count, but in this instance something had gone seriously awry.

He experienced a sharp pang of disappointment. She had to be a tart, coming here alone at this hour. How long had she been in the trade? Not long, he'd guess. She didn't have the weary look that characterized most of the whores he knew. Either that or she was a damn fine actress. Maybe that was her talent: to make every man think he was the first to touch that flawless skin, to taste that soft pink mouth.

He never engaged in liaisons with the demimonde. Never needed to. London's merriest widows and most accomplished courtesans flocked to him—whether he wanted them to or not. Still, he was bloody tempted by this one. She was beautiful, but not in the common way. There was something elfin about her appearance, almost fey, and he had the sudden, bizarre thought that if he moved too quickly she would simply vanish into thin air.

Her clothing was modest for a courtesan, though. There was nothing flamboyant about the dark blue dress, no frothy ruffles or frills. He couldn't see if she wore any rings—one small hand clutched the handle of a valise, the other was hidden in the folds of her skirts—but she wore no necklace or earrings. No adornment of any kind, in fact.

Richard frowned. She held herself too proudly to be a servant. There was no deference in the way she met his gaze, only a guarded watchfulness. His interest increased. An enigma.

She still hadn't said a word. Was she aware of the effect she had on him? Did she expect him to start stammering like an imbecile? He wouldn't. He'd been fifteen the last time a woman's beauty had reduced him to speechlessness.

She faced him squarely and tilted her chin. "You are Richard Hampden? Lord Lovell?"

Her accent was French, as Hodges had said. Her voice low and husky, with a slight musical inflection. A frisson ran down his spine at the way she said his name. Not the English pronunciation, with its precise, clipped syllables, but the French way. Smoother, more liquid; *Ree-shard 'Amp-den.* The way it rolled off her tongue was a caress in itself.

It was high time he took charge of this situation. He lifted one brow in a manner his younger sister, Heloise, assured him was both irritating and highly condescending.

"Indeed I am. But I don't believe I've had the pleasure, Miss . . ."

She bent her knees and set the valise down on the floor. "De la Tour," she said briskly. "Sabine de la Tour."

"Well, Miss de la Tour. Given your unaccompanied state and the lateness of the hour, I assume you're here to proposition me."

He waited to see how she would react to that outrageous pronouncement.

Her eyebrows rose and the corners of her lips tilted upward. "That's quite the assumption."

He shrugged. "I've been blessed with a combination of face, form, title, and fortune that seems irresistible. And I'm not sure what other conclusion I'm supposed to draw. Do you think it wise to visit a bachelor's lodgings alone at this hour of the night?"

She inclined her head, and he was momentarily distracted by the twinkle of amusement in her navy eyes. "Your concern for my welfare is touching. But I assure you, I'm perfectly capable of defending myself should the need arise. I have a pistol in my pocket, and I will not hesitate to use it if anything you do alarms me."

Richard glanced down. One of her small hands was indeed hidden in her skirts. Well, well. He felt a spurt of both anger and amusement. She was foolish to trust such a defense. He could disarm her long before she fired, if he wished. But he'd allow her to keep the fantasy of safety. For now.

"I'm afraid you've had a wasted journey. I'm not in the market for a mistress. And even if I were, I prefer to do the chasing myself."

She smiled, as if at some private joke. "I don't doubt it. You strike me as a man who is relentless in pursuit."

She raked him with a teasing, appraising glance, and for the first time he understood the acute discomfort young ladies at Almack's must experience when men subjected them to a leisurely inspection through their quizzing glasses. Her almost-innocent gaze slid over his shoulders and chest and his body heated in response. Her eyes dropped lower. Far from shying away from the front of his breeches, she calmly took in the whole of him until she reached the mirror shine of his boots. A hot wave of chagrin crept up the back of his neck. *Cheeky minx.*

She brought her gaze back to his, and there was mocking laughter in her voice. "I am tempted . . . but I'm here for an entirely different reason."

"And that is?"

"You were partly correct in your assessment. I do want your money. But not in exchange for my body. I have something you want far more."

He doubted it. His stupid body couldn't seem to think of anything it wanted more than hers wrapped around it, his hands on all that silky skin, his mouth on her—

He swallowed to clear his dry throat. She was still talking.

"I'm not a whore. Or at least, not in the conventional sense. I certainly have skills for which men will pay good money, but my particular talents only appeal to a very small minority."

The secretive little smile at the corner of her lips taunted him. He imagined putting his own mouth there, to wipe it off. What the hell kind of talents was she referring to?

The smile deepened mischievously. "I would hazard to say that you, Lord Lovell, are perhaps one of only ten men in the whole of England who could truly appreciate my skills. And pay accordingly."

She tilted her head, and he tried to ignore the smooth line of her throat the movement exposed. He really needed to engage a new mistress soon. Tonight, preferably. A fortnight's celibacy was turning him into an imbecile.

He narrowed his eyes. "And what skills might those be?"

She ignored the question. "I'm here because you have been seeking a certain Philippe Lacorte."

CHAPTER 4

*R*ichard stilled, jolted from his erotic perusal of her mouth. "How do you know that?"

"Why do you want Lacorte?" she countered.

He raised his brows at her demanding tone. "For the same reason I buy my boots from Hoby and my coats from Weston. I only employ the best."

His shirts were the finest linen. He paid the extortionate sum of ten guineas apiece for his cravats. And Philippe Lacorte was undoubtedly the best counterfeiter in Europe.

"How nice for Monsieur Lacorte," she said dryly. "I'm sure he should be flattered by your high opinion."

"I'd tell him to his face, but he's a very elusive man."

She gave an elegant lift of the shoulder. "Perhaps he did not wish to be found. Especially by the British secret service."

Richard suppressed another jolt of shock. Only a select few were privy to the fact that he worked as an agent for the crown. How had she known? Was she a French agent? He'd never heard of a female operative matching her description, but that wasn't to say it was impossible. What else did she know?

"Lacorte's the greatest forger in France. Or Europe, for that matter," he said carefully. "He's been a thorn in our side for years."

"Ah. Then perhaps you're trying to find him in order to kill him?"

He frowned. "No! We don't want him harmed. Far from it. The man's an artist. His skills are too valuable to waste by elimination. We want him to work for us."

Those dark brows lifted. "Indeed? And what makes you think he would work for you, monsieur? You are—or at least, you were until a few months ago—the enemy. Our countries have been at war, in case you hadn't noticed, for the past ten years."

She waved the hand that wasn't in her skirts to encompass the undeniable luxury of their surroundings. Her lip curled a little scornfully. "Perhaps you haven't noticed, living in such a place."

Richard felt his jaw tighten at her accusation. "I noticed. Believe me, madame, none of us have been unaffected by the war."

She shot him a disbelieving look, but let it pass.

He settled himself against the edge of his desk and tried to look nonthreatening. He wanted her to relax, to let down her guard. "Lacorte has no particular political allegiance, as far as I can tell. He provided as many forgeries for Napoleon as he did for émigrés fleeing the country. We know he created fake passports and travel documents."

"That is true. Monsieur Lacorte has worked for royalists and Bonapartists, Jacobins and Chouans. He does what he must to survive."

Richard crossed his arms over his chest. "So it seems to me that Monsieur Lacorte can be bought."

She smiled. "Indeed. Every man has his price. Or woman, for that matter."

Richard frowned at her soft insinuation. Was she a whore after all? The lower half of his anatomy urged him to pay whatever price she asked. His brain reminded him to ignore any suggestions made by his stupid crotch. "Why do you want to know about Lacorte? Did he send you?"

"Let's say I am in his confidence. Tell me more about the work you want him to do. And why? Does Britain not have her own perfectly competent counterfeiters?"

"Two reasons. Firstly, if Lacorte's working for us, then he's not out there working for someone else."

Her smile was distracting. "Ah. The old 'keep your friends close and your enemies closer' tactic. You want to keep an eye on Monsieur Lacorte."

"Indeed we do. The second reason is that we know he's already forged letters from Napoleon. I want him to do it again."

That surprised her. A slight crease formed between those dark brows. "Letters from the emperor? Why would you need them? He's locked away on St. Helena now."

"But his supporters still litter Europe. The network of spies he put in place over here is still active, working with British traitors who wish to prompt a revolution of their own." Richard shook his head. "I've been tracking a group of antimonarchists here in London. I want Lacorte's forgeries to lure them out."

"Hmm."

He shot her a calculating glance. "You must mean a great deal to Lacorte if he trusts you to act as his ambassador."

She regarded him warily. "Perhaps."

"So what's to stop me from detaining you?" he asked softly. "Then he'd be forced to come himself."

Her eyes twinkled. "You mean apart from my little pistol?"

"Apart from that."

She seemed annoyingly unperturbed by his implied threat. Her storm-dark eyes held his without fear, even with a hint of challenge. "You can hold me hostage if you wish, my lord, but I assure you, if you detain me Lacorte will never come."

"Doesn't he care for you?" he goaded. "What are you to him? His wife? A lover?"

She gave an elegant little snort. "I am no man's wife, monsieur, nor any man's lover. But you could certainly say that Monsieur Lacorte and I are intimately acquainted."

Richard quelled a growl at her deliberately obtuse answer. Had she been Lacorte's lover in the past, then? He ignored the little lift in his mood at the thought that she might be available now. Stupid groin. He had to—

"I am Philippe Lacorte."

Richard blinked. "I'm sorry, what did you say?"

She pursed her lips. "I said, I am the one you've been looking for. I am Philippe Lacorte."

* * *

THE ARROGANT DEVIL raised his brows in patent disbelief. Those tiger eyes bored into hers.

"You?" he drawled. "Philippe Lacorte? Really?"

He drew the last word out to its full extent and Sabine suppressed a frustrated huff.

"Such an attitude is precisely the reason I chose to work under an assumed name. Why is it that men cannot conceive of a mere woman being sufficiently skilled?"

She resisted the impulse to roll her eyes. She'd faced such idiocy for years, proved herself time and again in Paris.

Hampden settled himself more comfortably against the desk, as if preparing to listen to an entertaining fiction. "Forgive my skepticism, but you must admit it seems unlikely. In the entire history of counterfeiting I can't think of a single female of note."

She took a breath to control her simmering temper. *Condescending idiot.* "Of course you can't," she said sweetly. "You've only ever heard of the failures, the ones who were prosecuted. The men. The women were too good to get caught." She fixed him with a rebellious glare, just daring him to contradict her.

He inclined his head, vastly amused. "All right, I'll play. Let us suppose, just for a second, that you are Lacorte. Explain this." He lifted the forged invitation and waved it at her. "If you're responsible for this, where did you get my signature to copy?"

"Three months ago you left a message for Lacorte in Paris, at a print shop in Rue du Pélican. You signed it."

His eyes narrowed. "Was that you? That night? In the back room?"

Heat bloomed under her skin but she lifted her chin. "It might have been."

He muttered something that sounded like a curse. "Well, much as it pains me to contradict a lady," the tone of his voice betrayed that falsehood, "I don't believe you." He recrossed his long legs and she tried to ignore the distraction of the play of muscles under his tight breeches. "You say you're Lacorte. I say, prove it."

CHAPTER 5

*S*abine inclined her head. "I assumed you would require proof, of course."

She hesitated. She needed to loosen her grip on the pistol in her pocket if they were to proceed, but she was wary of relinquishing her advantage. Hampden's relaxed stance against the desk did little to diminish his intimidating physical presence. But what other option did she have? She forced her fingers to release the stock and let the weapon drop to the bottom of the pocket she'd sewn into her skirts. Its slight weight tugged on the fabric, and she had no doubt that Hampden would have noticed. He'd notice everything.

She withdrew the two banknotes she'd prepared.

Hampden uncrossed his arms and stood. Sabine tensed, but he merely stepped aside to give her room to use the desk. She approached him warily, unfolded the notes, and placed them side by side on the dark green leather top, acutely aware of his big body and hard shoulder right next to hers as he turned around.

She caught the scent of him, something masculine and subtle, a mossy base note overlaid with leather and grass and heat. Her knees turned to water. She took little sips of air in through her mouth, when what she really wanted to do was bury her nose into the fabric of his coat and fill her lungs with the delicious smell.

She bit the inside of her mouth. *Concentrate on the notes, idiot!* She had to make him accept that she was Lacorte.

"At first glance these two banknotes look identical, do they not?" she managed.

Hampden glanced down and she stole the opportunity to study his profile. Straight nose. Intriguing little white line of a scar just beneath his left ear. The fine, clean grain of his skin. He leaned forward, resting his weight on his hands. Strong hands, large and capable-looking. They would encircle her waist if he were to—No. She would not become distracted.

He took his time, studying both notes with intense scrutiny. "They do look the same," he conceded.

"Except one of them is real and one is fake."

Sabine watched with rising amusement as he picked both notes up and made another thorough inspection. He tested the paper, then rubbed the printed design to see if any ink came off on his hands. He held both of them up to the light to check the watermark in the paper. He sniffed them, although quite what he expected to determine by that, she had no idea, unless he was trying to detect the scent of fresh ink.

Sabine suppressed a sigh. Did he really think her such an amateur? She'd deliberately included one note that was more creased than the other. Would he be swayed by that factor?

After a full two minutes he stepped back and turned to her. "They still look identical to me," he finally admitted. "Can you tell the difference?"

She gave a snort of amusement. "Of course! That's like asking a mother if she can recognize her own children in a crowd." She pulled the right-hand note toward her and tapped it with her finger. "This one is the fake."

He raised a condescending brow, picked it up, and studied it again. "How can you be sure?"

"Admit it," she said confidently, "there is nothing that would alert you, is there?"

He narrowed his eyes. "How do I know they're not both real?"

She smiled at his suspicion. No agent of the British government would be a fool. "So cynical," she chided. "They're not. I made the fake one myself. Do you have a magnifying glass?"

"Yes."

He circled the desk and she breathed a sigh of relief as he put a little distance between them. He opened a drawer, took out a small brass-handled lens, and handed it to her. She took care not to touch his fingers as she took it.

"So now I will let you in on a secret. This note contains a mistake. A deliberate one, I might add. When I engraved the printing plates, I added one detail that would differentiate my fakes from real notes." She smiled. "Cartographers do the same thing to protect their work. They insert a completely imagined road—sometimes a little alleyway, sometimes an entire town—into their map as a safeguard to prove when they have been copied. 'Paper towns,' they're called."

He rounded the desk again and she tried to ignore the breathless sensation that standing so close to him engendered.

"And you have done the same thing on a banknote?"

She pointed to the small vignette that made up one corner of the inked design. "There, by the base of that tree. Do you see the initials? Hidden in the roots. *P.L.,* for Philippe Lacorte."

He leaned down and looked through the magnifier, then pulled the second note over to check the corresponding corner.

"You will not find initials on that one," she said confidently.

He lowered the glass and straightened. The look on his face was hard to define and her stomach clenched in dread. Was he surprised? Outraged? About to clap her in irons?

"That is perhaps the most arrogant thing I've ever seen," he stated coolly.

Her spirits plummeted.

And then the corners of his lips tilted upward. One cheek creased into a disarmingly boyish dimple that made her heart beat heavy in her chest. "I'm impressed."

Sabine inclined her head as relief rushed over her in a heady wave. "Unless you know to look for those letters, there is no way to tell my notes from the real thing."

He turned to face her fully and she had to tilt her head to look into his face again. His chest was only inches from hers, but she didn't dare step back. To do so would hint at weakness.

"This still doesn't prove that you're Lacorte," he said. "It just shows you know what to look for in one of his counterfeits. You could be a fence, an intermediary who got hold of a fake note and discovered how to spot the difference." His gaze focused on her face and she found it hard to breathe. "I don't believe in taking things at face value." His eyes narrowed accusingly. "However enchanting that face might be."

Her lips parted in astonishment and she felt an unwelcome flush rise on her chest. "Goodness, is that a compliment?" She stepped back, widening the distance between them. Weakness be damned. She had to breathe. "What else can I do to prove my identity?"

"Show me how you forged my signature." He reached across the desk and drew the inkwell, fountain pen, and a sheet of cream writing paper toward her.

"Fine." She shot him a look that indicated her displeasure at his continued skepticism, and positioned the original note she'd sent him in front of her so she had something to copy.

Acutely aware of him watching her every move, she picked up the fancy silver-barreled pen, dipped the nib into the ink, and wiped it on the side of the glass inkwell to remove the excess liquid.

"Since I'm copying a signature that is already, in itself, a forgery, you will allow me a little leeway," she said. "It is always best to counterfeit from a primary source. Unless you'd care to give me an example of your signature again?"

He shook his head. "Copy that one and stop making excuses. Unless you can't do it?"

She bit her lip and suppressed a flash of irritation at his gently mocking challenge. She made sure to move the pen swiftly, but not too fast, imitating the strong, boldly sweeping style of the original. She wasn't completely satisfied with the result, but considering the pressure she was under, it was passable.

She glanced up and was gratified to see a look of consternation on his handsome face. There. That should give Doubting Thomas something to think about. Time to remind him of exactly how much power she wielded. She shot him an arch glance. "I cannot tell you, monsieur, how tempted you have been to write me a nice, fat bank draft."

He stilled. She batted her eyelashes.

"I tell you this merely as a reminder of what I could have done with my skills, had I not been so honest. A gesture of goodwill, if you wish."

His expression turned sardonic. "I thank you for not defrauding me, madame," he said dryly, but there was the bite of irritation in his voice.

Good. He needed to take her seriously. "Yes. I have been excessively well behaved, I think."

He shifted. "All right. I accept that you are the counterfeiter Philippe Lacorte."

She inclined her head in regal acknowledgment. "Excellent. We progress."

His eyes ran over her, assessing her in a new, extremely distracting manner. "Well, well. I feel as though I'm meeting a creature of myth. A chimera. You have quite the reputation in the criminal underworld. One might almost call it legendary."

His eyes were bright with mockery. She feigned a careless shrug. "I apologize if I am a disappointment, monsieur. As you see, reality is far more prosaic."

That dimple flashed again and her insides curled.

"Oh, I wouldn't call you that." His wolfish smile made her abruptly aware that they were alone. Blood rushed to her face as his gaze flicked from her eyes to her lips and back again. "Far from it. You, Miss de la Tour, have surpassed my every expectation."

* * *

RICHARD KEPT HIS EXPRESSION NEUTRAL, but his pulse raced as if he'd been boxing or fencing for hours. *Bloody hell.* Philippe Lacorte was a woman!

France's greatest forger, the scourge of the British secret service, was a confounded bloody woman. And not just any woman, either, but an irritatingly beautiful one. Fate really was a perverse bastard.

Her ink-blue eyes twinkled with mischief and a faint smile played at the corners of her mouth. Richard felt a corresponding tug in his groin. What a tantalizing little baggage she was, standing there as cool as you please as she toyed with him. Enjoying it immensely, no doubt.

He caught a waft of her scent as she moved, a fragrance very different from the heady, cloying florals used by most women of his acquaintance. The unusual combination of lemons and ink tickled his nose and tightened his stomach.

He shook his head. Of all the times he'd imagined meeting the infamous forger—and he'd dreamed of the eventual capture many, many times—he'd never envisaged anything like this.

He narrowed his eyes at her dainty figure. "So what do you want?"

CHAPTER 6

*S*abine strolled over to a small side table and ran her fingers over the trinket box and a stack of books it held, trying to appear relaxed. "A deal, of mutual advantage."

He raised his brows in silent, autocratic question.

"I require money," she said.

"What for?"

She gave him a chiding smile. "I don't believe I'm under any obligation to answer that, Lord Lovell." She stroked the edge of a leather-bound book. "But I believe our interests are very much aligned. You wish to employ Lacorte. I wish to be employed."

"Ah." His lips quirked. "The British government is expected to pay for your enthusiastic cooperation. You had a figure in mind, perhaps?"

She lifted her chin at his dry tone. "I do. Ten thousand pounds."

If he was shocked by the outrageous proposal, he hid it well.

"That's rather expensive."

His face remained impassive. She had no idea what he was thinking behind those unsettling amber eyes. She made a mental note never to play cards with him. "I like to think of myself as better value—and certainly more exclusive—than a courtesan."

His lips curved in a smile she instantly mistrusted. "What makes you think we were planning on paying Lacorte?"

Her heart plummeted, but she managed a creditable snort. "You thought I'd work for free?"

"No," he said softly. "I never thought that."

His sudden predatory stillness sent a cold trickle of fear through her.

"I'm not sure you appreciate the vulnerability of your current position, Miss de la Tour," he said slowly. "Let me explain it to you. You have placed yourself entirely in my power." His gaze lingered on her face and he smiled. His teeth were white and straight. "With one snap of my fingers I could have you imprisoned as a Napoleonic supporter and an enemy of England."

He gave her a stare that probably reduced grown men to quivering heaps. It was extremely effective. Her own legs turned to water.

"You have no evidence."

He waved a hand. "A technicality. I'm sure I could come up with something. It's amazing what people confess to. With a little persuasion."

A frisson of fear skittered down her spine. She studied the hard line of his jaw. This was not a man to have as an enemy. He would be implacable. Utterly without mercy.

He inspected one perfectly clean fingernail. "According to English law, counterfeiting is one of the worst crimes a person can commit. A direct attack on the king's person. It's high treason, punishable by death." He picked up the fountain pen and turned it over and over in his fingers. "Lucky for you, burning at the stake was abolished a few years ago."

She felt the blood leave her face but managed a flippant tone. "We live in such enlightened and merciful times."

"You would merely be hanged, drawn, and then quartered," he finished softly.

She sighed. "And you call the French barbarous. At least the guillotine is quick."

His sleepy amber gaze lingered on her throat. "You have a pretty neck. Shame to see it stretched on the gallows."

Sabine pressed her palm to her chest and feigned insouciance. "Ah. Nothing makes a woman's heart beat faster than a man detailing all the grisly ways he'd like to watch her die."

His dimple reappeared at her scorn. He shrugged, not even pretending to be apologetic. "You can hang for treason or work with me. Your choice."

"What a delightful set of options," she cooed. "But it seems a little harsh. After all, counterfeiting is no worse than espionage. I'm no more guilty than you."

"That may be true, but you're on the wrong side of the Channel for that argument. There's no one to protect you here. Both Savary and Napoleon are in exile."

Sabine reached into her skirts for the reassuring presence of her little pistol. "Indeed, it is a sad state of affairs. Men once hailed as heroes are now unwelcome in their homeland."

He tilted his chin. "So tell me again, what's to stop me from arresting you and hauling you off to the nearest dungeon to await trial?"

He was so confident, so self-possessed. Sabine envied his sangfroid. She tried to match it. "I had considered that possibility, of course. I am not a fool. One thing you should know about me, Monsieur Hampden: I always have a plan."

"May I ask what it is? Because we both know I could over-power you in a heartbeat. Pistol or no pistol."

He barely moved. All he did was uncross his legs, one booted calf sliding negligently to the floor, and yet that somehow managed to convey an air of menace very effectively. That was all it took to focus all her awareness on the ripple of muscles beneath the pale breeches, the strength in his thighs. His lazy, relaxed pose only served to accentuate his power. No doubt about it, this was a dangerous man indeed.

She cocked the hammer of her gun. Her pulse was racing, her heart beating a frightened tattoo against her ribs, but outwardly she could be calm. "I read a translated Chinese book on warfare once. It said 'the supreme art of war is to subdue the enemy without fighting.'"

He looked momentarily thrown by the change of subject. "I've read it. That's a man called Sun Tzu."

She nodded, unsurprised that he knew the source. "To use force is a very inelegant solution. And you, Lord Lovell, are an elegant man. I do not think you will torture me."

But she wasn't sure. He was watching her with a calculating look in his eyes that was both assessing and terrifying. He still toyed with the fountain pen, threading it between his long fingers in a way that was strangely mesmerizing.

"Have you read many books on warfare?" he asked.

She shrugged. "Amongst other things. The theater of war has been my milieu for the past few years. A little study seemed prudent."

"Then perhaps you've read Machiavelli? He says 'never attempt to win by force what can be won by deception.'"

"I agree," she said sweetly. "You threaten me with violence. I counter with fraud."

He put down the pen, tapped his fingers on his braced thighs, and smiled, apparently enjoying their verbal sparring. "I would expect nothing else from a forger like yourself."

Sabine sighed, inexplicably saddened that it had come to this, but she refused to feel guilty. He was using her as much as she'd be using him.

"I hope you will remember that I gave you a chance to play— and pay—fairly. I did not wish to resort to such unpleasant measures, but you leave me no choice."

He raised his brows mockingly, challenging her to do her worst.

"You are going to pay me ten thousand pounds," she said evenly.

He laughed outright. "You think so? And what makes you so sure?"

"Because I have something you want even more than Philippe Lacorte. A million pounds in forged British banknotes."

CHAPTER 7

*H*ampden stilled, which was a gratifying response, but he recovered quickly enough.

"And how did you come to be in possession of such a princely sum?"

Sabine spread her skirts and sat without waiting for an invitation. "For five years I have made counterfeit notes under direct instructions from Napoleon himself. He planned to use them to destabilize your economy."

His amber gaze narrowed. "But now you've realized the error of your ways and have come to surrender this fortune to the British government out of the goodness of your heart?"

His tone was drier than the Sahara and she couldn't prevent a wry smile. "Sadly for you, no. If you do not pay me what I ask, I will be forced to put the emperor's plan into action."

A muscle flickered in his jaw. "What you propose is blackmail."

"No, it is business. Ten thousand pounds is a paltry sum for sparing your country from ruin."

He studied her for a breathless moment. Outwardly she kept her face composed, but inside she was quaking. This was like a game of cards: give nothing away, not by the flicker of an eyelid. If she showed weakness he would swoop in for the kill.

"Where is this fake fortune now?" he asked mildly. "Here in London?"

"Somewhere safe. I have friends who will release it if they do not hear from me in less than twenty-four hours."

He tilted his head. "Why don't you simply spend it yourself?"

Sabine pressed her lips together. "I do not wish to punish thousands of innocent citizens."

He shot her a disbelieving look. "A criminal with a code of honor?"

She shrugged and forced herself to hold his gaze to make sure he understood her determination. "I do not wish to ruin your economy, monsieur, but I will do so, if you force me." She released her pistol and crossed her arms, mirroring his aggressive stance. "I will work for the money. But the amount is not negotiable. Those are my terms."

He straightened from the desk. "It seems I have no option but to accept."

Disbelief and elation buzzed her ears. "I have some additional requests," she said quickly, before she lost her nerve.

"You mean demands."

She ignored that little dig. "We need to set out some ground rules."

He waved an airy hand. "Oh, I agree. I'm a firm believer in establishing the rules of combat very clearly. Whether in business or pleasure."

The way he rolled his tongue around the word *pleasure* did funny things to her insides. She cleared her throat and tried to sound businesslike. "For how long were you hoping to engage Lacorte's services?"

"Six months. Maybe longer."

She shook her head. "Impossible. I had not planned to stay in London for more than a few weeks."

"Three months, then."

"Three weeks."

He raised one eyebrow at her bartering. "Six weeks."

"One month."

A taut little silence ensued, a battle of wills. She refused to drop her gaze. A wave of relief prickled her when he finally inclined his head.

"One month then. Until the middle of May."

She exhaled. "Very well. I will lend my considerable skills to helping you rout your network of spies. You will pay me ten thousand pounds. In addition, you will provide me with decent lodgings, food, and clothing."

"Anything else?" he asked acerbically. "Perhaps you'd like chocolates and flowers delivered daily to your rooms? A white elephant? The crown jewels?"

Her lips twitched at his sarcasm. Oh, he was furious, under that cool exterior. No man liked to be manipulated. Especially not a man like this one, whose entire existence was based on tracking and cornering his prey.

She matched his dry tone. "That will not be necessary. My intent is not to bankrupt you, Lord Lovell. Although I imagine it would take more than a few cakes and baubles to do that. You hardly seem on the brink of penury."

She shot another brief glance around the sumptuous room. It was littered with gilt, fine art, and books. It even smelled of money: paper and ink, generations of wealth and privilege.

He smiled, acknowledging the hit. "Go on."

"I will be free to come and go without restraint."

"This is London. It's not safe for a woman to go anywhere unaccompanied."

"I have managed perfectly well in Paris for years," she said sweetly.

"You will have a maid or a servant accompany you."

She nodded to concede the point. "I will not be mistreated or physically harmed." She waited for him to nod. "And I want immunity from prosecution. I'm not having you arrest me as soon as our agreement is over. I want your word that I will be free to leave the country unmolested."

"So suspicious," he chided softly. "But all right. You have my word."

She moistened her lip with her tongue. "It will be a working relationship. Purely professional."

His eyes roved over her, an arrogant, dismissive sweep that discarded any other possibility. "If you say so."

Sabine was conscious of a little sting of pique.

He leaned forward. "I have a few terms of my own."

She raised her brows.

"The world of spying never sleeps. You will be at my disposal at any and all hours of the day and night. You will do whatever I ask of you, without question. For the next four weeks you will obey my rules. Is that understood?"

She swallowed a lump of fright at the steely menace in his tone.

He nodded, apparently satisfied. "And one last thing. Before you leave England you will surrender the counterfeit fortune to me."

She sighed, but it was no more than she'd expected. "Agreed."

"Good. Shall we put our agreement in writing?"

She glanced over at the forged letter on the desk with a wry smile. "I don't put much store in official documents." She stood and extended her hand toward him instead. "We can shake on it, if you like. A gentleman's agreement."

He stepped closer, looming over her. "Shaking hands is so formal." Her skin tingled as his fingers enveloped hers. "Let's seal it in the traditional manner. With a kiss."

Sabine jerked back, but he had a firm grip on her hand. Her gaze flew to his lips, and her heart thudded painfully. "I don't think so," she stammered.

His smile said he knew exactly the direction her thoughts had taken. He bent and executed a flawless, mocking bow, as if they were meeting in some elegant society ballroom. His warm lips grazed the back of her knuckles.

A jolt of awareness fizzed over her skin. She tugged her hand back and he released her with a lazy, knowing smile.

"Miss de la Tour, I'm looking forward to working with you immensely."

RICHARD SQUASHED his irritation at being manipulated by such a slip of a girl. She looked so damned innocent, with that slight flush on her cheeks, as if butter wouldn't melt in her mouth. He had to stop thinking about her mouth—she was a blackmailing little crook.

Of course, she could be lying about having a fortune stashed away, but the idea that Napoleon might have planned to flood Britain with fake currency was all too plausible. The despot had already used the tactic in both Russia and Austria before his abdication, and Richard's colleagues in the Foreign Office had long been wary of him trying something similar in Britain.

His uninvited guest had summed up the political situation with uncanny accuracy. The economy was on its knees after a decade of warfare. Coupled with a few bad harvests, the king's failing health, and the flagrant excesses of the Prince Regent, things were extremely volatile. Counterfeiting was taken so seriously by the government precisely because it was so dangerous. If all that money got loose it could lead to the downfall of the government. Or the monarchy itself.

The little baggage had backed him neatly into a corner, and she knew it. The satisfied quirk to her lips sent Richard's blood pressure soaring, and he wasn't sure if it was in desire, irritation, or reluctant admiration.

She wouldn't have it all her own way, though. Oh, no. Now that she was here, in his realm, he wasn't going to let her out of his sight. She'd have no chance to disappear until he'd uncovered all her secrets.

Richard strode to the wall and tugged the bell pull. Hard.

Hodges appeared so quickly he must have been loitering just outside the door. Richard shot him an amused, censorious glance. "Ah, Hodges. Let me introduce you to Miss Sabine de la Tour."

The majordomo bowed formally.

"She's going to be our guest. For the next month."

He heard her faint gasp from behind him, and was pleased to ignore it. "Please have the green room readied for her."

"Of course, sir."

She rounded on him as soon as the door closed behind Hodges. "What are you saying? I cannot stay here!"

"And I can't let you leave," he countered smoothly. "Surely you understand that?"

She sank back down into the chair she'd just vacated as if all the strength had left her. "My friends—"

"You will send them a note in the morning to let them know that you're safe," he interrupted. "You are not leaving this house tonight."

Her slim shoulders sagged, as if she realized she had no choice. "Very well."

He enjoyed the way she swallowed nervously. Good. Let her comprehend how tight a noose she'd walked into. She was his now.

He glanced at the small valise she'd been reluctant to surrender to the footman. "We can have the rest of your things brought over in the morning."

She tilted her chin in a defiant gesture he found oddly appealing. "I don't have anything else."

His astonishment was only partly feigned. "You have only one suitcase? One? I've never met a woman who could travel with anything less than two coaches, fifteen valises, hat boxes, band boxes, shoe boxes, and various household pets."

She scowled at him.

Hodges saved him from a scold with a discreet tap on the door, and Richard stepped aside so she could leave. "Hodges will show you to your room."

She stood and he bowed again, mocking her, as if she were indeed his honored guest instead of a semi-willing prisoner. Oh, this was going to be fun.

"Good night, Miss de la Tour. Sweet dreams."

CHAPTER 8

*S*weet dreams, indeed. Ha!

Sabine's heart pounded as she followed the servant up the wide staircase and into a palatial bedroom.

Hampden had driven a hard bargain, but she'd been expecting worse. She couldn't let her guard down now, though. Her adversary might be ridiculously handsome, but she had good reason to be suspicious of beautiful things. Her counterfeits were beautiful, but they were still lies. Nothing but thin air and promises.

Sabine shivered as she recalled the light of challenge that had kindled in those sleepy amber eyes. She'd won this first skirmish, but he looked worryingly confident that he could win the war.

She thrust her hand into her skirts and laid her pistol gently on the table by the bed. She'd bought it three years ago, after the brawny butcher's boy from down the street had cornered her in the back alley. He'd ground his mouth onto hers, all wet and slobbery, like a horse, reeking of stale beer and dried blood. Sabine had struggled, but he'd held her pinned with obscene ease.

Just when she'd been certain she was going to be raped, Anton had come charging out of the back door of the shop like an enraged bull. He'd shoved Guillaume into the wall, punched him

41

to the ground, then ushered her inside, shaken and utterly nause-ated. The next day she'd gone to a gunsmith on Rue de Rivoli and bought herself the pistol.

With any luck she wouldn't need to use it on the man downstairs.

Sabine leaned back and studied the room she'd been given. Such luxury! What a contrast to her room above the shop in Rue du Pélican. A scratching, snuffling sound at the door drew her attention and she stilled, afraid it was her host, but then came the click and scrabble of claws on wooden floorboards and an excited canine whine.

She crossed to the door and opened it just an inch. A wet black nose and a furry muzzle pushed its way through. She opened the door wider, stepped back, and allowed the animal to enter.

She didn't know much about dogs. This one had a long, aris-tocratic face, a shaggy silvery-gray coat, slender legs, and soulful black eyes. Its funny tufted eyebrows gave it a comical appear-ance and its wiry hair stood out from its body in random tufts, as though it had been struck by lightning.

It seemed friendly enough. It bounded into the room, pranced in a circle, then butted itself up against her legs. She put out a tentative hand. The dog sniffed then licked her fingers.

Sabine laughed. "Well, what's a scruffy mongrel like you doing in such an aristocratic household, hmm?"

The dog gave an "I have no idea" whimper.

"I'm sure your master would disapprove of you consorting with the enemy," she murmured, stroking the hound's lopsided ears.

The dog looked decidedly unimpressed.

She scratched beneath its chin and it closed its eyes with an expression that could only be described as doggy ecstasy. Its bony tail thumped painfully against her skirts.

"Have you been sent to guard me?"

His lordship would have given orders to prevent her leaving, she was sure. Doubtless there was a footman or porter downstairs with orders to remain vigilant all night. She could have told him not to bother. She wasn't going anywhere.

The dog gave a sigh, turned itself in a tight circle, and slumped down on the floor in an ungainly heap. It didn't seem to be going anywhere either, so Sabine washed her face with water from a pitcher on the washstand, stripped down to her cotton chemise, and crawled into the huge four-poster bed.

Her stomach rumbled. The last thing she'd eaten had been a hot meat pie of dubious quality from a street vendor near the coaching inn this morning. Still, she'd been hungry in Paris, too. At least here the bed was so soft it was like falling into a vat of whipped cream.

She prayed Anton was equally comfortable. They'd agreed he would find some inexpensive lodgings not too far away, but she doubted he'd be able to afford anything half this luxurious. She let out a deep, contented sigh. Ah, the wages of sin.

No doubt she should be feeling more apprehensive about sleeping under her enemy's roof, but she felt oddly protected from the world outside. At least within these stately walls the only thing she need be wary of was her host.

She pulled her valise up onto the bed and arranged it next to her, under the covers. She'd wake if anyone tried to remove it in the night.

Sabine closed her eyes. It had been surprisingly easy to slip back into speaking English, her mother's native tongue. Her chest ached. She recalled her mother more as a scent and a general feeling of nurturing happiness than by her features now. The rose petal soap she'd favored, the way she'd stroked Sabine's hair back from her face and hummed English lullabies as she drifted off to sleep.

One of her favorite English phrases flitted into her head. "Out of the frying pan and into the fire." Sabine sent up a drowsy prayer that it wouldn't be prophetic.

* * *

RICHARD POURED himself another generous brandy and sank into his favorite leather armchair.

Why had he always imagined he'd been chasing a man? He was surrounded by brilliant women. Hell, his own family was full of them. His sister Heloise was a talented code-breaker, and his brother Nic's wife, Marianne, had been an acrobat and spy. This was just the sort of thing he could imagine her doing. He ran a distracted hand through his hair and shook his head.

Philippe Lacorte was upstairs in his guest bedroom.

He became conscious of a fierce, savage elation. He'd been hunting the counterfeiter for the better part of eighteen months. Tracking him had been like the very best seduction: a long, taunting chase, by turns exciting, frustrating, tantalizing, and infuriating.

He'd admired Lacorte's skill for years. The forger's elusiveness had been a challenge, drawing him on, an insult he couldn't seem to let go. He'd relished their little game of cat and mouse. And if anyone had told him that Philippe Lacorte would simply walk into his study and announce himself, he would have laughed in their face.

And now he was a she.

He should probably be disappointed that she'd surrendered, but Richard didn't feel a sense of anticlimax. On the contrary. His heartbeat quickened in anticipation. This wasn't the end of the chase; it was the beginning of a whole new game. Sabine de la Tour was a fascinating enigma. Her coming to him had been incredibly risky; she was either very brave or very stupid, and he was certain it wasn't the latter.

He didn't trust her an inch. She'd walked into the camp of the enemy, but with what aim? Her professions of moral purity were highly suspect. She could be trying to wheedle her way in to his life to steal information, but for whom? Both of France's great spymasters, Fouché and Savary, had been ousted since Napoleon's defeat.

Still, it was hard not to applaud her audacity, the bravado it must have taken to face him down in his own study and blackmail him. Richard took another slow sip of brandy. Crafty little devil. He would probably have done the same thing, under the circumstances. It was a little disconcerting to find someone as good as himself, as his fellow agents, Raven, Nic, and Kit. He'd known gorgeous women and clever women, but never one with so much of both attributes at the same time. The combination spelled trouble, especially considering his physical reaction to her.

Richard narrowed his eyes. He'd underestimated her tonight. He would not make the same mistake again.

CHAPTER 9

here was no sign of her blue dress when Sabine awoke. Instead, a lilac morning dress lay over the back of a chair by the door, along with a petticoat, silk stockings, a matching spencer jacket, and a pair of leather gloves.

The sight irritated her, despite the fact that she'd requested new clothes. Donning them, bowing to Hampden's will, would be a small but significant capitulation, but she could hardly walk around all day in her shift.

She snatched up the dress, determined to throw it over her head and have done with it, but the softness of the fabric beguiled her. She gentled her movements with an appreciative sigh. She hadn't worn material this fine since before her father died. It would be churlish to rip it in irritation.

As she fastened the last buttons snugly over her bosom, she reflected that Richard Hampden was clearly a man well versed in sizing up the female form. The beast had gauged her dimensions with uncanny accuracy. The skirt was a fraction too long, but not enough to signify, and the color suited her pale skin and dark hair to perfection. She wondered if he'd specified the hue.

There was nowhere to stash her pistol, so she hid it under the mattress. She took a brutal delight in donning her serviceable black lace-up ankle boots beneath the exquisite dress, although the petty rebellion was foiled by the overlong hem, which hid them from view.

With a resigned sigh, Sabine picked up the butter-soft leather gloves and headed for the door, but a noise from outside stymied her exit. A female servant entered with a tray.

"Good morning, madame. I'm Jocelyn. Josie, for short. His lordship thought you might like to take breakfast in your rooms." The girl set the tray down on a side table and bobbed a curtsey. "He requests that you attend him in the library at your earliest convenience."

Requests, ha! Demands, more like.

Sabine smiled serenely. "Thank you, Josie."

"Yes, ma'am." The girl bobbed another curtsey and left.

Amazing smells wafted from beneath the domed silver covers. Sabine lifted them with a flourish, like a magician, and gave a deep sigh of contentment. Poached eggs balanced on a thick slice of ham and a strange circular sort of bread. Sabine poked it with a fork. This must be what her mother had once described as an English muffin. She'd never tried one, but it smelled divine. Toast, butter, and pots of both marmalade and jam completed the feast.

She gave a huff of disappointment when she discovered the steaming pot of liquid was tea, and not the strong black coffee she preferred, then laughed at herself for complaining. She was like poor Marie-Antoinette, agonizing over which delicious cake to nibble first while the rest of Paris starved. She attacked the meal with gusto.

When she'd finished, she tidied herself as best she could using the silver-backed comb and matching hand mirror that had been laid out on the dressing table. Sabine grimaced at her reflection in the glass. Her hair was wild, her eyes too wide set. Father had often teased her about her elfin looks—he'd called her his little pixie.

The memory reminded her. She crossed to the bed, opened the valise, and pulled out the two small oil portraits of her parents. She placed them carefully on the mantelpiece.

There was no sign of her doggy companion. She would have appreciated his stalwart support. A stone-faced servant directed her to the same room as before. Hampden was seated at the desk, the image of relaxed masculinity. He rose as she entered.

He was dressed as formally as he had been the previous evening, in a pristine white shirt, buff breeches, and a dark green jacket. No doubt the ensemble had cost a small fortune. The morning light caught the angle of his jaw and those amazing sleepy-tiger eyes, and Sabine cursed the way her stomach gave a nervous little flip as she met his eyes. His gaze traveled the length of her, and she felt her cheeks heat with a combination of anger and embarrassment.

"Ah, the dress fits. I sent a maid to purchase it ready-made from one of the modistes on Bond Street and I had to guess at your dimensions." His eyes roved over her in a manner that made her skin prickle. "It will suffice until we can get you properly measured up." He indicated the seat opposite him, as if he were about to interview her for a position, and retook his seat. "I trust you slept well?"

Sabine sat. "Yes, thank you."

"The untroubled slumber of the guiltless, no doubt." His voice was pleasant, well-modulated, with the merest hint of a laugh beneath the lazy, mocking tone.

She raised one eyebrow. "What is that proverb? Ah, yes. 'People in glass houses should not throw stones.' Can you honestly say you've never blurred the line between what is legal and what is necessary in the service of your country, Lord Hampden?"

He inclined his head in wry acknowledgment. "Perhaps."

"The only difference between us is that your illegal activities are currently sanctioned by your government," she sniffed. "Mine were, too, until recently. It is very difficult, to be on the losing side."

His lips curled. "You have my sincere condolences." He regarded her with an uncomfortable intensity. "You are a puzzle, Miss de la Tour. A counterfeiter who does not want to be a criminal."

"There is nothing puzzling about it," she said. "I did what circumstances dictated I had to do to survive. Believe me, if not for the war, I would have happily become a portrait painter like my grandfather, or a museum curator like my father."

Hampden pushed a blank sheet of paper and the inkwell toward her, apparently uninterested in her genealogy. "First things first. Write to your friends and tell them you are safe."

Sabine shot him a scornful glance. "You think I'm so stupid that I will give you their names and addresses so you can send someone to arrest them? I think not. At ten o'clock I will walk to the end of the street, toward the park. My friend will be watching to see that I am unharmed. You will not see him," she warned quickly, "so do not think to send your men to intercept him. He is extremely good at staying out of sight."

She glanced at the ormolu clock on the mantel. It was ten past nine.

Hampden leaned back in his chair and extended his long legs. "Fair enough. That leaves us a little time to chat."

Her stomach clenched. How delightful. A polite interrogation. "How old are you?"

"Twenty-four," she said coolly. "How old are you?"

He seemed amused by her direct attack. He steepled his fingers in front of his mouth, but she caught the telltale twitch of his lips. "Thirty-two. Tell me what you did in Paris. You must have worked at Vincennes."

So, he knew about Napoleon's counterfeiting operation. He seemed to know a lot of things he shouldn't. The British intelligence service was well informed. She lifted her shoulder. "Amongst other places."

"What did you counterfeit?"

She glanced pointedly at the clock again and raised her brows. "You require a full history?"

He nodded.

"Very well. My first job there was forging Austrian banknotes. My colleagues and I made over a hundred million francs' worth, which were introduced into circulation to weaken the economy."

Hampden raised his brows.

Sabine chuckled. "That created quite an awkward situation for the emperor a few years later, when he married the Austrian princess Marie-Louise. He was forced to issue a public ban on printing fake notes, but by then it was far too late."

"You mention colleagues," Hampden said smoothly. "Who else was in your merry little band of counterfeiters?"

Sabine bit her lip. The team had disbanded months ago, all gone their separate ways when Napoleon's defeat had become clear, but she had no wish to bring trouble to their doors. She shrugged. "Oh, a whole bunch of interesting characters. Artists, engravers, jewelers, satirical cartoonists."

"And who's the friend awaiting you in the park?" Hampden prompted gently. "The one who will release your fake banknotes if you fail to make an appearance this morning?"

Sabine's pulse quickened. "You do not need to know his name."

He didn't push her, as she'd expected. He seemed content to watch and wait for her to slip up, like a spider in his web. Patient. Implacable. Sabine fidgeted in her seat.

Hampden stood. "It's almost time to go."

She glanced up. "There's no need for you to accompany me."

"You're in no position to argue."

She narrowed her eyes. "If I must have an escort, I will walk with one of the servants."

"No. You will walk with me. It will be my pleasure."

CHAPTER 10

*S*abine muttered under her breath but followed him out into the checkerboard hallway. He gave a shrill whistle, a summons that was answered immediately by the scrabble of claws. Her scruffy companion from last night burst from below stairs.

Hampden bent to greet the animal's enthusiastic welcome, apparently unconcerned for his immaculate breeches as it leaped up and placed its huge front paws on his muscular thighs. Not that she was noticing his thighs, of course.

"What kind of dog is that?"

His one-sided dimple made an appearance and her insides liquefied in response.

"I'm not entirely sure. He was a gift from one of my tenant farmers. He claimed the pup was greyhound crossed with a Bedlington terrier, but there's lurcher somewhere in there too." He ruffled the animal's fur fondly.

"What's his name?"

"Argos."

The dog eyed his master with tongue-lolling, tail-thumping adoration. Sabine couldn't seem to look away from the way

Hampden's long fingers threaded through its fur. Argos left his master and pressed against her legs. She stroked his scruffy head absently.

Hampden raised a brow. "He likes you. And he's usually such a good judge of character."

She narrowed her eyes, but there was no malice in his teasing. "Maybe I bribed him with some breakfast ham," she said lightly.

His expression hardened. "It wouldn't surprise me. Blackmail's your preferred mode of business, is it not?"

Her pleasure faded at his barb, but he didn't give her a chance to reply. "Come on, time for that walk."

Argos knew that word. His ears pricked up. He bounded to the door and back with an excited yelp. Hampden retrieved a leather collar and leash from a hook by the door and fastened it on the dog. Then he took a firm grip of her elbow.

To anyone else, it would appear as if he were politely escorting her down the front steps. Only she could feel the strength in his fingers, the implicit warning in his grip.

They turned right, toward Hyde Park, and Sabine took a deep breath. The morning air was cool and brisk. Little clouds were blocking the sun, but a few patches of blue peeked through. London smelled better than Paris—fresher, less smoky. Or perhaps that was just in the rarefied environs of Mayfair.

The streets were wider, too, the pale stone of the houses a glistening white. Hampden nodded politely to the maid brushing the steps of the house next door, and acknowledged the boy on the corner who was sweeping the crossing with a twig broom.

"Don't even think of trying to run," he said casually. "I'll have no trouble at all catching you."

They walked on in silence until they reached the corner of Park Lane. Sabine couldn't help but notice the admiring, sidelong looks he received from the women they passed, the deferential hat-doffs from the men.

"There, you have reached the end of the street."

Sabine squinted to catch a glimpse of Anton across the way, but she couldn't see him amongst the dense trees of Hyde Park. Was that a flash of clothing by the railings? In one of the thicker areas of greenery?

She sighed, hating her faulty vision. If she'd been alone she would have pulled out the magnifying lens she wore on a chain around her neck, but the thought of rooting around in her cleavage with Richard Hampden so unnervingly close was not something she wanted to contemplate.

She'd simply have to hope that Anton had seen them. He'd said he'd find a way to spring her from Hampden's clutches if she appeared to be in distress, but she couldn't imagine what he could do. Hampden was not a man one could easily escape. She pasted a smile on her face to reassure Anton if he was watching.

"Now we will return home."

Hampden released her arm only to circle her, transfer Argos's leash to his right hand, and retake her other elbow, automatically placing himself on the side nearest the traffic, shielding her from the splashes of mud and potentially dangerous wheels of the carriages.

Sabine frowned. He probably wasn't even aware he was doing it. She doubted he considered her a lady worthy of such gentlemanly attentions. Such things were doubtless ingrained in lords and viscounts, as natural as breathing. A traitorous curl of pleasure warmed her chest anyway. She sighed. Things would be so much simpler if he were a complete bastard.

CHAPTER 11

*R*ichard kept a tight rein on his temper as he escorted the treacherous little Frenchwoman along the street. She held herself rigid, back straight, head high, avoiding bodily contact with him as much as possible. Her stubborn aloofness made him want to push her up against the side of the house and do something utterly uncivilized. Like kiss that haughty look right off that primly pursed mouth.

He clenched his jaw. God, the woman had the most ridiculous effect on him. He breathed a sigh of relief when the Ravenwood carriage rounded the corner and drew up outside the house. Raven jumped down and raised one black eyebrow at the sight of him arm in arm with his visitor from last night. His gaze was amused, inquisitive, but he bowed politely to Sabine and they all ascended the steps together.

"I need a word," he murmured in Richard's ear.

Hodges opened the door, his timing immaculate as ever, and Richard turned to Sabine. "You will await me in the library."

She stiffened at his peremptory tone but didn't argue. "As you wish."

Richard suppressed a smile. He wasn't fooled by her sudden

acquiescence. She hated taking orders from him, but she'd clearly accepted the need to appease him, at least for now. He watched her ramrod-straight back as Hodges escorted her into the library, then indicated for Raven to go through the opposite door, into his study.

"What is it?" he asked, dropping into one of the dark leather armchairs by the fire.

Raven's lips twitched in amusement. "Oh, no. I'm not saying anything until you tell me what happened last night. And why I arrived here this morning to find your mysterious visitor still here, and wearing a completely different outfit."

Richard bit back a curse. Raven would notice that little detail. He was a perceptive bastard. Those emerald-green eyes missed nothing.

Raven's eyes glimmered with interest. "Who is she?"

Richard filled him in.

Raven let out a long whistle and leaned back in his chair. "Oh, this is priceless. The great Lord Lovell, bested by a French pixie." He shook his head with a gleeful chuckle. "Do you know how long I've prayed for you to meet your match? Years, my friend. Years."

Richard briefly considered throwing his friend out of the window. Sadly, past experience told him that even defenestration wouldn't be enough to divert Raven.

"Who do you think she's working for?" Raven asked.

Richard shrugged. "I don't know. Decazes succeeded Fouché as minister for police, but he's got enough on his plate right now dealing with ultra-royalist insurrections. He hasn't time to stir up trouble here. And why send one of France's best assets over to us? It doesn't make sense. He'd want to keep her in Paris working for him." He frowned. "I think she saw the chance to get out with the money, and took it."

"Think she's acting on her own?" Raven sounded skeptical.

"No. She claims to have friends who will flood the market with the fake money if she's harmed. I don't think she's bluffing."

"We have to find them, then."

Richard nodded. "I'll have her followed."

Raven shot him a wicked grin. "Or maybe you can convince her to tell you where the money is. Put those famous good looks to use, for once."

Richard's stomach clenched at the thought of seducing the information out of his "guest." It wouldn't exactly be a hardship. She couldn't be a virgin; she was too poised, too brazen, too self-assured. And by her own admission she was no man's wife or lover. She'd presented herself on his doorstep, placed herself in his clutches. Surely that meant she was fair game?

"So what are you going to do with her?" Raven's question interrupted Richard's heated thoughts.

"Use her, of course. She can start forging documents right away."

Raven raised his brows. "You're keeping her here? Not putting her in a safe house?"

Richard drummed his fingers on the armrest. "I don't want her to run. I need her close."

Raven shot him a sardonic look. "Purely in the interests of national security, of course," he said, deadpan. "Poor Richard—forced to endure the company of a beautiful little traitor, day after day. Night after night. My heart bleeds for you." He shook his head with a grin. "I saw the way you were looking at her. Enforced proximity's going to be just the thing to keep a lid on all that simmering attraction."

Richard narrowed his eyes at his friend. He wasn't the only one affected by a tiny, infuriating woman. "Why are you here so bright and early, anyway? It's not like Heloise to let you off the hook."

Raven had married Richard's little sister Heloise only a few months ago. Out of choice. Richard still couldn't fathom it. Still, they seemed nauseatingly happy together. He tamped down a tiny wistful twinge of envy for their contentment.

Raven's expression sobered. "I came because I have news. Visconti's here. In London."

Richard straightened in his chair, all teasing forgotten. "Visconti? Christ, are you sure?"

Raven nodded. "Castlereagh's been tracking him since the Congress of Vienna. He must have run out of people to assassinate on the Continent. No confirmed sighting yet, but I've heard enough whispers to believe it's true. He's here."

"I doubt he's come to enjoy the smog or the cuisine," Richard finished darkly. "He'll be here for a job."

Raven leaned back in his chair. "Exactly. So all we have to do is figure out who his target is and who's hired him. Unfortunately, with the country in the state it is, there are any number of candidates. The prime minister. The cabinet. The entire royal family. Anyone in the public eye."

This gloomy pronouncement was interrupted by a discreet knock on the door. Hodges entered. "I searched our guest's room, as you ordered, sir."

"And?"

"It appears she brought very little with her, my lord. Three dresses. Some serviceable undergarments, a pair of gloves, one hat. A small case of artist's materials: sketchbook, paints, pastels, brushes. And some travel papers in the name of Marie Lambert."

Richard frowned. "No jewelry? Coins? Bundles of money? Nothing sewn into her clothes or the lining of the valise?"

"No, sir. Her pockets contained only a handkerchief and a ticket stub for the Dover-to-London coach."

"That's it? No perfume? Powder? Rouge?"

"No, my lord. Nothing of that sort. There are two small framed portraits, which I assume to be of her parents, on the mantel, and a pocket pistol hidden beneath the mattress."

So, she hadn't been lying about the pistol.

Richard experienced a faint pang in the region of his solar plexus. So little, to start a new life. He shook his head. He would not feel sorry for his captive. She'd chosen to come here. And, as the pistol evidenced, she was more than capable of taking care of herself. He glanced up. "Thank you, Hodges. That will be all."

When the servant bowed and withdrew, Richard turned back to Raven. "I want an update on Visconti's whereabouts as soon as we have it."

Raven nodded. "You have my word. God knows, I'd like to put a bullet in the bastard, but we all know you've got prior claim. We'll catch him this time, Richard, I swear it."

Richard nodded grimly.

CHAPTER 12

$\mathcal{S}$abine took her time studying the library.

Tall wooden ladders on brass wheels allowed access to the highest shelves of the floor-to-ceiling bookcases. A pair of terrestrial globes on splayed feet flanked a mahogany card table, the top inset with a circle of green baize and little indents for the players' mother-of-pearl counters.

It was a decidedly masculine room, designed to put the inhabitant at ease. A pair of green wing armchairs had been grouped around the fire. The leather on the arms was a darker color, polished to a high shine with age and constant use. She wanted to curl up in one and read the day away.

The smell was familiar, too, the same aroma as Jacques's print shop—a comforting musty mix of leather book bindings, paper, and beeswax.

Sabine scanned the shelves. They boasted an impressive array of titles, from the Ancient Greeks to a range of modern periodicals. But more surprising was the large section in French. She tilted her head to read the spines. Descartes, Balzac, Molière. A tragedy by Racine, Voltaire's amusing *Candide*. She even spied some of her favorites, including *Manon*

Lescaut by the Abbé Prevost and *Les Liaisons Dangereuses* by Laclos.

Her brows rose as she spied a copy of the erotic novel *Justine* by the Marquis de Sade. No wonder Hampden kept the French section so high up. She glanced farther upward. If de Sade was only halfway up, what on earth did he keep on the top shelves? She climbed a couple of rungs up the ladder and strained her eyes, but alas, it was too hard to see.

Her gaze alighted on the collected works of Roger de Bussy-Rabutin. He'd written one of her favorite quotes: "Absence is to love what wind is to fire; it extinguishes the small and inflames the great." Sabine grimaced. She'd had quite enough bonfires recently.

She climbed back down.

What was Hampden talking about with his friend in the study next door? Her, most probably.

Her eyes went to the pictures on the walls. One could tell a lot about a man by the pictures he chose to hang in his house, the things he chose to see every day.

In France, the nouveau riche who'd prospered under the emperor had raced out to auction and bought up all the family portraits of exiled and guillotined aristos. *Voilà.* Instant ancestors, to counterfeit a long and illustrious family heritage. The hypocrisy made her sick. The bourgeoisie who'd so detested the upper classes now seemed determined to emulate them as ostentatiously as possible. They had all of the money and none of the élan.

Richard Hampden's family portraits probably hung in some endless picture gallery at his ancestral home, no doubt complemented by gloomy Dutch still lifes and the bloodthirsty hunting scenes the English seemed so enamored of, with the poor fox pursued by baying hounds and red-coated huntsmen on lathered mounts.

Sabine turned her head and her mouth dropped open in

shock. Good God. Was that a Rembrandt van Rijn? She hurried over to take a closer look.

She'd studied Rembrandt's works at the Louvre, copied him on many occasions, but she'd never been satisfied with the results. This portrait was of a woman wearing a red hat. Sabine suspected it was Rembrandt's wife, Saskia. The artist had often used her as a model, and she looked vaguely familiar.

She stepped closer. The woman wasn't beautiful, by any stretch of the imagination. Her face was plump, with doughy features and the hint of a double chin, but her expression was kind. There was love in every brushstroke, a warmth in the way the artist had portrayed her that made her luminous, despite her flaws.

Sabine swallowed an unexpected tightness in her throat. Lucky Saskia, to be so loved.

The door clicked and she turned with a start.

"Admiring my Rembrandt?" Hampden drawled.

She didn't bother to hide her appreciation. "I am. It's wonderful."

"I hope you're not thinking of stealing it."

She shot him an irritated look. "I'm a forger, not a thief."

He grinned, apparently pleased with having needled her. "As an artist, no doubt you have a far better understanding of his skill than a philistine like myself. I know I like it, but I can't explain what makes it so extraordinary." He stepped closer and she drew in a breath. "Tell me, what do you see?"

He sounded genuinely interested, so Sabine decided to humor him. She turned back to the painting to avoid looking at him. "It's a deceptively simple painting. Rembrandt's using a whole host of complex techniques to manipulate you, the viewer."

Hamden's brows rose. "Really? Can paintings be deceptive?"

"Anything can be deceptive," she said briskly. "Some paintings are pure propaganda. Why, Napoleon's own court painter, David, depicted the emperor leading his troops across the Alps on a fiery, rearing steed. In truth, he rode an ass."

Hampden's lips twitched in a smile.

She pointed to Saskia's collar. "There. Notice how some parts are more in focus than others? That's deliberate. The less important areas are left blurred and vague. The sharper areas draw the eye. It's misdirection, the way a street magician misleads you to perform a trick."

She gestured to the woman's face. "The eyes are the most important part, so he paints them in more detail than the rest. That is where we focus."

Sabine resolutely kept her gaze on the painting, determined not to succumb to the temptation to study Hampden's extraordinary eyes. They were the most unusual color. She couldn't quite decide which paints she'd need to replicate them; burnt sienna, maybe? Flecked with charcoal and umber.

She cleared her throat. "His use of color is masterful too. People who have never painted always think human flesh is one single tone, but to paint skin well you need a whole range of colors."

She leaned forward. Next to her, Hampden did the same, not touching her, but his solid presence was a disturbance in the air, impossible to ignore. She caught the faintest whiff of his clean, masculine scent. Her stomach knotted.

"If you look closely you can see spots of red, blue, and yellow on the face. Blue in the shadowed areas, red on the nose, cheek, and eyebrow, and yellow in areas he wanted to lighten."

"Fascinating," Hampden murmured, and even though she didn't turn her head she had the unnerving suspicion that he was studying her rather than the painting. She stepped back and cleared her throat. "This is one of his later works, I would imagine."

"How can you tell?"

"Later in his career the brushwork is looser. Less detailed, but more confident."

She moved away, intensely aware of the fact that they were alone. Sometimes retreat was the better part of valor. She side-stepped to the bookcase and ran her fingers over the lowest shelf. "You have an excellent selection of books in French."

He shrugged. "My mother made me read a lot in her native tongue."

"Ah. My mother made me read a lot in English. Shakespeare. Marlowe. Chaucer."

He gestured to the large leather-topped desk she'd sat at before and pulled out the chair for her, another automatic gesture. "Feel free to borrow something another time. Now have a seat. It's time to get to work."

Sabine settled into the chair he indicated, across the desk from him. "What is it you want me to do?"

"As I said last night, I want to catch a dissident group who have been plotting against the government. We've identified most of the members, but they've been careful not to get caught doing anything treasonous. I wanted Lacorte to forge some incriminating papers that would set them fighting amongst themselves. Evidence of an affair, perhaps, or of double-dealing, to break up the gang."

He smiled, a crafty look that made her immediately nervous. He looked like a fox contemplating a gap in the chicken-coop fence. "But now I realize we can do something much better. Your fake fortune has given me an idea. We're going to encourage the plotters to complete Napoleon's unfinished work and ruin the economy by distributing your fake money."

Sabine frowned. "How are you going to do that? You're certainly not having my money. I won't tell you where it is."

He shot her a patronizing look. "I don't need your fakes to draw them out. All I require is that they incriminate themselves

64

by agreeing to the plan. When they do, we'll arrest them for plotting treason."

"So what do you want from me?"

"A letter from Napoleon, detailing his intentions."

"How will it get to the plotters without arousing their suspicion? Do they take their orders from France?"

"No. They're English. But they sport the same addle-brained, revolutionary ideas as your beloved countrymen." His tone was sweetly mocking. "And the letter is going to come via someone with intimate knowledge of the counterfeiting scheme. Someone with plausible access to the fake money and a proven loyalty to the emperor."

Sabine raised her brows, already suspecting his next words. "And that would be—?"

"Philippe Lacorte." Hampden leaned back in his chair and steepled his fingers.

She narrowed her eyes. "You're going to have someone pose as Lacorte?" A surge of anger warmed her chest at the thought of some stranger trying to emulate her professional competence. "Won't these men be wary of a trap? Surely they'll test whoever is sent?"

Hampden nodded placidly. "Doubtless they will. If they suspect whoever they're meeting isn't really Lacorte, they'll probably kill him."

Sabine's throat closed in dread. This was a human life he was talking about so casually. "Then if these men know anything about the technicalities of forgery—which, as criminals, I'm sure they will—they'll realize your man isn't Lacorte within minutes."

"I agree," Hampden said mildly.

Sabine frowned. His imperturbable calm was supremely annoying. How could he risk one of his men in this way? She placed her hands on the desk and tried to make him see sense.

"It is arrogance and stupidity to send someone who is not

proficient in counterfeiting to deal with them. You'd be sending your man to his death."

"I agree," Hampden said again, and his amused tone penetrated her righteous ire. "I doubt any of my agents could pull off the deception. As I said, I'm going to send someone I'm certain will be convincing."

Sabine curled her lip. "Yourself, I assume?"

His smile stopped her heart for a fraction of a second. "Your confidence is heartwarming," he mocked, "but no." His eyes never shifted from hers and her stomach lurched unpleasantly. "I was going to send the real Philippe Lacorte."

Her heart thudded to a stop. "Now, wait a minute. You just said these men will kill anyone suspected of being a spy or an impostor!"

His smile widened. "You'd better be convincing, then."

Her head reeled. When she'd first decided to offer her services to Hampden, she'd thought it would be a simple case of forging a few documents, taking payment, and getting out of London. Now, at every turn, she was becoming embroiled deeper and deeper in his world. A frightening, dangerous world.

She crossed her arms. And wished she'd bought her pistol. "This isn't at all what I agreed to."

His amber eyes bored into hers, unblinking. "You came to me. You agreed to work for me. It was your choice. You will write me that letter. And then you will offer the traitors the forgeries so they can carry out Napoleon's wishes."

"I'm a counterfeiter. Not a secret agent, or a spy, or whatever it is you call yourself."

His broad shoulders lifted in an elegant shrug.

She cast around for obstacles to the plan. "How would Philippe Lacorte even know about the existence of a bunch of English dissidents?"

"Leave that to me. The criminal underworld's a very small

place. A few whispers in the right ears and the plotters will seek you out."

"Oh, wonderful," she murmured darkly.

Hampden stretched like a lazy cat. "So, first things first. Let's write that letter, shall we?"

CHAPTER 13

*H*ampden leaned back and opened the central drawer to the huge desk. "You've forged the emperor's hand-writing before." He made it a statement, not a question.

"I might have done," Sabine hedged.

He withdrew a sheaf of documents. "Come now, no need to be modest. Castlereagh sent over a few examples of your work." He opened a file and picked up the topmost piece of paper. "Like this one. A passport for the Comte de Noailles. We recovered it last month, during a raid in Seven Dials."

Sabine narrowed her eyes. "What makes you think it's one of mine?"

He smiled at her defensive tone. "Not any technical flaw, I assure you. It's just that the Comte de Noailles was guillotined in '94. Odd, then, that he should have sailed into Portsmouth six weeks ago." His lips twitched at the corners.

She glanced over at the paper as if she'd never seen it before, but couldn't prevent the tiny smile of pride that tugged at her lips. "That was one of the last ones I did before leaving Paris."

"For whom did you make it?"

"I have no idea. Those using Lacorte were rarely forthcoming with their names. And I never met the clients. It was always An —" She bit her lip before she betrayed Anton's name. "An associate of mine," she amended quickly, hoping Hampden hadn't noticed the slip, "who dealt with the customers."

He flicked through a few more sheets.

She had no need to defend her actions to this man, and yet she felt the urge to explain herself. That alone made her angry.

"Apart from the fake currency—which I was forced to make—I only produced documents that helped people," she said. "Travel papers, hospital receipts, certificates of residence for returning émigrés who needed to prove they hadn't really left the country. Other, less scrupulous forgers faked 'deeds of gift' so illegitimate heirs could fraudulently claim an estate, or forged wills to give people an inheritance to which they weren't entitled. I never did anything like that."

That dimple appeared in his cheek. "Yes, we're lucky you're such an honest criminal," he drawled. "A regular saint."

She straightened in offended dignity. "What's legal and what is right are sometimes not the same thing. I may be a criminal, but I think of myself as a highly moral person."

"Now there's female logic at its finest."

She gave him a hard stare. "I am aware of the contradiction. Nevertheless, it is true."

He seemed disinclined to argue the point. "So, what do you need to fake a letter from Napoleon?"

"Apart from paper and ink, several authentic examples of his handwriting to copy."

He nodded and opened a second folder. "I'd anticipated that." He slid it across the desk, and Sabine caught a faint whiff of lemon verbena and the clean-starch smell of his cravat. Her stomach fluttered traitorously.

"This is some of his correspondence that we intercepted. As

you can see, there's all sorts. Dispatches. Personal papers. Even several letters he wrote to Josephine from Egypt. The contents of those were published in our national newspapers at the time to humiliate him. While he was writing breathy love letters, the empress was having an affair with a cavalry lieutenant called Hippolyte Charles."

Sabine studied the first document and frowned down at the scrawled lines. "There are two different people's handwriting here. This section was written by his private secretary." She drew her finger downward. "This is Napoleon's own hand. He's short-sighted, and writes very quickly. It affects his penmanship."

Hampden shook his head. "Such intricacies."

She nodded absently. "Learning to copy something is like learning a language. You need to repeat it over and over again until you are fluent enough to converse at a decent level."

"Do you need any special type of paper?"

"Not really. The emperor never used parchment or vellum. It just needs to be high quality." She arched a brow, unable to resist a sly jibe. "Exactly the sort of paper a pampered aristo would have lying around in his desk, I would imagine."

He opened a drawer and slid several pristine sheets of undoubtedly expensive paper across the desk. Sabine lifted one to the light and nodded at the evidence of the faint translucent lines that showed the paper had been dried on a wire rack.

She pulled the ink pot and fountain pen toward her across the desk. "As to which ink to use, this will do. Unlike drawing ink, which discolors with age because it contains iron, writing ink is still made to the ancient Greek formula, which consists of a carbon, like soot, plus gum arabic and water. It doesn't fade."

Hampden tapped one long finger over his lips. "It occurs to me that a counterfeiter must be many things. A chemist, to understand the composition of inks, as well as an artist and a draughtsman."

"Indeed," she murmured, warmed by the compliment and the fact that he seemed to appreciate her depth of knowledge. "So, what do you want this letter to say?"

"Use this one as a basis." He flicked through the folder and passed her a handwritten page. It was a letter from Napoleon with instructions on setting up the Vincennes counterfeiting operation.

Sabine hid her shock. So that's how he'd known about it. How long had the British had this information?

"That letter is dated 1809, but make yours later, from early last year."

Sabine dutifully wrote *January 1815* at the top of the page.

The letter read:

To Count Fouché, Minister of Police, Schonbrunn, 23rd September 1809.

Maret is sending you what you ask for. I repeat that, whether in peace or war, I attach the greatest importance to having one or two hundred million's worth of notes. This is a political operation. Once the house of Austria is shorn of its paper currency, it will not be able to make war against me. You can set up the workshops where you please—in the Castle of Vincennes, for instance, from which the troops would be withdrawn and which no one would be allowed to enter. The stringent rule would be accounted for by the presence of state prisoners. Or you can put them in any other place you choose. But it is urgent and important that your closest attention should be given to this matter. If I had destroyed that paper money, I should not have had this war.

Napoleon.

Hampden glanced at her. "I want your letter to be similar, except instead of talking about crushing Austria, I want it to discuss crippling England." He tilted his head. "Can you do it?"

Sabine sat up straighter. "Of course. If something has been made by human hand, it can be reproduced. And if one has talent and patience—which I do—it can be made so that no one suspects the difference."

She wrote a rough draft of the letter, conscious of his regard the whole time, and held it out for his inspection. "Will this suffice?"

He read it through. "Yes."

"How should I sign it? Napoleon uses several different methods." She indicated the documents he'd fanned out across the desk. "On this one he's just signed *N*." She prodded another. "Here he's used the shortened form, *Nap*." She tapped the letter she was copying. "And here he signs in full."

"Write *Napoleon* for clarity," Hampden said. "I want the plotters to have no doubt."

Sabine practiced a few more sentences on a blank piece of paper, trying to emulate the French leader's erratic style. The first three letters of his signature ran together so the *Nap* looked more like the letters *Nq*. She would take care to copy that.

She glanced up and met Hampden's gaze. "Don't you have something else to do? I work best in solitude."

He relaxed back in his chair, legs crossed in front of him. "Oh, no. I'm savoring this opportunity to see a master at work."

She scowled and proceeded to ignore him as best she could. Twenty minutes—and three unsuccessful attempts—later, she'd managed to create a letter she was proud of. She let out a sigh and leaned back in her chair.

"Now for the final touches. We must take into consideration where this is supposed to have been. How many people would have handled it? Too-perfect condition will arouse suspicion. It must look as if it's been opened and read a few times. Will you ring for tea?"

Hampden blinked at the apparent non sequitur. "I'm sorry?"

She shot him a serene smile. "Tea. If you wouldn't mind."

"If you wish." He rose and tugged the bell pull by the door. A maid appeared and, to Sabine's delight, he ordered not only tea, but sandwiches and cake, too. How wonderful to be able to demand such luxuries!

"Did you not eat the breakfast I sent up for you?" he asked.

"I did. It was delicious. But I wouldn't refuse a cup of tea now. And in any case, staining the paper with cold tea is an excellent way to add age to documents."

CHAPTER 14

*W*hat an extraordinary girl, Richard thought.
Watching her work had been a revelation. He couldn't recall the last time he'd been so impressed. Or so enthralled.

She rolled her shoulders in a delicate motion—which naturally drew his attention to the curve of her breasts beneath the taut fabric of her dress. His blood throbbed. Hodges's timely arrival with the tea tray provided a much-needed distraction.

Richard cleared his throat. "Here on the desk, please, Hodges."

Argos ambled in after the servant and with a brief, dismissive glance at Richard, trotted over and collapsed in a tangle of long limbs at Sabine's feet. The traitor.

Sabine, however, pounced on the sandwiches as soon as they were set down. She demolished one, barely taking time to breathe, and Richard experienced a sudden pang of guilt. She was so thin. Had she gone hungry in Paris? The idea made him feel sick.

She took one of the little cakes. Cook had sent up his favorites, little almondy things topped with icing. Sabine bit into one, stopped chewing mid-mouthful, and gave a groan of pleasure he found ridiculously erotic.

He dragged his eyes away from a crumb that trembled at the corner of her top lip and concentrated on pouring the tea like a normal person. Like a person who didn't have a vision of pulling her over the desk and licking off that crumb. She finished the cake and took another.

"You'll be sick if you eat so quickly," he chided.

She gave a guilty start, caught with an entire cake crammed in her mouth. He suppressed the desire to laugh. Clearly realizing she couldn't take it out with any degree of dignity, she started to chew, watching him with a faint blush staining her cheeks. She shot him a defiant glare and swallowed. He handed her a cup of steaming tea.

"That's the first time I've ever seen anyone try to inhale one of those," he said mildly.

She took a hurried sip of tea—and cursed under her breath when she scalded her tongue. "I never ate many cakes in Paris."

"Nor drank much tea," he teased. "One does not cradle the teacup between the palms of both hands as if it is a bird we are trying to keep warm. I'm reliably informed that a lady holds the handle delicately with just two fingers and thumb. Just so." He picked up his own cup and demonstrated.

She narrowed her eyes, as if she were considering smashing the teapot over his head. "I never claimed to be a lady."

He sent her a condescending smile that was sure to irritate. "So it would seem."

She rearranged her hands and took another tiny sip of tea. "So, I have finished your letter. What now?"

"I will make sure it gets into the hands of our traitors."

She brushed ineffectually at the crumbs in her lap. "Will that be all for today?"

He smiled at the hint of desperation in her voice. She wanted to get away from him. *Not a chance, Miss de la Tour.* "No. I wish to discuss your sleeping arrangements."

A new blush crept up her throat. The hand that raised her teacup trembled, ever so slightly. "What do you mean?"

"I mean you cannot publicly stay in this house with me for the next month."

Her shoulders sagged in relief. She shot him an impish grin. "Afraid I'll ruin your reputation, Lord Lovell?"

"In a sense. If I install you here, you'll be labeled my latest mistress, and neither of us wants that."

She stiffened in apparent affront, and he bit his lip to prevent himself from smiling. "To that end," he continued smoothly, "you're going to move next door."

She blinked in surprise.

"My parents own number six. My father's still at the family home in Dorset, but my mother's currently in residence for the season. For the next four weeks you will be living there, with her. You can be a distant French cousin, visiting us now that the war is finally over."

"You seem to have it all worked out," she said. "But your mother cannot possibly want a stranger forced upon her."

"You will not be forced upon her. Your residence will be in name only. The two properties share an interconnecting door. You will work and sleep here, but for appearance's sake you will leave from my mother's side of the house whenever you go out."

Sabine frowned. "If you're so worried about appearances, why don't you simply put me up in a hotel?"

"Because I don't trust you," he said. "Not one little bit. Now come along." He rose, expecting her to follow.

He heard her sigh. "I can't get up. Your dog is sitting on my skirts."

Richard glanced down. Sabine tried to extricate her feet, but Argos wasn't cooperating in the slightest. He gave an enormous yawn and lowered his head back onto his crossed front paws.

Richard gave a low whistle. "Move," he scolded the dog. "Go and see if Cook has any more cakes."

That had the desired effect. If there was one word Argos knew better than *walk* it was *cake.* The dog shot him a disgusted look, as if to indicate his scorn for such blatant bribery, but hauled himself to his feet and trotted out.

Richard led Sabine to the door in the hallway that connected to his mother's house. Both sides had a key, but he was the only one who ever used it. His mother never locked her side, protesting he was always welcome.

They stepped into a near-identical hall to his own, except that the walls were a powder blue instead of bottle green. Two animated female voices emanated from the front salon, and he headed in that direction. Perfect. Out of the corner of his eye he caught Sabine trying to straighten her skirts and smooth her hair into order, and hid a smile.

This was going to be fun.

CHAPTER 15

Two women looked up as Sabine entered a sunny yellow drawing room, hot on Richard's heels. Both wore polite, if surprised, expressions, but her stomach sank as she saw how beautifully dressed they were, even when they were just relaxing at home.

"Ah, there you are," Hampden said cheerfully. "Maman, Heloise, may I introduce to you Mademoiselle Sabine de la Tour." He turned to her. "Sabine, my mother—Therese Hampden, Countess of Lindsey, and my sister, Heloise Ravenwood, Marchioness of Ormonde."

The two women each bobbed a curtsey. Sabine copied the gesture, dredging the half-forgotten knee bend and head nod from distant memory. She realized with a sudden pang that she hadn't curtseyed since her mother died.

Hampden continued speaking as they all straightened. "Miss de la Tour is one of our French counterparts. A colleague of mine. She will be assisting me, as my guest, for the next month."

He shot Sabine a bland look, just daring her to contradict him.

A hot wave of embarrassment heated her cheeks. Oh, God, he

may as well have introduced her as his mistress. What other conclusion could the women draw from such an outrageous arrangement? She opened her mouth to try to explain, then shut it. What could she say? The she was a counterfeiter? A criminal? A fugitive from her own country?

To her surprise, neither lady appeared either disgusted or scandalized. In fact, they both wore identical expressions of amused intrigue. The elder of the two had the same warm amber eyes as her son. She barely looked old enough to have a child of his age. Sabine addressed her first.

"Forgive me, madame, for the intrusion. I am very pleased to make your acquaintance."

The woman smiled and extended her hands in greeting. "Welcome, my dear."

The girl, Heloise, stepped forward. A pale scar curved on one side of her forehead from hairline to temple but it in no way detracted from her beauty, which was enhanced by a pair of striking thunderstorm-gray eyes.

"The disreputable fellow you met next door is William Ravenwood, Marquis of Ormonde," Hampden said. "The poor bugger's married to Heloise, here."

"Richard!" The girl rolled her eyes at her brother's teasing. "We've just returned from our honeymoon in Egypt," she confided with a smile at Sabine. "It was wonderful. Now we're living at our London home, Avondale House. It's just a short walk away, in Berkeley Square."

Sabine nodded. "Congratulations."

Hampden addressed his mother again. "Miss de la Tour is going to be extremely busy working for me during the day . . ." he shot Sabine a taunting smile, " . . . but in the evenings she will be attending various ton functions, as our guest."

Sabine frowned. "That's not what we—"

His smile remained in place, but his amber gaze sharpened in warning. "Nevertheless, that is what I require, Miss de la Tour."

Sabine frowned, furiously aware that she couldn't tear him to pieces in front of his family. No doubt that was precisely why he'd mentioned it now, while they had an audience. She shot him a look that assured him they would continue the conversation later in private.

Heloise indicated a yellow upholstered sofa. "Won't you sit down, Miss de la Tour? I'm simply desperate to hear how you'll be assisting my brother."

Hampden sent her an amused, chiding look for her unsubtle attempt to pry. "We're not staying." He glanced over at his mother. "If anyone asks, Sabine's a distant Valette relative, come to visit now that the war's over."

"Of course." Therese nodded, accepting this as though she received such odd requests on a daily basis. Perhaps, being Richard Hampden's mother, she did.

His gaze returned to Sabine, and her skin warmed as he swept her from head to foot like a jockey eyeing up a racehorse.

"She's going to need something suitable to wear." His gaze switched back to his family. "I need you two to make her look presentable."

Sabine's eyes widened, but both women began nodding enthusiastically. Therese clapped her hands. "Of course we will help, Richard! I do so love a challenge."

Sabine stiffened, not sure whether to be insulted or not by such a frank assessment, but Therese seemed so genuinely delighted it was impossible to take offense. The older woman's avid gaze narrowed on her disordered tresses and her brow puckered.

"Her hair needs attention, of course, but that's easy to fix. Monsieur Travers can come at once." She clasped Sabine's hands in hers, inspected them, and gave a delicate little shudder. "And are these ink stains? Good heavens!" She glanced up at Hampden. "No matter. We can hide them with a nice pair of gloves."

She stepped back, tilted her head, and subjected Sabine to a critical scrutiny not unlike that of her son. "The rest will be easy. Oh, my dear, you are just too beautiful. The ladies will be tearing their hair out when they see you, I promise. You shall be a success *énorme!*"

Sabine was momentarily struck speechless. She was passably pretty, certainly, but no one had ever called her beautiful. Or even hinted that she might have the potential to be so.

Heloise shot her a conspiratorial grin. "Good luck. I know that look. Mother's spied her next victim and you're it!"

"Heloise!" Therese scolded gently.

Heloise gave her mother an unrepentant grin. "Don't try to deny it. My lack of interest in fashion has always been a sore disappointment for you. But now you have a new subject to torture." She turned back to Sabine with a chuckle. "I can't thank you enough for diverting her attention from me."

Sabine's own lips curved in response to the teasing. Heloise's smile was infectious.

Heloise stepped closer to Sabine so they stood shoulder to shoulder. "Look, we're almost the same size. I can lend you a few gowns until you get some of your own made up. You're a little shorter than me, but not enough to signify. Emma, my maid, can alter the hems. Unless you have any particular talent for sewing?"

Sabine gave a bemused shake of the head. "I once tried to darn a pair of my own stockings and sewed the toe completely closed."

Heloise snorted. "I can tell we're going to be great friends."

Sabine's heart warmed at the women's easy acceptance of her. What an extraordinary family! She hoped Richard Hampden appreciated what he had.

Heloise patted her arm. "Having a new friend to show off at all the parties is going to make things so much more fun. I can tell you all about everyone in the ton. Who's eligible, who's not."

"She won't be looking to catch a husband," Hampden said brusquely.

Sabine shot him an arch look. "And why not? Isn't attracting a suitor the primary motivation for going out?"

He returned her smile with a smug one of his own. "You won't need to look for a suitor. You'll already have one."

All three women turned to him in unison.

"What do you mean by that?" Heloise asked, intrigued. "Who?"

Hampden's lips twitched. "Me."

CHAPTER 16

*R*ichard watched Sabine closely for a reaction. He needed to tread carefully, but the idea that had taken shape as he'd lain in bed last night seemed the perfect solution to his problems with women.

Sabine blinked. "You're going to be my suitor?"

"Precisely. Not only are you going to assist me in a professional capacity, you're going to help me with a little social dilemma, too. You, Miss de la Tour, are going to be my human shield."

"I don't understand."

"I am going to court you, publicly, making it very clear that I have only the most honorable of intentions."

"Why on earth would you do that?" she asked, bewildered.

"To be blunt, I'm what's commonly referred to as 'a matrimonial catch.' I have only to look sideways at a debutante to have her parents mentally penning a notice to *The Times* and wondering what to serve at our wedding breakfast."

Sabine was regarding him with a look of speechless horror. His mother merely raised her eyebrows, while Heloise appeared thoroughly entertained.

"We are going to fake our engagement. Or, at least, our imminent engagement. You're going to keep the matchmaking harpies away for the next four weeks."

Heloise laughed. "A female chaperone? That's not a bad idea, Richard."

Sabine sent Heloise a filthy look for agreeing so readily. "Surely such a move will make the girls try even harder to get him? One last, concerted effort before he's lost to the shackles of matrimony."

Richard shot her a droll glance. "It's a risk I'm willing to take."

She raised her brows. "And when I leave, what then?"

"I'll tell everyone you've jilted me," he said. "You'll be long gone, and I'll have had four sweet weeks of liberty."

Of course, after that he'd probably be inundated with women desperate to console him, but that was a problem for the future. He watched Sabine's forehead furrow as she tried to think up objections.

"No one will believe for one minute that you'd fall in love with me," she said finally.

"Not in that outfit," he agreed sweetly. He watched her lips purse in annoyance and suppressed a smile. "Which is why you need their help," he nodded at his mother and Heloise, "to turn you into someone capable of capturing the heart of one of society's most determined bachelors."

"That would take a great deal more acting ability than even I possess," she said waspishly.

He took a step closer to her and enjoyed the way her eyes widened in awareness. "You do yourself a grave disservice." He treated her to a mocking bow. "I'm certain someone as adept at deception as yourself can feign anything you put your mind to. Even an engagement to a scoundrel like myself."

He'd backed her into a corner, Richard thought smugly. It was only fair. She'd done the same to him. Quid pro quo.

His mother gave an exasperated sigh. "The ton isn't that bad,

Richard. There are some very nice young ladies out there. You just never give any of them a chance."

Richard suppressed the desire to roll his eyes. His inability to settle down had been a constant refrain since he'd come into his majority at eighteen.

His mother continued. "But of course I'd be more than happy for Miss de la Tour to accompany us for the time that she is here. It will be our pleasure."

Sabine inclined her head. "Thank you, madame. You are very kind."

His mother nodded. "Tell me, are you by any chance related to the artist Maurice de la Tour?"

"He was my grandfather."

"Ah! I met him once, many years ago, when I was a young girl in Paris! He painted my portrait in pastels."

Sabine smiled. "I would like to see that, madame. He was an exceptional talent. Much like my father."

Therese patted her hand. "It's hanging at our house in Dorset. Perhaps you'll get to see it sometime." She shot Richard a sly, questioning glance over Sabine's head and he suppressed a groan. Mother was clearly hoping he'd turn this fake engagement into a real one. There was zero chance of that happening. Sabine de la Tour was the last woman he'd consider marrying, however physically attracted to her he might be. She was as trustworthy as a snake.

His mother's voice snapped him back to the present.

"Sorry, what was that, Mother?"

She frowned at him for his inattention, somehow managing to make him feel like a naughty ten-year-old instead of the thirty-two-year-old he was in truth.

"I asked you which events you wanted Miss de la Tour to attend."

"Isn't Lady Carstairs having a ball on Wednesday night?"

His mother nodded. "She is. It promises to be a great crush. I'm sure I can inveigle an extra invitation if you wish."

"Do that." Richard raked Sabine with a head-to-toe glance he knew would annoy her. He waved his hands in an airy gesture to encompass her slim figure and furrowed his brow doubtfully. "Do you think four days will be enough?"

Sabine's expression darkened.

His mother shot him a reprimanding glance. "Of course it will!"

"Then I'll leave it up to you to arrange for a hairdresser, modiste, and whoever else she'll need to make her presentable. Let me know when they will be here." He turned to Sabine. "Come along, Miss de la Tour. We have work to do."

Hampden's majordomo was hovering as they reentered his side of the house.

"The boy is here to see you, my lord," he announced. "I have put him in the study."

Hampden smiled. "Thank you, Hodges." He gestured for Sabine to follow him.

A small, scruffy boy, no older than twelve, was perched on the arm of one of the wing chairs, cap in hand, leg swinging. Sabine recognized him as the crossing-sweeper from outside.

"Morning, William. Do you bring good news?"

The boy shot Hampden a cheeky grin and bobbed his head at Sabine. "Indeed I does, yer lordship."

Sabine took in the lad's grimy hands and ragged outfit. She knew his sort from Paris, boys who knew how to make themselves indispensable. Savary had used them often, scamps who could blend into the shadows and slip seamlessly through a crowd. He appeared quite innocent, as angelic a choirboy, but Sabine gave a cynical snort. No doubt he was an accomplished liar. Just like herself.

"Skelton's agreed to the meeting. His shop, tomorrow, nine A.M."

"Well done, Will." Hampden ruffled the boy's hair affectionately, exactly as he did with his scruffy dog. "You getting enough to eat?"

"You know me, guv'nor. Never say no to a hot dinner."

Richard nodded. "Go and see Cook in the kitchens. She'll feed you."

"Yes sir. Miss." The boy slipped out the door as Hampden turned to her.

"Who is Skelton?" she asked.

"A pawnbroker in Holborn. One of the men we've been watching. Most of the plotters' finances come from stolen goods that pass through his shop. He's a fence. A money launderer."

"He sounds charming."

"He's not. But he's our way into the gang of traitors."

"Is your plan still to offer my counterfeit fortune to their cause?"

"It is. Skelton's going to be surprised to learn Lacorte's a woman. You'll have to work hard to convince him." His gaze turned calculating. "Of course, the best way to do that would be to take some of your fake money to the meeting. That way, you could show it to him and gain his trust."

Sabine raised a brow. She knew what he was doing: trying to ferret out where she'd hidden the bulk of the money. Well, he'd have to do better than that.

"I told you, I can't get access to it at present." She shot him a thin, patently insincere smile. "Sorry."

He made a sound of disappointment through his teeth. "*Tsk.* Now that's just not true, is it, my love? I'm beginning to understand the way your convoluted mind works. You always have a backup plan. So I can't believe you wouldn't keep a little money with you. A few thousand pounds, say? For emergencies."

Sabine quelled a flash of alarm. Damn him. He couldn't possibly know about the stash she'd hidden for just such an eventuality. It was a lucky guess, no more. She shrugged. "I'm sure you've already had your staff search my belongings, so you must know I brought no money with me. Only the notes I showed you last night."

"You can take those, then." That one-sided dimple made an appearance. "Don't look so worried. You won't be entering the lion's den alone. I'll be coming with you."

Sabine's lips twisted in scorn. She flicked a glance at his immaculate cravat. "I'm sure you'll blend right in."

"I'll be in disguise."

She eyed him doubtfully. There was no way he could hide all that arrogant self-assurance. No humble merchant or servant held himself the way he did, as if he owned the world and everything in it.

He strode to the door. "You may spend the rest of the afternoon at your leisure. Feel free to borrow some books from the library. I will see you for dinner at nine."

The thought of an intimate dinner made her pulse flutter. She shouldn't spend more time with him than necessary. To be drawn to him, her enemy, could only lead to disaster.

CHAPTER 17

a t precisely five to nine, Sabine left her room and found Hampden waiting for her at the bottom of the stairs. When he took her arm, she feigned a sudden interest in their surroundings so she didn't gaze at him like an imbecile.

The dining table could have seated fourteen with ease. Two place settings had been arranged at one end. Hampden pulled out a chair and indicated for her to sit. At least they wouldn't have to shout at one another down the mahogany expanse to converse, Sabine thought with a grim smile.

Two servants hovered by the door. At Hampden's signal, they began uncovering the domed silver dishes on the table to reveal a lavish array of food. "I requested service *à la Française* tonight in your honor."

Sabine nodded. The French style was to present all the courses at the same time, as opposed to the more recent fashion of service *à la Russe,* Russian-style, where courses were brought to the table sequentially.

At a nod from Hampden, the servants disappeared.

"Now eat."

Sabine was so hungry she could have consumed everything in

front of her, but Hampden was watching her with an expression of pained expectation, as if he were just waiting for her to embarrass herself. Did he imagine she lacked the ability to use a knife and fork? A small perverse part of her debated grabbing a chicken leg with her bare hands and tearing into it like a savage, but she repressed the childish urge. She picked up her fork.

The cutlery was heavy. She made a point of turning it over and inspecting it for hallmarks. Yes, there they were, the little stamped symbols that indicated the piece was solid silver. No rustic pewter for Lord Lovell.

Candlelight flickered off the ludicrously ornate centerpiece in front of her. It was shaped like a palm tree surrounded by camels, with three toga-draped women holding a cut glass bowl dripping with fruit. The luxury was intimidating, and Sabine felt a flash of anger at herself. She shouldn't be feeling daunted or uncomfortable. She'd lived like this for the first seventeen years of her life.

She forced herself to eat slowly so she could sample a little of everything. Soup, beef, turkey, ham, fried eggs, some asparagus. A pudding covered with an almond cream sauce. A custard tart topped with shining redcurrants. She couldn't remember the last time she'd had such a sumptuous meal.

Hampden watched her. Even though she kept her gaze resolutely fixed on her plate, she was acutely aware of his regard. With a conscious effort she stilled the betraying tremor in her hand, reached for her wineglass, and took a deep drink. She dared a glance at her companion and her heart twisted in her chest. Why did he have to be so good-looking?

"This is very good wine," she managed.

He inclined his head. "French, of course. It's from my eldest brother, Nic. He owns a chateau and vineyard just outside Paris." He studied her for a long moment. "I've a feeling you'd get on famously with my sister-in-law, Marianne. She used to be a criminal too."

She wouldn't rise to the bait, no matter how provocative his statements. He was mocking her, but his opinion meant nothing. He was the means to an end: the way to get Anton safely away from Malet. That was all.

Hampden raised his wineglass. "A toast. To a successful assignment."

She raised her own and took a sip. "To *entente cordiale*."

The food and soft candlelight was all designed to lull her, of course, but that was all right. For tonight she was quite content to be lulled. She hadn't been lulled in a very long time.

Hampden sat back in his seat and stretched his long legs out beneath the table. His foot brushed her ankle. She tucked her feet beneath her chair.

"Why did you choose the name Philippe Lacorte?"

She shot him a wry smile. "It was a joke. Inspired by your English story of Robin Hood. His friend was a giant named Little John, was he not?"

Hampden nodded.

"Well, it seemed a good idea to let everyone think that 'Philip the short' was a six-foot giant with a scraggly beard instead of a little, dark-haired French girl."

He looked her over, a brief, simmering appraisal that nevertheless managed to catalogue every salient point of interest from her crown to her waist. Her blood heated, but she schooled her expression to remain neutral.

"And did you rob the rich to feed the poor?" he asked lightly.

"I *was* the poor."

She glanced around the opulent room. So much to steal, if one were tempted. But she was not that kind of girl. Anton, however, would have had no such scruples. He would have slipped as many spoons into his pockets as possible.

A twinge of guilt twisted her stomach. Here she was, dining in the lap of luxury, while poor Anton was navigating the crime-ridden stews of London. His English was terrible. She'd taught him a few simple phrases, but he was unlikely to find himself popular, as a Frenchman on English soil.

She shook her head to banish the worrying thought. Anton could look after himself. He'd survived Savary and Malet in Paris. He would be all right.

CHAPTER 18

*L*ord, but she was tempting in that dress!

Richard watched as his "guest" selected a cherry from the fruit bowl and bit into it. Her lips closed around the crimson orb and his brain went a little fuzzy.

"Do people always do what you tell them to do, my lord?" she asked pertly.

Richard narrowed his eyes. Her use of his title was more insult than deference. "Generally speaking, yes. Which makes it all the more annoying when my orders are ignored."

The corners of her lips twitched. "Must be very vexing."

"Indeed," he growled.

She took another bite of cherry. The dark red juice stained her lips. He prayed for strength.

"We mere mortals must ingratiate ourselves with our betters to survive."

Her mocking tone indicated how little she viewed him as her better, but he found her lack of subservience refreshing. "I've yet to see any evidence of you making an effort to ingratiate yourself," he said.

"Yes, well, you," she raised an inky eyebrow, "are the exception. You're stuck with me whether I'm subservient or not."

"Lucky me," he drawled. "Obedience can get so tiresome."

She ignored his sarcasm. "I expect it does. That's why you choose to work as a spy. For the challenge. To feel alive."

Richard hid his surprise at her perceptiveness.

"I don't expect someone like you to understand my position," she continued. "What can you possibly know of hardship? Your idea of suffering is encountering a corked claret. Your mattress is probably stuffed with real hundred-pound notes."

He laughed. "War certainly creates some strange bedfellows, doesn't it?"

He raised his glass in a wordless salute and tried to ignore the mental image of her as his bedfellow, her naked body entwined in his sheets. "Your surname," he said, to distract himself. "De la Tour. It literally means 'of the tower.' Like that princess in the fairy tale. The one with all the hair."

"You mean Rapunzel."

"That's the one. Shut up in a turret, pining away for her prince."

She snorted. "I'm not pining away for anyone. I'd never sit around waiting for a prince to rescue me. I'd cut off my own hair and escape on my own."

He smiled at her spirit. "Of course. You'd forge an invitation to the prince's ball, turn up uninvited, kill his best dragon, and run off with his crown."

"Credit me with a little more talent than a thief," she sniffed. "Besides, princes are notoriously unreliable. In real life they'd get distracted by a tavern, or a horse race, or a buxom barmaid and forget all about rescuing the princess."

"You are far too young to be so cynical."

She shot him an arch look. "'All that glitters is not gold,' as Shakespeare said. Princes are spoiled and idle. And far too used to getting their own way."

Richard raised a brow. God, he loved the way she challenged him. "Are you talking about me, Miss de la Tour?"

She folded her hands piously in her lap. "It is not my place to judge you, my lord."

"And yet here you are. You think me everything that is bad about the aristocratic class: reckless, lazy, amoral, and dissolute."

She shrugged. "Even your name has the word *rich* in it, Richard Hampden." She took another slow sip of wine. "And I never said you were lazy."

He bit back a chuckle at that veiled insult.

"And since we're on the subject of names," she said, "Richard does not suit you at all."

"My parents will be so pleased you think so. What alternatives did you have in mind? Lucifer? Beelzebub? Mephistopheles?"

She shrugged. "History has not been kind to people named Richard. Just look at your English kings. Richard the Second was insane. Richard the Third was a hunchback who killed his own nephews."

"What about Richard the Lionheart?" he countered.

She waved a dismissive hand. "He was brave, but no one ever called him handsome. Handsome men are never called Richard."

* * *

HE SHOT her a look of breathtaking arrogance. "Are you implying that I'm ugly?"

Sabine bit her lip. To deny it would be one protest too far. But to confirm it would make him all the more obnoxious. She wrinkled her nose. "I've seen worse. Besides, it doesn't matter what your name is. A viscount can have a clubfoot, a lisp, and a facial tic and still be considered handsome." She shot him an assessing glance. "It's amazing how attractive a man appears when viewed through the lens of an unencumbered estate and twenty thousand pounds a year."

Hampden chuckled. "It's closer to thirty thousand, actually. And I'm pretty sure it isn't the size of my inheritance they're interested in."

Sabine raised her brows, even as she tried to ignore the hot flush that spread over her skin. Devil! How had the conversation veered to something so risqué?

Thankfully, Hampden drained his glass and rose from the table. "As delightful as this has been, Miss de la Tour, I must bid you good night. I'm engaged elsewhere for the evening."

Sabine became conscious of a sinking feeling. It was not disappointment. She didn't care where he was spending the rest of the night. She glanced at the ornate clock on the mantel—ten o'clock—and hid her pique behind sarcasm. "And here I was, praying for another hour of your exalted company."

"I doubt I shall return until after you're in bed."

He came around the back of her chair and pulled it backward so she could stand. There was a teasing glint in his eye as he reached forward and brushed her cheek with a casual flick of his fingers. Her breath caught in her throat.

"You should get some sleep, *ma chère.* You'll need to be at your most charming and persuasive tomorrow for Skelton. If you fail to convince him you're Lacorte, the consequences could be unpleasant for us both."

A shiver racked her as she sidestepped and escaped into the hall. His touch made her insides quiver, but she was under no illusion that he actually found her attractive. He was just playing power games, trying to intimidate and fluster her with his hot stare.

She knew men like him. They loved the chase but grew bored when they captured the prize. Right now her stubborn evasion had garnered his fleeting interest, but he would lose interest soon enough.

To her consternation, Hampden escorted her up the wide

staircase and down the corridor toward her room. He stopped at the door before her own. Sabine frowned. "Is that your room?"

He adopted an innocent expression. "Yes. You're in the duchess's suite. It's the mirror image of mine. Didn't you notice the connecting door? It's in the paneling to the right of the fireplace. I doubt you can hear anything through the wall, but I'll try not to wake you on my return." His sudden grin was pure devilry. "Sleep tight."

Sabine entered her own room and immediately rushed to locate the hidden door. There it was, neatly disguised in the wallpaper and wooden paneling, almost invisible unless you knew where to look. She ran her fingers over the seam and felt a tiny waft of cooler air seeping through the gap.

She didn't dare open it, though there was probably a second door on Hampden's side. He'd doubtless be waiting with some sarcastic comment about invading his bedchamber.

There was no handle and no key, so she slid a chest of drawers in front of it before she got ready for bed. Not that it would make much difference. She had no way of locking the door to the main passageway, either. Clearly, if Richard Hampden wanted to seek her out, he could. It was a sobering thought.

CHAPTER 19

*S*abine tried to stay awake and listen for Hampden's return, but the last thing she remembered was the clock on the mantelpiece chiming one. She awoke to sunlight, and wondered despondently where he'd been, and with whom.

He wanted to keep the eligible women of society at bay, but that didn't mean he was steering clear of women in general. No doubt he'd spent the evening with someone thoroughly ineligible. And enjoyed every minute of it.

Sabine tugged the brush angrily through her hair. She didn't care what Richard Hampden did in his spare time. All she cared about was that he paid her.

Another outfit had been provided for her; this one consisted of a rough hemp-spun skirt, a thin cotton shirt, and a whalebone corset. Presumably in London, as in Paris, pawnbrokers like this Mr. Skelton plied their trade in the less salubrious parts of the city.

She wrapped a drab woolen shawl around her and descended the stairs to find a stranger waiting in the hallway. From his broad shoulders, brown coat, and tousled hair she took him for some sort of groundsman or gardener.

"Good morning," she murmured politely, wondering whether Hampden would even be up at such an hour. Perhaps she should—

"Morning yourself."

The gardener looked up and Sabine gave a gasp of surprise as Hampden's laughing eyes met hers. She blinked. Good God! She wouldn't have thought he could disguise that arrogant air of lordly command that seemed so ingrained, but he'd achieved it.

He'd mussed his hair and neglected to shave; his jaw sported an intriguing shadowy prickle. Sabine curled her fingers into her palms against the urge to reach out and feel the texture of it. He looked thoroughly disreputable.

She descended the last step and wrinkled her nose. His clothes held the sickly sweet scent of the stables—hay and manure. He must have borrowed them from one of the grooms. She raised her hand to her nose.

"Would you care to borrow my vinaigrette?" he teased.

"You've missed your vocation," she said scathingly. "You should have been on the stage."

"I've spent my fair share of time roughing it. There are times when it's better not to be Richard, Lord Lovell, and be plain old Dickie 'Ampden, groomsman to 'is lordship, instead. Come on."

His coach awaited them outside. Sabine cast a dubious eye on the coat of arms emblazoned upon the sides. She opened her mouth to make a sarcastic comment on traveling unobtrusively, but Hampden beat her to it.

"Wilson will drop us off a few streets away from Skelton's," he said, handing her into the coach. "We'll walk from there."

It took only a few minutes to move from the wide, well-ordered streets of St. James's to the narrow, winding lanes of Spitalfields. Sabine shuddered as they descended the steps of the carriage and immediately had to step over a steaming pile of manure. At least she had on her sturdy boots.

Hampden turned down a dingy side street, and she took care

to avoid the twin channels of refuse running along either side. They exuded a pungent aroma best left unidentified. The buildings huddled together as if for warmth, or for protection. Traders called out incentives to buy from all sides, or haggled with housewives over their wares.

"Silk stockings for the missus, guv'nor? Lovely quality, see if they ain't."

"Oysters! Cockles! Fresh today!"

A group of apprentice boys crowded around a game of dice on a street corner, shouting encouragement and curses. A few people appeared to be staggering home, as if they'd never been to bed. Women walked among the crowd with steaming baskets of pancakes and dumplings. One cast a come-hither smile at Richard, the gesture marred by her rotten stumps for teeth.

"Tuppence a tup, me fine lad," she cackled as they went past, grabbing at his sleeve. Hampden deftly extricated himself with a wry shrug and a charming smile.

"I can't, sweeting," he joked, tilting his head at Sabine. "The missus would kill me. But I wish you good hunting."

Sabine pursed her lips. She could practically see the tart melting into a puddle on the cobbles.

They walked briskly, past barbers and peruke-makers, bakers and haberdashers. A swinging sign proclaimed the Spread Eagle Chocolate House, and the streets all had intriguing names like Bride Lane, Paradise Row, and Snow Hill.

She was glad of Hampden's broad-shouldered presence beside her. Even dressed as he was, in rough workman's clothes, people still moved out of his way. And for all her outward confidence she was a little scared of the press of people, the noise, and the almost overwhelming smells. There was a foreignness to this English city, with its strange guttural language and odd fashions, that made her conscious of how different it was from Paris.

Hampden took her arm to assist her around an upturned barrow of apples, but instead of releasing her, he slid his hand around until it rested at the small of her back. The gesture was both guiding and oddly protective. The light contact burned through the layers of her clothing.

Sabine cleared her throat just as Hampden spoke.

"Ah, here we are."

Skelton's shop was squeezed between a butcher's and a shoe-maker. The traditional sign for a pawnbroker, three brass balls hanging from a bracket, swung above the door. Curved mullioned windows bowed out into the street, their panes of glass showing shelves so crammed full it was impossible to see inside.

The grimy display held a random assortment of items: candlesticks, dinner plates, a violin and bow, linen curtains, a copper coffeepot, wooden crutches. There was even a great flopping parson's hat.

The bell above the door didn't so much tinkle as make a despondent, sullen thud, and the interior smelled of dust and human despair. Sabine stepped forward cautiously while Richard hung back, guarding the door to ensure no one else entered behind them. He turned the dog-eared cardboard sign around so it read *Closed.*

A glass-topped counter ran the length of the shop. Sabine leaned over to inspect the contents: tarnished shoe buckles, jewelry, gold watches, rings and snuffboxes. If the items weren't reclaimed by repaying the original loan with interest within a year, they would be sold by public auction.

A wave of melancholy swept over her. They made her sad, these tiny glimpses of once precious things that had been surrendered in desperation. A small silver vinaigrette, a child's ivory teething ring with three silver bells attached to it. Wedding rings and engagement rings. Were they from dead people? Or unwanted proof of a broken heart, a called-off engagement? So many small, sad stories.

She turned away.

Hampden came up behind her and leaned over her shoulder to inspect the contents of the case. His nearness sent a little shivery thrill through her. He indicated a silver spoon with an armorial engraved on the handle.

"That's Earl Gower's crest," he murmured in her ear. "Either he's lost heavily at the gaming tables and found himself in the river Tick, or someone on his staff is pilfering the silver."

"Mr. Skelton?" Sabine called into the gloom.

Richard stepped back as a figure loomed into view.

CHAPTER 20

Skelton was a man of epic proportions. A grimy brown waistcoat strained alarmingly over his protruding stomach and his greasy, gray-streaked hair was tied in a queue at the back of his neck. White specks of dandruff dusted the curled collar of his navy coat. Sabine caught a whiff of unwashed body and stale onions as he waddled toward her, his beady eyes suspicious in his jowly face.

He immediately gestured to several sets of false teeth on the counter.

"Them's the best 'Waterloo teeth' money can buy. Everybody wants 'em. Guaranteed to come from healthy young men, struck down in their prime."

Sabine suppressed an appalled shudder. "No thank you. My own teeth are perfectly good." Unlike Skelton's, she noticed. They were little more than brown stumps.

The shopkeeper gave a disappointed grunt. "Well, what can I do for yer then? You want some nice fabric for a dress?" He pulled forward a thick roll of scarlet cloth. "I got twenty yards of the best sarsenet, 'ere. For you, sixpence a yard."

Sabine shook her head. "No, thank you. I am here because we have an appointment. You wished to meet Philippe Lacorte."

Skelton stilled. "Maybe I did," he hedged. His squinty eyes flicked to Richard. "That 'im?"

Sabine smiled and brought all her acting skills to bear. She was Philippe Lacorte. She could do anything.

"Oh, goodness, no. That's just a friend of mine, Jacob." She waved a dismissive hand at Hampden and shook her head in mock sorrow. "He was hit on the head by a falling branch when he was a little boy. The blow left him an idiot." She gave a gusty sigh. "He hardly talks. I've barely heard him do more than grunt."

Skelton shot Hampden a suspicious glare. Hampden, to his credit, took her cue and stood staring vacantly ahead like the big dumb brute he was supposed to be, playing the part of village idiot to perfection.

Sabine suppressed a grin. Oh, this was going to be fun. A faint wicked smile curved her lips as she swept him with a slow, head-to-toe appraisal, just like the ones he'd given her.

She leaned toward Skelton and tried not to breathe in his repellent body odor as she pitched her voice to a conspiratorial whisper still loud enough to carry back to the door.

"He has a magic way with horses, though." She gave a little, feminine sigh. "I think it must be those hands. They're so very . . . capable."

She shot Hampden a cheeky glance and enjoyed the way his eyes widened slightly in shock. "He's as thick as two short planks, bless him, but I like to keep him around. He's so decorative. And brawny. Just look at those arms. I vow, it makes me positively dizzy." She fanned herself with her hand. "He's very popular with the ladies. All that manly exuberance." Her smile was thoroughly wicked. "They don't seek him out for stimulating conversation, if you know what I mean."

Skelton grunted, apparently unimpressed by Hampden's magnificent physical attributes.

"I brought him along for protection," she continued. "In these parts you can never be too careful."

Skelton sniffed. "I can see why. He's a brute."

She pressed her hand to her chest as if to contain her beating heart. "Isn't he, though?"

Skelton narrowed his eyes. "So where's Lacorte, then?"

Sabine shot him her best, most dazzling smile. "You're looking at him, Mr. Skelton. I'm Philippe Lacorte."

The pungent phrase Skelton uttered expressed his profound disbelief.

Sabine sighed. So it began. "No doubt you were expecting a man, but I can assure you, I am the forger you're looking for."

Skelton made another dismissive sound.

"I'm quite prepared to prove my skills," she said bullishly.

He shrugged, but gestured for her to come around the other side of the counter. "All right." He tilted his head at Richard. "'E can stay right there and guard the front door. Don't want no hinterruptions now, do we?"

He slid his fat body along the counter to make room for her. Sabine half expected him to leave a greasy trail on the glass top.

* * *

RICHARD STATIONED himself by the door, legs apart, and tried to compose his features into something resembling deaf and dumb.

He could still feel the heat of Sabine's cheeky glance on his body. He'd had to hastily fold his hands in front of his breeches to hide the humiliating evidence of his reaction. And he couldn't even retaliate.

Her shameless ogling had been clever, though. No well-born lady would exhibit her desire in public. Her bawdy appreciation of him neatly aligned her with Skelton as his social equal, a member of the lower orders. Someone who could be trusted.

Richard suppressed a grin as she turned her shoulder and

dismissed him as casually as if she were rejecting a misshapen pastry from the baker's tray.

"Let's get down to business, shall we, Mr. Skelton?" she purred.

CHAPTER 21

"*Y*ou know anything about jewels?" Skelton asked slyly. "What do you think of this lot? Just came in today." He pointed to a small pile of heaped jewelry on the counter.

Sabine gave it a desultory glance and pointed to a ring with three glittering stones. "I hope you didn't pay much for that."

"Why?" Skelton glared at her.

"Because the left-hand diamond has been replaced with paste."

He scowled, and fumbled in his waistcoat pocket. The fabric was stretched so tight against his belly he had a hard time getting his fingers into the opening, but he finally withdrew a jeweler's loupe. The magnifying eye glass had the unfortunate effect of grossly enlarging his eye; the sagging skin and bloodshot whites appeared even more grotesque under strong magnification. Sabine suppressed a shudder.

"See how the claw setting has been moved out of place?" she said. "And that stone bears several scratches on the top surface. Only another diamond is hard enough to scratch a diamond.

Plus, it doesn't sparkle like the other two. There's no internal fire."

Skelton gave a noncommittal grunt. His long, yellowed fingernails, discolored by years of tobacco smoke, tapped the counter. "All right, so you knows gemstones. But if you're a forger, you should be able to tell me which one of these is fake."

He reached beneath the counter and withdrew a sheaf of assorted foreign banknotes. Half a dozen currencies were represented, from French francs to Spanish asignados.

Sabine sorted through them. She bent to inspect a couple, then reached into the front of her bodice. Skelton's lascivious gaze tracked the move with interest, but he sagged in disappointment when she merely withdrew her own gold-rimmed lorgnette. The circular magnifying lens was surmounted with a pendant fastening shaped like a lady's hand. It was one of her most precious possessions, a gift from her father, and she rarely took it off.

She slid a Russian note away from the rest of the pack. "This one is a very poor fake. Definitely not one of mine. The paper's all wrong, for a start. It's too blue. And they have printed the signatures." Skelton inspected it through his own glass. "They should be signed by hand, by the clerk."

Skelton sniffed. "Humph."

"Also, they have misspelled the Russian word for *state.* Do you speak Russian?" she asked sweetly, already suspecting the answer. Skelton barely spoke *English.*

"No," Skelton grunted.

"I taught myself the Cyrillic alphabet," she said. "Quite a few Russian words are translatable if you know their alphabet. *Theater,* for example. *Coffee. Restaurant.*" She pointed to one of the longer Russian words on the note. "There, do you see the fifth symbol? The one that looks like an upside-down backward *L?*" She pulled over a genuine Russian note for comparison. "On this one it makes a complete loop, like a square."

Skelton nodded, his tone wondering. "I see it now. Yes. Very impressive."

Sabine resisted the urge to flash a triumphant grin at Richard, who was still hovering in the doorway. She lowered her eyes demurely instead and opened her reticule. "Thank you. Now, I've brought an example of one of my own counterfeits for you to inspect. To eliminate any doubt of either my identity or my skills."

Skelton placed the loupe in his eye again and examined the note she handed him carefully. He grunted. Tested the paper between his fingers. Sabine suppressed a shudder when he licked his thumb and tried to rub off the ink. His tongue, she noticed, was white with fur. She made a note to burn that particular note as soon as possible. He brought the paper up to his nose and sniffed, just as Richard had done.

Why did people do that? Money generally smelled revolting, passed from one grubby hand to another. Unless it was newly printed money, of course. That smelled like fresh ink and victory.

Sabine gave herself a mental shake. No. No more printing money. That was her old life. She was an honest woman now. At least, she was trying to be. She showed Skelton the initials hidden in the corner vignette.

"All right," Skelton sniffed finally. "I accept that you're Philippe Lacorte. Now what do you want from me?"

Sabine tried to quell her elation and lowered her voice to a conspiratorial whisper. "I've heard that you are in touch with a group of people who might be—shall we say—sympathetic to the emperor's cause?"

Skelton gave an abrupt nod and leaned closer, as if afraid of being overheard by the longcase clock behind him. "Maybe I am."

"I would like to meet them. I have a business proposition."

"What kind of proposition?"

She leaned even farther forward and Skelton mirrored her move. "Napoleon may have been exiled, but he still has his supporters," she whispered. "Loyal friends who are working to rescue him from his island prison and return him to power."

Skelton gave a knowing nod.

"They believe that Britain must be weakened, to eliminate the chance of another shameful defeat like that at Waterloo. You've heard of Savary?" she said. "The emperor's chief of police?"

Skelton nodded.

"He entrusted me with this." She reached into her pocket and withdrew the note she'd forged. She handed it to Skelton. His lips moved soundlessly as he read, shaping the words; clearly reading was a laborious process.

"Savary ordered me to seek out men like yourself who might help bring the emperor's plan to fruition. I know there are Englishmen who wish to see this country undermined quite as much as my own countrymen."

Skelton narrowed his eyes. "You truly have this fake fortune?" His eyes raked her body as if he somehow expected her to have it secreted about her person.

"I do. Half a million pounds' worth of fake British banknotes, right here in London." She paused for a beat to let that penetrate his thick skull. "What I propose is a deal, Mr. Skelton. I have the banknotes. You and your friends have the means of dispersing them. I suggest we work together to ensure a favorable outcome for both sides."

Skelton nodded. "All right. Get yourself to the White Lion, Haymarket on Friday evening, nine o'clock. I'll see to it the people you want are there."

It took a concerted effort not to look over at Hampden in triumph. She could gloat later. Sabine stepped back from Skelton's overwhelming presence and tapped the fake ten-pound note he'd inspected instead. "Thank you, Mr. Skelton. I'll leave you this, as an example of my work." She certainly didn't want to touch it again. "You can show it to your friends. Along with that letter."

Skelton's expression turned sly. "One more thing. To prove you ain't lyin' about the money, you can bring five hundred pounds' worth of it to the meeting."

Sabine cursed inwardly, but nodded her head. "Of course. If you wish." She edged out from behind the counter and sauntered toward Richard. "Nice doing business with you, Mr. Skelton. Until Friday. Come along, Jacob. Let's go."

CHAPTER 22

Sabine took a gulp of fresh air as she stepped outside, relieved to be away from Skelton's nauseating presence. His demand for an extra five hundred pounds was a complication she hadn't anticipated, but at least she'd managed to set up a meeting with the other plotters.

She glanced upward. Ominous clouds had gathered while they'd been in the shop; a rumble of thunder overhead confirmed an approaching storm.

Hampden heard it too. "Bloody hell," he muttered. "Come on!"

He grabbed her hand and set off, pulling her along in his wake, but they were still streets away from the carriage when the heavens opened. Sabine screeched in dismay as fat raindrops began to patter down.

The thoroughfare emptied. Vendors threw covers over their wares and wheeled their barrows to shelter while children ducked under the overhanging eaves and huddled in doorways to avoid the deluge.

Hampden shrugged off his rough overcoat and threw it around her shoulders as they raced along, dodging newly forming puddles. The coat was still warm from his body. The heat wrapped around her like an embrace and tightened her insides.

The carriage finally came into view. Sabine threw herself up the steps and slumped back on the velvet squabs with a sigh of relief as Hampden clambered in after her. She gave a laugh of sheer elation, buoyed up by their success.

He took the seat opposite her and stretched his long legs out in front of him. "Congratulations. You passed the first test."

Raindrops still trickled down her face. Sabine tugged the lace fichu from her neckline and used it to blot her face and neck. Her wet hair stuck to her cheeks; she pushed it back and sent Hampden a teasing, laughing glance.

"Oh dear! When was the last time the high-and-mighty Lord Lovell got caught in the rain?"

"I can't remember." He smiled ruefully. "And it's hard to be lordly when you're soaked to the skin."

He plucked his soaking shirt to peel it away from his chest—which drew her attention to the fact that the thin cotton had become almost transparent. It molded to the hard planes of his chest and abdomen like a second skin, allowing a tantalizing glimpse of tawny flesh and intriguing ridges beneath.

Her mouth went dry. His hair was rumpled in artless disorder, falling wildly over his forehead. He looked even more devastating than he had when he was perfectly attired. Disheveled suited him to perfection, damn him.

He sprawled negligently in his seat, taking up far too much space. Sabine tucked her legs together to avoid touching him.

He knocked twice on the carriage roof to signal the driver to move, and shot her a lazy grin. "So, you admire my big hands and broad shoulders, do you?"

She couldn't help it: she looked at his hands. And imagined them on her. Her stomach twisted into knots, but she managed a creditable shrug. "You're deaf. I never said any such thing."

He opened his mouth to argue.

"And if I did," she said quickly, "then it was only to convince Skelton you were a useless lump."

What a lie. The rhythmic hiss and patter of rain on the roof and the close confines of the carriage enclosed them in their own little world. Sabine was acutely aware of his body—and it was categorically not useless. It was strong and big and horribly tempting. She shivered.

The carriage rocked forward and she tried to concentrate on the sounds outside—the splash of the wheels through the puddles, the cries of the pedestrians—instead of the sudden tension that had thickened the air inside.

She took a steadying breath. She could not lose sight of her goal. Now was the perfect time to take advantage of his good mood. "I think I deserve a reward for convincing Skelton."

It wasn't her imagination: his eyes slid to her lips for a heartbeat before he looked up and met her eyes.

"You do, do you?" he said slowly. "What did you have in mind?"

There was no mistaking the predatory look in his eyes. He was watching her with an intensity that made her pulse flutter in her throat. All sorts of scandalous suggestions crowded her brain.

He leaned forward and she mirrored the action unthinkingly, drawn toward him as if by some invisible string. Desire thrummed in her blood. They were only a foot apart. If she just leaned forward—No. She did not feel this response to him. It was primitive and entirely unwelcome.

RICHARD CURSED UNDER HIS BREATH. His damn carriage was far too small. All he could smell was warm, wet woman. All he could hear was Sabine's panting breaths in the semidarkness.

Her wet eyelashes looked like spiky starfish against her pale skin. A droplet of water slid from between her eyebrows, down the side of her nose, and collected in the tiny indent at the corner of her lips. His body reminded him how long it had been since he'd had a warm, willing woman in his arms.

His lungs seized up. Desire shot straight to his groin. He imagined closing the space between them and pushing her back down onto the seat. Imagined licking that drop away, following it inside her mouth. She'd taste of cool rain and red-hot desire. His heart pounded heavily in his chest.

Sabine stared at him, unblinking. The tip of her tongue slid out and collected the droplet, and he almost groaned aloud. He'd just tensed the muscles in his stomach, ready to move across to her, when the wheel of the carriage hit a rut in the road. He grasped the leather strap on the wall to stop himself from falling right into her lap.

Sanity returned. He slumped back in his seat, focused his gaze resolutely out of the window, and forced his expression into one of bland interest.

"What did you have in mind?" he repeated gruffly.

She cleared her throat and sat back herself. "I wish to go out."

"Where?"

"The British Museum."

He turned and studied her for a tense moment, trying to sense a catch. His immediate response was to refuse, but he shouldn't be churlish. She'd played her part with Skelton beautifully, and now he had what he'd been after for months—a legitimate lead to the group of British plotters. It was another four days until they were due to meet. He couldn't keep her locked away in his study for the entire time, however much the idea appealed.

He nodded. "All right. I suppose you deserve a little leeway since the first stage of our plan met with success. You may go tomorrow. But only if you take a servant."

She inclined her head, as if she were the one bestowing a favor. "I will. And thank you, my lord."

CHAPTER 23

The British Museum was housed in a handsome building that had once been Montagu House, a late seventeenth-century mansion in Great Russell Street. Its foundation had been the collections of the English scientist Sir Hans Sloane, but subsequent acquisitions of manuscripts, sculpture, and art had made it a rival for the Louvre. Her father had always expressed an interest in visiting it.

Sabine suppressed a wistful pang and strode away from the bored-looking footman who'd been assigned to accompany her. She withdrew a small, ivory cloakroom token from her pocket and handed it to the attendant on duty.

In addition to stowing visitors' hats and cloaks, the museum had several cupboards and shelves for storing guests' bags. When the clerk located hers and deposited it on the counter, she let out a faint sigh of relief.

"Ah! Thank you. My sketching materials," she said brightly.

She was a firm believer in the old adage "hide in plain sight." In her experience, slapping a padlock on something was an invitation to have that very thing stolen immediately. One might as well post a flyer on the side saying "this contains something worth stealing."

Ergo, a battered brown leather bag in an unlocked pigeonhole in a barely guarded public cloakroom was the safest possible place for her fake money. If it looked as though nobody would care if it were stolen, no one would pay it the slightest heed.

Her theory had proved correct. Sabine shot the footman an innocent smile as she withdrew a sketchpad and a small wooden box of drawing instruments from the top. She barely glanced at the cigar box full of fake money nestled at the bottom.

A thousand pounds took up very little space. Sabine knew exactly what was in there: two hundred-pound bills, two fifties, forty tens, forty fives, and a hundred one-pound notes. One hundred and eighty-four small pieces of paper, barely an inch thick, that represented her safety net. Her alternative plan.

She gave the cloakroom attendant a wide smile as she handed him back the bag. "I won't be needing my oil paints today. Please keep them until I return."

"Of course, ma'am." The servant returned the ivory token with a nod.

Satisfied that her money was still safe, Sabine tucked the sketchbook under one arm and, conscious of the footman following her every move, strolled through a few rooms, idly studying the exhibits. She made her way up to the gallery, settled herself in front of a magnificent Tiepolo drawing, and proceeded to make a copy. She'd have to stay for a good few hours, at least. To arrive back at Brook Street too soon would arouse suspicion.

Some time later a dark shadow fell across her paper. Sabine, who had been lost in concentration, glanced up and suppressed a groan of annoyance when she saw Richard Hampden lounging in front of her.

"My lord," she managed. "What a pleasant surprise." Her tone indicated it was anything but. "Fancy seeing you here."

His lips quirked as he gave a casual shrug. "Just thought I'd make sure you weren't getting into mischief."

Sabine lifted her brows and made an impatient gesture at her paper and pencils as if to say "how, exactly?"

He didn't mistake her meaning. "Oh, I think you could get into trouble in an empty room, Miss de la Tour," he chuckled.

Sabine bit back a curse. She glanced around for her footman companion and found he'd disappeared. Dismissed, no doubt. *Merde.* Still, at least she'd checked her money. She'd never have dared to do so under Hampden's eagle-eyed scrutiny.

She sighed and went back to her drawing. Perhaps she could bore him into leaving her alone. "This place reminds me of the Louvre," she said placidly. "I spent many happy hours there when I was a girl, waiting for my father to finish work. I'd sit around all day, sketching. For hours," she repeated, hoping he'd take the hint. "It's how I honed my drawing skills."

He glanced down at her sketch. "You're exceedingly talented."

There was no trace of irony in his tone, only admiration. Sabine steeled herself against the tingle of warmth that spread through her at the compliment. "Thank you. I'm considering portraiture as a means of supporting myself now that the war is over."

"As opposed to blackmail?" he drawled sweetly.

She ignored the urge to poke him in the eye with her pencil.

"There are very few professions a woman can engage in without censure," she scolded. "Thankfully, being a portrait painter is one of them. Look at Madame Vigée Le Brun or Angelica Kauffman. They're recognized as among the best in their field. I'm going to return to Paris and set up a little gallery, somewhere near the Louvre."

"You can lead a life of spotless virtue," Hampden agreed amiably. "After you've finished fleecing me out of ten thousand pounds, that is."

She narrowed her eyes and pressed slightly too hard with her pencil. The lead broke in a little gray puff, and she cursed under her breath.

Hampden lifted the tails on his jacket and settled himself beside her on the marble bench as if he had all the time in the world. "Hodges mentioned there are two small portraits in your bedroom. Did you paint them?"

She scooted away from him as surreptitiously as possible. He seemed to take up an inordinate amount of room. "Yes. They're of my parents."

She expected him to make some further comment, but he gazed at the painting in front of them and for a moment they sat in a silence that was almost companionable.

"It occurs to me that drawing is just another form of trickery," he said presently. "It fools the eye into believing a two-dimensional object is three-dimensional."

Sabine stiffened, unsure whether that was a veiled insult or not. "I suppose you're right. But wasn't it Plato who said, 'Everything that deceives may be said to enchant'? Are you not enchanted by these paintings?" She waved her hand at the masterpieces around them.

"Of course. I have nothing but admiration for those born with such talent."

He sounded sincere, and Sabine sniffed, slightly mollified. "Drawing someone's portrait isn't so different from printing money. In both cases I am using my artistic skills for profit."

"Except one's lawful and one isn't."

She selected a new pencil from her bag and began sketching again, mainly to avoid looking at his hands, which were resting on his knees, tantalizingly close to her own. For some reason she found the veins running along the back of them particularly fascinating. She shot him another sideways glance from beneath her lashes. "Such an innocent pastime, drawing . . . and yet it's how I got into forgery."

Hampden raised his brows at her unprompted admission. "I

must admit, I'm curious to know how one goes about becoming a notorious counterfeiter."

She shouldn't tell him anything. The less he knew the better. But a perverse part of her wanted to see how he'd react to her additional misdemeanors.

"I had no choice. My mother died of a fever when I was eleven, my father when I'd just turned seventeen. I had no relations to protest when the emperor requisitioned the family house on Rue Saint-Honoré and granted it to one of his generals instead."

Sabine bit her lip against the bitterness of the memory, the awful sensation of powerlessness. "A friend of my father's took me in. He owned an art gallery and print shop on Rue du Pélican." She met Hampden's gaze squarely. "You've been there, monsieur. In addition to picture restoration, printing pamphlets, and selling antiquarian books, Jacques Carnaud had a rather lucrative sideline in forgery."

She went back to sketching.

"Jacques used to send me to the Louvre three times a week to improve my draughtsmanship. One day I made a copy of a Bernini sketch on some original fifteenth-century paper I'd taken from the flyleaf of an old book. Not with the intent to deceive, you understand. Just a technical exercise to see if I could do it. I used the same color charcoal, the same loose style as the original."

She peeked up at him again. As usual, she couldn't tell whether he believed her or not.

"Jacques was impressed. He said he couldn't tell mine from the original—and he was an expert at handling old master drawings. He put it in the window of the shop, unsigned, with no claims as to its genuineness, and sold it the very next day for thirty sous to the French foreign minister."

Sabine shook her head. "To a trained eye there are many differences between a copy and the original. The original is fluid, like your Rembrandt. A copy is more . . . deliberate, somehow. It's hard to explain, but the strokes are different, constrained, because you're trying to replicate what you see in front of you, not simply capture a moment." She shot him a conspiratorial smile. "Ah, but a drawing in the style of an artist, that's much easier. I sold quite a number of those to Napoleon's ministers and friends."

"You don't seem particularly repentant."

She chuckled. He didn't seem at all shocked or censorious of her admission. "None of those uneducated upstarts would know a Rembrandt from a rat's arse." She blew a speck of charcoal from the corner of her paper. "They had no interest in the artwork itself. It was just something to brag about at dinner parties to impress their friends." She folded her arms. "Once I even added a mustache to a portrait and the buyer still didn't notice!"

Hampden shook his head. "You are truly subversive." He made it sound like a compliment.

Since he didn't seem particularly scandalized, Sabine decided she might as well confess the worst of it. "I even swindled Napoleon once."

Hampden covered his eyes with his hand and let out a deep groan. "Go on, tell me."

"He sent to the Louvre demanding a painting be cleaned and restored. It was a big job, and while it was in Jacques's workshop I made an exact copy. Same size, same colors, everything. We took the original out of the frame and replaced it with the copy. Jacques excused the smell of new varnish as left over from the cleaning process. Napoleon never suspected a thing. He even said how delighted he was with the restoration and commented on how bright the colors were after it had been cleaned."

Hampden shook his head. "You are a dangerous woman, Sabine de la Tour."

She inclined her head in a graceful nod. "Why, thank you. I think that's the nicest thing you've ever said to me."

CHAPTER 24

*H*ampden stood and offered his arm. "Come on, I need to stretch my legs."

Sabine laid down her pencil and sighed in resignation, even though her bottom had been going numb on the marble seat. "Very well, I'll give you a quick course in how to identify the various artists." She laid her fingers on his forearm and tried to ignore the prickle of awareness that pulsed through her fingertips. They began a leisurely tour of the upper galleries.

Sabine had spent much of her life in the presence of great art, but until that very moment she'd failed to appreciate how many of them featured nudes. Everywhere she looked, nipples peeked out from diaphanous dresses. Naked putti waved their peachy little bottoms in the air; nymphs and satyrs chased one another, hands outstretched to grasp fleshy buttocks or bobbing breasts. Scantily clad ladies reclined suggestively on velvet sofas or lounged in verdant gardens. Even the canvases depicting warlike scenes were filled with glistening thighs and bulging biceps. She fanned herself discreetly with her hand.

Hampden slowed in front of a pen-and-ink study of a muscular woman in an exotic headdress.

"Ah. Michelangelo Buonarroti," Sabine said, not even glancing at the small explanatory label beneath the picture. "He really can't draw women. You can always tell which ones are his; they look like brawny men with breasts stuck on later as an afterthought."

Hampden chuckled.

"Michelangelo was a forger, you know. He buried his own statues in the ground to age them and then sold them to the Medici as antique Greek and Roman ones. When he was found out his works only got greater acclaim. It just proved his superior skill."

She drew him toward the next painting, a huge canvas of cavorting nudes. "Rubens. His women are all fat and red-haired, with enormous bottoms and hardly any clothes."

She distinctly heard him stifle a snigger and suppressed a smile of her own. She'd only ever spoken so freely with Anton. To do so with Hampden was surprising. Exhilarating. Except she really shouldn't be having this much fun with her persecutor.

They came to the next canvas. "If it's a dark background and all the men look like pale, sick, cow-eyed women," she said, "it's Caravaggio."

She pulled him farther along the wall. "If it's a dark background, but everyone has a tortured expression, it's Titian."

They reached a frothy garden scene with a woman on a swing. "If it's got cherubs, sheep, and garlands of flowers, it's French. Either Boucher or Fragonard. There, your lesson is complete."

"Irreverent chit," Hampden murmured, but it sounded more like an endearment than a criticism.

Unfortunately for Sabine's heart rate, the sculpture gallery was no better in terms of flesh on display; it was full of writhing, muscled bodies. Honestly. Did nobody wear any clothes in ancient times? Didn't they have winter in Classical Greece?

Hampden stopped to admire a particularly provocative piece by Bernini, entitled *The Rape of Proserpina*. Good Lord. Sabine stepped sideways to study it from a new angle, marveling at the artist's astonishing skill in capturing such frenzied movement. Pluto's hands encircled Proserpina's waist just as she threw her arms out in an attempt to escape.

There was something disturbingly erotic about the way Pluto's fingers pressed indents into the flesh of her waist and thigh. How could cold, unyielding marble be coaxed to look like heated, dimpled skin? Even the natural striations in the stone resembled faint veins. There was something about the pose that reminded her of all those dreams she'd had of Hampden chasing her, catching her ... kissing her.

Sabine cleared her throat and tried to banish the awful thoughts swimming through her brain. Of Richard Hampden's hands on her waist. Her thighs. She dragged her gaze away from the statue to the equally provocative man beside her.

"Art is in my blood, you know," she said, desperate to focus on anything other than the coiling sensation in her stomach. "My grandfather was court painter to King Louis. He painted Madame Pompadour, Voltaire, Rousseau. Have you ever seen any of his portraits? His sitters all look as if they're about to laugh, which is a lovely way to be captured for eternity, don't you think? There are far too many glowering portraits in this world."

Hampden tilted his head. "I've seen the portrait he did of my mother, back at Hampden House in Dorset. She does look like she's smiling. I always liked it." He turned to face her fully. "And what of your father? Did he paint too?"

"He did. But his main job was acquisitions director at the Louvre—except it was called the Musée Napoléon back then." Sabine couldn't keep the bitterness from her tone. "The emperor renamed it in his honor."

She shook her head and forced her voice to be matter-of-fact. "Father survived the revolution by being irreplaceable. No commoner had the necessary education to work as art director, or had his skills in restoration. He was too knowledgeable to be disposed of. Napoleon needed talented men like him."

It was a lesson Sabine had learned early and well. Aristos with no skills perished. Those who sullied their hands with trade, with a profession, survived. It was imperative to make yourself indispensable.

She allowed Hampden to escort her to the entrance and into his waiting carriage. As they rolled along Bond Street, she gazed out at the rows of galleries and antiques shops, all filled with outrageously expensive items only a lucky few could afford.

It had been the same in France after the revolution. What the aristos had sold in haste, the newly rich merchants had snapped up, eager for the appearance of centuries of inherited wealth. Shops like these provided them with portraits of other people's descendants they could pass off as their own to hide the fact that their money came not from land and property, but from munitions factories, shipping empires, and textile mills.

The general who'd been given her family home in Paris had kept her family's furniture and paintings. Generations of de la Tours now gazed down on ill-bred strangers. Sabine clutched her pencil box on her lap and refused to think about it. It was too depressing.

Hampden's voice interrupted her thoughts. "You'll be dining alone this evening. I'm out again tonight."

Sabine shrugged, as if it mattered little to her, and returned her gaze to the window. He'd probably be going to a woman. Unmarried men like him always had a mistress to see to their physical needs.

She told herself she was grateful he wasn't focusing his attentions on her. And knew she lied.

CHAPTER 25

*R*ichard was not, as Sabine's lurid imagination would have it, disporting himself with a team of experienced harlots. He sat, instead, in one of the smaller private rooms at White's, his club, with Raven and his superior at the Foreign Office, Robert Stewart, Lord Castlereagh.

"Any more news on Visconti?"

Castlereagh shook his head with a frown. "Nothing yet. He's keeping a low profile. But he's here. And he'll make a move soon." He glanced at Richard over the rim of his half-empty brandy glass, his gaze shrewd. "I know how much you want to bury that bastard, Richard. Not one of us doesn't, after what happened in Paris, but I want no bloody heroics from you, you understand?"

Richard bit down a curse. "When the time comes to take him down, he's mine."

Castlereagh nodded. "Agreed. But you're not to face him alone, is that clear? When he surfaces we will find him and eliminate him. But we will do it as a team. I will not have you going off on some half-cocked crusade on your own."

Richard gave a reluctant nod. He, of all of them, had the most reason to want the French assassin dead. The scars from that disastrous mission in Paris were seared into his brain. He shook his head to banish the familiar ball of grief and rage that churned in his gut whenever he thought of it. Eight years, it had been, but it was still as fresh in his mind as if it had happened yesterday. That murderer Visconti had lived far too long.

Castlereagh gave Richard one last, hard look, drained his glass, and stood. "I'll keep you informed. In the meantime, keep an eye on your guest. She could prove useful to reel in Visconti when we find him." He nodded. "Good evening, gentlemen."

Raven poured himself another brandy and slouched back in his chair. "So how are things going with your lovely little counterfeiter? Heloise tells me you're taking her to Lady Carstairs's ball as your soon-to-be-announced fiancée." He took a sip of his drink and shot Richard a wicked, teasing glance. "That was fast work, Dickie, even for you."

"It's not what you think," Richard said irritably. "I'm just using her to keep the tabbies away for a few weeks, that's all."

Raven's smirk was full of cynical disbelief. "Of course. The fact that she's talented, fascinating, and beautiful enough to give a man heart palpitations has completely escaped your notice."

Richard ran a hand through his already disordered locks. "She's dangerous and unpredictable."

Raven smiled into his drink. "I find peace and tranquility awfully overrated. And so do you."

Richard sighed. Raven was right. Working for Castlereagh provided them both with the challenge that had been missing from their daily lives. Richard deliberately endangered himself in plots and treasons because he needed an outlet for all the frustration and aggression he could not show in the ton. He loved the excitement of spying, the intellectual challenge of pitting his wits against other competent men. Or women. He relished the chance to use his skills. Not in a carefully choreographed dance like fencing, with no real danger of being hurt, but real, dirty, back-alley fighting. Those brawls were real in a way the artifice of the ton was not.

He'd worked hard to overcome his gentlemanly reluctance and the spirit of fair play that had been ingrained in him since his days at Eton. He'd had to learn how to fight. Not gentlemanly fighting, all form and elegance, but no-holds-barred boxing, street fighting, where the goal was survival, not glory. He and Raven had engaged in scuffles in parts of the capital few gentlemen dared to go. He'd seen the seedy underbelly of the city, honed his reflexes with a knife and brass knuckles. He knew how to fight dirty. And win.

Richard took a slow sip of his drink, savoring the warm burn of the brandy down his throat. He still hadn't answered Raven.

"I admire her, if you want to know," he admitted finally. "Life dealt her a terrible hand, and instead of folding, as most people would have done, she played on, bluffing when necessary, doing whatever she had to do to survive." He took another swallow. "And she's done more than just survive. She's thrived."

Raven nodded, but his smile was sly. "But you're a man who loves to chase, to pursue. You love the satisfaction of bringing criminals like her to heel."

Richard narrowed his eyes. "What's your point?"

His best friend chuckled. "Only that Sabine de la Tour is that rarest of things: an enemy you failed to catch." He ignored Richard's narrow-eyed glare and carried on. "She gave herself up voluntarily. In fact, if you think about it, she's your only official failure. She beat you, my friend. Fair and square."

Richard frowned into the amber liquid. "She scored points this first round, but the bout is far from over."

Raven raised one dark brow. "Are you sure you're the one in control?" he taunted softly.

Richard scowled. "Yes. Being in control is the best way I know to keep the people I care for safe. Tony went beyond my reach. I couldn't save him. All the money and influence in the world couldn't prevent his death."

He rubbed the tight muscles at the back of his neck with his free hand, surprised at what he'd just said. He rarely discussed losing his younger brother with anyone, even Raven. "The situation in Paris, with Visconti, was the same. We lost control of the situation and innocent people died. That's just unacceptable."

Raven nodded his agreement. "So what are you going to do about your little forger?"

Richard knew what he wanted to do with her: take her to bed and keep her there for a week. Screw her until neither of them had the strength to care which side they were on. He frowned, irritated with himself. He could use sex as a weapon to bind her to him. What stopped him was how much he wanted to. It wouldn't do to become emotionally attached to her. Sabine de la Tour couldn't be trusted. He might as well take a cobra to bed.

"I'm not sleeping with her, if that's what you mean," he growled.

Raven grinned, perfectly aware of his frustration. "Well, if you're not sleeping with her, have found a new mistress yet?"

"No."

"Ah. That explains it."

"Explains what?"

"Your current mood."

"I'm not in a mood."

Raven shot him a look.

Richard sighed. He didn't want to find a mistress. Or go to a whorehouse. He wanted Sabine. His cock ached, just thinking about her. He got hard as a nail whenever she came near. But spending any more time with her in his volatile condition was just plain stupid. He ground his teeth. "Bloody women."

Raven raised his half-full glass in an ironic toast. "Bloody women. How we love them."

His friend's faintly pitying expression made Richard want to smash his fist into Raven's jaw. Or throw him out the window. His fingers actually curled into a fist as he contemplated it.

It was all right for Raven. He had a wife to assuage his lust whenever he felt like it. The fact that the wife in question was his own little sister, Heloise, was not something he ever wanted to contemplate in great detail. Some things were better left unimagined.

Raven rose and straightened his jacket, apparently satisfied with his meddling. "I take it we're still on for our usual training session?

Richard bared his teeth in a feral smile. Maybe beating the stuffing out of Raven would take the edge off his current state of seething lust.

"Absolutely. I'll see you there."

CHAPTER 26

*S*abine jumped when the hidden door to her room opened and Hampden strolled in, as if he had every right to visit her chambers uninvited. She dropped the book she was reading and yanked the edges of her heavy velvet dressing gown together.

"Do you mind?" she snapped.

He grinned. "Not in the slightest."

His gaze traveled over her unbound hair, which she'd left loose, and her skin, which was undoubtedly still an unbecoming pink from the bath.

Sabine glanced pointedly at the clock. It was relatively early by ton standards, only ten o'clock. She hadn't expected him back before midnight. He couldn't have spent much time with his mistress.

He prowled closer and her heart contracted. He smelled of a subtle mix of cologne and brandy—with no overlaying hint of any feminine perfume. Sabine frowned. Maybe he preferred his women unperfumed?

His dark coat created a stark contrast to his white shirt, the dramatic effect like a canvas by Caravaggio. She belatedly noticed that he was holding a wooden box, about the same size as a writing slope. He offered it forward.

"I brought you a present."

"Your own attempt at bribery?"

He shot her a chiding look. "Stop being so cynical. It's a 'thank you' for your work with Skelton. A reward for a job well done. Accept it with grace, without questioning."

It was a handsome new box of artist's materials. The mahogany case had inset brass corners and the paper label inside the lid read *T Reeves & Sons, 150 Cheapside.* It contained a series of watercolor pigment squares and indented ceramic trays. The drawer below held numerous tubes of oil paints.

Sabine bit her lip. "Thank you."

Was he trying to buy her cooperation? This was far more personal than cold, hard cash. Was it a tentative peace offering? A gesture of friendship?

Unwilling to look at him, she inspected the thin sticks of red, white, and black chalk for sketching and highlighting. There were pencils, brushes, little screw-top bottles of linseed oil and turpentine. It was perfect. Exactly what she would have chosen for herself. And far more expensive than she could ever have afforded.

"I was assured by the shopkeeper that it contains everything a serious artist might require," he ventured.

Sabine blinked. The idea that he'd chosen it himself, instead of simply sending a servant to purchase it, made her even more uneasy.

"Do you really use all those colors?" he asked.

Sabine nodded, inexplicably unsettled. "You'd be amazed at the number you need to recreate human skin. Not merely pink and white, but also ochre, vermilion, umber."

She glanced up. He was watching her finger slide over the paints.

"Umber comes from the Latin word *umbra,* meaning 'shadow'

or 'shade.'" She trailed her finger slowly along the line, allowing it to dip into the little grooves between the blocks. She imagined she was trailing it over his skin, over the ridges of his chest, his stomach. "Dragon's blood. Vermilion." The names rolled off her tongue, seductive in their very exoticness. She moistened her lips. "Alizarin crimson." The color of fresh-spilled blood.

Was that really her voice? That breathy, sultry whisper? She suddenly felt as if she were reciting an incantation, summoning some fearsome alchemy that could bind him to her with nothing but words. "Venetian red." The color of love.

Sabine lifted her hand and broke the impromptu spell.

Hampden cleared his throat and blinked as if coming out of a trance. "You like it, then."

She smiled. "I love it. Thank you."

"So. Will you draw me?"

She glanced up in surprise. There was something intensely personal about a portrait. Looking at someone with such close scrutiny forged a link between artist and sitter that was not easily broken.

He saw her hesitation and a twinkle entered his eye. "I'll pay you."

Curse him. He dangled the hint of money in front of her like a carrot in front of a donkey. Sabine gave an inward sigh. She couldn't turn down the offer of more cash. "I'm very expensive."

His mouth quirked. "I know. Pricier than a roomful of whores at the Palais Royale," he said sardonically. "I can afford it."

Of course he could afford it, Sabine thought waspishly. He could furnish every tart in London with diamonds and silk underwear if he wanted to.

He must have sensed her silent acceptance. "Where do you want me? On the bed? The chair? The floor?" His eyes gleamed with teasing merriment at his deliberate double entendres. "Feel free to arrange me however you like. I'm completely at your mercy. Any position you choose will be perfectly acceptable."

Sabine sent him a quelling look. "Not the bed."

The last thing she wanted was an image of Richard Hampden lounging like some well-fed lion on her pillows. Or the scent of him on her sheets to drive her to distraction. She already dreamed about him far too often.

He shot her a knowing glance and she busied herself in finding a clean sheet of paper from the bureau. When she looked up, he'd already removed his jacket and was sliding his cravat from around his neck. The gesture made her pulse quicken.

"I'll keep the rest of my clothes on, shall I?" he teased.

She shot him a glare. "Please do. I don't do nudes." She pointed to the wing armchair near the fire. "There will do fine."

He settled himself in it with a contented sigh.

Sabine repositioned a lamp to give herself better light, selected a pencil, and began to draw, determined to ignore the cozy intimacy of the scene. She'd work fast. Get this over and done with as quickly as possible.

For a while the only sound was the faint scratch of the charcoal over the paper. She made a few initial, sketchy outlines, light strokes to define his overall shape, the planes and intersections of his face.

"You're used to studying things with great precision," he said quietly. "What do you see?"

"I see an annoying, autocratic, overbearing—"

"Never mind," he chuckled. "Just draw."

It was strange to have the excuse to look at him full on, not sneaking sideways glances when she thought he wasn't looking. Sabine studied him the same way she would have studied a drawing by Leonardo or Raphael. He had a face that would not have looked out of place on a Renaissance prince or an Italian mercenary: clever, shrewd, brilliant. Except the line of his nose was irritatingly perfect. A mercenary would have had it broken a time or two.

She noted the texture of his jaw, the fine, clear grain of his skin. The gradation of highlights and shadow in his shirt, his hair. The tiny lines at the corners of his eyes, the bones in his wrist where he rested his hands lightly on the arm of the chair. Her pencil flowed over the paper.

She could be an impartial, objective observer. Like a physician. Yes, he was a good-looking man. Obviously, if one were susceptible to broad shoulders and a narrow waist and big hands and generally splendid proportions—which, drat it all, she was—

She bit her lip. No. She could remain perfectly composed. She'd drawn from life. Never a male nude, certainly, but her anatomical studies had given her a decent understanding of the way the muscles in the body worked. It was only lines and angles. Bone and sinew. Nothing to get all hot and bothered about.

Except studying all those marble statues had furnished her with a graphic idea of what those elegant breeches and that superfine shirt concealed. She'd glimpsed it under his wet shirt in the carriage—sleek muscular perfection.

Her pencil faltered as she sketched in his collarbone—just a glimpse of the jut and hollow where it met at the base of his throat. If only he'd remove his shirt. She imagined him as a boxer, stripped to the waist, chest bare, fists bound by leather strips like some ancient gladiatorial combatant.

Her throat went dry. She was far too aware of him lounging at ease, the even tenor of his breathing in the quiet room. He seemed to be stealing all the air. His jaw was slightly stubbled. What would it be like to touch it?

She clutched the pencil tighter, a weapon against temptation. She was not Pygmalion, to fall in love with her own creation. She had more sense than that. But her pencil slowed as she sketched in the bow of his upper lip, the dip of his philtrum, the smooth line of his fuller lower lip. Her own lips tingled in response.

She cleared her throat and gestured at the box of paints. "Most of those colors come from less than romantic sources, you know. Shellac, for instance," she pointed to a little pot, "is a resin secreted from an insect." The ground flakes were mixed with an alcohol and used as a varnish. "And this brown color comes from the ink of the cuttlefish, a relative of the octopus."

Hampden's slow smile told her he knew just how much he affected her. And how much he enjoyed it.

"You are a woman of surprising knowledge and talent."

Her hand trembled slightly as she shaded in his thick, diabolic eyebrows. She bit her lip. How best to draw his eyes? Pencil couldn't hope to capture their color, that warm-honey, burnt-caramel brown.

It bothered her more than it ought that she couldn't define the exact color of them. They were changeable, dependent on his mood and the lighting and the color of his clothes. When she stared very closely she could see a wicked warmth: sherry, not quite golden brown, nor yet burnt orange.

And really, what grown man should have a dimple? He didn't even have one on each cheek, to balance out the austere perfection of his face, just the one, on the left-hand side. It should have been a disruption, but when he smiled that rare and sudden smile it was like the sun emerging from behind a cloud. It made those in the vicinity want to bask in its warm glow.

Sabine closed her eyes and prayed for strength. She wasn't allowed to bask. This man was her enemy. She couldn't forget it.

CHAPTER 27

*H*aving Sabine draw him was a ridiculously erotic experience.

Richard fought the urge to fidget in his chair. He'd only suggested it on a devilish whim, a means of spending more time with her, of gaining her trust.

He felt her scrutiny keenly, almost like a caress. She alternated her attention between his face and the paper, and every time her eyes fell on some part of him he became acutely aware of that particular area, as if she were actually touching him there.

He, in his turn, took the opportunity to study her. The long, dark sweep of eyelashes that shadowed her eyes. The way she bit her lip in concentration made him squirm. Her hands were small, delicate yet strong, and he allowed himself the indulgence of sinful imagination. Those hands on him, those lips. What if he were nude? Would she be as detached and analytical then?

She pushed back a wisp of hair with an impatient, absent-minded swipe, leaving a smudge of chalk on her cheek. Richard imagined wiping it off. Then he imagined stripping her, covering her in the paints. Not the weak, insipid watercolors, but the slippery, color-intense oils. Perfect.

In his mind he dipped his forefinger in the paint and smeared a semicircle of bright blue over the top swell of her breast. He dipped his thumb and used the pad to describe a sweep of yellow over her nipple. No. Mistake. If he did that he couldn't put his tongue there. He erased the mental image and amended it to his satisfaction, leaving her nipple free for his mouth.

He closed his eyes and allowed himself to sink into the fantasy. His hands would leave a trail of color wherever they went. He'd mark every inch of her skin. The jut of her collarbones, the ridges of her ribs, the curve of her waist, the smooth line of her belly, the inside of her thighs. He took a deep breath, lost in the erotic reverie. Hands sliding up, up—

Sabine dropped her pencil.

Richard opened his eyes and adjusted his pose while she retrieved it from the floor, relieving the aching evidence of his lurid fantasies. He transferred his hands to his lap and forced his mind into less dangerous territory.

He cleared his throat, but his voice still came out lower than he'd have liked. "Don't you think it's ironic that it took a war to reveal the extent of your skills?" he managed.

She tilted her head. "Sometimes I wonder who I might have been if circumstances hadn't made me a criminal." She gave a dainty shrug. "We'll never know. I am what I am. A forger. A traitor. A thief." She met his gaze, challenging him to dispute that, and the intensity of her navy eyes sent a jolt through him. "I've been Philippe Lacorte for so long, I've forgotten what Sabine de la Tour was like." She returned her attention to the drawing.

"Why did you come here, Sabine?" he asked softly.

She didn't look at him. "I always wanted to see London. The land of my mother. I have a hankering to visit the opera."

"No. Not to London. Why did you come here, to me?"

* * *

Aн, what a question that was, Sabine thought ruefully. Perhaps she should tell him the truth: that she'd been frightened, and bored, and lonely. That she'd wanted to find others like her, who understood the dangerous game they played. Someone else who balanced on the sharp knife edge between what was strictly legal and what was morally right.

When she didn't answer, he filled in the silence.

"I have a theory that all criminals secretly want to get caught."

She snorted. "That's ridiculous! Of course they don't. No one has a yearning for the gallows. Or the guillotine."

He raised an incredulous brow. "Really? You don't want someone to recognize your talent? Isn't that why you put your initials on the fake notes? So someone equally clever would notice and appreciate your skills?"

It was unnerving, the way he seemed to read her mind. She managed a dismissive shrug. "Perhaps you're right. Since public recognition is out of the question, a little private admiration from a peer who understands the complexity of what I do might be nice."

His expression was taunting. "Poor Sabine. All your successes are, by their very nature, unsung."

"It's no different from being a spy," she shot back. "Your victories are private too. You get the satisfaction of a job well done, but nobody knows your name."

He refused to let her look away. "Did you want me to catch you?" His voice was sinuous, an enchantment.

Sabine sighed. Was she so vain? Maybe. She did want him to look at her with respect. And with a little bit of fear and awe, too. She wanted him to comprehend the brilliance of what she could do. She forced her hand to keep moving on the paper. "I'd have thought that at the very least you might appreciate the restraint I've used. It would have been so easy to spend the counterfeit fortune I made. I could have ruined your country."

The knowledge that she'd had such power made her head

spin. The fact that she'd chosen the morally virtuous path made her proud. She still had some purity left in her soul after all. Of course, she should have known the one time she tried to do something honest it would all go horribly wrong. "No good deed goes unpunished," they said. How true that was. Now here she was, entangled with this man like a fly in a spider's web.

His eyes bored into hers, and his voice was a smoky whisper. "You love it, don't you? That tingle of triumph when you pass off a forgery. It's like a drug, isn't it, Sabine? You want more."

She shot him an angry glare. "Then we're the same, are we not? Don't you love the chance to test your skill against a worthy opponent?" She pointed her pencil at him for emphasis. "Don't tell me the easy victories are the ones you remember fondly, because I won't believe you. It's the hard-won battles that give you the greatest amount of satisfaction." She raised her brows, daring him to contradict her. When he did not, she let out a small huff. "Molière said it: 'The greater the obstacle, the more glory in overcoming it.'"

She returned her pencil to the page and tilted her chin. "I will admit to a certain amount of pride in my work. Outwitting the so-called experts has been one of the few real pleasures in my life."

It was the delight she'd taken in it that worried her. It seemed to highlight a terrible contradiction in her personality. As much as she wanted to start doing the right thing, she really loved being a criminal.

Her skills were what made her extraordinary, what set her apart. She didn't want to be like all those other vapid girls of the ton, with no thought to anything other than fashion and beaux. What would she do all day if she gave up counterfeiting? She'd be bored within a week.

But she was also tired of always looking over her shoulder, of expecting to be denounced, arrested, or even killed. Tired of sleeping with a pistol under her pillow.

Sabine shook her head and smiled at her own indecisiveness. She didn't know what she wanted. But one thing was certain: She couldn't be both Philippe Lacorte and Sabine de la Tour. Philippe Lacorte was invaluable, whereas Sabine de la Tour was . . . what, exactly?

"I can't imagine what it would be like to be blind," she mused. "I could live without smell, or hearing, or taste. But what if I could no longer see? What if I lost the use of my hands? To be unable to draw would be like death to me. Who would I be, if I didn't have my skills?"

She bit her lip. She hadn't meant to reveal so much, but Richard Hampden had a way of looking at her that made her want to bare her soul. It was terrifying. She turned the portrait around for him to see, hastily trying to conceal her confusion. "There. I've finished."

For a long, painful minute he simply studied it, his expression unreadable. She scratched her nose and resisted the urge to ask whether he liked it.

"I could have made you much less attractive, you know," she said, unable to bear the silence any longer. "Just a shade larger nose. Eyes a little closer together. I could have made you look like one of the gargoyles on the corners of Notre-Dame."

His laughing eyes flicked to hers. "Instead, I am a veritable Adonis."

Sabine narrowed her eyes. She could hardly deny it; he was a physically handsome specimen, but he had no need of anyone to puff up his sense of self-importance. "It's what's inside that counts," she said severely.

He stood and pointed to the edge of the paper. "You haven't signed it. I want proof I own an original Sabine de la Tour. Just in case you get famous for something other than counterfeiting."

With a put-upon sigh she signed a simple *S. de la Tour* in the lower right corner. It felt good to sign her own name, instead of hiding behind the initials *P.L.* Maybe this was the first small step in her transformation from criminal to honest woman.

Hampden's fingers brushed hers as he took the paper and a little tingle ran up her arm. He stepped closer. "Hold still."

Sabine's legs turned to water at the hungry intensity of his look. She barely breathed as he steadied her chin and brushed her cheek with the pad of his thumb.

His smile was a lazy glitter. "You had a smudge."

His gaze dropped to her mouth. Awareness thickened the air between them, a bright, expectant tension, like the hush before a thunderstorm. He leaned closer. Sabine could feel the warmth of him against her lips and sucked in a drowning breath. Oh, this was wrong. So wrong. She had to step away. She didn't move.

His thumb came to rest at the outer edge of her mouth. Sabine closed her eyes, lost in the thrall of the sensation. Her body felt like melting wax. His breath mingled with her own, hot as hellfire, tempting as the devil. Only the width of a piece of paper separated them.

"Would you like me to kiss you?"

His voice was a rough whisper against her mouth, more sensation than sound.

Yes! her heart screamed. *Yes yes yes.*

"No."

He turned his head, and his lips slid against her cheek. She shivered at the faint rasp of his jaw against her skin.

"Liar," he chuckled softly.

She almost did it. Almost turned her head and met his mouth, and to hell with sense and safety. But sanity prevailed. She drew back and opened her eyes. For one brief moment he stared down at her, his expression unreadable. And then he dropped his hand and strode to the door.

"Good night, Miss de la Tour."

The panel closed behind him with a quiet click.

Sabine drew in a shattered breath. *Good God.* Such monstrous lust was insupportable. She was a fool, wanting to kiss him. She should be keeping him as far away as possible, not wondering how good he would taste.

She was here for only another few weeks. She would control her attraction.

CHAPTER 28

Sabine stood in her petticoats in the center of her bedroom and surveyed the new hairstyle she'd been given. Mr. Travers, the *coiffeur,* had just left, having cut and styled her hair in a tumble of artful curls around her face.

Behind her, reflected in the mirror, Heloise and Madame Hortense, London's most celebrated modiste, nodded their approval.

Madame 'Ortense, it had transpired, was as French as Napoleon himself—which was to say, not French at all. When Sabine had first introduced herself in her own language, saying how nice it was to meet a fellow countrywoman, the woman had cheerfully admitted that she'd never been farther than Gravesend. She'd adopted the pseudonym when the original Madame Hortense, her former employer, died, having cannily realized that a French "modiste" got twice as much trade as much as plain old Sally-Anne Clackett, seamstress.

From the quality of the dresses that the woman had already provided for Heloise, it was clear that her skills at dressmaking were just as good as her skills of self-promotion. Sabine thoroughly approved of the woman's shrewd tactics. A girl had to get ahead any way she could.

Heloise tapped her lips. "Now, about the gown for Lady C's ball? I'm so glad you're not a debutante, Sabine. You can wear something dramatic that will have all the men fighting for your attention."

They'd already selected three day gowns and three evening gowns. Sabine had tried to refuse them for being too elaborate, but Heloise wouldn't hear of it.

"I promised Richard I'd help you get a suitable wardrobe," she said firmly.

"I have just the thing," Madame 'Ortense said. "New style, from Vienna. The pattern book's downstairs. If you ladies will excuse me for a moment?"

She bustled out of the salon and Heloise turned to Sabine. "You must teach me how to swear properly in French. I love languages. I can speak several quite fluently, but there's nothing like learning colloquialisms from a native."

"I'm not sure your brother or your mother would approve."

"That's exactly why I need to know! Who else can I trust? I can't even ask my own husband. Raven's so perverse he'd probably tell me something completely wrong, just for his own amusement. He'd have me saying 'I love your hat,' instead of 'go to the devil!'"

"All right." Sabine tried to think of the least offensive phrases she knew. "If someone is drunk we say they are *allumé*—'lit up.'"

"Excellent. Go on."

Sabine pursed her lips and racked her brains, beginning to enjoy herself. She hadn't had many female friends in Paris. It was fun to have someone with whom to giggle and share secrets.

"Well, a girl's breasts, showing out the top of her dress, is her 'balcony.' Her *balcon.* If she has a big chest the men might say, 'There are lots of people on her balcony.'"

"I should be taking notes." Heloise gave a wicked chuckle.

"And what about terms for the male member? There must be lots of those."

Sabine nodded, grinning too. "Hundreds, but I expect most of them are the same as in English. Men can't stop talking about it, no matter what nationality they are. They call it their 'tree branch,' their 'spade,' their 'bow,' 'cigar,' 'rod.'"

Heloise gave Sabine a spontaneous hug. "Oh, I wish I'd had you as a sister! It would have been such fun. Growing up with three older brothers is just not the same at all."

"Three brothers?" Sabine asked, surprised. "Richard mentioned your brother Nicolas, but—"

Heloise's face fell. "Tony, our other brother, died in France as a prisoner of war."

Sabine's stomach tightened with a heavy knot of guilt and compassion. Guilt that it had been her countrymen responsible for his death. Compassion for the thread of anguish she heard in the other girl's voice. She squeezed her arm lightly. "I'm sorry."

Her thoughts veered to Richard Hampden and she experienced another sharp stab of guilt. She'd taunted him about not being affected by the war. But he'd been as affected as herself, as the thousands of other families who'd suffered the loss of a loved one. What other hurts was he hiding from her? What other scars?

Heloise gave a sad, resigned smile. "It wasn't your fault. But we all miss him." She took a breath and brightened, apparently determined to banish the maudlin mood. "Now tell me something truly shocking. And remember, I am a married woman."

"But I'm not," Sabine said primly.

Heloise shot her a knowing glance. "Well, you've hardly been living in a nunnery, have you?"

When the door clicked open neither of them paid it any heed, assuming it was Madame 'Ortense returning.

"What are you two giggling about?"

Heloise gave a gasp of shocked outrage. "Richard! Get out this instant!"

Sabine scowled and clapped her hands over her almost-exposed bosom, humiliatingly aware of the fact that she was wearing nothing but her chemise.

Hampden ignored their protests. He strolled into the center of the room as if he owned it. Which—technically—he did, Sabine thought waspishly.

"I've come to help you choose a dress for Lady Carstairs's ball. If I'm going to be seen in public with you, I need to be sure you're appropriately dressed."

"I don't need your assistance!"

"Now, now. I know you have a wonderful, artistic eye, but even you must admit you aren't up to date with the latest fashions. I wish you to be *comme il faut*." He flicked back the tails of his coat and settled himself comfortably in a chair. "There's nothing improper or scandalous about it. Women have allowed their intimates to assist in their toilette for years." He shot Sabine a triumphant smile that said he wasn't going anywhere. "Now, why don't you tell me what was so funny?"

The two women glanced at one another. Both adopted innocent-as-nuns expressions. "Oh, nothing. Just fashions and gossip."

Heloise nudged Sabine's elbow and stifled a giggle. Sabine nudged her back.

"Miss de la Tour was just educating me on the intricacies of Parisian culture," Heloise snorted.

"I'll just bet she was," Richard muttered dryly.

Heloise shot him a dazzling smile. "She was. It's been an extremely enlightening conversation."

"I think it was a very bad decision to introduce the two of you." Hampden gave Sabine a hard stare. "Isn't there somewhere else you need to be, Heloise? I'm sure Raven's anxiously awaiting your return."

Heloise looked from him to Sabine and sighed. "If you want to get rid of me, just say it, Richard."

"I want to get rid of you."

She threw her arms up in the air. "Fine. I'm going. But don't you dare be mean to Sabine, or you'll have me to deal with."

"I'm quaking in my boots," Richard drawled. "Besides, Miss de la Tour can take care of herself. Goodbye, sister dearest."

Heloise shot one last, apologetic glance at Sabine. "Now do you see what I mean about brothers? I'll see you soon."

She left in a flurry of skirts.

Sabine's earlier merriment faded as she faced Hampden, horribly aware of how little she was wearing. "I don't need your help," she said again.

"I'll have no companion of mine dressed in anything but the first stare of fashion." He tilted his head and his gaze lingered on her face. "Our poor debutantes must languish in lavenders and creams. You, however, shall wear a deep midnight blue."

Madame 'Ortense chose that moment to reenter the room. "I've brought the—oh! Gawd! Yer lordship!" she gasped, as she caught sight of Richard. "I mean—I beg your—"

"Do come in, madam," he said serenely.

The modiste straightened. Richard waved an airy hand at Sabine.

"As I'm sure you've surmised, Miss de la Tour is something quite out of the ordinary. I want a dress to reflect that. Something unique. Something stark and simple. Nothing too obvious. No hint of the ingénue." He picked up one of the books of fashion plates that had been left on the side table, flicked through it, and tapped a design with his forefinger. "Something like this. But without all the bows and the frills."

The dressmaker peered over his shoulder, then glanced back up at Sabine. She narrowed her eyes as if trying to visualize the finished product. "Yes, my lord. I see what you mean."

He shot Sabine a wicked glance. "And lower the neckline."

"Yes, m'lord."

He selected a fabric swatch next, a dark indigo shot silk. "In this fabric."

"It shall be done, your lordship."

Hampden rested his elbows on the chair and his fingers obscured his mouth. Those amber eyes studied her. Sabine ground her teeth and tried to maintain an impassive countenance, but inside she was seething at his high-handed behavior.

He glanced at the dressmaker. "Have it ready by tomorrow. You may leave us now." He dismissed her with a languid flick of his fingers.

Madame 'Ortense bobbed a deferential curtsey. "Of course, m'lord."

And suddenly they were alone.

CHAPTER 29

Goose bumps broke out over Sabine's skin. Technically, there was no more of her on display than if she'd been wearing a ball gown, but she still felt vulnerable, dressed only in her silk under-dress and petticoats. Heat bloomed in her cheeks as Hampden regarded her. She could feel her pulse beating erratically in her throat. He stood and came toward her, lazy, relaxed. All her muscles, in contrast, tensed for a fight, but she couldn't move, caught by the look in his eyes.

She moistened her lips. "You should leave. I wish to dress."

"Don't let me stop you."

She glared at him. "What do you want, Hampden?"

"Now there's a question," he mused softly. "I want so many things." He held her gaze until she looked away. "Can you dance?"

"Well enough."

"Waltz?

She paused. "I never learned."

She heard him sigh and cursed the combination of anger and embarrassment that flushed her cheeks.

"Forgive me if I'm not up to your exacting standards, my lord," she said with acid sarcasm, "but my life has been rather lacking in elegant soirées of late. My country's bloody revolution and subsequent war with yours deprived me of a come-out at Versailles."

He took another step toward her. His chest was a scant inch away from hers. "Ah, but you must learn to waltz. Wasn't it Molière who said, 'All the ills of mankind, all the tragic misfortunes that fill the history books, all the political blunders, all the failures of the great leaders have arisen merely from a lack of skill at dancing'?"

Sabine tried to think of a witty comeback and failed. How annoying that he should be able to out-quote her. On Molière—a fellow Frenchman, of all people. "We have no music," she said stubbornly.

"I'll hum."

Clearly there was no escape. Had she been fully dressed, his closeness would have been unremarkable. Or at least more bearable. But she was not. Proximity heightened her acute awareness of him. Something dark and twisting uncurled in her stomach. She raised her chin. "All right. I'll make you a deal."

His sigh was heartfelt. "Everything is barter and exchange with you."

"That's how the world works. It's commerce. You never get anything for nothing."

"Except when it's fake money," he said.

She inclined her head to acknowledge the hit.

"What do you want?" he asked.

"Since working for you is proving more dangerous than anticipated, I think I should improve my skills of self-defense. Heloise says you box and fence. Will you teach me how to fight?"

"Agreed," he said abruptly.

One of his hands slipped around to the back of her spine, the other caught her right hand and held it slightly away from her body. Sabine had no option but to lift her own free hand to his chest to keep him at a respectable distance.

He pulled her closer, fitting her thighs to his, fusing the lower halves of their bodies together. She fixed her gaze on his shoulder and tried to ignore the smooth fabric of his coat beneath her hand, the hard muscles beneath. The alarming, fluttering heat warming her. Impatient with him just standing there, she made the first move—and promptly stepped on his toe.

He chuckled. "There can only be one leader in this dance, Sabine."

That was the first time he'd ever used her given name, she realized. The intimacy of it made her shiver.

He swept her into an impromptu whirl.

Sabine caught her breath. The waltz was positively indecent. Their palms were touching; she could feel her own pulse in her fingers, in her throat, in the tips of her breasts as they brushed against him. His soft humming reverberated through his chest and into her. His thigh insinuated itself between her legs. They might as well have been naked, for all the space there was between their bodies. It was a dizzying, intricate whirl, all curlicues and arabesques, like the scrolling borders of a banknote. Sabine closed her eyes and allowed herself to be swept away.

Finally, Hampden swung them to a breathless, panting stop.

There was a beat of silence; the thread of something bright and expectant hovered between them. Sabine held her breath as Hampden leaned forward . . . and then his eyes crinkled at the corners in the way she'd come to recognize heralded a joke.

"Want me to kiss you?" he whispered.

She wanted to kick him, for teasing her. And for how much she wanted to say yes. She pinned a bright smile on her lips. "Not in the slightest."

He tilted his head, maddeningly confident. "You will."

Sabine sucked cool air into her lungs as he stepped away and narrowed her eyes. "Don't think I've forgotten your promise. You have to teach me to fight."

"Tomorrow morning. Nine o'clock. Meet me in the ballroom at the back of the house."

"I'll be there."

He strode to the door and turned back, his hand resting on the knob. "I'll keep asking, you know."

"Asking what?"

"Whether you want me to kiss you." His smile was diabolical. "Sooner or later you're going to say yes."

Before she could summon up a suitably scathing retort to that arrogant statement, he pulled open the door and disappeared. Sabine sent up a silent prayer for patience. And for the strength to resist.

CHAPTER 30

The ballroom was located at the back of the house. Sabine approached silently, intrigued by the grunts of exertion, the scuffle of feet, and the metallic clash of blades that met her ears.

She peered around the door, hoping to spy a little before announcing her presence. There were three men in the room. Raven was shouting encouragement and insults from the side. Hampden, dressed in shirtsleeves and pale breeches, was sparring fiercely with another blond man she didn't recognize. He was as tall as Hampden, but thinner, almost gaunt.

Her eyes slid back to Hampden and a hot wave of agitation curled her stomach as she watched the violent display. His face was a picture of concentration. He fenced with a relentless determination that was both precise and utterly unforgiving.

It was a guilty pleasure to watch him, the easy way he inhabited his body, all loose-limbed, fluid elegance. He looked like one of Canova's marble statues brought to life. She could imagine him as the artist's model for some Homeric hero. Achilles maybe, or Hector. She vividly recalled that body, up against hers as they'd waltzed. It had taken her ages to fall asleep last night.

Sabine shook her head at the contradiction he presented. Hampden's public persona was charming and erudite. He was affable to everyone—except her. But here he radiated barely repressed fury. He gave no quarter and expected none in return. He drove forward, pressing his advantage with the scrape of steel on steel. After a particularly brutal attack his opponent swiped a mop of golden hair from his eyes and backed away, arms raised in surrender.

"Pax!" he panted. "That's all I can take for today."

He turned to one of the chairs that stood at regular intervals along the side of the room and tugged his damp shirt over his head.

Sabine gasped in horror. The man had stripes across his back that made her wince in sympathy. He'd been beaten—tortured—with what looked like a rope or leather whip. Or a chain. The skin was raised and puckered in permanent welts. Poor man, the pain he must have endured. Those were scars he would carry for life.

Her in-drawn breath gave her away. Hampden turned and caught her watching. His face was flushed, two red slashes running high on his cheekbones, and his hair was damp with perspiration, curled and disordered in a way that made him even more attractive, curse him.

Sabine stepped into the room. A bank of high windows took up one side, letting in the early morning light. Mirrors flanked the opposite wall, doubling the space. The effect was impressive, like the Galerie des Glaces her mother had once described, at Versailles.

Hampden pierced her with his amber gaze, but addressed his companions. "That will be all for today, gentlemen."

Raven glanced over at her and grinned. The other man nodded politely, his blue eyes full of friendly speculation. Raven gave her a jaunty salute as they left. "Miss de la Tour. Enjoy your morning."

Hampden scooped up a towel from one of the chairs and used it to wipe his face, then draped it around his neck, holding one end in each hand as he advanced on her.

Sabine swallowed. His shirt was open at the throat and he had a bead of sweat on his cheek. She wanted to reach up and wipe it away, to touch her fingertips to his lips, to taste the salt. He stopped directly in front of her and she caught his scent—not the unpleasant smell of stale body odor, but the clean, hot smell of man that made her light-headed with desire.

He threw his towel onto the nearest chair and narrowed a glance at her attire. "Where the hell did you get those clothes?"

She gave a mocking twirl. "Shirt and breeches. Same as you. Mr. Hodges was kind enough to borrow them from your night porter, Minton. He and I are much of a size. I couldn't very well learn to fence in skirts, could I?"

Hampden frowned, but thankfully didn't argue. "So, fencing or boxing, which is it to be first?"

"Fencing, if you please."

He inclined his head. "All right, let's cover some basic terms." He picked up one of the blades propped against the wall and handed it to her. "A foil is a blunt sword for practice."

He held the weapon in front of his face and Sabine mirrored the stance, angling her body to the side and placing one leg behind the other.

"*En garde* is the position to take to prepare to fence." He pressed his blade against her own so she felt the slight pressure in her wrist and forearm. "And this is to 'engage.'"

His lips curved. "According to the great Italian fencing master Morricone, engagement is 'a firm but gentle sustained contact of the opponent's blade in preparation for combat.'" His eyes creased at the corners and she knew he was about to say something wicked. "Is the contact of my blade firm enough for you, Miss de la Tour?"

Sabine responded with a pressure of her own and bit back a

smile at his provocative teasing. "Perfectly, thank you, Mr. Hampden."

He backed her toward the wall with a slow advance. "Fencing is elegant, deadly, refined. It's like a courtship. A dance."

She pushed back against his blade.

He smiled. "Your favorite, Molière, says 'the essence of fencing is to give, but by no means to receive.' Do you prefer to give, Miss de la Tour? Or to receive?"

Sabine ignored the flush that warmed her skin. "I've found one rarely experiences one without the other."

Fencing, it turned out, was a sport fraught with innuendo, full of touches and thrusts, flicks and glides. Hampden took perverse pleasure in rolling his tongue around the various phrases, as if he knew precisely the images he was conjuring up in her feverish mind.

He showed her how to assault and parry, the *passe avant* and *passe arrière*—passing steps forward and backward. The *prise du fer*, to trap the opponent's blade. He demonstrated each with an animal grace that made it hard to concentrate.

The tiny, almost inconsequential touches he gave her as he corrected her stance or touched her with his blade muddled her senses. They had a cumulative effect, a slow build, like a banked fire. She knew precisely where he was at any given moment.

After twenty minutes, he stepped back and set down his blade.

"As fun as this is, it's unlikely you'll ever need to fight with swords. If you're serious about self-defense, you need to know how to use your fists."

Sabine nodded. "I know how to fight. A friend taught me."

"A male friend?" His eyes narrowed, but not before she saw a flash of some primal, fierce emotion, swiftly checked.

"Yes."

"Why did he need to teach you? What happened?"

Ah, he was too perceptive. Sabine shrugged. "Paris, like

London, has areas that are not so safe. I had to learn to fend for myself. That was before I got my little pistol, of course."

He stared at her for a long moment, then shot her a cheeky glance. "Bare knuckles, bare chests? I'm game if you are."

She scowled at him.

He shook his head and sighed. "It was worth a try. All right, show me what you've got."

Sabine swung at him. He dodged the blow in a lightning-fast reflex and caught her fist in his. She tried to pull back, but he merely uncurled her fingers and repositioned them with her thumb on the outside.

"I doubt Tom Cribb or Tom Belcher are quaking in their boots just yet," he said dryly. "Bend your body toward me. Head and shoulders forward, fists up, knees slightly bent."

Sabine did so.

"Use your arms to defend your face and body. Keep your elbows in and your fists up near eye level to block side attacks." He aimed a few light taps at her head so she could practice blocking. "A hit isn't effective unless you judge the distance correctly. Too close and you won't have any power behind it." He demonstrated, then stepped back. "You're at a disadvantage because of your size, so you'll need to find other ways of bringing down your opponent."

"Like what?"

"Pull his ears, or better still, bite them. Jab his eyes. Punch his throat; if he can't breathe, he can't fight."

Sabine nodded earnestly.

"If you can grab his nose, snap it to the side. It'll bleed like the devil. Stamp on the top of his foot. Or bend his fingers back—you might break a few bones that way."

Sabine shuddered.

"And use your elbows and knees in close quarters. They're hard for an opponent to grab, and they pack a lot of force. Knees are easy to break if you kick them hard enough. And a foot in the groin is especially effective. Kick like you're kicking down a door."

"I have never felt the slightest inclination to kick down a door."

"Use the bottom of your foot. A solid kick can incapacitate your attacker long enough for you to get away."

She twisted her lips. "I'd have thought someone like you would consider these underhand tactics rather ungentlemanly."

He shook his head, his eyes serious. "No. You win. By whatever means possible." He circled her, throwing out punches to keep her on her guard. "Use whatever you have to hand as a weapon. Rocks, bottles, anything. If you're grounded, pick up a handful of dirt and throw it in your attacker's eyes."

Quick as a flash he stepped close, hooked one of his legs behind hers, and twisted her over backward. Sabine found herself arched over his thigh, suspended awkwardly above the floor, completely at his mercy. Only his arm around her neck and his thigh behind hers prevented her from falling. She grabbed the front of his shirt.

His face hovered above her, inches from her own. Sabine's heart was hammering against her ribs, but she shot him her most devastating smile.

He narrowed his eyes in immediate suspicion.

She leaned upward, closer, closer. So close she could feel the exhale of his breath. In the instant before her mouth made contact with his, she turned her head and touched her lips to his jaw. His breath hissed out. His skin was smooth and rough at the same time. Heat flashed through her body. "Do you want to kiss me, Richard Hampden?" she whispered in his ear.

He stilled. "You know the—"

She bit him on the ear. Hard.

He thrust her away like a sack of hot coals. "What the—! You devil!"

He clapped his hand to the side of his head and scowled at

her. Sabine skipped back, well out of reach, and shot him a taunting grin.

"I'm a fast learner."

A muscle ticked in his jaw. "I should spank you for that."

Her heart leaped in alarm at the threat—or was it a promise? —but she managed to send him a saucy, provocative look.

"Perhaps some other time, my lord. I'm afraid I need the rest of the day to get ready for Lady Carstairs's ball. You did say how important it was for me to look my best, and I wouldn't want to disappoint you. I'll see you this evening . . ."

She practically ran from the room.

* * *

RICHARD HISSED OUT A LONG, frustrated breath and counted to twenty in Greek. It did absolutely nothing to quell the pounding lust racking his body.

He couldn't believe he'd become so distracted that he'd actually let her gain the advantage. Cheeky little baggage! She really did deserve a spanking. Unfortunately, the thought of turning her over his knee, skirts thrown up, soft, rounded bottom wriggling under his palm, had him taking a deep breath and counting to twenty in Latin too. That didn't work either.

His blood throbbed in his veins; his heart pumped furiously. He'd trained hard against Kit and Raven, but instead of feeling tired, he felt energized. He was aroused, like after sex—all sweaty and flushed and panting. Pleasantly aching in every muscle. Only, unlike after sex, he was still unsatisfied.

That woman was a bloody menace.

CHAPTER 31

The dress Hampden had chosen for her was astonishing. Sabine stared at herself in the mirror in silent disbelief. This, surely, was the ultimate counterfeit; she looked like a well-bred lady of the ton.

The color of it hovered between deep azure and the inky blue-black of indigo. It made her pale skin seem luminous, her eyes huge, her hair darker. The stiff silk had a silvery sheen, like the touch of moonlight, and it rustled mysteriously when she moved.

It was breathtaking in its simplicity. There were no frills, no bows or lace. Just some subtle pleating at the scandalously low neckline. It draped across her chest to a line of ribbon beneath her breasts, then dropped straight over her hips to the floor. Sabine had never worn anything so sophisticated in her life.

The corset was tight. The hard whalebone spines dug into her ribs. She felt like a sheet of paper being squashed in a printing press, but the effect was worth the discomfort. Madame 'Ortense was a genius.

Heloise and Therese had come over to help her get ready—no doubt under orders from Hampden to make her look presentable, but Sabine was still warmed by their kindness. She stood obediently while her hair was curled and pinned in an intricate coil and Heloise lent her a string of pearls to thread through the dark strands.

It didn't matter what she looked like, however. The evening was sure to be a disaster. The polite, fashionable world was not for her. Its rules were as restrictive as her corset. She turned to Heloise and made one last appeal.

"I tell you, this is a bad idea. I'm not used to polite society. And I'm certainly not good with rules. Just ask your brother. I'll break one every minute, quite without knowing it."

Heloise shot her a reassuring grin and handed her a pair of elbow-length gloves. "You'll be fine, I promise. Raven and I will be there to help you. And so will Maman." She turned and went over to a side table. "Oh, I almost forgot! Richard told me to give you this." She handed Sabine a flat jeweler's box.

Sabine gasped at the contents.

Heloise leaned over to see and let out a low whistle of appreciation. "Now *that* is spectacular."

Sabine could only nod in agreement. The necklace was fit for a princess. Three huge teardrop-shaped sapphires hung suspended from a necklace of graduated diamonds. A pair of matching earrings, oval sapphires surrounded by a ring of brilliant diamonds, completed the set.

There was no doubt that the stones were real. Still, Sabine couldn't prevent herself from making doubly sure. She brought the necklace to her mouth, huffed on it, then quickly inspected the diamonds.

"What are you doing?" Heloise sounded half amused, half horrified.

"Testing the diamonds."

"You think Richard would give you paste?" Heloise sounded almost comically insulted on her brother's behalf.

Sabine shrugged, even though she knew the answer. Of

course he wouldn't. Hampden would never accept anything but the best. He'd never settle for a pale, cheap imitation.

"Diamonds dissipate heat very quickly. If you breathe on a real diamond there will be no hint of moisture, no condensation. Breathe on glass or paste and it will stay fogged up for a long time."

"Those aren't foggy," Heloise said smugly. She bent to read the name on the silk-lined lid. "Rundell, Bridge & Rundell. They're jewelers to the king. I'll say this for Richard: he never does things by halves."

Sabine closed her eyes. He certainly didn't. Her hands trembled as she fastened the necklace around her throat and the stones warmed to her skin. The central sapphire was a precise match for her dress, for her eyes. It nestled between the top curves of her breasts, where they were pushed together by her corset. Her heart fluttered. This set was worth a fortune. What was Hampden thinking, to give her such a thing? Was it a test? Was he waiting to see if she would run off with it in the night?

Heloise gave a low chuckle. "He said to tell you it's only a loan for tonight, so you won't embarrass him in public."

Sabine gave an unladylike snort. *Arrogant ass.*

Heloise gave her hand a brief squeeze of encouragement. "Don't worry about tonight. Believe me, I know what it's like to be a stranger in a foreign land. You'll be fine, I promise." She glanced at the clock. "Now, let's go down to the carriage. I'm coming with you and Maman—Richard and Raven had a meeting with Castlereagh this afternoon. They said they'd meet us there."

Sabine fought a little twinge of disappointment. Richard was the only reason she was going to this infernal party, and he'd abandoned her. She tossed her head. Well, she'd faced worse than a room full of bored, inbred aristocrats. She didn't need his support.

* * *

SABINE PAUSED at the entrance to Lady Carstairs's ballroom as terror vied with excitement. She quelled the impulse to turn on her heel and run. This was a mistake. She would never fit in. These people weren't fools; they would see past her fine clothes and jewels to the fraud underneath. They would know that her pristine white gloves concealed ink-stained fingers, divine the criminal core hidden beneath the thin veneer of respectability. She'd rather face Savary and Fouché together, and General Malet, too, than these harridans who would shred her with their tongues.

Sabine straightened her spine. *Non.* She'd duped Napoleon himself. She would feign confidence until it came to her. Besides, she had as much right to be here as anyone. The de la Tours had an ancient, noble lineage. Her mother might have been a governess, but she'd been the daughter of a gentleman, too.

Her favorite Oriental text on warfare had clearly grasped the fine art of faking it. "Appear weak when you are strong, and strong when you are weak." Now was not the time to appear weak. She would exude confidence, pretend to be on the inside what she appeared to be on the outside—poised and utterly delighted to be here in this room full of bright, inquisitive eyes and brittle smiles.

She raised her chin. Bah! What did she care for their opinion? They knew nothing of danger, of excitement. They led such boring lives. She pitied them.

She'd spent half her life skulking in the grim alleys of Paris, but here it was nothing but flirtation and frivolity. Hundreds of candles glimmered from the crystal chandeliers and glinted off silver punch bowls and fruit-filled centerpieces. There were at least twenty attendants, all dressed in blue liveries trimmed with lace. Without her lorgnette, the room blurred into a great, dizzying sweep of diamond-studded heels, flittering fans, and feather-plumed turbans.

Sabine's tension dissipated. This wasn't real. It was a fairy tale. She would enjoy it as a wonderful dream. With or without Richard Hampden.

She descended the steps and allowed Heloise to introduce her to a nearby group. She smiled until her cheeks ached, laughed at the gentlemen, nodded at the women. Much of the gossip centered around the upcoming royal wedding: the Prince Regent's daughter, Princess Charlotte, was marrying the impoverished but handsome Prince Leopold of Saxe-Coburg and Gotha. The general consensus was that it was a famous romance —a flighty, headstrong, impulsive girl tamed by a steady, dashing foreign prince.

Sabine suppressed a snort. Romantic? Ha! There was nothing romantic about a dynastic marriage—two rich families uniting to get even richer. Or perhaps, as they said, it really was a love match? She hoped so, for the princess's sake. She couldn't imagine much worse than being married for your money. Not that it was a problem she'd ever face, of course.

There was still no sign of Hampden, and the room was overly warm. Sabine sidled behind a pillar, closer to the open French doors where a cool breeze wafted in from the gardens.

A number of conversation stools had been placed around the edges of the ballroom for those who chose to watch the proceedings rather than dance. A pair of elderly matrons gossiped happily on the other side of the pillar, unaware of Sabine's unintentional eavesdropping.

". . . the ceremony itself is in two weeks' time. The second of May."

"At Carlton House?"

The first lady nodded. "Rumor has it the princess's wedding dress is costing upwards of eight thousand pounds!" She issued a disapproving sigh. "Of course, Prinny loves putting on a show. His daughter's wedding is the perfect excuse."

Her companion smiled placidly. "Well, I, for one, cannot wait. If it's anything like the Jubilee celebrations two years ago, it will be extraordinary. Don't you remember, Lydia? We watched that miniature naval engagement they staged on the Serpentine. The one with all Lord Nelson's victories."

The first dowager nodded, causing the ostrich feathers in her coiffure to wobble excitedly. "The *Times* reports that more than ten thousand fireworks have been ordered for the displays."

Her friend inhaled sharply. "Terribly dangerous. Why, only a few weeks ago I read about an accident in Westminster Road. Two neighboring fireworks manufacturers exploded. The roof was blown clear off one of them! It was a miracle nobody was killed."

"Let us hope this celebration is more carefully planned."

Their turbans bobbed in unison.

Heloise sidled up. "Why are you hiding over here? Come on, everyone's clamoring for an introduction to my gorgeous French 'cousin.'"

"I can't think why."

Heloise grinned wickedly. "Oh, I think it might have something to do with the fact that I've been circulating the rumor that not only are you beautiful, talented, and sweet-natured, but also an heiress."

Sabine gasped. "Why would you do that?"

Heloise looked smug. "Because Richard gets his own way far too often, that's why," she said cryptically. "He needs a little healthy competition."

Sabine opened her mouth to explain just how unnecessary that was, but Heloise grabbed her arm.

"Oh, goodness! Do you see that man coming toward us? The one with the curly hair? That's Edward Hughes Ball Hughes. I know, it's a ridiculous name, but he was up at Cambridge with Richard. He's in line to inherit a considerable fortune. And he's been begging for an introduction to you for the past ten minutes."

The young man stopped in front of them and bowed. He had

a pleasant, rounded face, though his complexion was a little florid. "Evening, Heloise. You're looking lovely. Won't you introduce me to your friend?"

"Of course," Heloise said with a beatific smile. "Edward, this is my cousin, Miss Sabine de la Tour."

Sabine gave him an encouraging smile.

Heloise shot them both an overly innocent glance. "She was just telling me how much she was longing to dance—"

Edward took his cue with a wry smile. "Was she really? Well, in that case—may I have the honor of the next, mademoiselle?"

Sabine shrugged inwardly. No reason she couldn't have some fun. Especially since Hampden hadn't even bothered to turn up.

She smiled and took his hand. "Sir, I'd be delighted."

CHAPTER 32

*R*ichard scanned Lady Carstairs's ballroom. It took him less than a minute to locate Sabine, whirling around the floor with his old schoolmate, Eddie Hughes Ball Hughes.

Of course it was a bloody waltz. Richard watched her glide across the floor as naturally as if she'd danced it a hundred times and swore under his breath. "Everything that deceives enchants," he muttered darkly. She'd done a bloody good job of enchanting Eddie. He had a soppy, besotted smile on his ruddy face.

Richard's mood darkened as he catalogued Sabine's transformation. He'd known it was going to be bad. She'd looked good enough to eat in the unadorned rags she'd arrived in. In decent clothes, she was ravishing.

Her dress was a masterpiece of suggestion: just diaphanous enough to hint at the body beneath it without actually revealing anything scandalous, a promise that if she moved in just such a way it might afford an unrestricted view of something pink or something white.

Richard frowned. How on earth was that bodice held upright? The tiny sleeves offered no visible means of support. It was a miracle of structural engineering.

The midnight-blue color was the perfect foil for her dark hair, which was pinned up in a way that looked deceptively haphazard but which had doubtless taken a great deal of effort to achieve.

The effect was beyond tempting. Richard curled his fist against the impulse to reach out and unpin it, to let it slide down over his hands and the pale skin of her shoulders in a blue-black wave. The image brought a rush of blood to his head.

She was wearing the necklace he'd provided. Seeing her in something he'd picked out gave him a primitive thrill of satisfaction. Unfortunately, it also drew attention to the perfect curve of her breasts and provided salivating devils like Eddie an excuse to drool down her cleavage.

The dance ended and Sabine returned to the side of the room. A group of young bucks lingered in the vicinity, clearly hopeful for an introduction. Heloise beckoned a few of them forward, and Richard watched with a mixture of amusement and contempt as Sabine reduced the newcomers to dumbfounded, stammering idiots. All she had to do was smile, apparently, and their gray matter ceased to function.

Heloise introduced Sabine to Reverend Twiggs and Richard shook his head. The vicar didn't stand a chance.

Sure enough, Sabine smiled and said a few words. Twiggs blinked slowly, like a boxer who'd taken one too many hits to the head. He flushed a deep red. His Adam's apple disappeared into his dog collar, then bobbed up again like a fishing float.

Richard chuckled darkly. He sincerely hoped the man was reminding himself of the sin of mortal lust and the evils of fornication. What was that quote from the Bible? "But I say to you that everyone who looks at a woman with lustful intent has already committed adultery with her in his heart."

The vicar was guilty as sin.

And what about that bit in Proverbs? "Do not desire her beauty in your heart, and do not let her capture you with her eyelashes."

It was too late for old Twiggs. Sabine had lethal eyelashes, and a way of looking up at a man from under them that liquefied his insides.

Raven sidled up and Richard shook himself out of his trance. He was gawping like a bloody schoolboy.

"God, these affairs are boring," Raven drawled. "I only agreed to come tonight because of your damn sister. Half an hour, I told her, no longer. I swear, Richard, if I didn't love her quite so much I'd strangle her with my bare hands."

"You married her," Richard murmured unsympathetically. "It's your own bloody fault."

Raven grinned. "I have no regrets, I promise you. In fact, I see my darling wife over there, with your little criminal. What are they up to?"

Richard tilted his head. "Fending off Eddie Hughes Ball Hughes, amongst others."

Raven raised his dark brows. "Even Lacorte would have a hard time printing enough money to rival *his* fortune."

Richard ignored his friend's wicked smile and the sudden, primitive urge to stride over there and throw Eddie through the French windows. He shot a murderous glare at his sister across the room. "Why the hell is Heloise introducing her to Drummond? The man's a fortune-hunter!" He watched with rising irritation as Sabine threw her head back and laughed at something Drummond said. It set his teeth on edge. "He's a penniless rogue. You know he doesn't have honorable intentions!"

Raven shot him a sly, knowing glance. "And you do, I suppose?"

Richard opened his mouth, but Raven didn't give him a chance to answer.

"Liar! You're thinking of exactly how many seconds it would take to get her out of that dress. You're counting the number of ties and tapes and ribbons and hooks—"

"I am not," Richard growled.

Raven raised his brows at him.

"Eighteen seconds," Richard conceded grimly, watching her. "Twenty-five at most."

Five covered buttons at the back of her dress, two tapes to untie at the shoulders, one side tie holding her petticoat closed. The front lacing on her short stays, one knee-length chemise to pull over her head. And then skin. Glorious, naked, heavenly skin. He bit the inside of his cheek.

Raven chuckled. "You couldn't be more obvious if you bared your teeth and beat your chest."

Richard felt a muscle twitch in the side of his jaw. It was time to put a stop to this. Sabine was supposed to be his fake fiancée. He needed to put his woman-deterring plan into action.

* * *

SABINE'S PARTNER returned her to Heloise's side, bowed, and excused himself. Heloise handed her a glass of champagne and tilted her chin across the crowded dance floor.

"Raven and Richard have arrived."

Sabine picked out Hampden's dark curls and broad shoulders, and wished she'd brought her lorgnette. He bent his head to listen to something Raven said, then smiled—a lazy, cynical smile that caused his cheek to crease into that almost-but-not-quite dimple. Her heart gave an irregular kick. He was so full of vitality, so ludicrously handsome, that she felt momentarily dizzy.

The simple cut of his coat and unfussy cravat made the ruffles and posturing of the younger men in the room seem ridiculous. It was easy to see why the ladies found him irresistible. He was a man supremely confident in his skin. He carried himself as if he were a prince, like Lucifer himself, addressing his cohorts. Sabine envied his assurance.

Heloise rolled her eyes at the females clustering around him. "Sometimes," she said darkly, "I am ashamed to call myself a woman. Look at them. They're like a covey of quails. The younger ones are all swooning and sighing, and the older ones are trying to catch his eye to make an assignation." She shook her head. "Evenings like this remind me of throwing bread crumbs to the carp in the pond; it's a feeding frenzy."

Sabine snorted at the apt description.

Heloise wrinkled her nose. "Word's got out that he finished with Caro Williams. They're all angling to be next. The eligible ones, that is."

Sabine frowned. "Eligible?"

"Richard's famous—or, rather, infamous—for his mistress rules: three months maximum. No virgins. No wives. No exceptions."

Sabine raised her eyebrows.

Heloise shrugged. "He says being so straightforward makes it easier all around."

"My God!" Sabine gave a horrified gasp, caught between laughter and despair.

"Raven says the betting books are already filling up at White's. Money's favoring Mrs. Winters, the new opera singer at Covent Garden."

Sabine's heart gave a painful little wrench.

Heloise continued. "The ones who aren't mistress material are just as bad. The stunts some of them play! You wouldn't believe what they'll do to try and wring a proposal out of him."

"You mean they try to force him into marrying them?"

Heloise nodded grimly. "Only last week Henrietta Tilton threw a glass of ice water over herself. And Sophia Alwell "accidentally tripped" on her hem and practically threw herself into his arms."

Sabine chuckled. "Isn't that rather shortsighted? I mean, surely forcing a man into marriage results in contempt, not affection?"

"All they can think of is being addressed as Viscountess

Lovell." She took a meditative sip of champagne and studied her brother with a critical eye. "It doesn't help that he's as rich as Croesus. If he were a penniless dolt it wouldn't be half so bad. But some wicked genie present at his birth decided to play a great joke on everyone by adding charm and intelligence into the mix."

Sabine studied him gravely. "Don't forget the dimple," she added judiciously. "Even I can see the potential allure of the dimple."

Heloise sighed. "Richard could be stranded on a desert island, walk off into the wilderness, and return a day later with a beautiful woman on his arm." She shot a sideways glance at Sabine. "I know what you're thinking—that you're immune. Just because you've seen a part of him that he rarely lets others see—namely the grouchy, overbearing, insufferable side of him—you're still in danger." She nodded. "Believe me, as someone married to a handsome, arrogant, overly intelligent bounder myself," she glanced across the room at Raven, who caught her eye and responded with a raised eyebrow and quirk of his lips that made Heloise snap open her fan and vigorously cool her heated cheeks, "you are still very much at risk."

Raven's smile widened as he took note of his wife's obvious loss of composure. He bent and murmured to Richard, who also glanced over in their direction. His eyes narrowed on Sabine and her breath caught. She shot him her most imperious stare.

"Your brother's interest in me is purely professional," she managed weakly.

Heloise snorted. "Poppycock! He hasn't taken his eyes off you the entire time we've been standing here. He just looks away when you look over at him. The whole thing is highly diverting, I assure you. If I weren't such a wonderful sister I would tease him mercilessly."

Sabine's heart thumped in hope, which was beyond stupid. The man was her enemy.

Heloise tapped her lips with her fan. "Forgive me, but Raven told me who you are."

Sabine stilled, suddenly wary, but Heloise shot her a conspiratorial smile. "Oh, don't worry—your secret's safe with me," she whispered from behind her fan. "I wanted to thank you, actually." She kept her gaze on her brother. "Richard's relished having you as an adversary. You've obsessed him—or rather, Philippe Lacorte has—for the better part of three years." Her eyes twinkled with mischief. "I always thought it would be something of an anticlimax when he finally found Lacorte, but you're even better than anyone could possibly have imagined."

Sabine didn't know what to say to that.

Heloise squeezed her arm. "Pursuing you across Europe gave him a purpose, something to focus on after Tony's death." She sighed. "His position as the heir sets him apart, you know. People treat him with equal parts envy, respect, and awe." Her lips twitched into a smile. "But you have absolutely no reverence for his title. You're neither intimidated nor impressed by his wealth —because you can simply print your own fortune, if you want it." She gave a gurgle of laughter. "It's wonderful!"

Hampden chose that moment to push off the wall. He straightened and, along with Raven, began to circumnavigate the room, stalking toward them like two graceful panthers.

Heloise nudged her arm. "Don't look now, but they're coming this way!"

Sabine took a fortifying swig of champagne.

CHAPTER 33

*H*ampden stopped directly in front of her, bowed low, and kissed her knuckles. The heat of his lips burned through her evening gloves. Sabine snatched her hand away.

"Why were you scowling at me from across the room?" he demanded.

"I wasn't scowling. I was squinting. Anything over ten feet is a blur. It's better if I narrow my eyes."

Raven chuckled. "I can think of several people here tonight who improve dramatically if you narrow your eyes."

Heloise smacked him on the arm. "Hush, you beast! Someone will hear!"

"I wasn't talking about you, my lovely." He grinned down at her, then nodded at a rotund lady in a silver dress and heavy jewelry who was holding court at the far end of the salon. "Lady Carstairs, our hostess," he added helpfully to Sabine.

Sabine raised her brows in surprise. "Her diamonds are paste!"

"You're the only one here who can tell." Hampden shrugged. "The real ones are probably stored in a bank vault somewhere."

She pursed her lips. "What's the point in owning something

beautiful if you lock it away? No artist wants his creation hidden in a safe deposit box. It should be seen and enjoyed."

Heloise nodded in agreement.

Hampden shrugged. "What matters is that everyone thinks they're real. The ton is all about appearances. Everything around us is fake, to some degree or another." He shot a teasing grin at Sabine and Heloise. "You ladies are the worst offenders."

"How so?" Heloise demanded.

He gave her the kind of smile that older brothers employ merely to infuriate their younger siblings. "A cynic would argue that no woman is ever truly honest."

Heloise took a deep breath to argue, but he held up an admonishing finger and forged on, a wicked gleam in his eye.

"Everything about you is artifice. You use corsets to disguise unsightly bulges, padding to give you curves you don't naturally have. You pluck your eyebrows, hide your complexion beneath powder and rouge. And that's just your appearance. In conversations you feign interest in us men and our hobbies. Sometimes you even pretend to be stupider than you are, just so you don't intimidate us." He raised his brows, which gave him a wicked look—the perfect devil's advocate. "Why, some of you even fake innocence—until the wedding night. And when the poor new husband discovers his 'virginal bride' is anything but, it's too late."

Heloise punched him on the shoulder. "You're right. That's very cynical. And completely untrue. Don't you think so, Sabine?"

Sabine tilted her head. "Oh, I don't know. External appearances *can* be deceptive. For example, no one would imagine that beneath your brother's lordly exterior lies a man whose sole delight is tormenting Frenchwomen."

Richard gave a snort of laughter. "I wouldn't say it's my *sole* delight, but yes, tormenting Frenchwomen—especially traitorous, criminal Frenchwomen—is a particular hobby of mine."

Heloise rolled her eyes.

Hampden let his gaze skim over Sabine's cleavage. The expression on his face made her blood slow and heat, like molten lava.

"Why are you looking at me like that?" she snapped.

"I'm making my interest in you perfectly clear." He sent her a wide, openly admiring smile. "For all those women who seem to find me irresistible."

"It's inexplicable," she said witheringly.

He raised an amused brow. "You wound me. I can be irresistible when I choose."

"I'm assuming now is not one of those times."

He laughed, impervious to her needling. "Those sapphires look magnificent on you, by the way. Don't tell me they're fakes. They were eye-wateringly expensive."

Sabine gave a nonchalant shrug. "They'll do."

She reminded herself that *this* was fake. His flirting was all for show, to deceive the casual observer into thinking there was something between them. She gazed out over the crowd so she wouldn't keep staring at Hampden's jawline and wondering what his lips would feel like against her own.

RICHARD CHUCKLED. Sabine's irreverence lightened his mood. In fact, he was enjoying the evening far more than he'd enjoyed a ton function in years. She put every other woman in the shade, like a real diamond compared to a paste stone. She was sparkling, vibrant, breathtaking. Beautiful enough to rouse envy in man and woman alike.

He shook his head. She was an astonishing woman, by turns worldly wise and innocent. Every so often he glimpsed a haunted, lost look in her eyes and a certain wry cynicism that made his chest ache. She'd been hurt, disappointed, bullied, and yet she'd still managed to keep her sense of humor and unbroken spirit. She reminded him of a quote from Shakespeare's *A Midsummer Night's Dream*: "And though she be but little, she is fierce."

He studied her as she took a sip of his drink. She wasn't a young girl in the first flush of youth, not one for maidenly blushes or stammering. He liked that—her slightly sarcastic control. She was brave, resourceful, and stubborn, all traits he admired immensely. And her mind was as sharp as a razor.

His first impression had been to liken her to a pixie, but that wasn't right. She was more sly than that, more dangerous—like a harpy, with sharp little talons, or a siren, luring men to their doom against the rocks. He certainly wasn't immune. He needed to strap himself to the mast so he didn't jump overboard and drown.

She shifted, and the scent of her drifted to his nose, acerbic and tart. That combination of lemons, ink, and skin that was uniquely her, all mixed together with the sole purpose of driving him mad.

Several women were sending him come-hither glances, or giving him suggestive peeks from behind their fans. None of them appealed. And even if they had, he couldn't very well go off and engage a new mistress while he was busy keeping Sabine under surveillance.

He was wound tighter than a spring because of her distracting presence. It was her fault he was in this highly charged state, with no way of expending his energies. The only sensible solution would be to take her as his mistress.

Richard paused, mentally cataloguing all the reasons that was a good idea. It would be a mutually beneficial decision between two consenting adults. She was already living under his roof, so it resolved his problem with the least amount of effort on either behalf. She would have no unrealistic expectation of him falling in love with her. And it was very unlikely that she would fall in love with him. She seemed to hate his guts most of the time. That was no bar to a satisfying sexual encounter, however. She might not like him, but she certainly wanted him. A little animosity just made things all the more interesting.

There could be no question of an inadequate performance from himself. He wanted her with bloodcurdling intensity that was downright terrifying, if he cared to examine it closely. Which he didn't. More worrying, though, was the suspicion that his desire for her was as intellectual as it was physical. He loved her sneaky, conniving brain as much as he lusted after her body.

Richard smiled. It was an excellent plan. Time to make himself irresistible.

CHAPTER 34

*S*abine held her breath as Hampden leaned closer and stole all the air in the vicinity.

"We need to dance."

She opened her mouth to argue, then froze as she glanced over his shoulder and recognized a horribly familiar face heading toward them with Lady Carstairs. All the blood drained from her cheeks.

Hampden turned to see what had captured her interest. "Someone you know?" he asked, an edge to his voice.

Sabine forced herself to speak through numb lips as the couple drew nearer. "Uh, yes. I mean, I've seen that man before. In Paris. His name is General Jean Malet."

She pressed closer to Hampden's side, assailed by the feeling of impending doom. What was Malet doing here? Had he followed them to England? How? Oh, God, was he going to arrest her?

Malet was wearing a new uniform; he must have been promoted. He'd probably slipped a dagger in the back of his predecessor, Sabine thought wildly. She glanced around for an escape route. Malet drew level with them, and for a brief minute she dared hope he would pass them by, but then his gaze alighted on her face and he stopped mid-stride.

"Lord Lovell," Lady Carstairs said breathlessly, addressing Hampden. "So glad you could make it to our little soirée. We are honored. May I introduce General Jean Malet, one of the key architects of that monster Napoleon's downfall."

Sabine barely suppressed a snort of derision. Politically, Malet was as inconstant as the English weather, always swapping sides to save his own skin.

Hampden bowed and Malet did the same, although more stiffly. His florid cheeks spoke of a fondness for claret. His eyes roamed Sabine's face as he straightened.

"I do not believe I have had the honor," he said, in highly accented English.

Hampden tugged her forward by the arm. "My cousin, Mademoiselle de la Tour."

Malet bowed again. "A pleasure to meet a fellow French-woman." He narrowed his beady eyes and studied her with a puzzled air. "Have we met before, my dear? You look familiar."

Sabine pinned a bright smile on her face while her pulse beat against her throat. "I don't think that's possible, monsieur."

"Of course not," he agreed readily. He bowed low over her hand and took the opportunity to ogle her cleavage. His mustache quivered as he gave her a jovial grin. "I would have remembered such a pretty face."

Sabine relaxed as the threat of exposure passed and she suppressed an impish desire to tell him everything. *Oh, we've met, Monsieur Malet. I'm the assistant you barely noticed at Carnaud's gallery in Rue du Pélican. I'm the girl who sold you Giorgione's study of a nude twice. I'm the forger who's been working for you for the past eight years. The thief who beat you to all that lovely money at Vincennes.*

She treated him to her best curtsey as he and Lady Carstairs drifted away, but her heart was still hammering at the close call. She glanced up at Hampden, suddenly in need of a moment alone. "If you'll excuse me, I need to visit the powder room."

Hampden inclined his head. "Go ahead. I need a word with Lord Simms, anyway. I'll meet you back here in five minutes." His eyes crinkled at the corners. "For that dance."

* * *

SABINE DIDN'T GO to the ladies' room. She stood near the open French doors instead and took several calming breaths while her pulse resumed its normal rhythm. A thrill of elation warmed her insides. What a close shave!

She scanned the blurry swirl of dancers, then the guests at the edge of the room, but couldn't see Hampden anywhere. Perhaps he and his friend had withdrawn to the card room. With a little squinting she located Raven and Heloise, chatting at the center of a lively group. Raven watched Heloise as she talked, his hard features softening as they rested on her face. Heloise glanced up and caught him looking, and they shared a secret smile.

A pang of wistful longing balled in Sabine's chest at the way they seemed able to communicate with only their eyes. She wanted that. That closeness of souls, the ability to hold a whole conversation without ever moving her lips. Her heart cracked a little; her parents had been the same. It was hardly surprising that she'd crave it too.

With a sigh, she turned to find a liveried servant hovering at her elbow. "Miss de la Tour?"

She frowned. "Yes?"

"There is a gentleman requesting your presence in the gardens." His face was completely impassive, and he bowed and withdrew before she could ask any more.

Her heart began to pound again. Had Malet somehow discovered who she was and laid a trap for her? She glanced around—and found him talking animatedly with the Russian ambassador.

She bit her lip. If not Malet, could it be one of her previous dance partners, trying to lure her into the gardens for a kiss? The idea was rather flattering, even if he was doubtless only doing it because he thought she was an heiress worth pursuing, thanks to Heloise's ridiculous meddling.

Curious, but wary, she slipped out into the gardens. There were plenty of people on the terrace, escaping the crush and heat inside. A few tables and chairs lit by lanterns had been artfully arranged to encourage conversation down on the lawn, and she descended the shallow stone steps toward a garland-swagged gazebo.

The shadows darkened as she slunk deeper into the gardens; there were several invitingly dark corners for the amorously inclined. Sabine spied the edge of a lady's dress disappearing behind a large willow tree and heard a giggle, hastily hushed.

She skirted the tall mass of a yew-tree hedge, trying to blend into the shadows. At least her dress was dark.

"Psst!"

An arm snaked out and clasped her around the waist. A hand covered her mouth. Sabine gave a muffled cry, but before she could even struggle she was hauled behind the hedge and pulled up tight against a broad chest.

"Shh! It's only me."

She sagged in relief at that dear, familiar voice. As the pressure on her mouth eased, she whirled around and threw herself against her best friend's chest.

"Anton!" she gasped. "You almost frightened me to death! It's so good to see you. I've been so worried Where are you staying?"

Anton removed her arms from around his waist with a muffled groan. Sabine stepped back just as he shifted position, and the faint light from one of the lanterns picked out his misshapen features. She gasped in horror.

"My God! What happened?" She lifted her hand to touch the swollen side of his cheek, then thought better of it when he flinched back. "Look at your eye!" she wailed. "Who did this to you?"

CHAPTER 35

*a*nton had been beaten black and blue; his handsome face was almost unrecognizable. His left eye was ringed with a livid bruise and so puffed up his eyelid could barely open. His ear was lumpy and misshapen, like a hideous flesh-colored cauliflower. He looked like a boxer who'd gone twenty rounds and lost.

Sabine's eyes hardened in fury. "Who beat you?"

Anton shrugged, then clutched his ribs as though even that movement pained him. Sabine winced in sympathy.

"Five lads. They heard my accent. Ex-army, they were, just roiling for a fight with a Frenchie to avenge all their friends killed in the war. They followed me back to the lodgings I'd found and set upon me."

"Oh no."

"That's not the worst of it," Anton sighed, giving her a sidelong glance from his one good eye. "The bastards ransacked my room. They took all my savings, and found my half of our emergency money."

Sabine sagged back against the hedge and swallowed a few choice curses. "Oh Anton!"

Anton gave an angry shake of his head, clearly frustrated with himself. "I know, I know. I'm sorry. But I couldn't fight them off."

Sabine sighed. "Well, what's done is done. And at least you weren't killed. Besides, we still have my half of the money." Anton nodded and she let out a sigh. "I hate to say 'I told you so,' but this is precisely why I said we should split it up. In case of unforeseen mishaps such as this."

"Where's your half?" Anton asked.

"I hid it in a locker at the British Museum."

"You sure it's safe?"

"Safer than at Richard Hampden's residence, I can tell you that," Sabine said grimly. "I'm sure he's already searched my rooms."

"I'm going to need some of it," Anton said. "I can't live on nothing."

Sabine scowled. She hated the idea of introducing the fake money into circulation, but what other choice did they have? "Very well. I'll go back to the museum and get it."

"Can't I go?"

"No. It's in the coat check, and you need a little numbered ivory disk to release it. It's back in my room."

"Can you leave it somewhere for me to find?"

Sabine shook her head. "Not really. I don't want to risk you being caught. It will have to be me." She peered at him through the darkness. "Have you found any ships sailing to America yet?"

Anton shook his head. "We just missed one that sailed last week. There's another company I'm trying tomorrow, down by the Thames docks, that sounds promising, though."

Sabine frowned. "How did you know I'd be here, anyway? And how did you get in?"

He started to smile, then hissed as the movement cracked his split lip. "I slipped in through the garden gate. And I knew you'd be here because I've been watching Lovell's house from Hyde

Park. I followed that fancy coach of his. Those crests on the side are pretty distinctive."

A peal of feminine laughter rippled from the terrace and Sabine jerked as another, terrifying thought struck her. "Oh, God. You can't be seen here with me! Malet's here, in this very house!"

Anton frowned. "Malet? Shit! Did he see you?"

"We were introduced. He said I looked familiar, but he couldn't place me."

Anton let out a relieved sigh. "I'm not surprised. I almost didn't recognize you!" He took her hand and raised it so she was forced to give him a twirl. Sabine spread her skirts and made a deep, sarcastic curtsey. He winked at her with his good eye. "You look *extraordinaire, ma belle.* Who'd have thought there was a ravishing woman under all that printing ink?"

Sabine laughed and shook her head. "You are a Frenchman through and through. Even beaten to a pulp you cannot help issuing outrageous compliments."

He meant nothing by them. Flirting came to him as easily as breathing. He'd flirt with a tree if there wasn't a woman close by. Ironic how his most outrageous comments failed to arouse her, but the slightest hint of appreciation from Richard Hampden made her pulse flutter alarmingly.

Anton gave one of his classic Gallic shrugs. "Bah. A man would have to be dead not to notice a beautiful woman."

The voices of a couple strolling their way interrupted his discourse. Sabine peered cautiously around the side of the hedge. The dense foliage of the yew made it the perfect screen, thick and impenetrable, but anyone could stumble across them.

"You should go, before Hampden catches us."

Anton frowned. "He's treating you well?"

"As well as can be expected. But he doesn't trust me an inch. He barely leaves me alone for a moment."

He nodded. "All right, I'll go. When do you think you'll be able to get the money?"

"I'll go tomorrow, first thing. I've already visited the museum once, so there's no reason to think that he won't let me return. Let's meet in Hyde Park tomorrow afternoon. The fashionable set don't go there until at least half past four, and even then they usually just parade up and down Rotten Row in their carriages." She saw Anton's frown and clarified. "It's the bridle path, next to the big lake. Anyway, I'll meet you just inside the northeast corner, by Tyburn tree, where the gallows used to be. I'll aim for around half past two."

"Will Hampden let you out without an escort?"

Sabine's eyes twinkled. "Probably not, but don't worry, I'll think of something. Richard Hampden needs to learn that I will not be contained."

Anton shook his head in mock commiseration. "I almost pity the man."

She plucked at his sleeve, half-turning him. "Go! If Hampden catches you he'll . . ." She couldn't even finish the sentence. She couldn't imagine what he would do.

Anton stepped close and gave her a quick hug, which she returned, careful not to crush his injured ribs.

"Until tomorrow, *ma chère.*"

* * *

RICHARD STEPPED onto the terrace and swept an irritated glance around the shadowed gardens. Where the hell had Sabine gone? He'd seen her slip out of the French windows. Had she made an assignation with one of the wealthy fops like Eddie who'd been fawning over her? The idea of her with another man made his fingers clench into a fist. He strode down the steps to look for her, his mood black. Damnable woman. What was she up to now?

CHAPTER 36

*S*abine brushed down her skirts and was about to step back onto the path when a tall shadow blocked the way. The moonlight briefly illuminated Hampden's austere features and her heat gave a guilty start against her ribs. "Oh! It's you." She resisted the impulse to glance over her shoulder after Anton.

Hampden joined her behind the yew screen. "Were you expecting someone else?" he asked tersely.

She realized with a sudden plummeting dismay that he was furious. Oh, *merde*. Had he seen her with Anton? No. Surely if he'd seen them together he would have been rushing past her, trying to catch her accomplice. Sabine backed up until the prickly needles of the hedge stopped her escape. "Of course not," she managed. "I just needed a little air."

He followed, a slow prowl like a wolf approaching an injured fawn. The shadowed gap between the hedges formed a tunnel of privacy and Sabine swallowed as he pressed close, invading her space. She caught his scent—warm male overlaid with a smoky tang of liquor.

He tilted her head up to the moonlight. "You look flushed, my sweet."

Sabine moistened her lips with her tongue and watched with a thrill of alarm as his eyes followed the move hungrily.

"Yes, I, ah," she stammered. "It's all so . . . overwhelming. My first ton ball. And it's so hot in there . . ." She trailed off at his skeptical expression.

His thumb swept over her jaw and her insides melted like candle wax.

"You shouldn't be out here alone," he chided softly. "Who knows what unsavory characters might be lurking about in the bushes?"

She couldn't tear her eyes away from him. The stroke of his thumb against her cheek was an erotic caress, but he hardly seemed aware that he was doing it.

Sabine swallowed. "You know I can take care of myself, monsieur. There's no need to cosset me like an English debutante. Men have tried to lure me into dark corners before."

A muscle ticked in his jaw. "Have they? Who?" The silky question held a distinct undertone of menace.

"Oh, I shall name no names. Suffice to say they found the experience extremely disappointing." She tugged away from his hand and started walking, but he sidestepped, blocking her way.

"You promised me a dance."

"In public," she protested. "What good will it do if we dance here? There's no one to see."

His teeth flashed white. "That means we can do whatever we like."

Sabine closed her eyes against temptation. He sounded so seductively reasonable. The serpent in the Garden of Eden would have spoken just like this. *Just bite the apple, Sabine. One tiny, forbidden taste.*

He bent his head. "Who are you meeting, out here in the dark?"

"No one."

"Liar."

He was still angry. It vibrated between them, thickening the air, mingling with the tug of desire. His lips brushed her ear, then nuzzled the soft skin at the side of her neck.

Sabine stilled. Her pulse slammed against her throat and slow, delicious heat curled her insides. She wanted to reach up and grab his hair and hold him to her skin.

"As long as we're pretending to be courting," he murmured, "I'm going to have to insist that you stay away from making assignations with other men."

Sabine opened her eyes wide. Was he jealous? Did she have that much power over him? Or was it merely that he considered her his possession, under his control?

The frothy white lace of his cuffs brushed her cheeks as he lifted his head and framed her face. "If it's a kiss you want, Miss de la Tour, your fiancé should be the one to provide it."

Sabine bit her lip. Oh, this was wrong, so wrong! "You're not my fiancé," she managed shakily. "And you're only doing this because you don't have a mistress to entertain you."

He tilted his head, but his eyes never left her lips. "That's not true. There are any number of women in that ballroom who would be more than willing to accommodate me. But I want you."

"Am I supposed to be flattered?" she snapped. "You have not bought my body with your money, Monsieur Hampden. Only my counterfeiting skills."

He chuckled darkly. "Oh, I'm well aware of that. Your body you have to give to me for free."

She opened her mouth to berate him, but he wasn't finished. "What's the problem, Sabine? There's no harm in playing. We're both adults."

He bent and pressed his lips to the very corner of her own. His tongue flicked out to taste her. Her stomach somersaulted. "Admit it. You want to. Just as much as I do."

Oh, he was a wicked, wicked man.

"One kiss," he taunted. "I'll stop whenever you say."

She knew how he would kiss her—with practiced, leisurely ease. He'd do what he doubtless did with all his other women: tease her, drive her to distraction—and never lose a scrap of his own composure. That was unacceptable. She wanted all of him. Uncontrolled. Unrestrained. She wanted him to go up in flames like a bonfire made of money.

Sabine threw caution to the wind. She was Philippe Lacorte. She dared anything. She went up on tiptoe, grabbed the lapels of his immaculate coat, and tugged him close. "Stop talking, Richard Hampden."

She pressed her mouth to his.

For one brief second he froze. And then he broke. With a wordless sound of need he pulled her to him, tilted her head to the perfect angle, and kissed her back.

The rest of the world disappeared. This was no practiced, tentative exploration. This was darkness, heat, and total abandon. His lips shaped hers, his tongue swirling inside.

Sabine closed her eyes in delight. They fit together perfectly, concave to convex, dip and curve. She pulled him closer, melting into his wonderful warmth. His heart pumped fast under her palm and she wished his clothes gone—wanted to feel him, all of him, body to body, skin against skin.

On a wicked impulse she caught his bottom lip between her teeth and felt the jolt that ran through him with a surge of dark delight.

* * *

BLOODY HELL, Richard thought dazedly. Kissing Sabine had to be the stupidest thing he'd done. And the most glorious.

His body was on fire, desire roaring through his bloodstream, pounding in his head, and he tried to remember all the many, many reasons he shouldn't be touching her.

They were enemies. She was a blackmailer, possibly a spy, and she had a Frenchwoman's soul—ungovernable, subversive. Full of rebellion and revolution. People like her threatened the very bastions of Englishness he held dear: cricket, and White's, and roast beef.

But Christ, she tasted good. Nothing mattered when she made those soft little sounds of pleasure and her body pressed into his as if she couldn't get close enough.

His head swam. He'd known it would be good, but this blistering intensity, this pounding need, was unsettling. He hated wanting her so badly. Still, he felt a rush of savage satisfaction. At least the desire wasn't all one-sided. This woman faked everything, but even she couldn't feign indifference to his touch.

Her dress exposed the creamy top swells of her breasts. He traced them with his fingers, cupping her through the fabric, finding her nipples with his thumbs. She arched up into him with a moan of delight and he dropped his head and kissed her, where the central sapphire nestled between her breasts.

It wasn't enough. Suddenly impatient, he pushed down her bodice and freed her breasts to the cool night air. Thank God he'd ordered her dress cut so low. He ignored her gasp of shock and cupped her. She was small and perfect, and her nipples pebbled against his palms. He wanted to devour her. Giving in to the impulse, he bent and took her into his mouth, flicking with his tongue, and she surged against him with an incoherent moan. The sound inflamed his blood. The world narrowed to his hands on her skin, his mouth, sucking, biting, licking. The scent of her: ink and paint and lemons.

He wanted to be inside her. Wanted her on the ground, skirts up, with him buried deep between her legs. In one impatient move he pulled up her skirts and gathered them at her waist in a frothy mess. He reclaimed her mouth and drew her leg upward, curving it around his hip. His body slid between her legs, a perfect fit, and he pressed his aching cock against her, grinding his hips so she could feel the effect she had on him.

She moaned and tugged him closer.

His fingers went to the buttons of his breeches. His hands were shaking so much he fumbled them in his haste and cursed his incompetence. He was almost dizzy with desire. Any second now he'd be inside her—

A sharp trill of female laughter on the other side of the hedge brought reality crashing down like a bucket of ice water. Richard froze. What the hell was he thinking? He pulled back, panting hard, his aching body protesting at the sudden lack of contact. His heart was thumping as if he'd just finished a fight.

Sabine's eyes were huge in her pale face, and in the dim light she looked as dazed as he felt. Her mouth was all puffy, her lips swollen from his kisses—which only made him want to kiss her all over again. With a belated gasp she tugged the front of her bodice back up, hiding those perfect breasts from view. Richard realized he was still gripping her hip and forced his fingers to release her. Her skirts fell back down to her ankles with an audible swoosh.

He took a deep breath of cool air. "You didn't say 'stop,'" he managed hoarsely, then cursed himself for sounding more accusatory than teasing. He hadn't exactly thought about stopping, either. Maybe she would hit him. He probably deserved it.

Instead, she tilted her head in wry acknowledgment and her lips quirked in a self-deprecating smile. "No, you're right. I did not say 'stop.'"

Richard felt a spurt of reluctant admiration for her fairness, swiftly followed by a hint of irritation. She appeared to be recovering very quickly from what had been—for him, at least—an earth-shattering event.

Bloody hell. What was it about this woman that made him lose all sense of control? He'd been like a randy schoolboy cornering a dairymaid in the stables. A hot wave of humiliation heated his cheeks. Where had Richard Hampden, consummate lover, gone?

Sabine smoothed the front of her skirts and set about re-pinning her hair. He'd dislodged several pins with his hands; she tucked a few loose strands back into the elaborate mess. Determined to appear equally unfazed, Richard plucked a leaf from her hair, annoyed to realize his hand was still not quite steady.

"We should get back inside," she muttered.

He shook his head. "Not together. That would create a scandal." Not to mention the fact that he was still sporting an erection hard enough to hammer nails into steel.

Her lips gave a sarcastic little quirk. "Of course. We wouldn't want to ruin your reputation, would we, Lord Lovell?"

"Debauching young women in the shrubbery is certainly not my usual mode of operation," he said bluntly. "But you returning to the ballroom slightly . . . mussed," his eyes lingered on her hair and lips, "will only help my plan. The ton generally turns a blind eye to a little dalliance if there's the expectation of an impending marriage announcement."

"There will be no marriage announcement," she said coolly.

"Of course not. But you'll be long gone by the time they realize that. I'm the one who will have to put up with the whispers and knowing looks that accompany a jilted suitor."

* * *

SABINE ESCAPED to the powder room without encountering anyone and tidied herself as best she could. She met Heloise on her way back to the ballroom, and the other girl readily accepted her excuse that she was tired and wanted to leave.

"Maman was just saying the same thing. She's having the carriage brought around now. Did you enjoy your first ball?" Heloise asked brightly.

Sabine was certain her flushed cheeks and throbbing lips

betrayed exactly how much she'd enjoyed herself. An indecent amount.

"I haven't seen Richard for a while—" Heloise's eyes sparkled mischievously and Sabine had the uncomfortable suspicion that the other girl knew exactly what she'd been up to. And with whom. Heloise gave an elegant shrug. "I expect he's still closeted with Lord Simms. Don't bother waiting for him. Just send his carriage back later." Heloise kissed her cheek. "Good night, Sabine. I'll see you soon."

CHAPTER 37

*S*abine couldn't sleep. It was beyond stupid to have kissed him. Even stupider to admit that she'd wanted more. The shameful truth was that she'd been only seconds away from letting him take her, there, up against a tree, like some back-alley doxy.

She shook her head. The one time Anton had kissed her, years ago, he'd been ardent, gentle. And when he'd tried to slip his tongue inside her mouth she'd pulled away, laughing and protesting at the same time. To his credit, he hadn't pushed her. He'd laughed too, albeit shakily, and run his hand through his hair. Sabine's momentary worry that he perhaps felt more for her than she did for him, or that the experiment might affect their friendship, had been unfounded. The following night he'd bedded a pretty army officer's wife and never mentioned the kiss again. They'd settled back into the easy familiarity of friends.

Sabine buried her face in the pillows with a groan. What she felt for Richard Hampden was entirely beyond her scope of experience. She knew what it was, of course. She'd listened to the gossip of the women in the markets and the taverns, heard the giggles and bawdy jokes. It was lust, pure and simple. Or, rather, impure and complex. An animal attraction that was both natural and highly inconvenient.

One conversation in particular had been an eye-opener. She'd been seventeen, sitting in the Louvre beneath a large marble statue of a contorted Greek warrior wrestling some fierce snake-like creature. She'd been making a pen-and-ink study of a Piranesi architectural drawing.

Two young women had seated themselves on the bench on the opposite side of the statue. They clearly had no notion of her presence, because the first, whom Sabine quickly inferred was recently married, proceeded to launch into a litany of excruciatingly personal information regarding her intimate relations with her new husband. Her friend—also presumably married—tried to counsel her.

Sabine stopped drawing and held her breath, listening in rapt silence.

"I promise you, Clara, it was such a disappointment!" the first girl wailed. "I never want to do it again. It was awful!"

"And I promise you it will get better, my love. Men always botch the first time. Despite the fact that they've undoubtedly done the deed many times before with other women, when faced with a virgin on their wedding night they're seized with some kind of temporary insanity that renders them completely useless. My own dear Edouard was exactly the same."

"But what shall I do?"

Yes, thought Sabine, from the other side of the pillar. *Tell her. I'm dying to know.*

"Do you know what a climax is? *La petite mort?*"

"No," the friend sniffled.

Sabine wrinkled her nose. The little death?

Clara, the friend, gave a sigh. "It is the pleasure you can experience with your husband in bed. It is, quite simply, the most wonderful feeling imaginable. Like racing to the top of a mountain and flinging yourself off."

"That doesn't sound very nice," the friend said doubtfully. "It sounds dangerous."

I agree, mouthed Sabine, chewing the end of her pencil.

"It's quite hard to explain. It's like a lovely throbbing, tingling explosion that starts between your legs, where your man is, and spreads throughout your whole body. It makes you feel all happy and glowing, like your veins are full of melted butter and honey."

"Well, that does sound quite pleasant," the first girl conceded.

"It is. Now I'm going to let you in on a little secret. The first thing you must learn is that no man can give you a climax."

"What?!" her friend stuttered. "But you just said—how on earth do you get one, then?"

"I should have said, no man can give you one unless you know how to find it yourself."

"That doesn't make any sense."

"What I mean is, there's very little chance of a man being able to make you feel that way if you, yourself, don't know what it feels like. How will you know if you're nearly there? It's like asking someone for directions to Versailles and then not knowing to look for an enormous chateau when you get there. Am I making any sense?"

"Not really," the friend said.

Sabine shook her own head in silent agreement.

"Fine. Then let me tell you this. There are any number of ways you can achieve pleasure in bed. Did Claude put his hand down there, between your legs? Or his mouth?"

The friend gave a scandalized gasp. "What? No! He just sort of fell on top of me and squashed me and pushed his . . . his thing into me and . . . it hurt. And then he moved around a bit and then he went all rigid, and then he rolled over and fell asleep. He'd had a lot to drink at the wedding reception."

Clara snorted. "What an idiot. But all is not lost, dearest. Things can only get better from now on. But it's up to you. You must take responsibility for your own enjoyment. You must discover what you like, learn how to get this feeling on your own, and then train Claude to do those things to you. Let me tell you what to do . . ."

For the next half hour Sabine listened in rapt astonishment as her education in female anatomy was increased exponentially. There, at the stone feet of Hercules, or Achilles, or Perseus, she'd learned that a man could give a woman pleasure by placing his hand between her legs, and by kissing her there, too.

She also deduced that a woman could find her own pleasure, with her fingers, even without a man. The very thought made her skin flush and her stomach clench. Could she find her own pleasure? She'd left the museum in a kind of daze.

The first time she'd been brave enough to try it, alone in her tiny darkened attic room, she'd been amazed at what she'd discovered. With barely a touch she could make herself shiver and throb, gasp and explode. It was a revelation. If this was the feeling women got from lying with men—this wonderful, warm, breathless glow of repletion—then it was quite clear why they did it. And kept on doing it. Even with the wrong man.

The noises she'd heard emanating from Anton's bedroom suddenly took on a whole new significance. Anton had never been short of female company. The walls of the print shop were so thin she'd often resorted to covering her head with a pillow to muffle the sounds of enthusiastic lovemaking coming from his room. He had a different woman every month—and not one of them seemed able to keep quiet.

Sabine knew what her body could feel. But until she'd met Richard Hampden she'd never felt the slightest desire to try it with a man. Recently, however, she'd spent an inordinate amount of time wondering what his body would feel like against hers. Their little contretemps in the garden had settled that question once and for all: absolutely wonderful.

Now she wondered what it would be like to have something other than her own, familiar fingers between her legs. His fingers, for example. His mouth? The very thought made her dizzy. Sabine punched her pillow.

By midnight she'd decided to simply pretend the kiss had never happened. It was a moment of madness never to be repeated. She had Anton to think of. There was no time for messing around with Hampden. From now on she would concentrate on the job in hand.

Mmm. Hands, her wicked mind whispered, wonderful, skillful, talented hands . . .

Sabine scrunched her eyes closed and willed herself to sleep.

CHAPTER 38

When Sabine strolled into the breakfast room the following morning, she was greeted by a veritable florist's shop of flowers. At least seven or eight bunches decorated the tables and mantelpiece, and the smell was almost overpowering.

"*Dieu!* What is all this?"

Hodges, who had trailed her from the foyer, gave her a congratulatory smile. "For you, madame. Her ladyship sent them over from next door. I have placed the relevant card with each one."

Sabine picked up the nearest and read it aloud: "Delighted to have made your acquaintance. Lord Hughes Ball Hughes." She glanced up at Hodges, astonished. "Goodness."

"It appears you have a whole raft of admirers, madam," Hodges beamed.

She examined the next bouquet and let out a sound of irritation. "Someone has removed the thorns from these roses!"

Hampden chose that moment to saunter into the salon, looking as effortlessly elegant as usual. "I sense disapproval. What's making you so cross this morning?"

Her heart leaped at seeing him, but she managed a frown. "A rose without any thorns isn't really a rose."

Those perfect lips quirked. "Didn't Shakespeare say that 'a rose by any other name would smell as sweet'? What does it matter? They're easier to handle that way."

"It matters because it has been changed from what it was meant to be," Sabine said. "They've made it defenseless." She flushed as she realized how stupid that sounded. She wasn't even certain she was still talking about the rose. She was so out of sorts from last night's kiss that she could barely look at him. Her whole body was a seething mass of confusion.

He plucked a lilac stem from a nearby vase and sniffed it. "I see your point. Maybe the real reason we appreciate roses isn't because they smell nice, but because they're so bloody difficult to grab hold of? The sense of accomplishment when we tame them is all the greater."

His expression was bland, but she had the feeling he was laughing at her. Beast. She shrugged. "Cut flowers make me sad. They fade so soon. The man who truly loves me will plant me a garden, not give me a bouquet."

"I'll bear that in mind," he said. "I trust you can amuse yourself today. I have a meeting with Castlereagh to finalize the plan for capturing the plotters tomorrow."

She waved him away. "Of course. I thought I might go back to the museum."

He shook his head. "Not today."

Her brows—and her temper—rose. "Why not?"

"Because I'm not free to accompany you and keep you out of mischief."

Sabine scowled. "Fine. I'll make use of the library here. Provided that's permitted," she added pointedly.

He nodded. "That will be fine. I'll see you later."

As soon as she heard the front door shut behind him, Sabine went into the library. Irritating man! Did he honestly think she would do as he ordered? A short search through the shelves produced what she was looking for: *The London Directory and Register*, "containing the names, residence and occupation of the citizens &c." She flicked to the sections for Bond Street and St. James's, withdrew a thick sheaf of writing paper from the desk, and started to write.

A wicked smile hovered on her lips. Lord Lovell was about to make some spectacular purchases.

She wrote fifteen letters in all and tied them up with a piece of ribbon. There was no point in trying to give them to the servants—Hampden had doubtless left orders to confiscate her correspondence—so she opened the sash window and whistled to one of the sweeper boys loitering about on the corner. Thankfully it was not Hampden's little ally, Will Ambrose. The lad skulked nearer as she beckoned him forward, looking suspicious.

"How would you like to earn a shilling?" she asked.

The boy's scrawny little face lit up in delight. "Yes, mum!"

"All you have to do is deliver these letters. But it must be right away. Can you do that?"

The lad nodded eagerly. "'Course, mum."

She tossed the bundle of letters down to him. "I'll have payment waiting when you come back."

A gleeful laugh bubbled up inside her as he hurried off. The notes had been made to an assortment of different tradesmen, and while the items she'd requested varied greatly, all the letters had specified the same time for delivery. The esteemed Lord Lovell required them at precisely two o'clock that afternoon.

Now all she had to do was wait.

She'd just settled into reading a particularly fine copy of Chaucer's *Canterbury Tales* when Hodges appeared at the door.

"You have a visitor, ma'am."

Sabine straightened.

"A French gentleman," Hodges added. "I have put him in the blue salon."

Her heart plummeted, but she pasted a serene smile on her face. "Thank you, Hodges—I'll be there directly."

She was going to strangle Anton. Why on earth would he risk coming here now? Especially since they'd already agreed to meet later on in the park. Thank goodness Hampden had already left.

Sabine strode into the salon quite prepared to give him a good scolding, but came to a sudden stop when she realized it was not Anton bending over one of her bouquets. It was General Jean Malet.

Merde.

Malet straightened and his expression was distinctly unpleasant. Sabine's stomach turned to lead, but she affected an expression of polite inquiry. "Good morning, monsieur." She dropped him a neat courtesy.

Malet's smile was chilling. "Let's dispense with the niceties," he said, in French. "I knew I recognized you last night, but I just couldn't place you. And then it came to me: you're the girl from Carnaud's."

Sabine schooled her face to show faint surprise. "I don't know what you mean, monsieur. I'm afraid you are mistaken."

The general's brows lowered. "Don't play games with me, girl. I don't know how you've managed to wheedle your way into Lovell's home, but I know who you are. You're Anton Carnaud's friend. Which means you're Philippe Lacorte's friend." His eyes gleamed with triumph. "Oh, yes, I know Carnaud is Lacorte. He thought to hide it from me, but nobody fools Jean Malet for long." His lips tightened beneath his bristling mustache. "I followed him from Paris, you know. Spoke to some of his old contacts, found out he used a fake passport to come to England, under the name Christian Lambert."

He plucked a tall daisy from one of the bunches of flowers and twirled the stem idly between his fingers. "And he wasn't traveling alone. No, he was with his 'sister,' Marie. That was you."

Sabine's hands were clammy, but she lifted her eyebrows the

way Hampden did when he wanted to express genteel incredulity. "I say again, monsieur, you are mistaken. What you say is a fantasy. I have never met this Monsieur Carnaud. Or this Lacorte of whom you speak."

Malet's smile would have made a snake recoil. "*Eh bien.* If that's how you want to play it. But you should pass on a message to your friend. He has my money and I will get it back. I tracked him here. I will track him wherever he goes until he returns what is mine. If he does not, well . . ." The daisy snapped in half under the pressure of his thumb, and Malet bared his teeth in the semblance of a smile. He gave a mock start of dismay. "How careless of me. I am staying at Grillon's. Tell Lacorte that he has ten days to return my money or I will bury him." He bowed. "I know where you are now. Don't think that Lovell's lofty position will shield you if Lacorte does not comply. Good day, madame."

A chill ran down her spine, but she merely tilted her head as Malet swept past her. She dimly heard Hodges open the front door as she sank into a nearby chair. Her stomach churned. *Merde, merde, merde.* They had seriously underestimated Malet.

Sabine pressed a hand to her stomach and took a deep breath. *Oh, God.* Which of her friends had he threatened in Paris to extract the information about the passports? She hoped they were all right.

She'd have to tell Anton of this new, unwelcome development this afternoon. There was no question of them returning the money to Malet, of course, but now it was even more imperative for Anton to leave England as soon as possible.

CHAPTER 39

*S*abine brooded over Malet's visit so much that two o'clock came almost before she was ready. At five minutes to the hour, she listened to the growing clamor in the street outside and her mood lightened. She pushed up the sash window of her bedroom, leaned out, and gave a sigh of delight.

Ah, sweet chaos.

Upper Brook Street was as crowded as the Place Vendôme before an execution. Fifteen assorted tradesmen all trying to deliver to the same address at the same time had created a traffic snarl of epic proportions. The road was full of confused, jostling merchants, all desperate not to irritate their lordly customer by being late.

The crates of wine and enormous grocery hamper she'd ordered from Messrs. Fortnum and Mason were visible on the back of the nearest cart. The driver was trying to negotiate his way past a second cart, painted *J. Broadwood,* containing a beautiful new pianoforte. Sabine had no idea whether Hampden even played the pianoforte, but she'd noticed the ballroom was in dire need of an instrument when they'd been fencing the other day.

The nurserymen's cart was instantly recognizable by the

sixteen large orange trees protruding from the sides. Two men in aprons—possibly the butchers from whom she'd ordered a large haunch of venison—were trying to back up their agitated mare to allow other representatives carrying an assortment of boxes to reach the front door.

Sabine chuckled. No doubt those were the boots from Hoby and the new superfine jacket she'd ordered from Weston. Lord Lovell bought only from the best.

Two burly apprentices were struggling to unload a handsome longcase clock, hampered by several dogs that were darting in between the horses' legs and barking excitedly. They almost tripped a young man bearing a paper-wrapped package that Sabine deduced to be the small but exquisite Raphael drawing she'd seen in the window of a gallery on Bond Street on the way home from the museum. It would look lovely opposite the Rembrandt.

She felt a brief twinge of guilt for spending so much of Hampden's money, and brutally quashed it. He could afford it, and it served him right for trying to keep her under house arrest.

The front door knocker was banging incessantly. Sabine slipped downstairs and found a harassed Hodges directing the nurserymen toward the back garden. She pressed herself against the wall to make room for two more boys carrying cylindrical rolls of upholstery fabric—all in deliciously feminine shades of pale rose and lavender. Sabine snorted. Heaven knew what Hampden would do with those. She'd love to see him redecorate his lordly bedroom in pastel pink.

With the rest of the servants rushing to and fro dealing with the unending stream of purchases, it was easy to slip out of the door. Using the tangle of carts as cover, she weaved through the baying crowd and hailed a hansom cab at the corner of Park Lane. "The British Museum, please," she called gaily.

"Right-o, miss." The driver tilted his head toward the chaos behind her. "What the 'ell's 'appenin' there? Beggin' yer pardon," he added as an afterthought for his ungentlemanly language.

Sabine shrugged innocently. "I have absolutely no idea."

It took a mere ten minutes to get to the British Museum, and no time at all to retrieve her bag of "artist's materials." She'd told the driver to wait for her, and on the return journey he dropped her off at Hyde Park Corner. The church clock struck half past two just as she entered the park through the tall wrought-iron gates. Perfect timing.

Sabine inhaled deeply, glad to be outdoors. It was easier to think with the peaceful tones of green around her. She passed the spot that had once held the infamous gallows, now commemorated by a small round plaque, and shivered. Doubtless they'd hung counterfeiters on that murderous gibbet, as well as highwaymen and thieves.

At this hour there was hardly anyone around, just a few harried nurses chasing after their small charges, who in turn were chasing the hapless ducks. Anton was waiting for her along one of the tree-lined walks. His injuries looked even more alarming in daylight: a grotesque rainbow of shades ranging from jaundiced yellow to deep bruised plum. He looked thoroughly disreputable, an effect heightened by the hat he wore pulled down low over his forehead to try to disguise the worst of it.

"I've found a boat going to Boston," he said by way of greeting.

Sabine returned his friendly hug and tugged him off the path between a clump of trees.

"The Black Ball Line has a brig, the *Falcon,* under a Captain Lewis, leaving on the eighth of May from the Pool of London docks. It costs five pounds and takes about thirty days, depending on the weather."

Sabine frowned. "That's in twelve days' time. You need to be on it." She told him of Malet's unexpected visit and his ultimatum.

Anton pursed his lips. "The wily old bastard. I never thought he'd have the brains to follow us here."

Sabine rummaged in her bag for the box full of cash. "Here, take it."

"I don't need it all. You have to keep some for yourself." Anton carefully counted out half the money and returned it to her. He folded his five hundred pounds inside his waistcoat.

Sabine nodded. She'd been willing to let him have it all, but what he said made sense. She'd have nothing to fall back on until Richard paid her otherwise. She hated the fact that they were being forced to use the fake money, but there was little hope that Hampden would pay her an advance and Anton couldn't wait until her arrangement with him was done. Every moment he stayed in London increased the chances of discovery by Malet.

Sabine studied Anton's profile in the dappled sunlight. Even battered and bruised, he was handsome. He'd been her best friend for more than half her life. She blinked back the hot sting of tears. "I don't know what I'm going to do without you," she said bleakly.

He put his arm around her shoulders and she recalled the first time they'd met, at the Louvre. She'd been ten, Anton thirteen, and both of them had been left to draw the same classical statue while their fathers discussed a newly acquired painting in one of the back offices. Anton had wryly remarked that her drawing was better than his. Then he'd taught her how to wolf-whistle. It had been the start of a beautiful friendship.

Sabine swallowed the painful tightness in her throat. Anton had saved her from the butcher's boy, that night in the lane, and shielded her in so many other ways, too. They'd been together, watching each other's backs, for eight long years.

Anton let out a deep sigh. "You could always come with me, you know." He lowered his chin to see her expression. "Forge a new life in the Colonies? It's a land of opportunity for people like us. Think of it, Sabine. We could start again, be anyone we want to be."

Sabine shook her head sadly. "No. I still have things to do back in Paris. You know that. And besides," she said, "I gave my word to Hampden that I would work for him for a full month. I still have three weeks left."

Anton gave one of his patented shrugs, using both shoulders for full dramatic effect. "Bah. What can he do if you just disappear? He won't have any idea where you've gone. You need to get away from Malet, too. If I leave the country who will protect you from him, eh?"

Sabine put on a brave face. They'd discussed the future at great length on the way over from Paris. Dealing with Malet would be unpleasant, certainly, but she could manage it. If only she didn't feel as if everyone she cared for was abandoning her. It wasn't Anton's fault, of course, but she couldn't help the wave of despair that swept over her.

He deserved to find happiness. She'd always suspected that one of the reasons he'd never settled down in Paris was because he didn't want to leave her. He'd taken his responsibilities as her adopted brother seriously, and she'd had no desire to be a burden to him. He needed his freedom, and as much as it pained her to see him go, she had no desire to accompany him. In three weeks she'd be going back to Paris with her ten thousand pounds and keeping the promise she'd made to the memory of her father.

Anton shot her a deceptively innocent look. "Sure it's not because you want to stay with Hampden?"

Sabine whacked him on the arm with her bag. "Of course not! I'm only using him for the money."

Anton ruffled her hair. "I saw you with him in the garden, *chèrie*. That didn't look much like work." He shook his head, pretending to be scandalized. *"Oh la la!"*

Heat flashed across her face. "*Dieu!* You were spying on us? You . . . pervert!"

Anton chuckled. "Only for a moment. I wanted to make sure he wasn't going to hurt you. But he kissed you. Or rather, you kissed him." He let out a long, low whistle. "My God, Sabine, that man wants you! I could feel my hair curling from the heat!"

As embarrassed as she was that Anton had witnessed the kiss, Sabine was also strangely pleased that he'd confirmed Richard's desire for her. She hadn't been imagining it.

"You be careful with him, little one," Anton warned, his voice suddenly gruff. He chucked her under the chin. "Hampden is not a man used to hearing 'no.' If he wants something, he gets it. Just be sure you know what you're doing, all right? You're playing with fire and I don't want to see you get burned."

She didn't want to discuss Hampden with Anton. The clock struck a quarter to three. "I have to go. I've been away from the house for too long already." Her lips quirked. "I'm supposed to be preparing for tomorrow's outing." She briefly told him of the English plotters and the emperor's letter she'd written for Hampden.

Anton's brows drew together. "These are dangerous men you're dealing with, Sabine. Are you sure Hampden can protect you?"

Sabine remembered the way he'd fought in the ballroom. "Yes," she said. "He can. But it won't just be him. Several of his men will be there too. As soon as the plotters accept my offer, they'll arrest them."

"Be careful." Anton gave her another swift hug and kissed the top of her hair. "Is this goodbye?" he said softly.

Sabine pulled back. "No. I'll come to the docks to see your boat leave." She smiled grimly. "Even if I have to knock Hampden unconscious and tie him up, I'll be there." She punched Anton playfully on the arm. "Try not to get beaten and robbed again, if you please. That means keeping a low profile—no seducing ladies or rescuing damsels in distress. And only spend as much of that money as you need."

Anton nodded dutifully. "Yes, Maman," he teased.

They reached the eastern exit to the park. Anton gazed across the road at Upper Brook Street. "There was quite the commotion over there earlier. Your work?"

Sabine nodded proudly. "All mine. I knew practicing Hampden's signature would come in handy." She bit her lip. "He's going to be livid when he finds out what I've done—he'll guard me even more closely from now on. I'm not sure how I'll get out to meet you at the docks, but I'll think of something. A doctor's note, an urgent summons from his banker . . ."

"Good luck," Anton laughed, and disappeared into the trees.

With a sigh, Sabine started back toward the house. She was not looking forward to the inevitable confrontation with the irascible Lord Lovell.

CHAPTER 40

"There is a boy to see you, sir."

Richard glanced up from his newspaper with an irritated frown. He'd come to White's for an hour of uninterrupted reading—a feat impossible in his own house due to a certain irresistible Frenchwoman. Even when she wasn't physically haunting his library he felt her presence, somewhere in the house, calling to him, urging him to stop reading and start— doing other things.

"Afternoon, guv'nr."

Will Ambrose's cheeky face peeked around the doorman's portly bulk. Richard dismissed the man with a nod and Will took the empty seat opposite. He glanced around the opulent room with interest. "Didn't fink they'd let me in 'ere. But your name opens doors, it does."

"Don't even consider stealing anything." Richard gave a wry smile. "So what brings you here, scamp?"

"Nuffin' much," Will grinned. "Just thought you might be interested to know that that lady o' yours spent the afternoon in the park. Wiv a man," he added smugly.

Richard lowered his paper. "Which man?"

"Didn't recognize 'im." Will shrugged. "And they was too far away for me to 'ear anyfink, like."

"What did he look like?"

Will's nose wrinkled. "S'pose if I was a girl I'd think 'im 'andsome. Dark 'air, afletick figure, broad shoulders. Tall—not unlike yerself, guv'nr," he added cheekily. "'ard to see 'is face, on account of 'is 'at, but looked like the cove'd taken a right beating. Black an' blue, 'is neck was."

"And what did they do?" Richard asked grimly.

"She 'anded 'im summit out of 'er bag. Paper. Looked like money. They talked a while, then went their separate ways."

"Did they embrace?"

"Kiss, you mean?" Will shook his head. "Nah. Hugged a few times, but no kissin' like." He stood and tugged down the front of his scruffy waistcoat with an air of importance. "Anyway, fought you might like to know."

"Thank you, Will," Richard said grimly. He reached into his waistcoat and flipped the boy a shilling, which Will plucked from midair and pocketed in the blink of an eye. "You were right. The whereabouts of that woman is of very great interest to me indeed."

When Will left, Richard stared moodily into the fire, then glanced at the clock on the mantel. Was four in the afternoon too early to start drinking? Probably.

He ascribed the sudden roiling in his gut to hunger, not jealousy. What was she up to? Hadn't he told her to stay at home? Who had she been meeting?

He didn't trust her any farther than he could throw her.

That was just a phrase, of course, but his fiendish brain began to imagine it literally. To throw her he'd have to wrap his hands around her tiny waist, span his fingers under her ribs, and lift her. He wouldn't want to hurt her, which meant he'd have to throw her onto something soft, like a sofa. Or a bed.

Richard shook his head to dislodge the kaleidoscope of erotic images that naturally followed that imaginary event. He beckoned a footman. Four o'clock be damned; he needed a brandy. And then he was going home to find out exactly what game little Miss Counterfeit was playing.

* * *

FATE SMILED ON SABINE. Cook was so preoccupied dealing with the contents of the picnic hamper that she barely spared Sabine a glance when she slipped in through the kitchen door.

"It appears we have quite a bit of food," Sabine said innocently as she headed for the servants' staircase. "Would you send a tray up to my rooms, please? I think I'll eat up there this evening."

Cook beamed. "Of course, madam." She held aloft two muslin-wrapped packets. "You can 'ave some o' these lovely Scotch eggs and a nice bit of cheese. I'll send up a bottle o' this new claret, too." She indicated a newly opened wooden crate on the floor.

"That sounds lovely, thank you."

A piercing squawk from the hallway above them almost made Sabine drop her bag of drawing tools—until she recalled the parrot. She stifled a chuckle. Oh, yes. Hampden was going to love that purchase.

She found Hodges overseeing two footmen carrying a large, domed metal cage, the inhabitant of which was a handsome gray parrot with a coral-pink tail and white patches around each of its beady eyes. Argos skipped excitedly around them, offering assorted woofs and growls and generally getting in the way.

"Must've been in his cups," the first footman muttered.

Hodges shot the young man a disapproving frown. "I am certain his lordship was no such thing, Henry."

The bird let out an ear-splitting shriek, then, quite clearly, said, "Fall to, boys. Ready about! Hard alee!"

Hodges's eyebrows shot toward his hairline.

The parrot bit the wire bars, flapped its wings, and added in a jovial, booming voice, "Come on board, sir! Come on board."

One of the footmen laughed in amazement.

"Yer buffle-headed boat-licker!" squawked the bird.

Hodges gasped. The footmen chuckled in delight.

"That bird should go straight to his lordship's rooms," Sabine said decisively. "I distinctly recall Lord Lovell saying that he wanted it in his suite. As a companion."

She escaped up the stairs to conceal her giggles.

Once in her room, Sabine glanced around for somewhere to hide her money. After much consideration, she got on her knees in front of the fire grate and pushed it up the chimney shaft. It lodged an arm's length up, where the flue angled backward into a smallish sloped shelf.

There was a tense moment when Josie entered with the tea tray and noticed the mess of soot Sabine had dislodged on the carpet, but Sabine fobbed her off with a story about hearing birds in the chimney and begged her not to light any fires until it had been swept by a chimney sweep.

CHAPTER 41

*I*t was, of course, too much to hope that Hampden wouldn't have something to say about the afternoon's activities. Sabine had just finished her dinner and poured a second glass of the rather tasty Bordeaux, when the door to her room banged open.

She treated Hampden to a welcoming smile. "Good evening, my lord. Would you care for a glass of claret?"

He closed the door behind him with a controlled click and narrowed his eyes. "No, I would not like a glass of claret," he said. He held up a sheaf of what she supposed must be bills for the purchases she'd made. "What I would like is for you to explain why I am now the proud owner of two pairs of new riding boots, a dozen orange trees, and"— he consulted the invoices—"a rosewood pianoforte?" His voice was dangerously calm. "I don't play the pianoforte, Miss de la Tour."

"Your future wife might," Sabine said reasonably.

He ignored that little provocation and riffled through the assorted pages, reading aloud. "A folio of erotic drawings from Orme & Co., Old Bond Street?"

"Improvements to your library," Sabine said. "The top shelves looked a little empty."

A muscle ticked in his jaw. "A large order of loose leaf tea from Bennet & Tolson, tea merchants?"

"In case I need to age any more documents."

"One solid gold timepiece from Francis Perigal, watchmaker to His Majesty."

"Wouldn't want you to be late to all those routs and balls you so enjoy." She gave him an innocent smile. "The ladies would be devastated."

"A mahogany-cased set of dueling pistols from Charles Grierson." He glanced up, looking sorely tempted to use them on her. "I already own a perfectly good set of pistols by Manton."

Sabine shrugged. "I thought you might need a spare pair. But I'll have them, if you don't want them. They sound much better than my little pocket pistol." She shot him a bland look, but inside she was quaking with laughter.

A loud, reproachful squawk echoed from the adjoining rooms. Hampden closed his eyes as if in acute pain.

"And the parrot?" he inquired softly, but with distinct menace. "Would you care to explain the parrot? A bird that appears to have been brought back from the tropics in the company of a bunch of foul-mouthed sailors and whose vocabulary consists of little more than maritime instructions and curse words."

"Bugger me down dead!" squawked the parrot, right on cue.

Sabine bit her lip. "I thought you might find it entertaining."

"Turn out, ye cock-chafing bastards!" screeched the bird.

She offered a plate forward, struggling to keep a straight face. "Do try a Scotch egg."

A muscle ticked in the side of Hampden's jaw. He looked like a man pushed past the limits of his endurance. It was a marvelous sight. Sabine could only pray he would crack. She very much wanted to see him lose his fabled cool. Sadly, however, he took a deep breath and appeared to regain control.

"You forged my signature," he said evenly. "You bought these things pretending to be me. Why?"

What could she say? *So I could escape and meet my friend? So I could retrieve some of that counterfeit fortune you so want to get your hands on?* Hardly. She gave a careless shrug. "I was bored. Women shop when they're bored."

His amber eyes bored into hers and her heart beat wildly against her ribs. Oh, she was enjoying teasing this wolf immensely. She was half frightened, half exhilarated. Any second now he would pounce. She took a fortifying sip of wine. "I was merely helping your deceit of the ton."

One dark eyebrow rose. "How so?"

"These are the purchases of a man setting up home. Extra cutlery, glasses, upholstery fabric. All evidence of an imminent intent to start entertaining. It adds credence to your story that you're courting me with a view to matrimony."

He didn't blink. "The furnishing of this house is to be left to my actual wife, Miss de la Tour. It is not your prerogative. Is that clear?"

Sabine suppressed a scowl. *Condescending idiot.* Someone like her would never occupy that lofty position, evidently.

"Very clear, your lordship." She gave a helpless little shrug. "It's just that I hate sitting around all day. You could at least have given me something to forge while you were out. You're paying me ten thousand pounds, and all I've done so far is write one letter from Napoleon and convinced that fat slug Skelton I'm Lacorte. You're not precisely getting your money's worth out of me."

His eyes narrowed in a way that made her insides heat. "Oh, I fully intend to get my money's worth, Miss de la Tour."

He crossed the floor and she tensed in anticipation, but he merely sank into the seat opposite her with a sigh. She caught the faintest tang of brandy and wood smoke.

"We need to discuss the plan for meeting with the conspirators tomorrow."

"Now?"

He glanced pointedly over at the bed, then back at her. The corners of his mouth twitched. "Is there something you'd rather do instead?"

His gaze lingered on her mouth and she tried to banish all the wicked suggestions swirling around her brain. She swallowed and shook her head. "No. Of course not. Go ahead."

He nodded and used her wineglass to pour himself a generous helping of claret. "According to my sources, two other men should be at the meeting tomorrow with Skelton."

He took a sip of wine and grunted appreciatively. It was a good thing he liked it; it was an exorbitantly expensive Château Palmer, and as of this afternoon he was the proud owner of three crates of the stuff.

"They're both English. The first is George Levy. He's ex-navy, with a fondness for ale. Been shooting his mouth off in taverns for months, criticizing the way our veterans have been treated after the war. He blames our 'profligate prince' for wasting money on lavish ceremonies while injured soldiers are left to starve on the streets."

Sabine raised her brows. "You can hardly fault him for that."

Hampden nodded. "No, I can't. But his suggestion—assassinating the prince and doing away with the royal family altogether—is not the way to effect change." He frowned. "The second man is John Maynard. He owns a betting shop in Spitalfields and organizes horse races all around the country. He distributes the proceeds of stolen goods sold through Skelton's shop. His brother was killed at Waterloo, and he's been organizing protests out in the provinces, trying to stir up civil unrest. He's as keen to see the government topple as Levy. That's why I'm sure he'll agree to the suggestion of using your counterfeits."

Hampden took another sip of wine. "Speaking of which, are

you sure there's no way you can get even a small amount of your fake currency? You promised Skelton you'd take a sample of it to show him."

Sabine didn't even glance toward the fireplace. "I told you, I don't have access to it." Her heart thudded guiltily at the lie, and she was sure her cheeks were turning pink, but Hampden seemed to accept her word.

"Pity. Oh well, we'll just have to take some real money and hope they don't notice the difference. I should be able to rustle up five hundred pounds or so. Provided you've left me some funds in my account after your zealous shopping spree," he added pointedly.

Sabine ignored the jibe and grinned. "It will be an interesting change, passing real money off as fake."

Hampden finished his wine and stood. "My men will be stationed in the inn and across the street. As soon as the plotters incriminate themselves by agreeing to buy your counterfeits, I'll give the signal and they will storm in and arrest all three of them."

Sabine nodded. "All right."

He looked down at her for a long moment, his face unreadable.

"Show a leg, ye cadger!" the parrot screeched.

Hampden shot her an exasperated look. "If you'll excuse me, I must have that thing strangled." He offered her a formal bow. "Good night."

* * *

THE FOLLOWING MORNING, Richard dispatched Sabine next door to visit his mother and slipped into her bedroom.

According to Will Ambrose, she'd exchanged something with her mysterious male friend in the park yesterday and he was determined to discover what it was. She wouldn't have chosen anywhere obvious to hide it; she was too sneaky for that. Even so, he searched her paint box, her drawers, under the mattress, and behind the small portraits of her parents on the mantelpiece.

Nothing.

He stood in the center of the room, hands on hips, lips pursed. Her maid had reported sweeping up a sooty mess in front of the fireplace. She said Sabine had given explicit orders not to light a fire because she suspected there might be a bird's nest up there.

Richard snorted. *Bird's nest, my arse.* There was something up that chimney, but he'd bet his boots it wasn't avian. He knelt in front of the grate and peered up the flue; it was pitch black, but he took off his jacket, rolled up his sleeves, and stuck his arm up the chimney. His fingers touched a large leather package and he chuckled in delight.

Nice try, little Miss Counterfeit.

With some judicious wiggling the package came free. It fell and hit him on the head, but his irritation vanished when he opened the leather bag and discovered the small wooden cigar box inside. A smile split his face.

He had her.

CHAPTER 42

*A*fter an enjoyable afternoon spent with Therese and Heloise, Sabine bathed and dressed in the same unremarkable outfit in which she'd met Skelton. It was almost dusk when she descended the stairs.

Richard had reprised the role of her dumb brute cousin Jacob, and embellished his outfit with a greatcoat, the caped shoulders of which added even more bulk to his already intimidating size.

He turned to her with a conspiratorial grin. "Ready?"

"I suppose so."

For one instant they shared a look of perfect complicity; they were in this together, accomplices in deception. Sabine's insides warmed. It felt good. She might not have much in common with Richard, Lord Lovell, but this man, this roguish vagabond, oh, she knew him. A man like him would be easy to fall in love with.

She shook her head. No. Nobody was falling in love with anybody. It was just the thrill of the chase that had her emotions on edge.

She brushed past him and stepped up into the nondescript carriage waiting outside. Hampden joined her, placing a leather satchel on the seat beside him and patting it indulgently. "Five hundred pounds of fake money."

Sabine wished she had the ability to conjure up that kind of cash with only a few hours' notice.

He shot her an intense, faintly questioning glance. "Nervous?"

She shrugged. "A little. I would be a fool not to be wary of these men." She gazed out of the window, mainly to avoid looking at his chest in that thin, almost transparent shirt. "I wish there were some way to counterfeit courage, but people either seem to have it or they don't."

She jumped as he leaned over and gave her arm a light, reassuring squeeze.

"You have it," he said softly.

It was a relatively short ride to the Haymarket. Sabine's eyes widened as they traveled along the broad street and she saw the crowds milling around outside the various theaters, coffeehouses, taverns, and hotels.

Posters advertised the skeleton of O'Brien, the Irish Giant, plus assorted waxwork figures and Weeks's Museum, containing "figures exhibiting the astonishing power of mechanism."

They passed the Haymarket Theater, with its pillared portico extending from the front of the building, lit with lanterns. It seemed to be offering *The Tragedy of Coriolanus,* with the celebrated Mr. Kemble as the title character.

Hampden knocked on the carriage roof and when the vehicle stopped, he helped her down onto the crowded pavement. He glanced around, presumably to locate the men he'd ordered to be on hand when his signal came. Sabine craned her neck, but the crowd made it impossible to see with whom he was communicating. It was a tumult of noise and accents, and all she could see was a scruffy-looking gingerbread vendor and a trio of overdressed tarts hanging around on the corner.

Hampden handed her the satchel full of money, caught her

free hand in his, and steered her toward a building whose swinging sign proclaimed it the White Lion coffeehouse.

The interior was extremely crowded. Sabine wrinkled her nose at the strong blast of warm bodies and weak ale that assaulted her nostrils. Sawdust had been strewn onto the floor to absorb spilled beer—and probably blood and spit, too—but her shoes still stuck to the sticky boards. A pall of tobacco smoke hung like a gray fog between the exposed wooden beams, and the air was filled with the clatter of dice shaken in tin cups and raucous, drunken laughter.

It was a predominantly male domain. Only a couple of other women were visible: a slatternly-looking barmaid with lank hair serving the customers and a red-haired doxy perched on a man's lap, her breasts spilling out of her low top. Sabine pressed closer to Hampden's back.

"Over here."

Skelton loomed into view and Sabine sucked in a breath. His collar was damp with sweat, and beads of perspiration glistened on his forehead and nose. He barged past Hampden and grabbed her arm.

"Come on," he said, tugging her forward. "We've a room upstairs."

Hampden stepped between them, breaking Skelton's grip, and the man stepped back with a grunt of apology.

"Thank you, Jacob," Sabine said sweetly. She turned to Skelton. "He doesn't like to see me manhandled. Lead the way, Mr. Skelton."

Skelton pushed his way through the crowd and up a rickety flight of stairs at the back of the taproom. The wood creaked with his every step. At the top, he opened a door off the landing and ushered them both inside.

Two men sat at a rough oak gateleg table. Neither rose as Sabine entered the room, but both regarded her with an air of wary suspicion. She gave them her warmest smile.

"This is 'er," Skelton said, by way of introduction. "The forger."

He nodded dismissively at Richard. "Yer man can wait over there."

Sabine nodded and made a shooing motion with her hands toward the window. Hampden took his cue. He crossed the room and stationed himself in the bay, blending unobtrusively into the shadows.

"Yes, please ignore my bodyguard," she said mildly. "I keep him around because I hear there are dishonest men around these parts."

Skelton snorted in cynical amusement and introduced his two companions, George Levy and John Maynard. Hampden had been correct. The men nodded, their expressions closed.

"Levy was in the navy, till 'e was invalided out," Skelton said. "Maynard's a tout."

Sabine nodded. "A pleasure, gentlemen." She pulled herself a seat at the table and sat. Skelton lowered himself onto the fourth chair beside her; the wood groaned in protest.

"Let's get down to business, shall we? I'm sure Mr. Skelton has mentioned my proposition, so I won't beat around the bush. I hear that you have as much desire as myself to see England's currency weakened and her government and monarchy embarrassed."

Levy raised his brows, Maynard merely grunted, but neither of them outright denied it, which Sabine took as a good sign. She sat back and addressed Maynard. "Your horse races are the perfect place to distribute my fake fortune."

"Aye," he said slowly. "But first I want to see it. Skelton says you're good, but I want to see for meself."

"Of course," Sabine said brightly. She opened the satchel on her lap. "I promised to bring a small amount to show you, did I not?" She slapped a fat wad of money on the table. "If you gentlemen would care to inspect it, you'll see it passes every test with flying colors."

Of course it will, she thought wryly. *It's real money.*

Skelton pulled out his jeweler's loupe and handed it to Maynard, who bent over to study one of the notes.

"Good, ain't it?" Skelton said. "The only way you can tell them's fake is because o' the initials *P.L.* hidden in the corner. Look closely. In the roots."

Sabine bit her lip in horror. She'd forgotten she'd told Skelton about that particular detail.

"I can't see nuffink," Maynard grumbled.

Sabine shot Richard a quick, panicked glance over Maynard's bent head. How on earth was she going to explain the absence of her trademark?

And then, to her utter astonishment, Hampden sent her a cheeky wink and a smile.

Sabine blinked. Their deception was about to be exposed as a scam and here he was, winking at her? The man was mad.

"Ah, I see 'em now," Maynard said triumphantly.

Sabine stilled. Surely he was simply pretending to see the initials to save face? There were no initials on real banknotes.

Suddenly suspicious, she tugged on the chain around her neck, withdrew her own looking glass, and bent over the nearest note. She stiffened. There, hidden in the tree roots, were the initials *P.L.*

Fury and disbelief coursed through her veins. This wasn't real money. It was *her* money! That sneaky, treacherous, deceitful swine must have searched her bedroom and found her stash!

Sabine took a deep breath and cursed herself for being so stupid as to trust that cheating, lying son of a . . . She could not let her anger show. She smoothed her features into a bland smile and straightened. But her eyes flicked to Hampden with a look that promised retribution. Extremely painful retribution.

He sent her a taunting smile that made her blood boil. She

was going to strangle the deceitful wretch—just as soon as they got out of here. First, she had to concentrate.

Maynard finished his perusal of the note and handed the glass to Levy. "Looks good, I'll give you that." He sat back in his chair, hooked his thumbs into the waistband of his breeches, and surveyed her with a belligerent air. "So the real question is, how much is this fortune going to cost us?"

Triumph surged through her. They'd gone for it!

"Well, the going rate for fake currency in Paris is around one-third of face value," she said confidently. "So I should really be asking you for a hundred and sixty thousand pounds in exchange for half a million in fakes."

Skelton made an inarticulate spluttering sound. Maynard's brows drew together and Levy opened his mouth to argue, but Sabine held up a hand and gave them her sweetest smile. "But of course I wouldn't dream of extorting you gentlemen in such a manner. Not when your cause is so worthy."

Maynard's brow unknotted a little.

"All I ask is a small token of appreciation, for my time and undeniable craftsmanship."

"How much?" Skelton growled. "Name your price, girl."

Sabine tilted her head. "Let's say twenty thousand pounds, shall we? Does that sound fair? You get the means to protest against your government most effectively, and I get the satisfaction of seeing Napoleon's plan put into effect, plus a little compensation for my efforts. Do we have a deal?"

Maynard glanced at Skelton, then tilted his head at Levy. "Let us discuss it, for a moment." All three rose from the table and went to confer in the corner of the room.

While they engaged in a low-voiced discussion, Sabine stood and sidled over to Richard. "I am going to kill you, Richard Hampden," she hissed. "How did you find my money?"

His beatific smile was beyond irritating. "I searched your room, of course."

"That money is not yours!"

"It's not yours, either," he whispered.

"I need it."

"No, you don't."

The plotters returned to the table then, so Sabine turned her back on Richard and joined them.

Maynard stuck out his hand. "We agree to your terms. How do you want to be paid?"

Sabine's heart leaped, but she gave a wry smile. "Not in banknotes, I assure you. They're far too easy to counterfeit." She smiled at her own joke. "I'd like jewels. And be warned—I can spot a fake diamond as easily as I can spot a fake note. Your associate knows that to be true, don't you, Mr. Skelton?"

Skelton grunted. "Yes."

Sabine took Maynard's outstretched hand. "In that case, we have a deal. When and where shall we make the exchange?"

Sabine couldn't see Hampden from her position, but he had surely signaled his men to move in and make the arrests. She heard the door behind her open and tensed, expecting three or four armed men to burst in, weapons drawn, but instead a man she didn't recognize entered the room. When Maynard greeted the newcomer with a nod of welcome, Sabine grew even more confused.

"Perfect timing, Toulin," Maynard said easily. He turned back to her. "Allow me to introduce the last member of our merry band—a fellow Frenchman, in fact."

Sabine's stomach plummeted. The man did not appear English. His skin was olive, almost sallow, and he had a narrow, clever face, with thin lips beneath a pencil-thin mustache.

"This is Pierre Toulin. Mr. Toulin has had some experience disrupting things in your home country over the past few years, haven't you, Toulin?"

A chord of recognition tugged at Sabine's memory. The name

Toulin sounded familiar, but she was sure she'd never met the man before.

The newcomer shrugged modestly. "A few protests and organized riots, that's all . . ."

His dark gaze rested on Sabine's face and she quelled an immediate feeling of discomfort. His eyes roamed over her, almost as if he were cataloguing every part of her for future dissection. He made a small bow and caught her hand in his. "I am delighted to meet the infamous Philippe Lacorte. You are a credit to our country, madame."

His smile was disconcerting. It stretched his lips but didn't reach his eyes. There was something almost reptilian about him; maybe it was the way he didn't seem to blink. He retained Sabine's fingers for a fraction longer than was necessary and she stepped back, uneasy. Her palm was sweaty but her fingers were cold.

"In fact," Toulin said silkily, "I have Monsieur Lacorte to thank for my presence here tonight. You provided my travel documents, madame."

Ah. Now she remembered. She'd made false papers for a Pierre Toulin a few years ago. Her stomach gave a guilty lurch. She'd been responsible for allowing this criminal into the country. Still, he'd be imprisoned very soon.

She wanted to leave. The thick, smoky atmosphere was making her feel ill. From the corner of her eye she could see that Richard had withdrawn into the shadows by the window and tilted his head down so his hat almost covered his face.

Sabine took a calming breath. He must have given his men the signal through the window by now. They would be here any minute. She cleared her throat and started to gather the notes from the table. Toulin watched her movements with interest.

"Where would you like to make the exchange, Mr. Maynard?" she repeated.

Why weren't Hampden's men storming in and arresting

everyone? She glanced over and saw him give an almost imperceptible shake of his head. What did that mean?

"Here will do," Maynard said. "Friday next, same time."

Sabine nodded. "Excellent. I will bid you gentlemen good night." She closed the leather satchel and made for the door. "Come along, Jacob."

Toulin narrowed his eyes as Richard stirred from the corner, and Sabine noticed that Richard kept his head averted as he ushered her from the room. As soon as they were back in the corridor, he took her arm and guided her down the stairs and through the crowded taproom. He pushed through the sweaty bodies, pulling her along in his wake.

"What's the hurry?" Sabine panted.

He shook his head and tugged her out into the street. "I can't explain now. You have to go. Immediately." He gave a shrill whistle to summon a hackney cab and practically thrust her inside it.

"What?" she demanded in confusion as he slammed the door behind her. "Aren't you coming too?"

Hampden's face was grim. "Go home. I'll see you later."

He shouted the address up to the cabbie. Before Sabine could even protest at his high-handed behavior, the carriage moved off.

What on earth was going on? Hampden might not have expected that extra man Toulin, but that didn't explain why he'd aborted the mission. The plotters had agreed to treason. Had he wanted to get her safely out of the way before his men stormed the place?

Sabine's sense of gratitude quickly turned to anger as she realized he'd kept the satchel full of money.

It was her money, the thieving pig!

CHAPTER 43

*S*abine waited for Richard in the study, but two hours passed without a sign. Her righteous fury increased by the minute as she imagined giving him a blistering lecture on stealing other people's property. It was, admittedly, a bit like the pot calling the kettle black, as her mother would have said, but it was the principle of the thing. She didn't steal. She counterfeited. It was an important distinction.

Declining Hodges's offer of a cup of tea, she set about searching Hampden's desk. She'd half a mind to simply forge herself a promissory note to cash in at his bank, but her nerves were so agitated she doubted she could draw a straight line, let alone forge his signature.

She kicked the side of the desk in fury and stubbed her toe, which made her even crosser.

She'd done exactly what he'd employed her to do: forced the English plotters to incriminate themselves. It wasn't her fault he'd failed to seize the moment. And nothing excused him retaining possession of her forgeries. He owed her. Not just the ten thousand pounds he'd promised her, but the return of her fakes as well.

His desk yielded a collection of bills, including those for her purchases the previous day. Sabine rifled through them. He paid how much for his cravats? Good Lord. She could eat for a week on that in Paris.

At the back of the drawer she discovered a leather-bound book, apparently some kind of payments ledger. Lines of his haphazard writing filled the pre-lined vertical columns.

Sabine began to read. He really did deal with some astronomical sums. She'd assumed he must have a man of business to do all this for him, but apparently Hampden preferred to keep a hand on the financial reins himself. Probably didn't trust anyone else.

He received rents and incomes from numerous properties—from tenants, livestock, investments, and bonds. He had shares in some unpronounceable Welsh railway, and part-ownership of a tin mine in Cornwall.

Sabine found an entry dated two weeks ago for Rundell, Bridge & Rundell, jewelers, and scowled. They'd made the sapphire and diamond necklace she'd worn to Lady Carstairs's ball, but this entry was for "a fine diamond and pearl bracelet." Presumably a parting gift for his previous mistress. The startling amount made her grind her teeth. He certainly was generous.

She flicked back a few pages, looking for further evidence of his spending on females. If Heloise was right about his "mistress rules," there should be a similar payment approximately every three months. Sabine told herself the angry feeling in her breast wasn't jealousy. Of course it wasn't.

A French name caught her eye; there was a payment of one hundred pounds to a Madame Pensol, Paris. No further explanation appeared in the adjoining column. She flicked back a few pages and frowned. There it was again—same name, same amount. More pages, and her suspicion and sense of nausea grew. The book went back only eighteen months, but the payments had been going on regularly, once a month, for all that time.

Sabine sat back in the chair, her mind working furiously. Why was Richard paying this woman? Was she a former mistress? A feeling of disappointment crashed over her as the obvious answer presented itself. Hampden must have an illegitimate child. Why else would he pay this woman a monthly stipend?

Sabine felt a tight ball form in her chest. For all his talk of trust and honesty, she wasn't the only one keeping secrets. A whole range of emotions churned through her. She felt betrayed, somehow. He'd manipulated her, taken her money, shattered her trust—and played merry havoc with her heart.

At that moment the front door opened and she heard the low rumble of his voice as he conferred with Hodges. The click of his boots approached the study and Sabine braced herself for confrontation.

"Making yourself at home, I see," he said.

His hair was disheveled and he looked weary, but she hardened her heart. She wouldn't feel sorry for the rotten, sneaky thief. She shrugged, unrepentant. "You went through my things. I don't see why I shouldn't do the same."

He stalked forward, unhurried, and her heart rate increased. "Find anything interesting?"

His mild tone was annoying. Why did he always have to be so composed?

"As a matter of fact I did. Why do you pay some woman in Paris every month? Is she your mistress on a retainer? Or are you supporting a bastard, Lord Lovell?"

She'd thought he would get angry, but he merely looked resigned. "I assume you're referring to Madame Pensol?"

His calmness made her want to shoot him. In the privates.

"You have been busy. If you must know, I've been sending her money for the past eight years."

Sabine blinked. He had an eight-year-old child? Was it a boy or a girl? And why had he left the poor thing in Paris?

He crossed the room and sank into one of the green leather

armchairs. "Eight years ago I was in Paris, on the trail of an Italian assassin named Carlo Visconti. Castlereagh had received intelligence that he was planning an attempt on Napoleon's life."

Sabine frowned. "I'd have thought the British would have supported such a scheme."

"Not at that particular moment. Napoleon was more useful to us alive than dead right then." He sighed. "You want to know who Madame Pensol is?"

Sabine nodded.

"She's the mother of a girl killed by Visconti when he blew up a cart, trying to kill the emperor. Her name was Marie-Jeanne Pensol, and she was fourteen years old."

Hampden's face was pale, etched with lines of pain. "Her mother sold bread rolls and vegetables from a stall on the Rue du Bac." His haunted eyes caught hers. "She died in my arms."

Sabine felt her own face leach of blood. "Tell me what happened."

Hampden rested his forearms on his thighs. "We knew something was being planned, but we didn't have enough information to stop it. It was a royalist plot, orchestrated by Visconti and four others. They loaded a barrel full of explosives with shards of metal onto a cart and attached a long fuse. It was designed to disperse shrapnel on detonation to inflict maximum injury. They chose a spot in the Rue Saint-Nicaise, north of the Tuileries Palace, toward the Rue du Faubourg Saint-Honoré."

Sabine nodded. She knew the spot. It wasn't far from the Louvre.

"Napoleon planned to visit the opera that evening, so they knew the route he would take. The passing of his advance cavalry guard was the cue for the bomb to be set off. But one tiny event foiled the whole thing. Josephine was wearing an Egyptian-style cloak, and one of her aides pointed out that she was wearing it incorrectly, so she had to re-pin it. Napoleon became impatient and went without her, in the first carriage. He left in such a hurry that the guards were riding behind him instead of in front.

"The bomb exploded when the second carriage was passing by, carrying Josephine and Napoleon's sister, Caroline, but apart from a few cuts from flying glass and wooden splinters the ladies were unhurt."

He lowered his head. "Those outside weren't so lucky. We arrived just after the bomb detonated. At least fifty people were wounded. I tried to save the girl, but she was beyond help. There was nothing I could do."

He squeezed his eyes closed, doubtless reliving the carnage, then raised his head and pierced Sabine with a despairing glare. "Visconti had paid her ten sous to hold the horse that pulled the cart." His voice cracked. "A man like that deserves no mercy."

Nausea rose in her throat. Sabine wanted to get up and put her arms around him, but she had no doubt he would spurn the offer of comfort. He still seemed lost in the past.

"The girl's mother received no compensation from the government. All she had was a meager widow's pension—her husband had been killed fighting for Napoleon in Russia. She couldn't even afford to bury her only daughter. So I paid for a headstone in Sacré-Coeur. I thought about paying someone to lay fresh flowers on her grave each week, but cut flowers never last. I dislike them as much as you do."

The faint up-curl of his lips as he attempted levity made hot tears burn behind her eyes. Sabine blinked rapidly, wincing as she recalled making the same complaint about the flowers her admirers had sent. It was so frivolous compared to this.

Richard took a deep breath. "I have someone tend her grave and commissioned a garden around it in memory of her." He ran his fingers through his hair and rolled his shoulders. "I pay Madame Pensol a modest sum every month. I can afford to do it, and it seemed the right thing to do."

Sabine's throat ached. She felt awful for doubting him, for

jumping to the wrong conclusion. He was a good, decent man. A few hundred years ago he would have been one of those courtly knights who entered the lists and fought for the honor of their lady with jousting or swords.

Hampden's next words made her swallow, though. His expression hardened. "I vowed that I would make Visconti pay for what he'd done. What kind of heartless bastard pays a child to stand next to a bomb? It's one thing to kill an enlisted soldier in the heat of battle, but to kill a defenseless child is the meanest sort of cowardice."

He glared at her across the room. "There were five men in the group. I tracked them down. I caught them. And I sent them to the gallows. Only Visconti escaped."

Sabine hardly dared breathe. His expression was bleak, unreadable. "Eight years, I've been tracking him." He rubbed a hand through his hair, disordering it further. "The man who came to the meeting tonight? Toulin? That was Visconti."

Sabine felt all the blood drain from her face.

"That's why I had to get you out of there. He's a dangerous man, Sabine. A murderer. A month before the attempt on Napoleon's life, he was involved in the assassination of the bishop of Quimper. The month before that, he'd kidnapped the French senator Clement de Ris in Touraine. After Paris he worked all over Europe. He doesn't care who he kills. He'll work for whoever will pay him."

"Do you think that's why he was there tonight?" Sabine whispered. "Do you think the plotters are paying him to kill someone?"

"That would be my guess." Richard shrugged. "And they're using your money to do it."

Her guilt at creating the man's passport doubled. "He used travel papers I made to get here," she said quietly.

Hampden nodded. "And you also provided the passport he

used four years ago. Does the name Joseph Berthier ring any bells?"

Sabine nodded miserably.

Richard's voice was harsh. "Do you know what he did while he was here?" He didn't wait for her to answer. "He murdered the Comte d'Antraigues, right here in London."

He was forcing her to take responsibility for her criminal actions, but how could she have foreseen such awful consequences? She'd asked as few questions as possible about those who'd requested her fake papers, always salved her conscience by telling herself she was helping people. Innocent people.

Sabine closed her eyes. Was she any better than Visconti? She'd worked for whoever could pay her, too. They'd both sold their dubious skills, like mercenaries. Misery and guilt tightened her chest.

He glared at her. "You helped Visconti come to this country, Sabine. Which means you have a responsibility to help me now. You can bloody well help me track him down."

She nodded, numbly.

"If we don't stop whatever assassination he has planned, Britain will be plunged into chaos, maybe even civil war, a revolution just like in France. There's already plenty of antiroyalist sentiment. I don't give a stuff about the politics, but I do care about all the innocent people who will be caught up in the subsequent violence."

Back in her room, Sabine threw herself down on the bed in frustration. She wanted her old life back. This complicated mess of emotions Richard Hampden stirred in her was exhausting.

How dare he be good and bad in equal measure? She admired his steadfast determination to right wrongs, the way he championed and avenged innocents, but in confiscating her money he'd made her life a whole lot more difficult. She didn't want to have sympathy for him. He was a stealing brute. And he'd left her with nothing but anger and guilt.

CHAPTER 44

*R*ichard pinched his nose and leaned back in his chair. He'd never told anyone what had happened all those years ago in Paris except Raven, Nic, Kit, and Castlereagh.

Hodges knocked discreetly on the door.

"What is it?" Richard asked wearily.

"Lord Ravenwood to see you, sir."

Raven sauntered in without waiting for an invitation. His expression was grim. "They found Anderson."

"Alive?"

Raven nodded, and Richard let out a relieved breath.

"Only just, though," Raven qualified. "Visconti realized he was being followed and ambushed him in a side alley. Stabbed him in the side. Barely missed his kidneys, but he'll live."

Richard cursed. "I told him to stay back. Christ."

When Richard had aborted the mission earlier, he'd ordered each of his men to follow one of the plotters. He and Anderson had followed Visconti, but they'd become separated in the warren of side streets and back alleys. Richard had eventually given up and gone to report to Castlereagh. He'd hoped Anderson had done the same.

"Anderson revealed your name," Raven said carefully.

Richard swore long and fluently. Raven, no stranger to profanity, raised his eyebrows, impressed.

"Visconti could be anywhere. He could be outside this very house right now," Richard said.

He wasn't so concerned about his own welfare, but he felt guilty for putting Sabine into the path of that madman. The thought of Visconti getting anywhere near her was enough to make him break into a cold sweat. It wasn't that he thought her incompetent, far from it, but she was no match for a killer.

Raven took the seat opposite him. "What's his plan do you think? Kill the king? The Prince Regent? The prime minister? It's only been four years since Spencer Perceval was murdered."

That was true. The prime minister had been shot dead in the House of Commons by a deranged man named John Bellingham, a veteran who believed he'd been unjustly imprisoned in Russia during the war and was entitled to compensation.

"The newspapers print when the royal family are expected to attend the opera, the theater, and the like. It would be easy to target them, as he did Napoleon," Richard said.

"Think he'll try another infernal machine, like in Paris?"

"He likes dramatic gestures, but he doesn't have a team to help him this time. It's too much for one man to organize."

"What then? A simple assassination?"

"That's all it would take. The country's so unstable." Richard steepled his fingers. "The royal wedding's less than a week away. That would provide excellent cover. Lots of crowds to hide in."

Raven nodded. "The ceremony's set for nine o'clock at Carlton House, with fireworks afterward in both St. James's Park and Green Park. The royal party will come out onto the front terrace of Carlton House to watch fireworks . . . "

Richard grimaced. "Perfect for a sniper. Lots of loud flashes and bangs to hide the noise of a gunshot."

"Plus everyone will be looking up at the sky."

"Who will be attending the wedding?"

"Pretty much everyone you'd want to assassinate if you were Visconti. The queen. The royal princesses, the Prince Regent, the bride and groom, most of the House of Lords. The archbishop of Canterbury is going to officiate."

Richard nodded grimly. "We'll tell Castlereagh to tighten security. And pray we catch Visconti in the next five days."

CHAPTER 45

Sabine was still angry the following morning. She listened until she heard Richard leave the house, then slinked downstairs and encountered a beaming Hodges in the hall.

"Another bouquet arrived for you this morning, madame. I put it in the drawing room."

Sabine sighed. More cut flowers. This particular bunch was already on the turn. The heads of the blooms were drooping and overblown, past their best. The hint of brown decay at the edge of petals made her feel slightly queasy.

It was probably from Malet, an unsubtle threat to remind her of his ultimatum. She unfolded the accompanying note and her blood ran cold.

M. Toulin requests a private audience with Philippe Lacorte at the White Swan, Vere Street, at ten o'clock this evening. Come alone and do not inform your friend Lovell. I would not wish anything untoward to befall him or his charming family. It was signed *Toulin.*

Sabine crumpled the paper in her hand. *Merde!* The irony that Visconti was blackmailing her, just as she'd blackmailed Richard, was not lost on her. But she'd never had any intention of making good on her threats, whereas she had no doubt at all that Visconti would truly harm someone if she failed to comply.

It served her right, she thought miserably.

She ought to tell Richard immediately. To face a man as dangerous as Visconti alone was beyond foolish. But if anything happened to Richard or his family because of her she would never forgive herself. Far better to put herself at risk than endanger them.

Visconti obviously knew her location—witness the flowers and the note. For all she knew, he could have a team of men watching the house. She glanced out of the window, looking for suspicious characters lurking around Upper Brook Street, but could see nobody unusual. She couldn't even contact Anton; she'd forgotten to ask him where his new lodgings were.

No. She would have to go alone and see what Visconti wanted. She'd dealt with unsavory characters in Paris. She would be fine.

The rest of the day passed in awful anticipation, dread curling in her stomach. It was almost a relief when Hodges brought her a pot of tea and cakes mid-afternoon and informed her that Richard sent his apologies but he would not be home for dinner.

He was doubtless out with Raven and the other agents trying to catch Visconti.

She prepared her pocket pistol with grim determination. Powder first, then the metal ball, then a patch of lubricated wadding. She rammed it down the barrel with the end of a paintbrush, then opened the pan protector, sprinkled a tiny bit of powder into the pan, and closed the lid. It was ready to cock and fire.

She still had the outfit she'd worn for fencing. At half past nine she slipped out of her room—and almost tripped over Argos, who'd stationed himself on the floor outside her door.

"*Dieu!* Argos!" she hissed. "Go! *Allez!*"

The hound regarded her expectantly. His tail thumped on the

carpet. Sabine sighed. "Guarding me, are you? Oh, come along then. Walk!"

The dog leaped up with a delighted yelp. "Hush, you awful creature!" she scolded. The two of them padded down the staircase and she winced at the loud click of the dog's claws on the tiles. Thankfully the hall was empty—sounds of the servants' dinner drifted from below stairs.

Sabine slipped out of the front door. From the map she'd consulted that afternoon, it was only a short walk from Brook Street to Vere Street, just off Oxford Street. Ten minutes at most. She set off, Argos trotting obediently at her heels, his tongue lolling. Despite the gaslights that illuminated the street she was glad of the dog. He was both protection and disguise. She was simply a street urchin out walking his pet.

She'd just turned into Vere Street and glimpsed the sign for the White Swan up ahead when a large body bumped her from behind. Sabine stumbled with a curse just as her assailant shoved her sideways, into the mouth of a dark alleyway.

For one awful moment she imagined she was back in Paris with Guillaume, the butcher's boy, and a wave of furious disbelief rolled over her. The man shoved her against the brick wall and she raised her pistol to fire, but he grabbed her wrist and pushed her arm above her head.

"What in God's name are you up to, you foolish woman?" Hampden growled in her ear.

Sabine sagged back in relief, even though she could feel the anger vibrating off him. "You madman!" she hissed. "I nearly shot you."

A muscle ticked in his jaw as he ground his teeth. "Sabine, I warn you, I am tired, cold, and brutally sober. Now tell me what the hell you're up to. Who are you meeting? An accomplice? A lover?"

She glared at him. "No! If you must know, I'm meeting Visconti."

That stopped him dead in his tracks. "What?" His eyes narrowed in a combination of sudden fury and suspicion. "Do you know him? Are you working with him?"

His lack of trust stung, but she supposed she deserved it if he believed she was underhand enough to double-cross him. "Of course not, you imbecile! I'd never seen the man before last night. But he sent me a note, telling me to meet him here, alone, or he'd hurt you and your family."

There was a tense pause as he weighed what she's said. "Not a nice feeling, being blackmailed, is it?"

That barb hurt, but at least he believed her. "I was trying to protect you, you dolt."

"And who will protect you?"

"I have my gun," she said with a defiant lift of her chin. "And Argos."

Hampden glanced down at the dog with a snort. "Fat lot of good he did. He didn't even bark."

"He must have recognized you," she said. "He would have bitten anyone else."

Hampden ran his hand through his hair. "God, Sabine. Why must you make it so bloody hard to protect you?"

"No one asked you to protect me," she fumed.

"No one needed to ask me. You're part of my team. That makes you my responsibility."

It was hard to argue with that.

His dark hair was falling wildly over his forehead and his eyes were intense. He was still holding her wrist, his warm body pushing her back against the wall. Her blood heated at the feel of him, pressed all down her front. Her attempts to squirm away failed. She was no match for the strength of his grip and they both knew it. Oddly enough, she felt safe with him. He would never offer violence toward a woman, despite his physical superiority.

"Where are you meeting him?"

"The White Swan."

His eyes widened in amusement. "So that's why you're in this fetching ensemble." He must have seen her confusion because he elaborated. "The White Swan is a house of ill repute. A low-class brothel."

"Oh," she gasped and he nodded, enjoying her embarrassment. She was horribly aware of the delicious scent of him; it made it hard to concentrate. "Let me go."

"Not until you promise not to do anything stupid. You will work with me, Sabine, or you won't go in there at all." He shook his head. "God, I wish you'd trusted me with this earlier. I could have had my men here and captured him. As it is, I promised Castlereagh I wouldn't confront him alone. Bloody hell."

"So now what?" Sabine asked.

"I can't go in there with you. At least, not where Visconti might see me, but I need to know what he wants. It might give us a lead on his plans."

He pulled out a pocket watch, and she noticed with a flash of pleasure that it was the gold one she'd bought the other day. "It's ten to ten. I'll go inside. You wait five minutes and follow me in. And when you meet Visconti, stay in the main rooms. Don't go off with him alone."

Sabine gave him a level look. "I know all the tricks men like Visconti use."

"Just because you can take care of yourself doesn't mean you should. It's not defeat to let someone help you," he said. "Being part of a team doesn't make you weaker—quite the reverse. You don't get lazy or complacent because you don't want to let down the rest of your team. They're your men. You love them. You'd die for them."

His impassioned words hung in the air between them like a promise. A declaration. Then Hampden shook his head, dismissing the moment. "Don't ask me to stand by and do nothing if someone under my protection is in danger," he said gruffly.

He reached forward and tucked a strand of her hair behind her ear, a casual gesture that nonetheless spoke of possession. "You don't have to do this alone, Sabine. I will be there, even if you can't see me."

Her throat constricted. He would always be there for her, she realized. She knew his tenacity, his sheer bloody-mindedness. Such traits had been a curse when he was tracking her, but as his ally they were a blessing. It was comforting to know he was at her back.

He bent and kissed her hard on the mouth.

"What was that for?" she breathed.

He looked deep into her eyes and she felt the intimacy and connection of it all the way to her toes, in a bloom of painful pleasure.

"I don't know. Good luck, maybe?" He shrugged and stepped back. "Wait five minutes, remember."

"What about Argos?"

He glanced down at the dog. "Go home," he said, pointing out of the alley. "Find cake."

Argos barked once and trotted off down the street.

Sabine watched Richard enter the White Swan and prayed Visconti wasn't already inside.

CHAPTER 46

*T*he bored-looking doorman barely spared Sabine a glance. She tightened her grip on the pistol in her pocket and peered around the crowded taproom. There was no sign of Visconti, so she took a place at an unoccupied table with a clear view of the door. Richard had positioned himself near the bar, huddled in the far corner.

Visconti entered a few minutes later. He saw her, and smiled thinly in greeting. Sabine's stomach roiled as he slid into the seat opposite her.

"Good evening, madame," he said in French, keeping his voice low.

Sabine decided on a direct attack. "Why am I here, monsieur?"

His smile widened. "Because I have a little job for you, *ma chère.* I need you to make me a new passport and travel papers."

Sabine raised her brows.

Visconti continued. "Not only that, but you're going to give me the fake fortune you promised to those English fools."

Ah, so that's what he was about. He meant to double-cross his English allies. Sabine almost smiled. Visconti reminded her of

General Malet; both were predictably consistent in their treachery.

Visconti leaned back, entirely at his ease. His dead eyes roved her face. "You will put your fake money into two traveling bags and have it ready for me on Thursday, along with the papers."

"That's the day of the royal wedding," Sabine clarified, hoping to prompt him into saying more.

He nodded. "Yes."

"Am I to meet you somewhere, then?" she probed.

He flicked her chin lazily with his finger. It was all she could do not to flinch. "Don't worry your pretty head over the details, *chèrie*. I will find you when the time comes, fear not."

Sabine suppressed a shudder. Visconti rose. "Until Thursday, then. It has been a pleasure doing business with you, Philippe Lacorte. And don't forget what I said about your friend. You wouldn't want anything to happen to him or his family, would you?"

Sabine cocked her pistol beneath the table. She could shoot him now. She'd probably be arrested for murder and hanged, but even so, it would be worth sacrificing herself to stop this monster. She thought of the girl he'd killed in Paris. Thought of Richard, Heloise, dead or wounded. Her finger tightened on the trigger.

But Visconti stepped away, and the chance was lost. Sabine watched him leave with a combination of relief and regret. She glanced over at Richard and saw him slip through a door leading off the main taproom. She rose and followed.

It was a private room. Sabine cast an interested glance at the shabby bed with its gaudy array of pillows and the battered velvet chaise longue that had clearly seen plenty of action. It barely looked robust enough to support one person, let alone two.

She related her conversation with Visconti. Richard nodded. "Well, at least that's confirmed our suspicions. He means to kill someone at the wedding, then flee the country."

He stepped closer and Sabine tilted her head to look into his face.

"Christ, seeing you with Visconti made me sick," he growled. "I wanted to run over there and murder him with my bare hands."

Sabine's heart pumped hard at the fierceness of his expression, the simmering tension so close to the surface. Relief and excitement coalesced inside her, and suddenly all she could think about was kissing him.

Almost as soon as the thought formed, his lips were on hers. Sabine didn't know if she'd been the one to initiate it or not, but she didn't care. Their mouths met in a kiss that was hot and hungry. Richard pulled her body hard against his, and without the encumbrance of her skirts she felt every part of him against every part of her. His chest crushed her breasts. His knee slipped between her breeches-clad thighs and rubbed against her in a maddening friction that made her want more. And more.

Sabine moaned into his mouth and slipped her hand down his body to investigate the front of his breeches. She curled her fingers around him tentatively. His hissed expletive could have been an expression of agony or delight. He rocked against her hand.

The click of the door opening had them springing apart like guilty schoolboys. A woman stopped dead in the jamb and gave a throaty, knowing chuckle. "Ooh, sorry, gents! Didn't know the room was taken."

She thought she'd disturbed two men, Sabine realized dazedly.

"You two carry on." The tart sent them a cheeky wink and retreated.

Sabine glanced at Richard, horribly aware that her breathing was irregular and her entire body was throbbing with desire. He returned her look with a simmering one of his own. Her knees turned to water.

She backed up a few steps, her mind churning. She was so tired of denying her desire for him. There could be no future for them, but what was to stop her from taking him as her lover?

She'd never slept with a man. Not because she valued her virginity overmuch, but because she'd never met a man she trusted enough to give her body into his keeping. Until now.

It wasn't for want of offers. Most of the men she'd met in Paris had been on the shady side of respectable, and some of them had been downright crooks. She had a soft spot for a rogue, but she'd hardly have shared a drinking glass with most of them, let alone allowed them access to her most intimate areas. Richard was the first man she'd ever been truly attracted to. Was it a result of their forced proximity? The ridiculous situation they were in? Probably. But she wanted his cunning mind and his dry wit and his beautiful body beyond anything.

She moistened her lips. "I'm eligible."

His brow puckered in confusion. "What?"

"According to your rules. Heloise told me about them. I'm not a wife. Or a virgin."

She didn't even blink at the lie. If he thought she was virgin he'd never sleep with her.

The intensity of his look made her breath catch in her throat. A potent silence stretched between them, a moment's suspension full of bright unspoken possibilities, emotion held savagely in check.

"Do you understand what I'm saying, Hampden?" she said when he didn't answer. "I want to be your lover. Tonight."

* * *

RICHARD INHALED SHARPLY, certain his ears deceived him. The way she was looking at him made his head spin. He could still taste her on his lips. Her scent curled around him, heady and exotic, like opium. It made him crazy. Just the sight of her long legs encased in those breeches made him itch to touch her.

"This isn't anything to do with me paying you for counterfeiting," he said slowly, needing to clarify that, at least, between them. "This is just you and me."

He held his breath, unable to recall the last time he'd been so anxious to hear an answer. God knows what he'd do if she refused.

"Yes," she said.

He resisted the urge to howl like a wild animal. Anticipation had the blood pounding thickly in his veins and he took a step back from her, afraid if he touched her again he wouldn't be able to think straight.

"Not here," he growled. A fleeting expression of disappointment crossed her face and he smiled with a twist of dark amusement. "Oh, I am going to have you in every possible way, Sabine de la Tour," he clarified gruffly, "but we are not doing it here, in the back room of some seedy tavern."

He strode to the door and yanked it open, practically taking the doorknob with him, and indicated for her to precede him. When they got outside, he put a good two feet of space between them. "Stay on your side of the pavement."

She speared him with a gaze both innocent and thoroughly wicked. "And why is that?"

His mouth went dry. "Because if I touch you, I'll be inside you," he said baldly. "Up against a wall or no."

God, his voice was low. It had dropped at least an octave, was gravelly with need. Her eyes widened in shock and he had to look away. They would be home soon. He forced his legs to keep on walking.

A tense silence stretched between them as they crossed Oxford Street and started down New Bond Street. Richard kept his gaze resolutely ahead.

"We are going straight up to my bedroom," he said quietly. "I have wanted you since the moment I saw you, and possibly long before that. I am mad for you."

His body was rigid with tension. He risked a glance at her and saw her cheeks were pink with anticipation. Her lips were still puffy from his kiss. He prayed for strength.

"It's six minutes until we get home," he said tersely. "In six minutes I am going to strip you naked and lick every inch of your skin."

CHAPTER 47

*S*abine could hardly draw air into her lungs.

"I'm going to touch you," Richard continued silkily. "All over. And you're going to touch me."

There really was no air in London at all. Around them carriages rattled by and people bustled to and fro, blithely unaware of the unbearable anticipation twisting inside her.

"You're going to scream out my name," he said darkly and smiled at her gasp. "And then you're going to beg me for more." He glanced toward the end of the street. "Three minutes."

His eyes met hers. They were glittering, almost feverish. Her own body was burning up. Between her legs throbbed. And he knew it. Knew what he was doing to her, the beast. She was out of breath, but whether it was from the brisk pace or desire she didn't know.

They turned into Upper Brook Street.

"Two minutes."

They reached the house. He caught her wrist and ran up the short flight of steps, pulling her with him. The door opened, but he didn't spare the night porter a glance. Sabine caught a glimpse of Minton's surprised face and then she was running across the tiled foyer, hurrying to keep up.

Richard strode up the stairs, down the corridor, his fingers still encircling her wrist. And then they were in his bedroom. He pulled her through the door and closed it with his back, leaned against the mahogany, and tugged her into his arms. "One minute," he whispered.

In a lightning move he reversed their positions so she was the one up against the door. He trapped her hands, entwined their fingers, and bent to take her mouth.

The hot kiss swept her away. Sabine lost herself in the tempest, craving the sinful thrust of his tongue. He groaned at the same time as she did and released her hands. He shoved his fingers into her hair, imprisoned her face between his hands, and kissed her as if the world were ending. Sabine explored the muscled slope of his shoulders, the sides of his neck, the hair at his nape.

His body pressed hers against the door and his fierce gaze caught hers as he pulled back. "I don't care if you've had one lover or a hundred," he panted. "You're going to forget every single one of them. You're going to think only of me. What I'm doing with my hands. And my mouth. And my body. You're mine."

Above her was a gilt metal wall sconce holding two candles. He ran his hands down her arms, then drew them up over her head and folded her fingers around the curved metal bars.

"Keep your arms there. Don't move."

Sabine shivered as he slid his hands down, skimming her armpits, traversing the bumps of her ribs. He shaped her waist and molded her hips as though trying to memorize the shape of her by touch alone. She made a low sound of yearning. Her fingers tightened on the metal sconce as she resisted the need to explore his body in the same greedy, shameless way.

He slid his hands around to cup her bottom, indecently

outlined by the tight fabric of her breeches. He clasped her waist and lifted her up, using the strength of his arms, until they were nose to nose.

"Wrap your legs around me."

It was easy without skirts. She released the sconce, twined her arms around his neck, and reclaimed his mouth. Her body was on fire, aching, hot. She could feel him between her legs, the marble-hard muscles of his abdomen, the aggressive jut of his erection rubbing between her thighs that both thrilled and frightened her.

He pushed off from the door, carrying her easily, and strode toward the bed, but stopped before his shins hit the mattress. He lowered her to the ground, a tantalizingly slow slide of her body down his.

He shrugged out of his jacket and threw it away, heedless of the expensive cloth, then pulled his shirt over his head. It went sailing to the floor and Sabine hid a smile. His urgency was oddly endearing. This was no leisurely, planned seduction. She'd made him *fou*—mad. Finally!

Her eyes roved over him, drawn to the absolute perfection of his form. He was even better than she'd imagined, one of Raphael's Greek warriors brought to vibrant life. Unable to help herself, she slid her hands over the ridges of his stomach, the bulge of his biceps, enjoying his sharp intake of breath and the way the muscles leaped under her explorative touch. His skin was perfection, tawny and smooth, raw sienna mixed with gold. A little thrill ran through her at the thought of how much physical power he wielded. He was much larger than herself, but she wasn't afraid that he would hurt her.

He reached up and undid the tie at the throat of her linen shirt. It fell open in a deep vee and Sabine stood motionless, fighting for breath, as he tugged it from the waistband of her breeches. She raised her arms to assist him and he pulled the shirt over her head. She wasn't wearing a corset, only a thin silk chemise, and her nipples peaked in the sudden chill.

"Christ," Richard muttered reverently under his breath. "You have been driving me insane."

His eyes lingered on her breasts. They felt full, aching, crying out for his touch. He reached out and cupped her, then bent his head. His breath pebbled her skin in a warm exhale she felt all the way down to her bones. His mouth found her through the silk. He sucked.

Sabine's knees buckled.

"Take off the breeches," he ordered huskily, and she complied, unfastening the front so the fabric fell down her legs. In one frenzied move he divested her of the chemise, and before she had time to become self-conscious over her nudity, he bent and recaptured her nipple.

This time there was not even a scrap of silk between his mouth and her skin. Sabine gasped as his tongue did wicked things, swirling and flicking. She grasped his hair to keep him there as he lavished attention on the other breast, while his hands skimmed up the long line of her back and down over her buttocks and thighs.

He made an animalistic sound of deep longing, a groan of pleasure that vibrated against her skin. Suddenly impatient, she wrapped her arms around his neck and tugged him backward, toward the bed, and he half-fell on top of her as he lost his balance. She laughed against the skin of his shoulder.

He loomed over her, trapping her within the cage of his arms, holding his weight off her while he plundered her mouth with a sense of rising urgency. The taste of him made her blood rush and her head swirl.

He urged her leg up to curve around his hip and she could feel his cock pressing at the junction of her thighs . . . those other words she and Heloise had laughed about, *stick* and *rod* and *cigar,* were utterly inadequate to describe something so potent. A sudden, dismaying thought struck her. Something that size was never going to fit.

Sabine tried to think, but it was hard to concentrate with Richard's mouth pressing butterfly kisses down her stomach and his tongue swirling in a wicked dance over her hipbones.

Would it hurt? She wasn't afraid of pain. It couldn't be worse than trapping a finger in a printing press, or getting lemon juice in a cut when cleaning ink from her hands. But perhaps she should tell him he was her first.

Presumably one of the reasons he eschewed virgins was because he'd be expected to marry them shortly afterward. Clearly he didn't have to worry about that with her. But perhaps another reason was that he was simply too big for a virgin to accommodate. Maybe only women with a little experience—

"Wait," she panted. "About all those 'other lovers.' I haven't—I mean, I've never—"

She didn't finish. His hand slid down between her legs. His fingers slid over her core. And he touched her exactly the way she touched herself.

Sabine's mouth opened in an astonished O of pleasure as he found the little button that made her jerk and writhe. She closed her eyes and heard a deep sound of longing, then realized with amazement that it had come from herself.

Oh, God, he was a master. He teased and tormented and she rolled her hips, urging him to go deeper, to ease the building, throbbing ache, but with a wicked, knowing chuckle he withdrew his hand and slid back up her body.

In one swift move he rolled to one side, removed his breeches, and rolled back on top of her, forearms bracketing her head. Sabine gasped at the feel of hot skin pressing full length on her. She'd never been naked with anyone before.

He slid against her, between her legs, and she shivered in both anticipation and trepidation. Suddenly impatient, she tilted her hips, urging him on. "Please," she breathed against his lips.

With a groan he caught her face between his palms and took her mouth at the same moment he pushed forward and entered her. Sabine tensed, expecting pain, but the slight resistance eased as he slid inside her with a smoothness that left her breathless. She stilled, partly in astonishment, partly in dread that he would call her out for lying to him.

"Christ, you feel so good," he whispered. "I have wanted you for so long."

Sabine slid her hand down the long line of his back and smiled in relief. The ridges of his muscles were delicious. "*Eh bien*, you have me, monsieur. Do your worst."

Her mocking challenge freed some demon inside him; he started to move.

"I have you," he echoed, the rough edge of triumph in his voice. He pulled back and thrust again. Little familiar shivers of delight raced through her.

"I have you, Philippe Lacorte." He slid back, then thrust again, plunging deep, and Sabine's breath caught in her throat. "I have you, Sabine de la Tour."

She couldn't deny it. His fingers pressed into the flesh of her thighs as Pluto's had done on the statue of Persephone. He drove her upward and she urged him on, recognizing the spark she knew from her own experimenting. When he hit one particular spot inside her that made her buck and writhe, she arched her back and wordlessly encouraged him.

She didn't care if this was what she was supposed to do. Didn't care if all his other women had simply lain beneath him, acquiescent and unmoving. She had to move.

"Say my name," he ordered huskily.

"Richard!" she gasped.

"Do you want more?"

Sabine could barely speak. She dug her nails into his back. "Yes!"

He reclaimed her mouth in a kiss that was both savage and

tender. Sabine wrapped her arms around him and gloried in the strength of him, the taste of his skin, the scent of him in her nose.

It was wonderfully overwhelming. Every sense was full. She wanted him with a fierce desperation that was almost unsettling. She threw her head back, mouth open, eyes closed, and reached, reached for that spark that would send her up in flames. Unbearable tension coiled through her body.

"God, I can't wait." He dropped his head to her shoulder as his movements became almost aggressive, thoroughly uncivilized. He drove into her, and his body shook with a deep and powerful passion. "You make me—"

He seemed unable to finish that thought and Sabine bit her lower lip, too close herself to even smile at his confusion because her own matched it. He made her something, too. Crazy? Happy? In love?

"Now, Sabine," he ordered roughly, "come now."

And she did. She hit the peak and trembled there for a split second before she was lost—and simultaneously found. Sparks exploded behind her closed eyelids as her body convulsed around his, the climax familiar, but so much better with him inside her; fuller somehow, all-encompassing.

In the midst of her own pleasure she dimly realized that he was pulling back from her. She clutched at him with her hands, trying to make him stay, but he withdrew and with a loud, shuddering groan of completion, he pressed himself hard against her stomach.

Sabine understood the warm wetness against her skin for what it was. Thank God one of them had been thinking of contraception. She hadn't been thinking at all.

CHAPTER 48

*S*abine blinked as her breathing returned to normal and she came to full awareness of where she was. Richard was a wonderful, heavy weight on top of her, but even as she tried to savor the feel of him he pushed himself up on his arms. She tensed, expecting him to say something, but he rolled away from her, off the bed.

She stared at his exquisite back as he walked naked across the room, totally unashamed. He was astonishingly beautiful. Her gaze roved his broad shoulders, the long line of his back, the intriguing shadowed indents on his buttocks. Her mouth went dry. She hadn't had time to really look at him before—everything had happened too quickly. Now she ogled him shamelessly. He was just as she'd imagined when she was drawing him: perfect.

He poured water from a pitcher into the bowl on the washstand, dipped a washcloth in it and wrung it out, then brought it back to her. Sabine couldn't tear her eyes away from his naked form. He gazed down at her, apparently amused by her regard.

"Here, let's clean you off."

Sabine was convinced it was possible to die of mortification. He was obviously used to such casual intimacy, but her cheeks heated as if she were in an inferno as he used the cloth to gently clean her stomach.

Why feel shy now? Considering what they'd just done, it was beyond foolish. She closed her eyes and pretended she lay naked in bed with men all the time. She was worldly, sophisticated. She'd done this a hundred times.

Should she return to her bedchamber now? What was the etiquette? She was just debating getting up when Richard drew the covers up and slid into bed next to her. He propped his head on his elbow and regarded her solemnly.

"That was—" he said, and Sabine tensed for his condemnation, "long overdue. And over far too soon." He made a rueful face and brushed her hair from her temple. "I place the blame entirely on you."

That sounded like criticism, but he bent and placed the softest of kisses on her lips. "You are completely irresistible."

Another kiss, this one clinging a little longer. She shivered.

"Next time, I promise, I will have a lot more stamina."

She shot him a haughty look. "I'm glad to hear it."

Richard rolled her over onto her side, then tugged her back against his body, fitting them together like nestled spoons. Sabine bit her lip, amazed at the intimacy of the gesture, at how right it felt to be held in the warm circle of his arms. Oh, this was a dangerous game. Far too easy to forget they were only temporary allies. She closed her eyes as he kissed the back of her neck. She had no regrets. But now that he'd had her, would he lose interest?

RICHARD CLOSED HIS EYES, bemused and yet oddly content. Making love to Sabine de la Tour had been as explosive and satisfying as he'd imagined. But at the same time, he couldn't quite believe his own loss of control.

He, who was usually the one drawing out his partner's pleasure, playing and teasing with consummate skill, had barely lasted five minutes. Never before had he been so desperate, so completely driven to have a woman, to take her to the peak of pleasure and give himself in return.

He felt as though he'd been hit in the head with a shovel—stunned and slightly disoriented. Thank God the one remaining shred of sanity he'd possessed had forced him to withdraw before he climaxed.

He shook his head, amazed he'd managed even that small gesture of self-preservation. He always used a contraceptive sheath with his mistresses—even though he hated them—because he didn't want to expose himself to either disease or an illegitimate child.

He hadn't even thought about using one tonight. He'd been so caught up in the intensity of the moment, in the savage, driving need to possess Sabine, that it was as if his body had sabotaged his brain. It had been an exquisite pleasure to be inside her with no barriers between them at all.

Richard frowned against her neck. There *were* barriers between them, though. Despite the fact that he wanted her again with almost devilish intensity—as though his body had been starved of her touch for so long that he wanted excess of her now —there were still the barriers of lies and half-truths between them. Still deception and mistrust.

He kissed her temple and enjoyed the way she gave a little shiver. "Where have you hidden the money, Sabine?" he murmured.

She stiffened in his arms and he cursed himself for having spoken the thought aloud. Her rib cage rose as she inhaled.

"You think I am so dazed and addled by your lovemaking that I have lost my wits?" she mumbled, and he could hear the smile in her voice. "You're good, but not that good, Richard Hampden."

He slid his hand over her shoulder and down the fascinating

undulations of waist and hip. "I don't suppose you deposited it anywhere as obvious as a bank?"

She made a scoffing sound. "You think I would trust the Bank of England?" She laughed, a rich, deep sound that he felt all the way down in his gut. And lower. "They're nothing but bewigged crooks. I'd sooner trust a highwayman."

He skimmed his hand back up and cupped her breast. She inhaled sharply and arched her back, pressing herself into him. He squeezed. "Clearly you're not addled enough," he teased. "I'll have to do better."

She made a purring murmur of appreciation. "By all means, try. But I warn you, I am not such an easy conquest."

He would have been disappointed if she'd caved in to his unsubtle fishing, Richard admitted to himself. He liked the fact that she continued to defy him, challenging him mentally even as she melted in his arms.

"Well, if we can't use your fake fortune, what are we going to give to Visconti?"

She rolled onto her back and frowned at him. "Surely you don't need any money. Just wait until he tells me where to meet him, then go there and arrest him."

"He's not such a fool. He'll be expecting to be duped. We're going to have to prepare some money, either real or fake, for him to inspect. I don't want any reason for him to think that you're leading him into a trap."

He sighed. "Despite what you think about the limitless depths of my pockets, even *I* can't get my hands on half a million pounds at such short notice. And I doubt Castlereagh will allow us to take real notes." He raked a hand through his hair. "How long would it take for you to forge that much money?"

"To engrave new printing plates? At least three weeks."

Richard swore softly. "Too long."

* * *

SABINE BIT her lip as the desire to help Richard warred with her sense of self-preservation. A man as evil as Visconti undoubtedly needed to be stopped, but if she trusted Richard with yet another of her secrets she would leave herself without a backup plan. Defenseless.

She closed her eyes in desperation. This unexpected closeness, this desire to share not just her body, but her thoughts and troubles as well, was something she both craved and despised. To be so unguarded and vulnerable was a grave mistake. And yet her heart told her it was time to trust. She'd opened her body to him. Maybe it was time to open her soul a little too.

"Wait here."

Richard made a sound of protest as she slipped out of bed, grabbed her chemise from the floor, and shrugged into it. She wasn't as comfortable as he was with running around the place naked.

She found the door by the fireplace that connected her room to his, grateful that she didn't have to venture into the corridor and risk being seen by the servants.

Richard gave a confused frown when she returned with her paint box and the two small portraits of her parents that had been on her mantelpiece.

"Are you going to paint my picture?"

She was very tempted. He looked delicious, sprawled amongst the sheets, his torso and muscled arms visible. "Not right now."

She opened the box, took out a rag, and soaked it in turpentine. He wrinkled his nose at the smell. With a deep breath—and a silent apology to her mother—she swept it over the surface of the first painting. Right across her mother's face. The paint dissolved beneath the solvent, smearing the delicate features into a hideous, streaky blur.

Richard sat up in alarm. "What are you doing?" His expression was horrified. "You're ruining it!"

Sabine ignored him. She applied more spirits to the rag and repeated the process, rubbing hard at the surface of the painting.

Richard gaped at her apparent act of desecration. Sabine glanced up at him and smiled. "These are not originals. The real portraits are stored safely in Paris. These are copies I painted myself just a few weeks ago."

There was almost no paint left on the surface now. She angled the wooden panel toward him so he could see the smooth layer of gesso, the chalk-based primer she'd used to create a nice flat surface on which to paint.

Richard still looked mystified, even more so when she dipped the wooden block in the basin of water and began scrubbing at it. The chalky layer gradually fell away to reveal the etched metal plate concealed beneath. Sabine returned to the bed. "It's a printer's block."

Richard regarded it, then her, in wonder.

"It is the front side of your English ten-pound note," she said.

"I suppose your father," he tilted his head at the other painting, "conceals the obverse plate?"

Sabine nodded. Her heart was pounding. "Nobody pays any notice to things that are left unguarded. I don't know why museums don't realize that. There's no surer way to get something stolen than to rope it off with a sign saying 'do not touch.' It is irresistible to human nature."

"It is to your nature," he said wryly. "What most normal people interpret as a polite warning, you translate as a direct personal challenge." He shook his head. "You're the sort of woman who sees a notice that says 'please do not walk on the grass' and immediately sits down for a picnic. You revel in disobeying authority."

Sabine couldn't help but smile at that. He knew her well.

Richard tilted his head and his tiger eyes warmed her from the inside out. Was she just imagining the approval and respect she saw in them?

"Are you suggesting that we print our own money, Miss de la Tour?" he asked gravely. "Because that would be counterfeiting. On a grand scale."

His face was serious, but the curl at the corner of his mouth gave him away.

"Can you think of another way of coming up with half a million pounds by next week?"

His hair flopped across his forehead as he shook his head, and Sabine's fingers itched to reach out and smooth it back. He collapsed on the pillows with a pained, resigned expression. "All right, you little criminal. You win. What else do you need?"

Sabine's heart stuttered with elation. "We'll need a press. Can you get access to a newspaper office or printing shop?"

"I expect so. What else?"

"Paper and ink."

"It shall be done."

A strange silence descended between them and Sabine cleared her throat, suddenly awkward. "Well, I, ah, suppose I should return to my rooms, then."

If he was disappointed, he didn't show it. She waited for him to issue a denial, to open his arms and beckon her back to the bed. He did neither.

"Good night."

She felt his gaze on her back as she crossed to the panel door, but he said nothing more. Back in her own bed, she buried her nose in the sheets and tried to assimilate the evening's astonishing chain of events. She was no longer a virgin. And Richard hadn't even noticed.

Perversely, she wasn't sure whether she was disappointed by that or not. It might have been nice for him to have appreciated the fact that she'd chosen him as her first lover. Then again, he might have treated her differently if he'd known. He might have stopped entirely, and she wouldn't have traded his passionate, uninhibited haste for anything.

It had been more than she'd ever imagined. Compared to her solo efforts, his lovemaking was a full-orchestra symphony as opposed to a single, scratchy violin. There was no doubt that he could be dangerously addictive. Her body was still warm, aching, pleasantly replete. She already wanted a rematch.

CHAPTER 49

"**W**here are we?" Sabine demanded as the carriage rocked to a halt. She peered out at a row of shop fronts.

"Cheapside." Richard lowered the step and jumped down, then turned to assist her. He led her to the nearest shop, whose many-paned windows displayed a proliferation of prints and satirical cartoons. The painted sign read *Thomas Tegg, Books & Prints*.

He produced a key from his pocket and unlocked the front door. Sabine followed him inside and immediately felt at ease. The shop smelled wonderfully familiar, like Carnaud's—a mix of leather, glue, sheet paper, and printing ink, vanilla with a faint overlaying mustiness.

Ignoring the shelves of books and easels displaying scurrilous prints, Richard rounded the wooden counter and beckoned her into the back room.

He swept her a magnificent bow. "Your workshop, madame."

A smile spread over her face as she rushed forward to examine the large iron-framed press centered in the room. "This is a new Stanhope press!"

Richard smiled. "It's pronounced 'Stannup,' not 'Stan-hope.' After England's very own Charles Mahon, third Earl Stanhope. The ton calls him 'Citizen Stanhope,' because of his sympathy for your revolution."

Sabine examined the machine with interest. "I've heard these can print over two hundred impressions an hour." She tugged on the wooden-handled lever at the front, which lowered the upper printing plate onto the lower, then turned and beamed at him, delighted with her new toy.

He peeled off his jacket and rolled up his sleeves. "Now what else do we need to get started?"

Sabine raised her brows. "Is the great Lord Lovell deigning to help?" she teased. "Are you sure you want to sully those lordly hands of yours with trade?"

The look he shot her made her stomach flutter. "Oh, I'm more than willing to get my hands dirty."

Sabine ignored the innuendo and stripped off her gloves, hat, and pelisse, and laid them on a workbench next to a long-armed guillotine used for slicing multiple sheets of paper. "Very well. Even with this wonderful press, there is still much to do. This prints only one side of the banknotes at a time, so we'll need to feed each piece of paper into the machine twice." She sucked in a breath at a sudden thought. "We do not have the right paper! It must be a very particular combination of cotton and linen rags. *Merde.* We will just have to use plain paper and hope that Visconti does not check for a watermark."

Richard shot her a superior grin. "Over there." He pointed to a wrapped rectangular package on a table.

Sabine untied the string and gaped at the sheets inside. She held one up and let out a soft whoosh of disbelief as she detected the faint watermark border. "Where did you get this?"

Richard's expression turned smug. "Only one printer in all of England has the contract to supply paper to the Bank of England. Henri de Portal at Laverstoke Mill in Hampshire."

Sabine sent him her own smug look. "Ah, another Frenchman. We are extremely good when it comes to money."

Hampden ignored her jibe. "Castlereagh managed to pull some strings. Don't ask me how, but I suspect that the Bank of England might be missing a bundle when they next take an inventory."

Sabine raised her brows. "Careful. That sounds awfully like condoning one crime to enact another. 'Pardon one offense and you encourage the commission of many,'" she quoted.

"Publilius Syrus," Hampden said with a smile, correctly identifying the source.

She inclined her head. "Next we need the right kind of ink. Printing ink is mixed with varnish, which gives it a distinctive sheen."

He pointed to several large bottles. "Over there."

Sabine busied herself setting up the room, then showed Richard how to feed each sheet of paper into one end of the press. "Be careful not to trap your fingers," she warned.

They settled into a companionable rhythm and she shook her head at the perversity of fate. She'd never imagined she'd be doing this again. And certainly not with him.

Richard discarded his cravat and untied the neck of his shirt. She tried not to stare. Seeing him doing manual labor made her hot and bothered. The man really was too handsome for his own good. She left the press and inspected a pile of new notes they had produced. Richard joined her.

"What do you think? Will they pass muster?"

She ran her finger over the surface of one and nodded. "They feel right."

"What do you mean?"

She caught his hand and directed his finger over the newly printed note. "Do you feel those tiny bumps and ridges? The plate presses the paper with such force that not only is the ink in the engraved scratches transferred onto the paper, but the paper itself is actually pressed up into the tiny gaps. It leaves that distinctive raised pattern."

Richard's finger brushed against hers on its path over the paper and her blood thickened. She knew she was babbling, but all she could think about was his body, there beside her. Heat fairly radiated off him.

"Amazing how one can detect the tiniest variations with touch," she croaked. "Our fingers are incredibly sensitive."

Sabine inhaled, imagining his fingers on her skin, learning the textures. *Stop it!* She forced herself to step away from him and pointed to the wording on the uppermost note.

"'I promise to pay,'" she read aloud and shook her head. "I always find it incredible that the entire system of money is based on something as nebulous as trust." She glanced at him, then swiftly away. "Promises are easily made and easily broken."

Richard caught her chin. "Not mine," he said softly. He turned her face up to his, forcing her to meet his eyes. "If I make a vow, I keep it."

She believed him. He would not take a promise lightly. He'd vowed to catch her, and here she was. He'd vowed to end Visconti, and she had no doubt that he would pursue him to the ends of the earth to get justice.

And when he succeeded he wouldn't need her anymore.

She pulled away from his hand. "Let's get back to work."

CHAPTER 50

*R*ichard straightened. "Time for a break."

He stretched, and Sabine tried to ignore the way his shirt tightened over his shoulders. She'd been intensely aware of his nearness for the entire time they'd been working. She found this new facet of him—the capable workman—just as appealing as the haughty Viscount Lovell. She forced her eyes away from the inviting line of his jaw and his perfect lips, and walked into the front room.

She studied the cartoons that decorated the walls. "You English have a great tradition of satirical cartoonists," she said over her shoulder. "Cruikshank, Hogarth. Gillray." She pointed to an image of a grotesquely fat Prince of Wales in bed with his mistress, Lady Hertford. "I'm a great admirer of your Mr. Rowlandson. Look at that—he only needs to draw two lines to make something look real."

Richard came to stand beside her. She could feel the heat of his body next to hers and her mouth dried up. Printing was sweaty, physical work. He looked as he had after fencing, mussed and utterly delectable.

She'd been naked next to that body. It seemed unbelievable.

She wanted to do it again.

"There you have it," Richard said with a grin. "Your new profession. Instead of engraving banknotes, you can cause social disruption quite legally by becoming a cartoonist. I'm sure you'd enjoy swaying the thoughts and opinions of the general populace."

Sabine wrinkled her nose. "Influencing the mood of the masses seems like a great deal of responsibility." She chuckled at an image of three gentlemen in a ballroom all bumping heads as they simultaneously bent to pick up a lady's fan. It was entitled "Miseries of High Life." "Your royal family does provide a great deal of fodder for mockery, however."

Hampden sighed. "I know. It's almost too easy to laugh at them. The Prince Regent would be quite enough on his own, what with his debts, his gambling, his bigamy, and his adulteries. He may or may not have been previously married to the twice-widowed Mrs. Fitzherbert when he married Princess Caroline."

Sabine shook her head.

"If Prinny's behavior wasn't bad enough, there are the ten other adult children of the king to provide entertainment. The Duke of York was investigated for his mistress's sale of military commissions. The Duke of Clarence has had ten children by his mistress, the actress Dorothea Jordan. The unmarried Princess Sophia is rumored to have had an illegitimate child, probably by an elderly equerry. The Duke of Sussex contracted a marriage that was promptly declared null and void. And the Duke of Cumberland was suspected of having murdered his own valet."

"I thought our French royals were bad. Still, you may rest easy in your bed. If the country hasn't risen up in revolution by now, it probably never will."

"No thanks to you," he said with a smile.

She felt the familiar, treacherous softening his teasing provoked and was swamped with an odd kind of despair. It would be dangerously easy to love him—and a fatal mistake. Her leaving was inevitable. She frowned at him. "I can't concentrate with you here."

The dimple made an appearance. "That's good to know."

She turned her displeasure to the stacks of neatly printed bills.

"What's the matter?" he asked when she shook her head.

"They're too new. There should be smudges and marks, folds and creases. A real banknote has been handled hundreds of times."

"Why is that a problem? Visconti will be expecting counterfeits, not circulated notes."

"We'd never leave them like this. They're too conspicuous. We need to rough them up a bit."

"I have an idea." Richard grabbed a handful and made his way to the back of the shop, where a narrow staircase rose to the upper level. Sabine had peeked up there earlier—it contained a small living quarters with a desk, an armchair, and a single, narrow bed, presumably for the printer's apprentice, or for the printer himself if he was working late.

Richard scattered the notes on the bed.

"You want to jump on them?" Sabine asked doubtfully.

A wicked light came into his eyes. "Not exactly." He shot her a sly, questioning look, and she felt the color rise on her cheekbones as she recognized his intent expression. It brought a flash of heat to her skin and a spearing sensation between her legs.

He took a step toward her and her eyes opened wide. "It's the middle of the day!"

He shot her an ironic, cynical look. "I know what time it is, Miss de la Tour. Come here."

"You are a very wicked man," she chided, backing away. Her heart pounded madly in her chest. He made a grab for her but she skipped sideways, out of his reach. She darted one way, he went the other, each of them on an opposite side of the small bed.

"I will catch you," he growled. "I always get my man."

"Or woman?" she teased.

She was thoroughly enjoying this childish game, the undeniable thrill of being stalked by such an attractive wolf. The low twisting in her belly wasn't fear. It was longing.

She feigned left, then changed direction and leaped up onto the bed, trying to dart past him, but he was too quick. He caught her around the waist, lifted her off her feet, and deposited her with a bounce on the narrow mattress.

Some of the notes went flying and the metal bedsprings creaked in protest. Sabine let out a screeching laugh. She couldn't seem to stop giggling. She was panting with exertion, her hand on her throat, gasping for breath. He took her hands, laced his fingers through hers, and spread them wide against the bed, over her head, holding her prisoner. The paper rustled beneath them.

"I've caught you," he leered in his best wicked-wolf voice. His deep baritone sent shivers racing through her body. "Now you have to pay."

"How much do you want?" she breathed.

His eyes burned into hers. "Everything you have."

He lowered himself with tantalizing slowness. His mouth brushed hers, gentle at first, feather light. As soft and sweet as the stroke of a sable paintbrush. Sabine moved up into it, pressing her body to the hard planes of his, wanting more.

She felt the touch of his tongue and met it with her own. Her laughter stilled as play became serious. He kissed her again and again, endless, drugging kisses, clinging and shaping, learning the contours of her mouth with a dedicated concentration that left her trembling.

She arched up, craving his full weight, but he held himself apart, above her. He pinned her hands and lowered his head to nuzzle her neck, the front of her gown. When he found the taut peak of her breast he lingered there, teething her through the fabric. Pleasure shot through her like fireworks.

He released her hands and stood, but she swallowed her

instinctive protest as he quickly stripped off his shirt. Then his breeches.

The late afternoon sun slanted through the grimy windows, illuminating his glorious body. Those long, lean legs, the hard muscles of his chest. The undeniable evidence of his desire for her.

Sabine shot him a slow smile.

His chest was smooth except for an intriguing line of hair arrowing from his navel down to his impressive arousal. Sabine drank her fill of him. He had a scar on his pectoral and a new scratch on his arm. Her heart clenched. He wasn't invincible, despite the air of invulnerability he exuded. She didn't want to think of how easily he could have been killed in his wartime activities. A stray bullet, a lucky punch. Arriving at the scene of a bomb just a few minutes earlier and being caught in the blast. She shivered.

Richard held out his hand. He pulled her to her feet, then turned her around so her back was to him. Sabine stood meekly as his fingers unbuttoned her dress; it fell at her feet in a rustle of fabric. Her short corset laced at the front. He turned her back around and bent his head, his expression intent as he loosened the laces.

The corset fell away. His fingers brushed her arm as he untied the bows of her chemise at each shoulder and she caught her breath as the thin lawn skimmed down, leaving her completely naked to his hot gaze.

This was entirely different from the passionate blur of before. This was slow and utterly deliberate. And just as arousing.

Her breath was coming in short, excited pants. She wanted to throw herself into his arms, but instead she simply stood there, enduring his silent scrutiny. A wave of self-doubt washed over her. Hers probably wasn't the best body he'd ever seen. She pushed the thought away. She was here; those other women were not.

She still wore her lorgnette: it lay between her breasts, suspended on its thin gold chain. Richard caught it and used it to draw her forward with a slight tug. Her breath hitched. He lifted the little glass and touched it to the side of her face, grazing the skin in a strange kind of caress. He followed the line of her jaw, then strayed lower, down her throat.

She could barely breathe for wanting him. Her skin pebbled as he used the magnifier to describe lazy circles around her breast, circling in a spiral closer and closer to her nipple. His face was a study in concentration. He pressed the cool flat of it to the tip, and her stomach clenched in anticipation.

"Please," she whispered achingly.

He glanced up. "Someone once told me that learning to forge something is like learning a language. You need to repeat it over and over again until you're fluent enough to converse at a decent level."

Sabine frowned on a flash of recollection. She'd said that.

The corner of his lips quirked. "It's the same with making love." He let the lorgnette drop and slid his arms around her waist. "Over and over again. Would you like to converse with me, Sabine?"

Oh, the beast! He was certainly fluent in this particular language. And she'd be a fool to refuse. Sabine wrapped her arms around him and pulled his mouth down to hers.

She held nothing back, kissing him with all the ardor in her soul, and he responded with gratifying enthusiasm. With a groan, he crushed her to his chest and lowered her onto the bed. The banknotes crumpled beneath them, but Sabine barely noticed. She was too intent on driving Richard beyond reason.

CHAPTER 51

*R*ichard surrendered to the madness.

Sabine bit his lower lip, sending a rush of blood to his groin, and then arched beneath him. He marveled at the perfection of her. She was small, so much smaller than him, but strong and supple and so vibrantly alive.

He couldn't stop touching her—the curve of her back, the line of her thighs, the silky-smooth texture of her warm skin. He closed his eyes and ran his fingers over her, depriving himself of sight, reading her body with touch.

She'd been right about fingers, he thought dimly. Their sensitivity. Fingers were astonishing things. He explored every dip of shoulder and collarbone, each hollow of rib and curve of breast.

Hunger was rising in him and he pulled back, panting, trying to find that cool distance. It wasn't there. She enchanted him, deceived him, bewitched him. He was addicted to the piquant danger of her.

Last night he'd barely lasted five minutes. Pride demanded that this time he retain some control. He slid down her body, determined to demonstrate at least some of his expertise.

She gasped when he settled between her legs and tried to pull him up by the hair, but he simply kissed the inside of her knee and told her to lie back and enjoy it. She almost bucked off the bed when he kissed her core, then sank back with a blissful sigh.

Richard bit back a roar of triumph as a wave of fierce possessiveness welled up inside him. This beautiful, vexing creature was his. He used his mouth on her, his tongue. And then his fingers, sliding and teasing until she was incoherent, twisting on the bed, lost in sweet abandon.

She cried out his name as her climax hit and he rose up and sank into her in one fluid movement. The sensation was so exquisite he stilled, needing a moment to regain the control that threatened to spiral away. Her inner muscles gripped him like a glove, and an odd emotion tightened his chest, something tender and grateful and oddly protective. This was where he belonged. Here, with this wonderful, impossible woman.

Richard shook his head. Impossible. He didn't need anyone. It was lust, that was all. Wonderful, glorious lust.

He moved with deliberate slowness, brought her to the very edge, then drew back, taking his time, pacing them both to heighten the moment of release until she was begging him, shivering with desire. Every stroke brought him nearer to exploding and with a low groan of defeat he plunged into her, over and over, relinquishing control.

There was nothing practiced or restrained about it. It was wild and abandoned. Free. He had no finesse at all. It was simply power and pleasure, unimaginable joy. He could feel the darkness pushing closer, sweet and rich, heard her cry out in delight—and he was lost. His own climax punched him in the back of the head like a prizefighter's winning blow, and he slid into that dark sparkle of scarlet and black with a muffled groan of pleasure.

* * *

SABINE LOST count of the number of times over the next three days that Richard demanded she tell him where her money was hidden to save them all the effort of printing their own. But she remained adamant; she would not give it up.

She wasn't helping him because of their stupid one-month agreement. She wanted to avenge that young girl in Paris as much as he did.

Raven and Will Ambrose both learned how to use the press, but she still had to be there to supervise. She was reminded of her old team at Vincennes: Peter, Claude, and Mathilde. She'd missed the camaraderie, the sense of working together for some shared purpose.

She missed Anton most of all, and prayed that he was staying out of trouble. He had only ten more days to wait until he could escape to Boston, but with Malet expecting his money in only four days' time, she hoped her friend remained well hidden.

She considered trying to print additional counterfeits to give to Malet, but it proved impossible under the watchful eyes of Raven, Will, and Richard. They knew exactly how many notes they had produced. And besides, Malet was unlikely to be fobbed off with anything less than the full amount they'd stolen from him, which was impossible. Sabine had no idea what she was going to do about that particular situation, but since the meeting with Visconti was imminent, she pushed it to the back of her mind.

CHAPTER 52

The money was ready, two bags neatly packed with five hundred thousand pounds. Neither she nor Richard had slept for more than a few hours, working solidly to print enough counterfeits to satisfy Visconti's demand. When she hadn't been printing, Sabine had busied herself making the fake travel documents for Visconti.

Finally, at midday on the day of the royal wedding, a message arrived addressed to Madame de la Tour: *A carriage will be sent for you at nine o'clock this evening. Bring the money, and come alone.*

Sabine handed the note back to Richard and glanced nervously through the window. "Do you think he's watching the house?"

Richard shrugged. "It's possible. Which is why we're going to appear to do just as he says. You will get into the carriage with the money and set off. Raven and I will follow, far enough away not to arouse suspicion. As soon as we see Visconti, we'll act."

Sabine nodded. She didn't want to know what Richard meant by "act," but she suspected it would be something more than simply arresting the man. And after what Visconti had done in

Paris, she didn't feel bad about that. He deserved everything that came to him.

Richard raked a hand through his hair. "Christ, I hate having to involve you in this."

She forced a confident smile, even though her stomach was in knots. "You want to catch him, don't you?"

His jaw tightened. "Absolutely. But take your pistol, just in case. If you feel threatened at any time, use it. Understand?"

The carriage arrived at the door at a quarter to nine. Raven, who had been there since breakfast, went to ready the horses, but Richard caught her arm in the hallway. He turned her to face him, his expression grim.

"I'll be right behind you, but don't try anything stupid. Let us deal with Visconti." He stroked her jaw with his thumb. "This will all be over soon, I promise." He pulled the hood of her cloak around her face and dropped a light kiss on her lips that made her stomach flutter with more than just nerves. Sabine rose up into it, but he stepped back and nodded to the two waiting footmen to load the bags into the carriage.

She studied the carriage driver intently, but he was not Visconti. She hadn't thought he would risk coming himself, but even if he were a master of disguise he couldn't have faked the man's crooked nose and numerous missing teeth.

"Where are we going?" she demanded imperiously.

The cabbie shot her a knowing grin and tapped the side of his nose with one finger. "Yer fine fellow told me Vauxhall. But if it's Gretna Green yer headin' for after that you'll need to take the stage. Never go further than Holborn, me."

Sabine raised her brows. The man thought he was participating in an elopement. If she hadn't been so tense she would have laughed.

"Might take us a while to cross the river," the driver prattled merrily. "Everyone's 'eading the same way, to see them fireworks for the weddin'."

His gloomy prediction proved true. The carriage had barely swung onto Park Lane when it became snarled in a great throng of traffic and slowed almost to a standstill. A huge number of vehicles of all shapes and sizes filled the thoroughfare, all heading in the same direction—south, toward the prince's residence, Carlton House.

Pedestrians crowded around, passing between the slow-moving vehicles like a great wave. Horses tossed their heads and reared in agitation as drivers shouted curses and admonishments and tried to settle their teams. Sabine's driver joined in, hurling colorful invectives at children ducking under the traces and hawkers pressing close to lean through the window to offer her gaudy colored ribbons or oranges with cloves pressed into the skins.

They crawled forward, barely faster than a walking pace. Sabine couldn't see Richard following her, but he'd surely have no difficulty keeping track of her carriage in such a slow-moving cavalcade.

The carriage rocked sideways on its springs as someone stepped on. Sabine turned to berate the hawker, then stifled a cry as the figure pulled open the door and swung himself in next to her. Her heart lurched as Visconti settled himself onto the seat opposite.

"Good evening, madame."

Visconti's face was calm, amused, but his smile didn't reach his eyes. Sabine's heart began to race. Had Richard seen him slip inside the carriage?

Visconti placed a slim, black wooden box on the seat beside him and withdrew a wicked-looking knife from his waist. Sabine pressed back into the seat.

"Ah, so you see my pretty knife, do you?" Visconti purred. "Don't forget it. I will cut you from ear to ear if you don't do exactly as I say."

The gentleness of his voice was extremely disconcerting—and

far more frightening than if he'd shouted. Sabine glanced into his dark eyes. In the gathering dusk they were like bottomless pools, utterly devoid of emotion. He truly wouldn't bat an eyelid if he had to slit her throat. Her palms began to sweat.

"Do you have my money?"

She cleared her throat. "Yes." She pointed at the bags at her feet.

"Open them," he said harshly. "I want to see."

Her hands were shaking so much that it took several tries to undo the buckles and open the brass latches, but she finally opened the lid of one. The money had been tied into neat bundles; the uppermost edges riffled in the breeze coming in through the window.

Visconti leaned forward and flicked through them, glancing at each note in turn, right to the bottom. Thank God they hadn't tried to dupe him by putting just a few printed notes on the top of each bundle and then filling the remainder of the box with blank paper. All that effort had been worth it.

He nodded. "Good. Now the other."

She showed him the contents of the second bag, and breathed a sigh of relief when he slumped back, apparently satisfied. "I commend you on the quality of your forgeries, madame." He held out his hand. "Now the fake papers."

Sabine handed them to him. He subjected them to intense scrutiny too, but she was confident in her abilities. He would have no complaints. She strained her ears, listening for any sign that Richard was outside and preparing to pounce.

A quick glance through the window showed they were opposite the gated entrance to Green Park. A great number of people were jostling to get inside to see the amusements.

Visconti picked up the wooden case, keeping his knife in his other hand. "Pick up the bags," he ordered.

When Sabine complied, he swung open the door and gestured for her to exit the still-moving carriage. Sabine took one look at his knife and jumped down. She stumbled as she landed and looked around frantically for Richard, but Visconti pressed the blade into her side and urged her forward, through the crowd.

"Walk," he ordered in her ear.

The park was a sea of people, all keen to get a glimpse of the princess and her fairy-tale prince. Charlotte, it seemed, was far more popular than her fat wastrel of a father. People loved a romance, after all. Or perhaps it was just an excuse for a party, Sabine thought wildly.

Her legs felt like water. She glanced over her shoulder, but there was still no sign of either Richard or Raven. *Merde!*

Stalls, like striped tents, had been erected all along the walks and around the edge of the great central lake. They passed gypsies selling bunches of lucky white heather, rabbit's feet, handkerchiefs, and scarves. The scent of nuts cooked in honey mingled with the aroma of spiced wine and whole roast pig, making her stomach churn.

Music and laughter filled the night air, and the general air of merriment was a disconcerting contrast to her own panicked state. Sabine briefly considered trying to run, to slip away from Visconti into the crowds, but she didn't dare, with his knife at her side.

Hundreds of glowing lanterns had been suspended on tall stakes and hung from the trees. Rows of them draped the ornamental Chinese-style bridge that spanned the water and illuminated the five-tiered pagoda that had been erected in the center.

Visconti steered her across the bridge. As the crowds thinned, he gestured her off the path and through a small copse of trees. Sabine's panic increased. Richard hadn't seen her. She was on her own.

She considered hitting Visconti with the bags of money she was holding, then rejected the idea. They were too unwieldy. She still had her pocket pistol, but how could she get it when she was holding these infernal bags?

They emerged from the trees next to a building that had obviously been erected for the festivities; the large wooden structure looked like a Grecian-style temple. Sabine glanced across the lake and realized they were opposite the entrance to Carlton House. A great crowd had gathered on the far side, awaiting the imminent appearance of the wedding party.

Her heart thudded against her breastbone. Did Visconti mean to kill her? He had his money and his travel papers. She was of no further use to him.

He urged her inside.

A single torch illuminated the interior. Unlike the outside, which was fully decorated, the interior was unfinished, like the reverse of a theater stage set. Angles of wood and tangled crossbeams propped up the exterior walls and an unsteady-looking set of wooden steps rose to an upper level. It smelled of new sawdust and fresh paint.

Visconti gestured for her to put down the money, then pointed at the stairs. "Up."

Sabine was torn between confusion, irritation, and terror. Up? Why on earth did he want her to go up there? If he was going to kill her, surely he could do it just as well down here. She opened her mouth to tell him precisely that, but he spoke first.

"You must be wondering why I brought you here."

When she merely raised her eyebrows, he chuckled, delighted by her refusal to be cowed. "I'm not going to harm you, *chérie,*" he chided. "You're far too valuable. I'd be a fool to kill the goose that lays the golden eggs."

A hysterical laugh welled up in Sabine's chest. She'd always wanted to be irreplaceable. Now, it seemed, her skills were going to save her life. She slipped her hand into her pocket and cocked the pistol. "I will never work for you," she said coolly.

Visconti pushed her toward the ladder. "Up."

"No." Sabine withdrew her pistol, turned, and pulled the trigger.

CHAPTER 53

The gun's retort was followed almost immediately by an enraged bellow from Visconti. Sabine barely had time to register disbelief that she'd missed when his fist caught her across the cheek.

Pain exploded in her skull. She staggered back into the steps as he twisted the gun from her grasp and grabbed her hair.

"You little bitch! Get up!"

Sabine let out a shriek of pain as he forced her up the steps. Her eyes were watering as they emerged onto an upper level and it took her a few moments to realize that it was open to sky, like the battlements of a castle. Visconti's breath was heavy in her ear as he thrust her against the wooden railings. She sank to the floor, her ears still ringing, furious and despairing all at once. How had she managed to miss? He'd been less than a foot away!

The wicked sliver of his knife flashed before her eyes as he yanked her head back. Sabine stilled.

"You don't lack for courage, I'll give you that," he said in a curiously detached voice. "But if you move again I will kill you, golden goose or not. You're not the only forger in Europe." His grip tightened painfully on her scalp. "Do you understand?"

Sabine moved her head just the smallest fraction in agreement. Visconti released her and stood. "Good. Now sit there while I take care of business."

Sabine glanced around. The platform was covered with an assortment of cardboard tubes laid neatly in lines, all facing upward, with what seemed to be string running between them. She squinted, trying to read the wording on those nearby: *Chinese Fountain, Yew Tree, Flaming Star.*

Understanding dawned; these were the fireworks for the display, joined by a single fuse. Each one would light the next. Sabine wondered miserably what Visconti had done to the person who was supposed to be lighting them.

At that moment a great cheer went up from the crowd across the water. A blurry group of figures emerged from between the pillars of Carlton House. Sabine could just make out the newlyweds: Charlotte in a silvery-colored dress and Leopold in the uniform of a British general. A group of other dignitaries and courtiers, many in military colors, flanked them. And there was the Prince Regent himself. A chair had been provided for his corpulent form and he seated himself in their midst—an unmistakable target.

Visconti set his wooden box on the balustrade, laid down his knife, and took out a short-barreled musket. He stroked the wooden stock like a lover.

"I was a marksman, you know," he said mildly, and Sabine shivered at the reasonable tone of his voice. He didn't sound like a madman. "In Russia. I can hit a target over three hundred yards away."

He glanced over at the steps of Carlton House, judging the distance. "Only two hundred to the prince," he said with a sick smile. He loaded the musket with frighteningly brisk efficiency.

"At first I considered an explosion of some kind," he continued. "But it's never easy to ensure the accuracy. A bullet is so much more . . . personal." His thin lips stretched wide at his own humor as he carefully removed his jacket and draped it over the rail.

Sabine's stomach churned at his casual boasting of cold-blooded murder. She had to stop him. Should she tackle him? Shout for help?

"Why are you doing this?" Her cheek hurt from where he'd hit her. "You already have money. Why don't you just leave?"

A bell rang, across the water. The music ceased and an expectant hush fell over the crowd. Visconti shook his head. "That's my cue, *chèrie.*"

Sabine realized that the entire crowd had turned to face the pavilion; hundreds of indistinct pale faces angled toward them. She braced herself to leap up, but Visconti shot her a lethal glare. "Do not move."

He placed the loaded gun next to his knife on the railing, lit a wooden taper, and touched it to the fuse on the nearest firework. Fire raced along the thin cord in a glowing fizz of sparks. There was a brief pause as it disappeared beneath the first firework, and then an ear-splitting shriek as the pyrotechnic shot up into the sky.

The crowd roared with approval.

The next firework followed, then the next, an unstoppable chain reaction. In a moment the whole air was ablaze, and Sabine clapped her hands over her ears to block out the deafening noise. The crowd gasped and cheered as the glowing sparks formed crowns, hearts, even the entwined initials *C* and *L* for the bride and groom, in the dark sky above.

The explosives gave off a thick gray smoke that caught in her lungs and made her double over, coughing. Sabine felt a brief spurt of hope that the smoke might obscure Visconti's shot at the prince, but he seemed unperturbed. Doubtless he was used to compensating for conditions like this during warfare, she thought desperately.

Through the smoke she saw him kneel and balance the musket on the balustrade.

She couldn't let him fire. Sabine pushed herself to her feet and launched herself at him, trying to remember every dirty move Richard had taught her. He toppled sideways, caught by surprise, and she followed, clawing and scratching at his face. Her hand found his ear and she twisted mercilessly, then wrapped her arms around his head to obscure his eyes while simultaneously trying to avoid the deadly barrel of the musket.

When he put an arm around her neck she bit his forearm. Hard. Visconti swore viciously—and her momentary advantage ended. He raised the musket and delivered an agonizing blow to her ribs with the wooden butt.

Sabine collapsed and curled into a tight ball as pain darkened her vision. She clutched her stomach, barely able to breathe as her muscles spasmed. Visconti staggered to his feet and delivered a brutal series of kicks to her back and ribs and she cried out, trying to shield her head and body with her arms.

"Bitch!" he cursed bitterly.

She tried to crawl away, but her limbs wouldn't obey. She dragged in an agonized breath and closed her eyes, waiting for him to use the musket on her. She could detect the flashes of the fireworks even behind her closed eyelids. She screwed them up tight and heard the hammer of the musket click.

Then came the explosion.

CHAPTER 54

*S*abine waited for the pain to hit, but there was none—at least, no more than she already had. She uncurled just in time to see Visconti stagger back, a dark stain spreading on the shoulder of his white shirt. He turned toward the staircase with a howl of disbelief.

Richard loomed out of the smoke and Sabine gave a whimper of relief. It turned to one of horror as Visconti lifted his own musket and fired. Richard dived behind a crate of still-exploding fireworks and Sabine craned her neck to see if he'd been hit. He staggered to his feet as Visconti threw down his gun and lunged.

The two men engaged in a vicious tussle. Richard landed several brutal blows to Visconti's kidneys, then concentrated on his injured shoulder. They crashed into another of the crates, knocking it over. The fireworks continued to explode, screaming up into the air like banshees. Some, knocked out of alignment, raced off across the floor and disappeared down the stairs, or set fire to their neighbors.

It was like a scene from hell. Smoke billowed everywhere, with the acrid smell of sulfur and charcoal. Flashes of red and gold briefly illuminated a terrifying series of tableaus before plunging them back into darkness: Visconti, teeth bared in murderous fury, his hands around Richard's neck. Richard, fists mercilessly pounding the other man's body. Grunts of pain and labored panting.

A Catherine wheel failed to launch and spun furiously along the ground, igniting even more of the display. Little fires sprung up everywhere.

Sabine crawled away from the stinging flames and found Visconti's knife where it had fallen on the floor. She staggered to her feet and approached the two men, looking for an opening. When Visconti exposed his back, she saw her chance. She raised her arm and stabbed the blade down hard into his shoulder.

Visconti gave a shriek of pain and arched back, his arm swinging furiously to knock her away. Richard took advantage. His next blow landed square on Visconti's temple and Visconti sagged like a puppet.

Richard pushed the limp body away and stood, his chest heaving. He bent over double, hands resting on his knees as he tried to regain his breath. He was spattered in blood. His own? Or Visconti's?

"Are you hurt?" he demanded fiercely. "Answer me, Sabine. Did he hurt you?"

Sabine shook her head, even though her ribs were aching and the pain in her head made her want to vomit. He sagged in relief.

"I'm fine. Thank God you got here in time." She dragged in a shattered breath and stared down at Visconti's prone figure. "Is he dead?"

Richard stepped forward, his face intent. "Not yet."

Sabine caught his arm. "Don't," she coughed.

Richard glared at her as if she were mad. "He deserves to die."

"I know. But not like this. He should swing from the end of a rope for what he did to that girl in Paris."

Richard gave Visconti's inert body a vicious kick. "He should burn in hell," he said darkly.

"He will."

Richard heaved a furious sigh, but Sabine knew she'd won. He didn't need Visconti's death on his conscience, however satisfying he imagined vengeance might feel. It would only leave him with more scars.

She turned toward the stairs and let out a gasp of dismay. Thick gray smoke was billowing up from below. "We have to go," she croaked.

Richard would gladly have left Visconti to burn, but when she stared pointedly at the body he cursed, grabbed the other man by the collar, and dragged him none too gently toward the stairs.

It was like descending into hell; orange flames fizzed out of a crate of unused fireworks and smoke filled the small room. Sabine put her hand up to shield her face and rushed toward the entrance, stumbling out onto the grass. Richard emerged close behind her. He deposited Visconti a few yards away, then ran over to help her, and together they staggered away from the burning structure.

Fireworks were still shrieking up into the sky, dozens at a time, reflecting in the rippling surface of the lake, a continuous stream of white fire. The noise was a wall of sound that hurt her ears, a volley of cracks that sounded almost like applause. Each explosion was so loud it reverberated through her chest.

The crowd roared their appreciation, presumably believing the accidental intensity of the show was all part of a spectacular final act.

Perhaps this was what war looked like, Sabine thought dazedly. Fire dripping from the sky, streaking and screaming like comets. Explosions like dandelion heads. Something fell to the grass near her feet, and she saw it was one of the cardboard cylinders that made up the body of the fireworks.

Richard tugged her arm. "We have to—"

A blinding explosion filled her peripheral vision, a flash of orange flame accompanied by a vibration that punched through her body like a fist to the chest. Something hit her head so hard it knocked her off her feet. Or was it Richard who knocked her off her feet? She felt his arms around her, felt him propel her backward toward the lake. And then came a sudden unwelcome splash as she hit the water.

At first she froze in disbelief. Icy darkness enveloped her. She heard the dull boom of the blast muffled by the water and jerked into action. She flailed her limbs and surged to the surface, gasping for air.

The noise increased tenfold above the water—the alarmed shouts of the crowd, bellows for a fire brigade. Small chunks of debris were splashing into the water all around her as she struggled to stand. The world flashed and dimmed as a great weakness tugged at her limbs.

She called out for Richard in the darkness.

* * *

THE WATER WAS ONLY WAIST deep. Richard stumbled to his feet and grabbed Sabine from where she was floundering about in the weeds. He caught her hand and splashed to the edge of the pond, wading through the bulrushes. It was a muddy scramble up the bank, but he managed to pull her up after him.

The temple was in ruins; plumes of dark gray smoke billowed up out of what remained. His ears were ringing and his soaked clothes stuck to his body, but a great ball of elation filled him. He let out a whoop of triumph.

People were running toward them over the bridge, but he dragged Sabine against him and kissed her, hard. She seemed too dazed to respond, but he pulled back and shot her an exultant grin.

"We did it!"

Her hair was plastered to her head and a dark rivulet of mud trickled down the side of her face. He didn't think she'd ever looked more beautiful.

She put a hand up to her temple, frowned when it came back covered in mud, and opened her mouth to say something. Richard braced himself for a lecture on throwing innocent Frenchwomen into muddy ponds.

"I can't see you," she said plaintively.

She blinked, and he wondered when he'd begun to see her shortsightedness as an endearing trait. He grinned. "That's because you're blind as a bat, sweetheart."

Then he realized she really was trying to focus. Her pupils were huge and in the flickering light she was as pale as death. Her lips were bloodless.

"Richard. My head."

All his elation evaporated as he realized the front of her white fichu was pink. *Shit!* That wasn't mud. It was blood.

Her eyes rolled up in her head and he barely caught her before she hit the ground. His veins turned to ice as he turned her limp body in his arms.

"I need light!" he bellowed.

A man with a lantern reached them, but Richard hardly knew nor cared about the gathering crowd. He swept Sabine's hair back and almost vomited at the red smear that covered his palm.

Oh, Christ, no. For one hideous moment he was transported back eight years, to Paris. The same acrid scent of burning in his nose, the screams and the wails, a girl bleeding to death in his lap, warm blood soaking into his breeches as he frantically tried to stop the bleeding even as he knew it was hopeless.

He shook his head. No. This was Sabine, not Marie-Jeanne Pensol. He dragged himself out of the nightmarish vision and back to the woman in front of him. He had to think.

"Sabine, sweetheart. Talk to me. Oh, God, it's all right. You're going to be all right."

Was he trying to convince her or himself? Panic wavered in

his voice. There was blood on his hands, on her face. He brushed it from the side of her nose, leaving an obscene streak on her cheek, a crescent of red.

"We have to bind her head," he heard himself say.

A dozen hands offered forth scarves and handkerchiefs. Richard grabbed the nearest one and bundled it into a pad. He couldn't see exactly where she'd been hurt, somewhere in her hair, but he pressed it to her skull, then pulled his cravat from around his neck and wrapped it around her head.

He glanced around and saw Raven pushing through the crowd, horse in tow, his face taut with concern. Richard gathered Sabine in his arms and stood. Oh, God, she barely weighted anything. She was so . . . breakable.

Raven started to mount, but Richard shook his head. "No, I'll take her. Hand her up to me."

He transferred her carefully into Raven's arms, loath to let her go even for a moment, then jumped into the saddle and reached back down for her. He positioned her across his lap, her legs draped over one side, her head and shoulders nestling in the crook of his arm. She didn't stir, as limp as a rag doll in front of him, and his heart constricted in terror.

"Move!"

Trusting the crowd to get out of his way, he dug his heels into the horse's sides and set off at a gallop, trying to shield her from the jolt of the animal's gait. "Don't you bloody dare die!" he growled down at her.

No response. Not even the flicker of an eyelid.

CHAPTER 55

The trip back to the house was a nightmare blur. The part of his brain not focused on Sabine dimly registered the direction he needed to take. St. James's Park adjoined Green Park—quicker to go through them than navigate the crowded streets. Richard bellowed invectives for people to clear the path; they took one look at his stricken face and leaped out of the way.

Past Hyde Park Corner and Apsley House, Wellesley's home. The wind whistled past, chilling his soaking hair and clothes. It matched the cold terror in his heart. His panicked breaths echoed the drumbeat of the horse's hooves as he panted out the same pleading refrain: "Don't die. Don't die. Don't die."

Despair clawed at him. He could feel blood seeping into his shirt and cradled her cheek to his chest. He crossed into Hyde Park, sending ducks and pedestrians running for cover. As he clattered up outside number five he slid off his mount and took the steps two at a time, ignoring a blur of anxious faces, a flurry of questions.

"A doctor! Quickly!"

His voice was hoarse, but he managed to get the order out.

He rushed upstairs and into his room and laid Sabine on his bed. His heart kicked in an irregular rhythm. She looked so small.

"Wake up for me, sweetheart. Please. You have to wake up."

His voice broke in the middle as he applied more pressure to the wound. She was so pale; her skin was almost translucent. He felt for a pulse at her throat and knew a moment of stark terror when he couldn't find it, then relief as he located it. It was faint, so weak and erratic. But there.

"Where's the doctor?" he snarled.

"Minton has gone for him, sir."

Richard blinked up at Hodges, who was hovering by the bedside.

Guilt and self-loathing surged over him. He shouldn't have risked her to get to Visconti. Shouldn't have let her get within fifty miles of that murderous bastard. Dimly he registered a commotion downstairs, the thud of hurrying feet.

"Dr. Foster's here, my lord."

The man looked familiar. Richard frowned, then recalled that the physician was his neighbor. He scowled as the younger man tried to push him aside. He moved just enough to allow him access to the bed, but refused to relinquish Sabine's hand.

The doctor peeled back the makeshift bandage and Richard forced himself to look. His stomach churned. Fresh blood, bright red, seeped from a nasty cut just above her ear.

"Hmm. How did this happen?"

"There was an explosion. Something must have hit her in the head. A bit of wood, maybe? I didn't see. And she fell in a lake."

Foster pursed his lips. "That may pose a problem for infection. Head wounds can be notoriously difficult." He probed the matted hair and Richard had to look away.

"I don't believe the skull is cracked, but injuries like this often bleed heavily. How long has she been unconscious?"

Richard tried to think. "Ten, fifteen minutes?"

Foster lifted Sabine's eyelid and looked into her eye. "It is probably better that she's insensible. I'll need to sew it shut."

Richard' stomach clenched. "Use laudanum," he ordered. "Make sure she doesn't feel anything, you hear me?" It came out as a fierce growl.

"Yes, sir," Foster said, apparently unoffended by his gruff tone.

Richard watched as the doctor dribbled laudanum down Sabine's throat, then cleaned and stitched the wound. He'd seen hundreds of injuries, suffered many himself, but seeing Sabine like this almost made him retch. His fingers tingled unpleasantly.

"When will she wake up?" he demanded hoarsely.

Foster finished tying off the end of the bandage he'd wrapped around her head and stepped back. "I cannot say, my lord. She's lost a lot of blood."

Take mine, Richard wanted to say. *Cut my arm open and pour it into her.* He'd give it all, his last drop, if it would save her.

Foster sighed. "That's as much as I can do. The rest is in God's hands. She'll wake up when she's ready. Have someone change her out of those wet clothes and watch over her until she regains consciousness. I will return in a few hours, if that is acceptable, to check for signs of infection."

Richard nodded. Sabine was so still it terrified him. She was usually so vibrant, so full of life; the contrast was awful. He wanted her to wake up and start sniping at him. "I'll stay with her."

"Might I also suggest you make yourself a little more comfortable?" The smile in the other man's voice finally penetrated his gloomy thoughts. "You're making a puddle on the floor."

He looked down at himself. His knuckles were red from his fight with Visconti, but apart from a few scrapes and bruises he'd emerged practically unscathed. Unlike Sabine. Water dripped from his shirt cuffs, and his sopping breeches had made a wet patch on the Aubusson rug. He nodded absently. "I'll deal with it."

When Foster left, Hodges bustled forward with one of the

maids holding a white linen nightgown. "My lord, if you'll just let us—"

Richard took the garment. "I'll do it. Go."

He ignored the maid's scandalized gasp. Sod propriety. This was his house. He'd do as he damn well pleased. Nobody was touching Sabine except him.

He stripped her himself, moving her limbs gently so as not to hurt her, wincing as he discovered bruises already forming on her ribs and back.

A fresh wave of fury warmed his chest. That bastard had beaten her.

Richard frowned as he tried to recall what had happened to Visconti. He remembered dumping his body on the grass before the explosion. Perhaps the bastard had been killed after all. He bloody hoped so.

Hodges returned a few moments later with warm bricks wrapped in blankets and Richard arranged them around Sabine's still form, then went to find clothes for himself, resenting even the few moments it took to locate a clean shirt and dry breeches. He growled at a knock on the door, but bit back his irritation as Raven's dark head appeared.

"What in God's name happened back there?" Raven asked by way of greeting.

Richard glanced up at his friend, then back at the bed. "Look at her." He raked a hand through his still-damp hair. "It's my fault. I should never have brought her into this. Never have put her in danger." His throat tightened as he swallowed. "I failed to protect her. Just like I failed to protect Tony."

Raven sat in the chair on the opposite side of the bed. His dark brows came together. "There was nothing any of us could have done to save Tony," he said quietly. "Or those people in Paris. Sometimes we just can't get there in time."

His green eyes bored into Richard's and his face was full of stoic regret. "You have to stop blaming yourself. You haven't failed her. Visconti would have killed her when he had no further use for her; you know that. And he would have murdered someone else tonight if we hadn't stopped him."

Richard knew his friend spoke the truth, but he looked at Sabine's pale face and felt all the hope draining out of him. "What if she doesn't wake up?" he whispered.

Apparently Raven was unwilling to even discuss that possibility. "Visconti's in custody," he said instead. "I took care of him myself. You put a nice hole in his shoulder, and a stab wound in his back, but other than that he's in perfect shape to face trial. Castlereagh's delighted."

Richard nodded at the bed. "It was Sabine who stabbed him, not me."

Raven's brows lifted.

"I wish I'd left the bastard to burn," Richard said savagely. "He hit her. You should see her ribs. They're black and blue."

Raven sucked in a breath. "It's over, Rich. He'll hang for what he's done."

Richard dropped his head. He'd always thought he'd feel some kind of savage elation when he finally caught Visconti, but there was nothing. No delight. No sense of achievement. He just felt empty. Hollow. Sabine had ripped out his heart and left him an empty shell.

Raven stood. "I'm going to get a drink."

When he left, Richard lifted his head and glared at Sabine. "This is no way to behave, Miss de la Tour. Don't think you can get out of working for me by staying unconscious for the next two weeks. I still have things for you to do."

She didn't move.

"If you don't wake up I'm going to track down your money. All of it, you hear me? I'll confiscate the lot. Then I'll find that secret bloody lover of yours—the one you met in the park—and have him thrown in the Tower."

Still nothing. He switched from threats to cajoling.

"I don't care about him. Really. You can have as many lovers as you want. Just wake up for me."

Even as he said it, he knew he lied. Sabine was his. He wouldn't share her with anyone. He dropped his head into his hands. "I wouldn't blame you if you wanted to leave me, after this. It's my fault you're hurt."

His throat hurt; his voice was an aching rasp. He must have inhaled a lot of smoke. His eyes were stinging too.

"I'm sorry I didn't come sooner. But the crowd slowed us down and it took me ages to work out where you'd gone. I should have known he'd need somewhere high up to take his shot." His voice cracked. "I'm so sorry."

Still no answer. Her inky-black eyelashes lay in stark contrast to the snowy paleness of her cheeks, but he thought perhaps her lips were a little pinker than they had been before. He stroked his thumb across her cheek and along her jaw, trying to infuse her with his strength, his warmth.

"Please wake up. I love you."

Richard held his breath as he realized what he'd said. It was so clear. So simple. Why hadn't he realized it before?

He studied her face, certain she would wake up now, if only to laugh at him for his admission. In fairy tales the princess always woke up at this point. He let out a jagged breath. Ah, but Sabine scoffed at fairy tales, didn't she? Trust her to be the princess that refused to conform. She'd wake up when she was good and ready.

For some reason that thought made him feel slightly better. Sabine never played by the rules. She was a counterfeit princess, but he'd wait a hundred years for her, give up his title, his kingdom, his gold.

He loved her irreverence, her jaunty walk, the way she tilted her chin, just so, when she disagreed with something he said. She was clever and brave, and he was completely unworthy of her.

But she would wake up. Because he needed her, with a soul-deep ache in his bones.

Richard positioned himself gently on the bed next to her, careful not to jostle the doctor's handiwork. He turned on his side and gathered her into his arms. He'd failed her, used her, bullied her, and seduced her. He didn't deserve her. But she had to wake up.

He was lost without her.

CHAPTER 56

Sabine awoke to darkness and confusion. Her eyes were open, so why couldn't she see? A core-deep terror gripped her. She reached up in panic, trying to touch her face, but strong hands covered her own, stilling her movements.

"Shhh, sweetheart, it's all right."

Richard's voice, sure and low. "Richard?" she croaked. Her voice sounded odd, unused. "Why can't I see? Oh, God, am I blind?"

"It's all right. It's just a bandage. Let me help."

Her panic ebbed away as the darkness eased, lightening with the removal of the bandages. She blinked as Richard's face came into focus.

"Hello," he said solemnly.

She frowned. He looked awful—at least by his own usually high sartorial standards. His jaw was stubbled with at least a day's growth of beard and his hair stuck out in wild disarray, like Argos's fur.

"What happened?"

She started to sit up, but a terrible pain slashed across her skull and she sank back, nauseated. Flashes of memory came and

went and she frowned, unable to sort one from another. A fire—
but not the one in which she'd burned the money with Anton.
Another one, with Richard. And Visconti.

Complete recollection came to her. The fireworks. The explosion. Visconti. Blood. She groaned. The two bags of money they'd
printed had been in there. They must have burned too. Sabine
closed her eyes. What a waste of good counterfeits!

She was so tired. Richard was holding her hand, and she
guessed the warm weight by her feet was Argos, curled up on the
bed. She smiled and slid back into the darkness.

It was daylight when she woke again and she became
conscious of a weight on her arm. She turned her head cautiously
and saw Richard next to her; he was asleep, his head resting on
the pillows, his hand in hers.

He stirred, as if sensing her regard. His amber eyes opened
and a look of sweet relief creased his face. The dimple appeared.

"You're awake."

His voice was gravelly, deep with sleep. It made her stomach
clench. She blinked. "How long have I been asleep?"

"Two days, give or take."

A jolt of panic made her sit up. The room twirled around her
like a waltz. "Two days! What day is it?"

He regarded her with steady amusement. "Sunday, the fifth of
May. Why do you ask?"

She bit her lip. *Merde!* Malet was expecting his money today.
She could only hope that if he came to the house, Hodges would
turn him away with the excuse that she wasn't receiving visitors.
And Anton's ship wasn't leaving until the eighth—thank God she
hadn't slept through that; she'd promised to be there to see
him off.

"What happened to Visconti?" she asked.

"Tried, convicted, and hanged," Richard said with grim satisfaction. "With all the evidence we'd collected on him over the
years, it took the jury less than ten minutes to find him guilty of

treason. Neither the Prince Regent nor the lord chancellor wanted the publicity of a public execution. He was hanged yesterday morning at Newgate."

Sabine squeezed his hand. "Good. And the plotters?"

"Arrested. They're all looking at lengthy prison sentences or transportation." Richard rose from the bed. "I'll go and tell Heloise you're up. She's been nagging me for two days to come and see you. Mother, too." He gestured at the side table. "I brought some books for you to read. And there's a drink of water there."

Sabine watched him go with a pang in her heart, then inspected the books he'd chosen for her. On the top was William Shakespeare's *The Tempest*. She opened it up and found her favorite passage:

> *Our revels now are ended. These our actors,*
> *As I foretold you, were all spirits and*
> *Are melted into air, into thin air:*
> *And, like the baseless fabric of this vision,*
> *The cloud-capp'd towers, the gorgeous palaces,*
> *The solemn temples, the great globe itself,*
> *Yea, all which it inherit, shall dissolve*
> *And, like this insubstantial pageant faded,*
> *Leave not a rack behind. We are such stuff*
> *As dreams are made on, and our little life*
> *Is rounded with a sleep.*

Hot tears stung her eyes. Her time with Richard was at an end too. It had been a brief interlude, a beguiling fantasy. But now it was time to return to real life. Anton had prior claim to her loyalty. She had to help him escape Malet.

Richard, of all people, should understand the power of such a bond; he shared the same link with his band of brothers, Raven, Nic, and Kit. His loyalty to those fortunate enough to have it was absolute.

Sabine closed her eyes. If only she could give Anton real money, so he wouldn't have to spend the fake cash she'd given him. She hated the idea of allowing her forgeries onto the open market. But Richard wouldn't pay her until the end of her month of service, and by her calculations she still had twelve days to go. She couldn't very well ask him for an advance.

And how on earth was she going to get herself to the Thames docks to say goodbye to Anton as she'd promised?

Her fretting was interrupted by Heloise, who breezed into the room with a delighted smile. She raced over to the bed, hugged Sabine gently, then settled in the chair to one side of the mattress in a flurry of skirts.

"Oh, I'm so glad you're recovering! We were all so worried. Richard barely left your side and Raven told me how brave you were, facing Visconti. And guess what?"

Sabine shook her head, bemused at the torrent of chatter. "What?"

"The Prince Regent has requested your personal attendance at a ball he's hosting on Wednesday evening. Castlereagh told him of your involvement in catching Visconti and the prince means to honor you for your bravery!"

Sabine's mouth fell open. "He does?"

Heloise nodded. "The recognition will need to be secret, of course, due to the sensitive nature of the circumstances. Very few people are aware that an attack was foiled and the prince doesn't want it made public. But he asked for you to be there. Do you think you'll be well enough to go?"

Sabine's heart sank. Anton's ship sailed on Wednesday. If everything went to plan, she wouldn't be here.

The thought of leaving her new friends, of leaving Richard, made her chest tighten up in misery, but she forced herself to sound enthusiastic. "Of course! It was only a little bump on the head." She patted the bandage at her temple and smiled, but she desperately wanted to cry.

Thankfully Heloise didn't notice her sudden pallor. "Good. Because I have the most wonderful idea for a dress . . ."

* * *

TWO DAYS later Sabine was feeling a lot better. She moved from Richard's bedchamber back to her own, and while she still had a small bandage on her head, her splitting headache had diminished and the bruises on her body were fading.

She spent the morning comfortably ensconced with Heloise, chatting and laughing, each moment bittersweet because Sabine knew how soon she'd be leaving. She was also humiliatingly convinced that the other girl knew exactly how involved she'd become with her brother.

Heloise put down the pattern book they'd been studying and tilted her head. "Did you know that etymology—the study of words—is a particular hobby of mine?"

Sabine made a little hum of interest. "Really?"

"Yes. In fact, my love of languages is what led me into code-breaking. Words are all linked, you know. They all have a common thread somewhere down the line. You just have to trace the right path backwards to find the answer to the puzzle, like Theseus following Ariadne's string to escape the Minotaur's maze."

Sabine wrinkled her nose, not sure what point Heloise was trying to make. "Hmmm?"

"Anyway, I was thinking about the word *forge* the other night," Heloise said. "In your honor." She shot Sabine a conspiratorial grin. "You, obviously, associate the word with forging money, or coins, or documents. You use it to mean 'making something fake.'"

Sabine shrugged. "I suppose so."

"But have you ever considered that the word isn't always used negatively? To forge also means simply to create, as in 'to forge something anew.' The way a blacksmith creates something with his hammer and anvil." Heloise cast her a sideways look. "One can forge a new life, for example. Something different from the life we thought we had planned."

Sabine narrowed her eyes. What was the other girl hinting at?

"Also to forge ahead," Heloise continued blithely. "To push your way through something difficult and emerge successfully on the other side. To do something no one else has done."

Her innocent expression was not very convincing. Heloise was meddling.

"I've never thought of it," Sabine murmured.

Heloise patted her hand and shot her a warm smile. "Perhaps you should," she said meaningfully.

An hour after Heloise left, a smiling Hodges arrived with a tea tray. "His lordship sent this up for you, Miss de la Tour," he said. "For the prince's ball tomorrow evening."

Sabine gave an inward sigh. She'd seen very little of Richard over the past few days, and now, it seemed, they were back to 'Lord Lovell' and 'Miss de la Tour.' She told herself it was for the best.

Hodges set down the tray and handed her a leather-covered box. Sabine's stomach dropped. When the servant left, she opened the lid and stared at the necklace inside. Two rows of perfect diamonds sparkled like fireworks against the night sky, a shower of pure color and light. She lifted it from the velvet and the pendant stones trembled with the shaking of her hand. She unfolded the accompanying note. Richard's negligent scrawl commanded the page.

Sabine,

These are for you. They are not paste: I'd never dare give you anything other than genuine stones. I know you can tell the difference.

With utmost respect and gratitude,

R.

Sabine closed her eyes, shutting out the beauty of the gift. She'd never seen anything so lovely. The elegant simplicity of the design was exactly what she would have chosen for herself.

Her throat felt hot and scratchy. She wasn't worthy of real diamonds. She was paste, a fake. Heloise might talk about forging a new path and creating a new life for herself, but there was no future for her with Richard. He was a wealthy, titled, respectable member of the ton. She was a criminal with nothing but lies and deceit to her name.

A tight knot of misery balled in her stomach. Tears stung her eyes. She couldn't keep this gift, however much she wanted to. What use did a counterfeiter have for jewels? She wasn't going to the prince's ball tomorrow. She was going back to Paris.

The very idea of giving them away, or selling them, made her feel physically sick, but what choice did she have? Anton needed them far more than she did. He could sell them, use the money. Sentiment had no place in her life. There was only necessity.

She found paper and ink in the library, and addressed a letter to the jewelers Rundell, Bridge & Rundell. Lord Lovell "respectfully requests to return these jewels" as they "did not find favor with the lady for whom they were intended."

Sabine bit her lip at writing that awful untruth, then added that "a cash refund paid to the bearer of this note would be perfectly acceptable." Not wanting the jewelers to think they had somehow offended their client, she added that they could be "fully assured of His Lordship's continuing patronage in the future &c." She signed it with Richard's name, blew on the ink to dry it, and carefully folded the missive.

Who could she trust to run this errand for her? She glanced out of the window. Will Ambrose was half-heartedly sweeping the crossing with his twig broom, obviously there to keep an eye on the street. Or on her. When he saw her at the window, he grinned and waved. Sabine beckoned for him to come to the house.

When a footman showed the boy into the room a few minutes later, Sabine handed him the letter. "Lord Lovell would like you to deliver this for him," she said, glad her voice did not quaver. "He's trusting you with collecting a large amount of money and bringing it directly back here."

The boy examined the outside of the letter and apparently accepted the handwriting as Hampden's. His cherubic, if grimy, face wrinkled. "'Ow come 'e ain't askin' me 'imself?"

"He had to go out," Sabine temporized. "I'd go myself, but as you can see, I'm still not fully recovered." She pointed to the bandage on her head.

Will shot her a calculating gaze. "Wot's in it for me?" His teeth were surprisingly white when he smiled.

Sabine sighed, well aware she was being manipulated by an adolescent felon. "Ten pounds," she said promptly.

The boy's eyes widened. "Done!" He headed for the door.

"Make sure you come straight back here," Sabine called. "And bring the money directly to me."

Will nodded and turned, his hand on the door handle. "I 'eard about wot you did, lady. Stabbin' that Frenchie. Nice job, that." He slipped out of the door before she could find an appropriate response.

Sabine sank into a chair and bit her lip to prevent herself from calling to the boy to stay. Richard would hate her when he discovered what she'd done. Selling his gift was the ultimate betrayal of his trust, an insult to everything they'd shared, everything she'd hoped. She hated having to do this to him.

She dashed away her tears. If nothing else, this just proved the impossibility of her staying with him any longer. He didn't deserve someone like her in his life. And he didn't need her anymore. Visconti was dead, the plotters arrested. Their worlds might have collided temporarily, but now it was time to part.

Better to leave now before he tired of her, as he'd tired of every other woman in his life.

Will returned less than an hour later with three hundred pounds, and Sabine quashed the stab of remorse that clenched her stomach. It was done. She would give half to Anton and keep half for herself. And as soon as she saw her friend safely onto his ship tomorrow, she would make her way back to Paris. She had promises to keep, broken heart or not.

CHAPTER 57

Sabine barely slept. All night she'd listened for an indication that Richard was in his room, hoping he would come to her, but dawn arrived with no sign of him. Her heart clenched in misery.

Her farewell note to him had been almost impossible to write. There was so much she wanted to say that in the end she said as little as possible. She simply told him that she was ending their agreement early and taking the diamond necklace in lieu of her ten thousand pounds. She signed it, *Adieu, Sabine.*

She hid her money under her skirts along with a few sketches she'd done of Richard, and the travel papers for Marie Lambert. She brushed off Josie's concerned fluttering, assuring her all she wanted was to read uninterrupted in the library for an hour or two.

With one last, longing glance at the portrait of Saskia, she pushed up the sash window. Argos, who'd followed her in from the hall, gave a miserable whimper, almost as if he knew what she planned. She bent and kissed the top of his shaggy head. "Take care of him, won't you?" she choked.

The dog pawed her skirts and shot her a look of heart-breaking disappointment.

"I can't stay!" Sabine groaned, knowing how ridiculous it was to be having a conversation with an animal that couldn't even reply.

Argos dropped his head on his crossed paws and eyed her reproachfully.

Sabine climbed over the windowsill, dropped to the ground, and sped down the street.

* * *

RICHARD OPENED his eyes to the disconcerting sight of his younger sister, Heloise. He frowned.

He'd spent the evening at Raven's house, determined to stay away from the temptation that Sabine presented by getting thoroughly and uncharacteristically drunk. Raven, good friend that he was, had matched him drink for drink. Somewhere around the third bottle, Richard had slumped back in his chair and regarded the fire dolefully. "Bloody woman."

Raven frowned. "Which one?"

"My one," Richard said.

"Ah."

Richard took another drink. "There was nothing wrong with my life before she came along," he muttered crossly. "It was perfect. I had a title. A fortune. Any mistress I wanted. No need for some bloody woman to come and turn it all upside down."

Raven nodded sagely.

Richard finished his glass and poured another. "That's what she does, you know—she creates carnage wherever she goes. If it's not forging my signature, it's causing havoc in a public street. She's like those typhoons at sea. The ones that suck a man up and carry him away, then spit him out a thousand miles from home, broken, bewildered, and exhausted."

Raven lifted his glass in a toast. "I know. She's marvelous."

Richard groaned, unable to refute it. "God, why her? She's socially inept, but so charming she wraps everyone around her little finger. She even has the bloody Prince Regent eating out of her hand!"

Raven shrugged. "You need a little madness in your life, Rich. And of course you find her irresistibly attractive—you've never encountered anyone like her. She refuses to do your bidding on an hourly basis. And she's probably the first woman not related to you who hasn't offered herself up on a platter."

Richard scowled into his glass. "She is not a restful woman."

"Ha. You can rest when you are dead."

"Every time I think I know what she's going to do—what any other, perfectly rational woman would do in her place—she turns around and does precisely the opposite!"

Raven refilled his glass. "Ordinary women don't interest you. It's the curse of men like us; we're fated to be attracted to extraordinary women." He took a deep swallow. "Admit it. Normal women have been throwing themselves at you for the past fifteen years and you've never felt more than a glimmer of interest in any of them. But this one stubborn, infuriating creature is utterly necessary to your future happiness."

Richard glared at him.

Raven grinned. "You are considering that a world without her would be bleak and unchallenging," he continued. "You are considering that the only way to keep such a vexatious creature near you is not with threats or bribery or brute physical strength, but with something even more drastic. By admitting that you love her. And by offering a legally binding, always-and-forever, till-death-do-us-part option: marriage."

Richard dropped his head back against the chair. "Oh, God."

Raven cuffed him playfully on the shoulder. "It happens to the best of us."

Richard had no answer to that. He uncorked anther bottle. After that things got a little hazy.

"Get up, you dolt!"

Heloise's voice brought him sharply back to the present. He closed his eyes as Thor's hammer pounded mercilessly on his skull. "Whaddyouwant?"

His thankless sister whacked him on the arm. "Will Ambrose just saw Sabine escaping out of your library window."

Richard sat up, instantly awake. "She what?"

He jumped to his feet, fury heating his blood. Infuriating woman! She couldn't be trusted an inch. Where did she think she was going? To meet that cursed lover of hers? She couldn't leave. They had an agreement, dammit. She still had ten days to go.

He stalked out into the hall, tugging on his crumpled jacket as he went. Will was waiting by the door.

"Which way did she go?" Richard demanded.

"Hailed a cab," Will said cheerfully. "Told the driver to take 'er to the Pool o' London, near London Bridge."

Richard swore. She was leaving the bloody country!

"Raven, I need a horse."

Raven appeared in the doorway, looking as rumpled and hung over as Richard felt. He nodded toward his stables. "Of course you do. Help yourself."

CHAPTER 58

*T*he *Falcon* turned out to be a large sailing vessel with two square-rigged masts. Sabine thanked her cab driver and stepped cautiously onto the wharf, dodging some sailors carrying crates of dry goods up the wooden gangplank.

A shout from above made her crane her neck and she smiled as Anton raced down the walkway and enfolded her in a smothering hug.

"You look much better," she commented. His face was back to normal, the swelling gone, save for a few small patches of yellowish bruising under his jaw.

"You don't," he said bluntly. His concerned gaze went to the bandage she still wore on her head. "What happened to you?"

Sabine told him of her adventure with Visconti. Anton whistled in astonishment. "*Dieu!*" he breathed. "You could have been killed."

Sabine nodded. "Yes, but Richard saved me."

She bit her lip and Anton tugged her hand, as if sensing her desire to avoid that particular topic. "Come and see my cabin. We don't sail for at least another hour."

Sabine smiled at his boyish enthusiasm as he showed her his

comfortable, well-appointed berth in the middle of the ship, complete with a deck skylight and whale-oil lamp. They met the captain, Mr. Lewis, and several of his fellow passengers, including a vicar and his wife. Anton introduced her as his sister Marie, come to wish him a bon voyage.

When they reemerged on deck, they went over to the green-painted rail and looked out at the bustle of activity along the riverfront. "You can still come with me, you know." Anton glanced sideways at her. "It's not too late."

Sabine shook her head. "I'm for Paris. I still have things to do."

Anton shrugged. They'd had this argument countless times on the trip from France.

"Oh, I have this for you." Sabine reached into the pocket of her cloak. "One hundred and fifty pounds of real English money. You shouldn't have to use the counterfeits at all."

Anton whistled. "How did you get this?"

"Legally," she said curtly. She didn't want to think about her betrayal; it made her chest hurt.

Anton pocketed the money and gazed out over the water. "I'm looking forward to a fresh start, you know. A new challenge. America is a land of opportunity for men like me." His eyes gleamed with roguish anticipation. "Just think—a whole continent of women desperate for the love of a good Frenchman." He chuckled. "It will be a great adventure."

Sabine smiled, even as her throat tightened at the thought of him leaving. "Behave yourself, Anton Carnaud!"

She couldn't hold him back anymore. He'd made so many sacrifices for her over the years; she had to release him from that obligation. He needed to live his own life without constantly worrying about her. She was twenty-four. Old enough to stand on her own two feet.

She would miss his easy friendship, though. This must have been how Richard felt when he'd lost his beloved brother Tony.

This wrenching, aching sadness at the thought that they might never meet again.

Anton put his arm around her and squeezed her to his side. "Stop looking so sad, little one. It's not forever. Just long enough for Malet to forget I exist. I'll be back in Paris before you can print your next million."

Sabine blinked back the tears that threatened to fall. "I know."

"I'll write to you," he said coaxingly. "In between making my fortune and beating off love-struck women, that is."

She gave a watery chuckle. "Oh, Anton, I'm going to miss you."

A commotion on the dock below drew their attention. Sabine leaned over the rail and then shrank back in horror.

"Oh no," she whispered.

Captain Lewis bustled to the side to investigate. "What's ado?" he shouted down.

Richard's voice carried with awful clarity in the crisp morning air. "I have reason to suspect you are harboring a fugitive, sir."

Sabine paled at his authoritative tone. Richard's footsteps stomped up the gangplank and she shrank back as his gaze found her unerringly across the deck. Her heart somersaulted. She caught Anton's sleeve, but instead of accosting them, Richard turned and addressed the captain.

"Allow me to introduce myself, sir. I am Richard Hampden, Viscount Lovell."

The captain bowed. "How may I help you, Lord Lovell?"

"I regret to inform you, Captain, but you have a woman on board who is attempting to flee the country."

The captain's brows rose. "Is that so?"

Richard nodded in her direction. "Her name—or should I say, one of her names—is Sabine de la Tour."

The captain frowned and glanced at her over his shoulder.

"There must be some mistake, my lord. Why, that is Christian Lambert and his sister."

"She's no more his sister than I am," Richard said dryly.

Sabine's cheeks burned with humiliation. The vicar, his wife, and the other passengers were now all regarding her with assorted degrees of suspicion and horror.

Richard strode up and grabbed her by the arm. She tugged away.

"Get off me!"

He turned back to the captain. "This woman has so many names I'm not surprised she finds it hard to remember them all," he said. "She's known as Sabine de la Tour. And Philippe Lacorte. And, most recently, Sabine Hampden—my lawfully wedded wife."

"Your what?!" Sabine gasped. "Your wife? I'm not his wife!"

Richard shot her a quelling look and glanced at the captain. "She recently sustained a blow to the head—you see the bandage?" He pointed at the dressing she still wore. "Alas, she seems to have forgotten not only me, but our recent marriage, too."

"Liar!" Sabine shrieked. "I might have had a bump on the head, but I would never forget if I'd married you! I would never be so demented. And you—" She turned to the captain. "He's Viscount Lovell. Don't you think if we *had* been married you would have heard about it? The newspapers would have been full of reports."

She shot Richard a superior smile.

"Well, that's true," the captain said, suddenly doubtful. He turned to Richard. "What proof do you have that she is your wife?"

Richard held up one finger. "Ah."

He drew a piece of paper from his waistcoat like a magician. A very smug, satisfied magician—and smiled down at her in a way that could only be described as Machiavellian.

"We were married by special license." He unfolded the parchment and angled it for her to see. "Your name: Sabine de la Tour, spinster, twenty-four." He shot her a pitying look. "And me, Richard Frederick Montague Hampden, bachelor, thirty-two. Dated Friday of last week, and signed by none other than the archbishop of Canterbury himself."

He showed it to the captain.

"This doesn't prove anything," Sabine said. "A special license merely grants permission to marry. It does not prove that the two people listed on it have actually done the deed."

Hampden addressed the captain again. His calm, assured tone made her want to kick him.

"The reason you haven't heard about it is because it was a private affair. I was so desperate to marry her that I couldn't bear to wait the three weeks necessary to read the banns in church, so I procured a special license."

"It's a fake," Sabine said stoutly.

Richard feigned insulted affront. "*Tsk.* Are you accusing me, an upstanding member of the House of Lords, of falsifying a legal document?" His dimple reappeared. "And what would you know about fake documents?" he added wickedly.

"This is a monstrous falsehood!" Sabine howled.

"She really does have problems recalling we are married." Richard smiled confidingly at the captain. "It was a very small service. Just a handful of close family and friends." He furrowed his brow in fake concern and gazed down at her. "Don't you remember it, darling? The tiny chapel at my parents' country estate? You looked so beautiful. You wore a silver gown like Princess Charlotte's, scalloped all over with beads. You looked like a star."

The vicar's wife sighed lustily and shot Sabine a reproachful look for daring to forget such a magical moment.

Richard's eyes filled with mocking laughter. He put his arm around her waist, pulled her close, tilted her chin with his fingers, and gazed down into her eyes. "I can forgive you forgetting the marriage ceremony, but surely you recall the wedding night?"

The vicar's wife gasped in scandalized delight.

Sabine opened her mouth to berate him, but he didn't give her the chance.

"Perhaps this will refresh your memory." He kissed her. Hard.

Sabine's knees buckled and for one dark, glorious moment she forgot she was running away and kissed him back.

He drew back, panting. "Ring any bells?"

She smacked him on the arm. "Let me go! I don't want you!"

His eyes flared, and she realized he was utterly furious beneath his urbane exterior.

"I don't want you!" she repeated fervently. "I came here to meet my lover!" She pointed at Anton, who had been standing back, enjoying the show. "I am eloping with him!"

This elicited more gasps from their avid audience.

"Now wait a minute!" blustered the captain. "I'll not be party to an elopement. Or to your planned adultery, madam. I apologize, my lord, for any insult."

Sabine groaned at his obsequious bow to Richard. The toadying idiot. "There is no adultery," she cried. "I tell you, I'm not married to this man!"

Richard shot her a quelling glance. His lips were a thin line and his eyes blazed. She quaked at the depths of emotion she saw there.

"Do you deny you could be carrying my child even now?"

All the blood left her face. Oh, God—she hadn't even considered that possibility. "I—it's—"

Her stricken pause was proof enough for the captain.

"Good Lord, what falsehood!" he thundered. "My Lord, please remove this woman from my ship at once!"

"I won't go!" Sabine shrieked, backing away.

Anton stepped in front of her and intercepted Richard's

advance. He held up his hand. "One minute, if you please, monsieur. If I might have a moment to speak with my friend?"

Richard glared at him as though he were trying to burn him to a cinder, but stopped. He folded his arms and gave a lordly nod.

Anton turned Sabine toward him. "Sabine, are you truly married to this man?"

He spoke rapidly in French and she answered in the same language, praying it would be too fast and too low for Richard to follow.

"No! I'm not, I swear!"

"He would like you to be," Anton whispered.

She gaped at him. "What? Are you mad? He doesn't want me. I'm nothing but a nuisance."

Anton shook his head. "He cares for you. Why else would he go to such lengths to chase after you?"

"I don't know!" Sabine hissed, exasperated. "He likes chasing people. That's what he does. But once he has them, he loses interest, believe me."

Anton gave a wry chuckle and glanced over her shoulder at Richard. "He hasn't lost interest in you. He watches you with a hunger that is almost painful to witness. He wants you so badly he aches with it. And he fights himself, because he thinks he is alone in his regard." He cupped her face and grinned down at her. "But he's not, is he?"

Sabine felt her cheeks suffusing with heat. "Of course he is! He drives me insane. He—"

"Do you love him, little one?"

"I don't—I mean—"

Whatever Anton saw in her face must have answered his question. He gave a delighted chuckle. "In that case, let me do you a favor."

The next thing Sabine knew, he'd pulled her into his arms and was pressing a fervent kiss on her astonished mouth.

"What are you doing?!" she gasped as he straightened her back up and gave a piratical grin. He leaned down to whisper in her ear. "You won't think so right now, but someday you'll thank me for that. I've just done you a great service."

He shot Richard a cocky look and Sabine was suddenly glad she stood between them. The hard set of Richard's jaw hinted at a longing to do bodily harm. He started forward, arm outstretched, as if to pull her away from Anton, but she sent him a warning glare. He stopped. Satisfied, she took the opportunity to give Anton a fierce hug.

"Goodbye, Anton."

Anton cleared his throat, his tone gruff. "We've had some adventures, you and I, eh?" He ruffled her hair in the same affectionate gesture as always. "You should go home, *chèrie*."

"I will," she muttered. "If I can get away from that awful man."

He shook his head and glanced over at Richard again. "I don't mean Paris. Home is wherever someone who loves you is waiting."

Her heart clenched in misery as she took his meaning. "I can't, Anton. It's impossible—"

"As touching as this little scene is," Richard's frosty tone cut through their farewell, "it's time to go. Madam?" He gestured grandly at the gangplank.

Sabine pulled back from Anton's embrace and scowled at Richard.

"I am coming, Lord Lovell," she said regally, and swept across the deck.

CHAPTER 59

The first ten minutes of the ride back to Upper Brook Street was accomplished in strained, furious silence. Sabine crossed her arms, not trusting herself to speak. Richard sat on his side of the carriage and glared broodily out of the window, as if the very sight of her sickened him.

"I wasn't leaving with Anton, you know," she muttered finally, unable to keep quiet any longer.

Richard turned and glared at her. "Pardon?"

"I said, I wasn't leaving with Anton. I was about to disembark when you so rudely interrupted us. I was saying goodbye. He is a dear friend. God knows when I will see him again." Her voice quavered and she bit her lip, but Richard ignored the embarrassing display of weakness.

"No need to kiss him quite so enthusiastically," he said acerbically. "I have plenty of 'dear friends.' I don't embrace any of them with such abandon."

Sabine shook her head. "You wouldn't understand."

Richard's gaze narrowed as he sat forward abruptly and she reared back into her seat. Her heart pounded in her throat.

"What I understand, madam, is that I have just allowed a man who is undoubtedly your partner in crime to leave the country unimpeded. I could have had him arrested on the spot. No doubt he's the one with whom you have been communicating these past three weeks, hmm?"

Sabine's temper snapped. She cursed him roundly in French, using every insult, every gutter word she could think of to disparage him. "You are an idiot!" she spat. "*Un bête.*" Stupid, a beast. "*Tu me rends fou!*" You make me crazy.

"*Et tu as la colère de diable,*" he snapped back. And you have the devil's own temper.

Her heart thudded to a stop. Hearing him speak in her native tongue was a shock.

He noted her surprise and raised his brows, mocking her. "I have a French mother. *Je le parle aussi même que toi, ma chère.*" I speak it as well as you, my sweet.

He had a melting liquid accent, utterly beguiling. Sabine's heart contracted. It was the aristocratic French of her parents. She'd forgotten how different it was from the rough Parisian dialect she'd grown accustomed to with Anton and his father.

And then another thought struck her. Oh, God, had he heard what she'd said to Anton? She'd practically admitted that she loved him. How utterly humiliating!

With one final, frustrated glare, Richard sat back and resumed brooding, and Sabine breathed a sigh of relief. When they reached the house she braced herself for the interrogation that was sure to follow, but they were intercepted in the hallway by Hodges.

"Ah, Miss de la Tour," he said, clearly relieved. "You are home. You have a visitor. The same foreign gentleman who called on you before. He has been insistent on seeing you for several days now."

Richard's brows lowered in confusion, but Sabine's stomach dropped to the floor. Oh, *merde*. She'd forgotten about Malet.

"I have put him in the drawing room." Hodges smiled serenely.

Sabine stifled a groan. Could the day get any worse?

Any hope of meeting with Malet alone was quashed as Richard trailed her into the drawing room. Sabine found herself torn between resenting his presence and being glad of his silent protection. Her knees were quaking.

Malet wasted no time on preliminaries. He leaped up and jabbed a stubby finger in her direction.

"Where is my money?" he boomed. "My patience has run out, madame. Where is Philippe Lacorte?"

Sabine steadied herself with a hand on the back of a chair. "Gone," she said simply. "He left on a ship for Boston this morning."

Feigning a coolness she certainly did not feel, she glanced over at Richard. "We saw him off ourselves, is that not so, Lord Lovell?"

Richard's face was inscrutable and for a moment she wondered if he would play along with her charade, but he answered politely enough. "It is indeed."

Malet's mustache bristled in fury. "And my money?"

"Lacorte burned it," she said.

Malet's face turned a mottled, unbecoming red. "What?"

"He burned it," Sabine repeated triumphantly. "Three weeks ago. On a bonfire in the Bois de Vincennes. I helped him do it."

From the corner of her eye she saw Richard's eyebrows rise, but Malet leaped forward. "I don't believe you! Tell me where it is!" he bellowed.

Richard caught him by the collar before he could touch Sabine. "I do hope you weren't thinking of assaulting my fiancée, General." His voice was smooth, but Malet didn't miss the edge of steel in it.

"Fiancée?" he spluttered.

Richard's smile was pure triumph. "Why yes, you're one of the first to know, actually." He shot Sabine an adoring look. "Miss de la Tour has accepted my suit." He patted Malet's lapels as he released him and stepped back. "Be a good man and keep it to yourself for a few days, won't you? We haven't told the family yet."

Malet appeared nonplussed. He opened and closed his mouth a few times like a landed fish. "I wish you happiness," he said finally.

"And I do hope," Richard said softly, moving to stand beside Sabine and threading his fingers through hers in an outward show of solidarity, "I do hope that you will cease tormenting Miss de la Tour with your foolish accusations. Sabine has no knowledge of Philippe Lacorte. Or your money. You will not disturb her peace again."

Malet's face was almost purple now, but he clearly realized he'd been thwarted. "As you say," he muttered. "I apologize for taking up your time, Miss de la Tour."

He bowed stiffly and made his exit.

Sabine almost sagged with relief. She didn't know if Malet had believed her about burning the money or not, but there was nothing he could do about it now. And at least Anton was safe from his wrath.

Richard was still holding her hand. She tugged her fingers free and stepped away. Standing so close to him caused a physical ache.

"I do wish you would stop telling all and sundry I am either your wife or your fiancée," she said crossly. "It is ridiculous."

Richard's face was granite. He gestured toward the door to the salon. "Into the library, Miss de la Tour. We still have some unfinished business."

Sabine bit her lip. It was time for the reckoning.

She stalked across the hall and into the library and was reminded of their very first meeting. Had it really been only three weeks ago? She felt as though she'd lived a lifetime since then.

Richard positioned himself behind his desk, every inch the powerful, autocratic Lord Lovell, and gestured for her to take the opposite seat. He picked up his fountain pen.

Sabine's stomach clenched in panic. Where was the passionate, teasing man who'd made love to her? She felt like a schoolgirl pulled in front of the headmaster for some expulsion-worthy infringement.

Richard's gaze caught hers and she couldn't seem to look away.

"Might I remind you of our bargain, Miss de la Tour?" he said softly. "You agreed to work for me for one whole month, in exchange for ten thousand pounds. And yet here we are, with ten days still to go, and you appear to be reneging on the deal."

His expression was polite, unreadable. He was a cold stranger. Sabine bit her lip and dropped her gaze.

"I am sorry," she said, relieved that her voice didn't waver. "But I have decided to forfeit the money and end the agreement now. You have achieved your objective, which was to entrap the English plotters. If you will excuse me—" She started to rise, but his next words stopped her.

"I will not excuse you," he said curtly. "You agreed to disclose the location of your fake fortune before you left."

Sabine's heart shriveled in her chest. So that was what he wanted. He didn't care about her leaving. He only wanted to ensure she didn't wreak havoc on the country with her counterfeits. His lack of faith in her made her chest ache. Surely he knew she would never do such a thing.

She closed her eyes. There was nothing for it; it was time to be completely honest.

CHAPTER 60

"All right. I will tell you the absolute truth."

"That would make a refreshing change," he said with searing sarcasm.

That stung. She'd given him her body, her heart, her soul—but he still didn't trust her. Not that she could blame him, of course. She'd done nothing but lie to him for weeks. She took a deep breath.

"There is no counterfeit fortune. It isn't hidden anywhere. What I told Malet was the truth. I really did burn it. The same day I stole it. Before I even came to England."

She braved a glance up at him. Those amber eyes burned into her like hot coals and she felt as though he were trying to read her soul.

Sabine clutched her hands in her lap to still their shaking. She'd never felt so vulnerable, so exposed. With the truth out, she had no leverage against him. There were no threats or promises she could make to manipulate him. She could only trust that he wouldn't harm her. Or imprison her.

"It has all been a bluff," she said. "There is no threat to Britain. The only fake money I brought from Paris was a thousand pounds. Five hundred was stolen from Anton. Of the remaining five hundred, I gave half to him, and you took the rest."

She glared across the desk, recalling that particular episode. Hampden wasn't entirely guiltless, either. "I kept one set of British printing plates, too—for the ten-pound note—which I gave to you to help catch Visconti."

Not that he'd appreciated the gesture. She raised her chin, refusing to be cowed. "I may not have stayed the entire month, Lord Lovell, but I have sacrificed more than enough on behalf of you and your country."

His expression showed neither surprise nor sympathy. Did he believe her about destroying the money? Or did he think she was lying yet again? She couldn't tell, but she couldn't seem to stop talking, now that she'd started.

"I never really lied to you." To her horror, she realized she was on the verge of tears. She curled her fists so her nails pressed into her palms. "I may have omitted certain pertinent facts, but I have never outright lied."

"Do you expect my thanks?" he asked sardonically.

She shook her head. "No. But I expect you to let me go. Our agreement is over. I wish to return to France."

The pen drummed on the desktop. "You didn't like the necklace I bought for you?"

She stilled. *Merde.* So he knew about that, did he? She swallowed the lump in her throat. "I did. It was very beautiful. But Anton needed the money more. It was the only way I could think of to raise some capital so he wouldn't have to spend counterfeits." She trailed off miserably.

Hampden's brows rose. "I suppose it never occurred to you to trust me? To simply ask me to help your friend?" His tone was light, as though he were merely curious about her answer.

"You might have arrested Anton for treason. I couldn't take the risk. He's my oldest friend. He saved my life."

Richard nodded, but didn't deny the charge. His long fingers turned the pen over and over. "I have an offer for you. A proposition, if you will."

She raised her brows.

"Castlereagh wants you to stay. The Bank of England has launched an inquiry aimed at finding an 'inimitable' design for their banknotes and they want you to help them design it. Who better than a counterfeiter to dream up new ways to stop counterfeiting? You know all the tricks, all the processes."

Sabine's head swam in disbelief. Of all the things she'd expected, it hadn't been this.

Richard seemed to realize she couldn't frame a response, because he continued. "It would be a crime to squander your extraordinary talents. They want to offer you the post of official engraver for the Bank of England. Based here in London."

A thousand possibilities flashed through her brain. Oh, she was so tempted to accept! To be able to use her skills without fear of arrest, to gain the security and stability she'd been craving her whole life, would be a dream come true. She could be part of a team again, doing something useful to bring criminals like Visconti to justice.

But accepting the job would mean staying close to Richard, and that could only lead to heartbreak. She loved him. To be relegated to nothing more than a work colleague would be torture. And the idea of watching him take another mistress or marry some suitable society heiress in the future would be beyond awful.

Richard was patiently awaiting her answer. She swallowed the hot tightness in her throat. "With regret, I must decline."

He shrugged, as if her refusal meant no more to him than Hodges telling him they were out of claret. "All right. I promised to make the offer," he said lightly. "I didn't think you'd take it."

Disappointment and misery twined together in her chest. Didn't he care for her at all? She started to get up.

"One more thing, Miss de la Tour," he said casually. "Before you leave, I'd like your professional opinion on this—"

He reached into his coat and pulled out the same special license he'd shown to the captain on the ship. He slid it across the desk and she took it automatically. "Does that look like a fake to you?"

Sabine frowned and bent to study the parchment:

Charles, by Divine Providence, Archbishop of Canterbury, Primate of all England and Metropolitan, by the Authority of Parliament lawfully authorized for the Purposes within written: To our well-beloved in Christ,

Richard Frederick Montague Hampden of the Parish of Saint Andrew in the County of Dorset, Bachelor, 32, and Sabine de la Tour, of Paris, Spinster, 24,

grace and health. WHEREAS it is alleged that ye have resolved to proceed to the Solemnization of true and lawful Matrimony . . .

An indigo tax stamp for ten shillings adorned the top left corner and the archbishop's impressed seal was enclosed in a paper fold at the bottom.

She shook her head. "You have omitted my middle names."

"I don't know them," he said mildly.

Her temper rose. "How can you even pretend to marry someone when you don't even know their full name? They're Marie Louise, if you must know."

His lips twitched. "I'll bear that in mind the next time I'm attempting to forge your signature. Which I did," he added, pointing to the back of the page. "Right there."

Sabine turned the paper over and her eyes widened in shock. Several examples of her own name adorned the reverse, next to his own confident scrawl.

"Don't you recall practicing to sign the marriage register, sweetheart?" he chided softly.

His smile was calculating, predatory, and her heart pounded

in sudden panic and confusion. What game was he playing now? She shot him an accusing glare. "That is not my signature."

"I know. But I think I made a rather good job of it, don't you think?"

"How did you do it?"

He looked extremely pleased with himself. "You signed the drawing you made of me. I copied that."

She curled her lip. "This is terrible. I never make my *s*'s like that."

"I like to think your hand was shaking with excitement at the prospect of being joined in holy matrimony with myself."

She snorted, but her mind was spinning furiously. "It wouldn't fool a blind man, that signature." She turned the paper back over and pointed at the date. "Besides, this cannot be real. The third of May was five days ago. I was unconscious, in bed."

His eyes bored into hers. "It's real. The archbishop of Canterbury is the father of an old school friend of mine. I went to see him."

"Why?"

He tilted his head. "I'd have thought that was obvious."

"You wish to blackmail me into working for your government by claiming I am your wife?" she hazarded angrily. "It will not work. You cannot hold me here against my will."

That damnable dimple appeared. "*Tsk.* You have such a suspicious mind. No. I was thinking of something rather less Machiavellian."

"What?"

He set down the fountain pen. "You are a remarkable woman, Sabine de la Tour. You are—"

"A liar? A forger? A thief?" she finished scornfully. "I know."

His mouth curled up at the corners. "All of those things. But that wasn't what I was going to say."

"What then?" she demanded, exasperated.

He tilted his head, as if searching for the right word. "Indispensable," he said finally. "You are indispensable. To England. And to me."

Sabine's heart stuttered to a stop. "You are cruel to mock me," she said stiffly.

He raised his brows. "I'm not mocking you. It's true. Five days ago—when you were unconscious in bed—I realized I wanted to marry you."

CHAPTER 61

Sabine pushed away from the desk and started for the door. She'd had quite enough of his teasing. Richard rounded the desk in two long strides, caught her elbow, and spun her back around to face him. She tried to ward him off with one hand, but the back of her legs bumped against one of the armchairs and stymied her retreat.

He took immediate advantage, stepping closer, trapping her with his body. "You told your friend you loved me," he challenged belligerently. "On the ship."

Her face heated. "I did not! I said you drove me insane. And that was a private conversation. You shouldn't have been listening!"

"He asked if you loved me and you didn't deny it."

She couldn't answer that without perjuring herself, so she tightened her lips together in a stubborn line.

His fingers tightened on her arm and he took another step, deliberately crowding her so they were almost nose to nose. She could feel the heat of him across the scant inches that separated them and her pulse rocketed in response. She cursed the fact that her body tightened in awareness despite her anger.

"You love me," he accused softly.

She glared at his perfectly tied cravat. "That has nothing to do with the situation in hand."

"It has everything to do with it." He caught her chin and lifted her face to his. "When I love you too."

Hope and desperation swirled inside her. She could barely breathe. "You don't mean that. Really. I'm a terrible person. I'm like fake money. I can't be trusted. Philippe Lacorte doesn't even exist."

The warmth in his eyes made her stomach flutter. "I don't care what your bloody name is. You're the woman I love."

She gestured at the opulent splendor around them, tried to make him understand how impossible it was, this thing between them. "I don't belong in this world. I'm your social inferior. And French."

"You're half French, just like me," he corrected calmly. "And you already have the approval of the Prince Regent. He was wholeheartedly in agreement when I told him I planned to make you my viscountess. And where he approves, the rest of society will follow. They can go hang if they don't. Do you think I care what they say? I'll marry whoever I see fit. And that's you, Sabine Marie Louise de la Tour." He gazed deep into her eyes. "You belong in my world," he said roughly. "Just as I belong wherever you are. I'll live wherever you want. Here in London, down in Devon. Hell, back in Paris. I don't care, as long as I'm with you."

"I have no money!" she wailed.

"You have three hundred pounds from selling that diamond necklace," he said dryly.

"I gave half of it to Anton."

His lips quirked. "Very well, I'll accept a hundred and fifty pounds as your dowry." His thumb stroked her jaw, a mesmerizing petal-soft caress. "Sweetheart, I have enough money for both of us. And if you marry me, half of everything I own will become yours anyway."

Her throat closed up at the expression on his face—fierce and tender at once.

"You already own half my soul," he whispered. "It seems only fair you should get half of everything else as well." The dimple reappeared. "And maybe giving you access to real money will curb your unnatural inclination to make your own."

His smile warmed her from the inside out.

"I cannot imagine anyone else as my wife. Show me another woman who could do what you have done. Show me a woman I can admire and respect as much as you. There is none."

She opened her mouth to argue, but he forestalled her with a teasing finger over her lips.

"And don't tell me you'll never get used to signing another name, because we both know that's not true. You already have my surname down to a fine art."

She stamped her foot in frustration. "Richard! You're not listening!"

"No. I'm not," he said amiably. "Because you're talking nonsense." He lowered his head so his lips were almost on hers. "I love the way you say my name. 'Ree-shard.' Say it always. Just like that."

Sabine gripped her skirts so she didn't throw herself into his arms. "I am going back to Paris," she said shakily.

"*Je t'aime,*" he whispered against her mouth.

"Oh, don't," she breathed desperately. The way he spoke French made her insides liquefy.

He switched back to English. "It doesn't matter what language I say it in. The meaning's the same." He pressed a kiss against her jaw and Sabine closed her eyes, hardly daring to trust the treacherous sensations unfurling inside her. Happiness was flowing through her like warm honey.

"*Ti amo,*" he murmured. "That's Italian. *Te amo.* That's Spanish." His large hands cradled her face. Another kiss, closer to her mouth. "I love you," he groaned. "I can't pinpoint the exact moment, but somewhere in the middle of all of this madness it stopped being fake and started being real. It's got nothing to do with my brain and everything to do with what's in my chest."

"Your lungs?" she added helpfully, unable to resist teasing.

"My heart, you wretch!" He scowled and tilted her jaw to press a hot kiss just below her ear. She shivered.

"Useless, disobedient organ that it is. My heart wants you. Needs you. And since I need it to keep on beating, you're just going to have to marry me. That's all there is to it." His breath warmed her lips. "You know how relentless I am when it comes to pursuing something I want."

Sabine felt like her heart was breaking and reforming at the same time. Elation and a wild recklessness bubbled up inside her. "I suppose becoming a viscount's wife would be a good way to avoid future prosecution—"

His lips cut her off. His arms went around her and his mouth plundered hers, demanding and coaxing a response, igniting the need that had been building between them for days. Sabine didn't even think of denying him. Her whole body rose to meet his, every sinew aching to get closer. Urgency replaced languor. His lips shaped hers and his tongue probed her mouth, advancing and retreating in a desperate rhythm that made her blood heat white-hot in an instant.

"Say yes," he panted, lowering himself into the chair and tugging her down so she straddled him in a flurry of rustling skirts. "Say you'll marry me."

Sabine caught his lower lip in her teeth and gasped as his hands slipped down her back and slid beneath her skirts. He cupped her bottom and arched his hips, bringing her into full, shameless contact with his arousal through his breeches. She rolled her hips, grinding onto him. They both groaned.

She speared her fingers through his hair and tugged his head back, struggling for control when all she wanted to do was surrender. "Your rules for bedding women need to change," she managed to gasp as his wicked fingers slid up her thighs.

"How so?"

She could barely speak—he'd found her core. He teased and slid. "No wives and no virgins, you said."

"Let me amend that," he panted. He fumbled with the buttons of his falls, impatience robbing him of his usual grace. He sprang free, hot and silky-hard between her thighs, and Sabine reached down and encircled him with her fingers, amazed at her own boldness. He felt wonderful—an intriguing contradiction of hard and soft at once. She gave an experimental stroke and he hissed through his teeth.

"God, that feels good."

A flash of exultant pleasure warmed her. She did this to him. She made him burn, lose control. "You were saying?" she prompted wickedly.

He fisted his hand around hers and guided himself to the entrance to her body. Sabine was light-headed, panting in anticipation.

"No virgins," he promised hotly. "No mistresses." He pressed himself against her. "And only one wife; mine," he growled. "You, Sabine. Only you."

His eyes met hers and Sabine read the truth in them, the sincerity. The adoration.

She caught his shoulders, reveling in the muscled strength beneath his jacket. "Then yes," she breathed on a ragged laugh. "Yes."

His eyes closed in relief even as he caught her hips and brought her down on his body in a slow, delicious slide. Sabine gasped at the sensation of him pressing into her, the sense of belonging, of fitting together so perfectly. Her skirts puffed around them, and the knowledge that they were so intimately joined beneath the formality of their clothing only added to the piquancy of the moment. She rose up on her knees and then eased back down, drawing another stifled curse from him.

He tugged at the front of her dress and freed her breasts, then rolled his hips and sank deep into her again. And again.

Sabine closed her eyes in blissful surrender and threw her head back. The pins in her hair lost the battle for control and the heavy coils fell down over her shoulders. Richard drew it forward and buried his nose in it, his tongue finding her peaked nipple unerringly through the silky mass.

"I love the taste of you," he groaned. "Ink and lemons."

He seemed intent on drawing out her response. Her nails dug into the bunched muscles of his arms as he rocked himself beneath her in a tantalizing rhythm designed to drive her mad. When she gasped out his name he laughed darkly against her skin and caught her head in his hands, pulling her down for a ravenous kiss.

"Always," he murmured against her lips. His tongue probed her mouth in perfect imitation of the way he drove into her body. Pleasure shimmered through her with every deep, possessive stroke.

She was his. He was hers.

It felt good.

"Come for me," he panted. His hand slid between them and Sabine felt herself spiraling away. She held her breath as the pressure built and built, and then, with a muffled cry, she hurtled over the edge. Beats of pleasure radiated through her, endless and infinitely satisfying.

Richard groaned as he joined her at the peak and she pressed her face into his shoulder, loving the feel of his powerful body shuddering beneath her in release. She collapsed against him, deliciously weary, her heart throbbing with a joy she could barely contain.

After a few breathless moments she raised her head. "Oh,

God, the servants!" she uttered in a scandalized whisper. "You didn't even lock the door!"

Richard gave a sleepy smile. "You're fooling yourself if you think they don't know exactly what we've been up to," he said. "There's not a thing that goes on in this house without Hodges knowing about it."

Her face suffused with heat as she struggled to disentangle herself from his lap. He laughed. "It wouldn't surprise me if they were already laying bets on the birth date of our first child."

"Oh, God," she groaned again, then stilled, half on, half off his lap. "You really want that? Children? A future? With me?"

He leaned his forehead against hers, then kissed the end of her nose. "Yes. I really do."

Sabine lowered her cheek to his shoulder with a sigh. Her eyes came to rest on the painting on the far wall. Was it just her imagination, or did Saskia have a satisfied, congratulatory look in her eyes? Richard didn't paint, of course. But if he could, she suddenly knew that he'd paint her the way Rembrandt had painted Saskia: beautiful in her imperfections, with love in every brushstroke. She sighed again in happiness.

Richard stroked her hair. "Come on, get up. Things to do. We've got the prince's ball tonight."

Sabine groaned. She'd meant to be long gone before that. Except now the whole world was different. She could face it with Richard by her side.

He helped her stand—her legs were still decidedly wobbly—and raised her hand to his lips. "You know, if you don't want a huge wedding in St. George's, we could go and get married today. I do have that special license."

His eyes met hers and her heart swelled at the tiny hint of uncertainty she encountered in his gaze.

"The prince's ball could be your first official engagement as Lady Lovell," he coaxed.

She tightened her fingers on his. "Yes," she said in an aching voice. "Yes, please."

He pulled her into his arms. "Bloody hell. I'd better go back to Rundell, Bridge & Rundell and tell them you've changed your mind about that necklace."

Sabine smiled against his chest. "Please do. I promise I'll never sell it again."

CHAPTER 62

A few hours later, Richard opened the connecting door and beckoned her into his room. Sabine suppressed a wistful sigh at the sight of him in his evening attire. The stark black of his jacket and snowy white shirt made him look thoroughly delicious. She still couldn't believe she'd actually married the man this afternoon.

His eyes lingered hungrily on her figure as he took in the dress that Heloise had ordered from Mrs. Triaud and Mrs. Bean, the same dressmakers who'd worked on Princess Charlotte's trousseau.

She knew she looked good: she shimmered like a firework. Silver lamé net sparkled over a gossamer-thin slip, and the entire gown had been embroidered with hundreds of tiny three-dimensional bellflowers fashioned from silk-covered wire and decorated with silver thread.

Richard held out a familiar flat velvet box. "I do hope you'll keep this rather longer than last time," he murmured softly. He fastened the diamonds around her neck and dropped a kiss in the hollow at her nape. "My beautiful wife."

Sabine opened her mouth to thank him, but he tugged her

through the door and into his bedchamber. A fire was burning in the grate, but her eyes went immediately to the leather satchel next to it. Her eyes widened. "Is that my money?" she demanded hotly.

He opened the bag and pulled out a handful of counterfeits. "*Our* money," he amended with a chuckle. "Half of everything you own is mine now, remember?" He pressed the paper into her hand and gestured at the fire. "Go on. Throw it on."

Sabine sighed heavily. "Oh, if I must."

She tossed the bundle into the flames and felt as if her soul were flying up the chimney with the ashes. A lightness settled about her, a great weight lifted from her shoulders. The past was done. It was time for the future. "Adieu, Philippe Lacorte," she whispered softly.

Richard stood behind her and gathered her in his arms. He kissed her bare shoulder. "Bonjour, Sabine Hampden."

She glanced up at him with a sparkling smile. "Bonjour."

EPILOGUE

Galerie Carnaud, Rue du Pélican, Paris

"*W*hy are we in a dusty Parisian cellar?" Richard demanded. He ducked his head to avoid a large cobweb and glanced around the gloomy vaulted room.

His wife of precisely ten days shot him a chiding glance over her shoulder. "I told you. To retrieve my father's legacy."

She set a bag of tools on a dusty table and raised her lantern. Richard did the same, and the combined glow illuminated the back wall of the underground room. He raised his brows. The entire wall was covered with an enormous mural painted directly on the plaster: a great writhing mass of soldiers and horses in the midst of a pitched battle.

He frowned. "Your father painted that? Why on earth did he do it down here?"

Sabine gave him a mischievous smile. "No. I painted that. It is inspired by a lost painting by da Vinci called *The Battle of Anghiari*."

"But—"

She selected a heavy-looking hammer and approached the

wall, and he was momentarily distracted by the sway of her hips as she moved. He didn't think he would ever get tired of watching her.

"You know I like to have a backup plan," she teased. "And how fond I am of hiding things in plain sight." She pointed to a soldier, high up in the top right corner. He was holding aloft a green flag inscribed with the words *Cerca Trova*.

"He who seeks, finds," Richard translated.

"Exactly." She raised the sledgehammer and aimed a blow straight at the wall.

Richard gasped in shock. "You madwoman! What are you doing?" He reached out and tried to grab her arm but she shook him off, laughing, and aimed another blow at the plaster.

"Trust me, Richard. Watch."

The wall crumbled. To his amazement the head of the hammer went straight through, leaving a gaping hole.

"It is not solid brick at all," she said, taking another swing. "Merely plaster and a wooden frame. The real wall is about two feet farther back."

Richard narrowed his eyes. "A false wall? Very sneaky."

"Why, thank you."

He took the hammer from her hands. "Let me do that." He enlarged the hole so it was at least a couple of feet wide, revealing a dark gap behind it. Sabine pushed the lantern through and he leaned forward, intrigued. The dusty gilded edge of a picture frame caught the light. The corner of a painted canvas—red drapery and a pair of folded hands—followed.

Sabine raised the lantern higher and let out a crow of delight. "They're all still here!"

Richard inhaled sharply. At least thirty or forty paintings hung from nails on the real wall or rested on the floor, stacked three deep.

"What are all these?"

Sabine glanced at him. "I told you that my father worked at

the Louvre, did I not? Well, whenever he knew that a work of art sent for restoration had been stolen, he or Jacques would copy it." Her eyes twinkled. "They would return the copy and hide the original, waiting for the day when it could be returned to its rightful owner."

"My God."

Her face fell. "But Father died before he could complete his task. Jacques and I hid the artworks and I painted the mural as a distraction, in case anyone came down here." She reached into the void and withdrew a small square bundle wrapped in cloth. "Ah, and here is the book."

The cloth revealed a leather-bound journal. She opened it up with a bittersweet smile. "My father's handwriting," she whispered reverently. "He risked imprisonment and even death to keep these records." She glanced up, her eyes sparkling with unshed tears. "This is a list of the original owners. Aristos who had them confiscated, or who were forced to sell them for a pittance. It was my father's wish to return their property after the war. Will you help me finish what he started?"

Richard leaned forward and placed a tender kiss on her mouth. "Of course."

After a breathless moment, Sabine pulled back and directed her light to one of the nearest portraits. "Actually, we don't need to return *all* of these paintings. A few of them belong to me."

Richard suddenly recognized the woman in the painting. She had the same lustrous eyes, the same vivid beauty, as the woman standing next to him. That same face had disguised Sabine's printing plates in London. "Is that your mother?"

She nodded proudly. "Yes. And that," she shone the light on the adjacent portrait, "is my father. They were painted by my grandfather, Maurice de la Tour. Anton and I stole them from my old house when it was given to one of Napoleon's men."

She lifted her chin in that defiant, unrepentant way he loved so well. "Don't they look like they're smiling? I think it's because they're finally proud of me."

Richard chuckled and pulled her into his arms. "Yes," he agreed softly. "I think so too."

THE END.

ABOUT THE AUTHOR

Kate Bateman, also writing as K. C. Bateman, is the #1 bestselling author of Regency and Renaissance historical romances, including *The Secrets & Spies Series* and the *Bow Street Bachelors Series*. Her Renaissance romp, *The Devil To Pay* was a 2019 RITA award finalist.

She's also an auctioneer and fine art appraiser, the co-founder and director of Bateman's Auctioneers, a fine art and antiques auction house in the UK. She currently lives in Illinois with her husband and three inexhaustible children, but returns to England regularly to appear as an antiques expert on several popular BBC television shows.

Kate loves to hear from readers. Contact her via her website: www.kcbateman.com and sign up for her newsletter to receive regular updates on new releases, giveaways and exclusive excerpts.

FOLLOW

Follow Kate online for the latest new releases, giveaways, exclusive sneak peeks, and more!

Amazon
Barnes & Noble
Apple Ibooks
Kobo
Google Play

Join Kate's Facebook reader group: Badasses in Bodices

Sign ip for Kate's monthly-ish newsletter via her website for news, exclusive excerpts and giveaways.

Follow both K.C. Bateman and Kate Bateman on Bookbub for new releases and sales.

Add Kate's books to your Goodreads lists, or leave a review!

ALSO BY K. C. BATEMAN

Secrets & Spies Series:
To Steal a Heart
A Raven's Heart
A Counterfeit Heart

Bow Street Bachelors Series:
This Earl Of Mine
To Catch An Earl
The Princess & The Rogue

Italian Renaissance:
The Devil To Pay

Novellas:
The Promise of A Kiss
A Midnight Clear
A Midsummer Night's Kiss

SNEAK PEEK

Read on for a sneak peek of *This Earl Of Mine,*
the first exhilarating historical romance in Kate Bateman's Bow
Street Bachelors Series. . .

THIS EARL OF MINE

CHAPTER 1.

*L*ondon, March 1816.

THERE WERE WORSE PLACES to find a husband than Newgate Prison.

Of course there were.

It was just that, at present, Georgie couldn't think of any.

"Georgiana Caversteed, this is a terrible idea."

Georgie frowned at her burly companion, Pieter Smit, as the nondescript carriage he'd summoned to convey them to London's most notorious jail rocked to a halt on the cobbled street. The salt-weathered Dutchman always used her full name whenever he disapproved of something she was doing. Which was often.

"Your father would turn in his watery grave if he knew what you were about."

That was undoubtedly true. Until three days ago, enlisting a husband from amongst the ranks of London's most dangerous criminals had not featured prominently on her list of life goals.

But desperate times called for desperate measures. Or, in this case, for a desperate felon about to be hanged. A felon she would marry before the night was through.

Georgie peered out into the rain-drizzled street, then up, up the near-windowless walls. They rose into the mist, five stories high, a vast expanse of brickwork, bleak and unpromising. A church bell tolled somewhere in the darkness, a forlorn clang like a death knell. Her stomach knotted with a grim sense of foreboding.

Was she really going to go through with this? It had seemed a good plan, in the safety of Grosvenor Square. The perfect way to thwart Cousin Josiah once and for all. She stepped from the carriage, ducked her head against the rain, and followed Pieter under a vast arched gate. Her heart hammered at the audacity of what she planned.

They'd taken the same route as condemned prisoners on the way to Tyburn tree, only in reverse. West to east, from the rarefied social strata of Mayfair through gradually rougher and bleaker neighborhoods, Holborn and St. Giles, to this miserable place where the dregs of humanity had been incarcerated. Georgie felt as if she were nearing her own execution.

She shook off the pervasive aura of doom and straightened her spine. This was her choice. However unpalatable the next few minutes might be, the alternative was far worse. Better a temporary marriage to a murderous, unwashed criminal than a lifetime of misery with Josiah.

They crossed the deserted outer courtyard, and Georgie cleared her throat, trying not to inhale the foul-smelling air that seeped from the very pores of the building. "You have it all arranged? They are expecting us?"

Pieter nodded. "Aye. I've greased the wheels with yer blunt, my girl. The proctor and the ordinary are both bent as copper shillings. Used to having their palms greased, those two, the greedy bastards."

Her father's right-hand man had never minced words in front of her, and Georgie appreciated his bluntness. So few people in the ton ever said what they really meant. Pieter's honesty was refreshing. He'd been her father's man for twenty years before she'd even been born. A case of mumps had prevented him from accompanying William Caversteed on his last, fateful voyage, and Georgie had often thought that if Pieter had been with her father, maybe he'd still be alive. Little things like squalls, shipwrecks, and attacks from Barbary pirates would be mere inconveniences to a man like Pieter Smit.

In the five years since Papa's death, Pieter's steadfast loyalty had been dedicated to William's daughters, and Georgie loved the gruff, hulking manservant like a second father. He would see her through this madcap scheme—even if he disapproved.

She tugged the hood of her cloak down to stave off the drizzle. This place was filled with murderers, highwaymen, forgers, and thieves. Poor wretches slated to die, or those "lucky" few whose sentences had been commuted to transportation. Yet in her own way, she was equally desperate.

"You are sure that this man is to be hanged tomorrow?"

Pieter nodded grimly as he rapped on a wooden door. "I am. A low sort he is, by all accounts."

She shouldn't ask, didn't want to know too much about the man whose name she was purchasing. A man whose death would spell her own freedom. She would be wed and widowed within twenty-four hours.

Taking advantage of a condemned man left a sour taste in her mouth, a sense of guilt that her happiness should come from the misfortune of another. But this man would die whether she married him or not. "What are his crimes?"

"Numerous, I'm told. He's a coiner." At her frown, Pieter elaborated. "Someone who forges coins. It's treason, that."

"Oh." That seemed a little harsh. She couldn't imagine what that was like, having no money, forced to make your own. Still, having a fortune was almost as much of a curse as having nothing. She'd endured six years of insincere, lecherous fortune hunters, thanks to her bountiful coffers.

"A smuggler too," Pieter added for good measure. "Stabbed a customs man down in Kent."

She was simply making the best out of a bad situation. This man would surely realize that while there was no hope for himself, at least he could leave this world having provided for whatever family he left behind. Everyone had parents, or siblings, or lovers. Everyone had a price. She, of all people, knew that— she was buying herself a husband. At least this way there was no pretense. Besides, what was the point in having a fortune if you couldn't use it to make yourself happy?

Pieter hammered impatiently on the door again.

"I know you disapprove," Georgie muttered. "But Father would never have wanted me to marry a man who covets my purse more than my person. If you hadn't rescued me the other evening, that's precisely what would have happened. I would have had to wed Josiah to prevent a scandal. I refuse to give control of my life and my fortune to some idiot to mismanage. As a widow, I will be free."

Pieter gave an eloquent sniff.

"You think me heartless," Georgie said. "But can you think of another way?" At his frowning silence, she nodded. "No, me neither."

Heavy footsteps and the jangle of keys finally heralded proof of human life inside. The door scraped open, and the low glare of a lantern illuminated a grotesquely large man in the doorway.

"Mr. Knollys?"

The man gave a brown-toothed grin as he recognized Pieter. "Welcome back, sir. Welcome back." He craned his neck and raised the lantern, trying to catch a glimpse of Georgie. "You brought the lady, then?" His piggy eyes narrowed with curiosity within the folds of his flabby face.

"And the license." Pieter tapped the pocket of his coat.

Knollys nodded and stepped back, allowing them entry. "The ordinary's agreed to perform the service." He turned and began shuffling down the narrow corridor, lantern raised. "Only one small problem." He cocked his head back toward Pieter. "That cove the lady was to marry? Cheated the 'angman, 'e 'as."

Pieter stopped abruptly, and Georgie bumped into his broad back.

"He's dead?" Pieter exclaimed. "Then why are we here? You can damn well return that purse I paid you!"

The man's belly undulated grotesquely as he laughed. It was not a kindly sound. "Now, now. Don't you worry yerself none, me fine lad. That special license don't have no names on it yet, do it? No. We've plenty more like 'im in this place. This way."

The foul stench of the prison increased tenfold as they followed the unpleasant Knollys up some stairs and down a second corridor. Rows of thick wooden doors, each with a square metal hatch and a sliding shutter at eye level lined the walls on either side. Noises emanated from some—inhuman moans, shouts, and foul curses. Others were ominously silent. Georgie pressed her handkerchief to her nose, glad she'd doused it in lavender water.

Knollys waddled to a stop in front of the final door in the row. His eyes glistened with a disquieting amount of glee.

"Found the lady a substitute, I 'ave." He thumped the metal grate with his meaty fist and eyed Georgie's cloaked form with a knowing, suggestive leer that made her feel as though she'd been drenched in cooking fat. She resisted the urge to shudder.

"Wake up, lads!" he bellowed. "There's a lady 'ere needs yer services."

CHAPTER 2.

. . .

BENEDICT WILLIAM HENRY WYLDE, scapegrace second son of the late Earl of Morcott, reluctant war hero, and former scourge of the ton, strained to hear the last words of his cellmate. He bent forward, trying to ignore the stench of the man's blackened teeth and the sickly sweet scent of impending death that wreathed his feverish form.

Silas had been sick for days, courtesy of a festering stab wound in his thigh. The bastard jailers hadn't heeded his pleas for water, bandages, or laudanum. Ben had been trying to decipher the smuggler's ranting for hours. Delirium had loosened the man's tongue, and he'd leaned close, waiting for something useful to slip between those cracked lips, but the words had been frustratingly fragmented. Silas raved about plots and treasons. An Irishman. The emperor. Benedict had been on the verge of shaking the poor bastard when his crewmate let out one last, gasping breath—and died.

"Oh, bloody hell!"

Ben drew back from the hard, straw-filled pallet that stank of piss and death. He'd been so close to getting the information he needed.

Not for the first time, he cursed his friend Alex's uncle, Sir Nathaniel Conant, Chief Magistrate of Bow Street and the man tasked with transforming the way London was policed. Bow Street was the senior magistrate court in the capital, and the "Runners," as they were rather contemptuously known, investigated crimes, followed up leads, served warrants and summons, searched properties for stolen goods, and watched premises where infringements of bylaws or other offences were suspected.

Conant had approached Ben, Alex, and their friend Seb about a year ago, a few months after their return from fighting Napoleon on the continent. The three of them had just opened the Tricorn Club—the gambling hell they'd pledged to run together while crouched around a smoky campfire in Belgium. Conant had pointed out that their new venture placed them in an ideal position for gathering intelligence on behalf of His Majesty's government, since its members—and their acquaintances—came from all levels of society. He'd also requested their assistance on occasional cases, especially those which bridged the social divide. The three of them not only had entrée into polite society, but thanks to their time in the Rifles, they dealt equally well with those from the lower end of the social spectrum, the "scum of the earth," as Wellington had famously called his own troops.

Conant paid the three of them a modest sum for every mission they undertook, plus extra commission for each bit of new information they brought in. Neither Alex nor Seb needed the money; they were more interested in the challenge to their wits, but Benedict had jumped at the chance of some additional income, even though the work was sometimes—such as now—less than glamorous.

He was in Newgate on Conant's orders, chasing a rumor that someone had been trying to assemble a crew of smugglers to rescue the deposed Emperor Napoleon from the island of St. Helena. Benedict had been ingratiating himself with this band for weeks, posing as a bitter ex-navy gunner, searching for the man behind such a plan. He'd even allowed himself to be seized by customs officials near Gravesend along with half the gang—recently deceased Silas amongst them—in the hopes of discovering more. If he solved this case, he'd receive a reward of five hundred pounds, which could go some way toward helping his brother pay off the mass of debt left by their profligate father.

He'd been in here almost ten days now. The gang's ringleader, a vicious bastard named Hammond, had been hanged yesterday morning. Ben, Silas, and two of the younger gang members had been sentenced to transportation. That was British leniency for you; a nice slow death on a prison ship instead of a quick drop from Tyburn tree.

The prison hulk would be leaving at dawn, but Ben wouldn't

be on it. There was no need to hang around now that Silas and Hammond were both dead. He'd get nothing more from them. And the two youngsters, Peters and Fry, were barely in their teens. They knew nothing useful. Conant had arranged for him to "disappear" from the prison hulk before it sailed; its guards were as open to bribery as Knollys.

Several other gang members had escaped the Gravesend raid. Benedict had glimpsed a few familiar faces in the crowd when the magistrate had passed down his sentence. He'd have to chase them down as soon as he was free and see if any of them had been approached for the traitorous mission.

Benedict sighed and slid down the wall until he sat on the filthy floor, his knees bent in front of him. He'd forgotten what it felt like to be clean. He rasped one hand over his stubbled jaw and grimaced—he'd let his beard grow out as a partial disguise. He'd commit murder for a wash and a razor. Even during the worst scrapes in the Peninsular War, and then in France and Belgium, he'd always found time to shave. Alex and Seb, his brothers-in-arms, had mocked him for it mercilessly.

He glanced at the square of rain visible through the tiny barred grate on the outer wall of his cell. Seb and Alex were out there, lucky buggers, playing merry hell with the debutantes, wives, and widows of London with amazing impartiality.

The things he did for king and bloody country.

And cash, of course. Five hundred pounds was nothing to sneeze at.

Tracking down a traitor was admirable. Having to stay celibate and sober because there was neither a woman nor grog to be had in prison was hell. What he wouldn't give for some decent French brandy and a warm, willing wench. Hell, right now he'd settle for some of that watered-down ratafia they served at society balls and a tumble with a barmaid.

A pretty barmaid, of course. His face had always allowed him to be choosy. At least, it did when he was clean-shaven. His own mother probably wouldn't recognize him right now.

Voices and footsteps intruded on his errant fancies as the obsequious voice of Knollys echoed through the stones. A fist slammed into the grate, loud enough to wake the dead, and Benedict glanced over at Silas with morbid humor. Well, almost loud enough.

"Wake up, lads!" Knollys bellowed. "There's a lady 'ere needs yer services."

Benedict's brows rose in the darkness. What the devil?

"Ye promised ten pounds if I'd find 'er a man an' never say nuffink to nobody," he heard Knollys say through the door.

"Are they waiting to hang too?" An older man's voice, that, with a foreign inflexion. Dutch, perhaps.

"Nay. Ain't got no more for the gallows. Not since Hammond yesterday." Knollys sounded almost apologetic. "But either one of these'll fit the bill. Off to Van Diemen's Land they are, at first light."

"No, that won't do at all."

Benedict's ears pricked up at the sound of the cultured female voice. She sounded extremely peeved.

"I specifically wanted a condemned man, Mr. Knollys."

"Better come back in a week or so then, milady."

There was a short pause as the two visitors apparently conferred, too low for him to hear.

"I cannot wait another few weeks." The woman sounded resigned. "Very well. Let's see what you have."

Keys grated in the lock and Knollys's quivering belly filled the doorway. Benedict shielded his eyes from the lantern's glare, blinding after the semidarkness of the cell. The glow illuminated Silas's still figure on the bed and Knollys grunted.

"Dead, is 'e?" He sounded neither dismayed nor surprised. "Figured he wouldn't last the week. You'll 'ave to do then, Wylde. Get up."

Benedict pushed himself to his feet with a wince.

"Ain't married, are you, Wylde?" Knollys muttered, low enough not to be heard by those in the corridor.

"Never met the right woman," Benedict drawled, being careful to retain the rough accent of an east coast smuggler he'd adopted. "Still, one lives in 'ope."

Knollys frowned, trying to decide whether Ben was being sarcastic. As usual, he got it wrong. "This lady's 'ere to wed," he grunted finally, gesturing vaguely behind him.

Benedict squinted. Two shapes hovered just outside, partly shielded by the jailer's immense bulk. One of them, the smaller hooded figure, might possibly be female. "What woman comes here to marry?"

Knollys chuckled. "A desperate one, Mr. Wylde."

The avaricious glint in Knollys's eye hinted that he saw the opportunity to take advantage, and Benedict experienced a rush of both anger and protectiveness for the foolish woman, whoever she might be. Probably one of the muslin set, seeking a name for her unborn child. Or some common trollop, hoping her debts would be wiped off with the death of her husband. Except he'd never met a tart who spoke with such a clipped, aristocratic accent.

"You want me to marry some woman I've never met?" Benedict almost laughed in disbelief. "I appreciate the offer, Mr. Knollys, but I'll have to decline. I ain't stepping into the parson's mousetrap for no one."

Knollys took a menacing step forward. "Oh, you'll do it, Wylde, or I'll have Ennis bash your skull in." He glanced over at Silas's corpse. "I can just as easy 'ave 'im dig two graves instead of one."

Ennis was a short, troll-like thug who possessed fewer brains than a sack of potatoes, but he took a malicious and creative pleasure in administering beatings with his heavy wooden cudgel. Benedict's temper rose. He didn't like being threatened. If it weren't for the manacles binding his hands, he'd explain that pertinent fact to Mr. Knollys in no uncertain terms.

Unfortunately, Knollys wasn't a man to take chances. He prodded Benedict with his stick. "Out with ye. And no funny business." His meaty fist cuffed Ben around the head to underscore the point.

Benedict stepped out into the dim passageway and took an appreciative breath. The air was slightly less rancid out here. Of course, it was all a matter of degree.

A broad, grizzled man of around sixty moved to stand protectively in front of the woman, arms crossed and bushy brows lowered. Benedict leaned sideways and tried to make out her features, but the hood of a domino shielded her face. She made a delicious, feminine rustle of silk as she stepped back, though. No rough worsted and cotton for this lady. Interesting.

Knollys prodded him along the passage, and Benedict shook his head to dispel a sense of unreality. Here he was, unshaven, unwashed, less than six hours from freedom, and apparently about to be wed to a perfect stranger. It seemed like yet another cruel joke by fate.

He'd never imagined himself marrying. Not after the disastrous example of his own parents' union. His mother had endured his father's company only long enough to produce the requisite heir and a spare, then removed herself to the gaiety of London. For the next twenty years, she'd entertained a series of lovers in the town house, while his father had remained immured in Herefordshire with a succession of steadily younger live-in mistresses, one of whom had taken it upon herself to introduce a seventeen-year-old Benedict to the mysteries of the female form. It was a pattern of domesticity Benedict had absolutely no desire to repeat.

In truth, he hadn't thought he'd survive the war and live to the ripe old age of twenty-eight. If he had ever been forced to picture his own wedding—under torture, perhaps—he was fairly certain he wouldn't have imagined it taking place in prison. At the very least, he would have had his family and a couple of friends in attendance; his fellow sworn bachelors, Alex and Seb. Some flowers, maybe. A country church.

He'd never envisaged the lady. If three years of warfare had taught him anything, it was that life was too short to tie himself to one woman for the rest of his life. Marriage would be an imprisonment worse than his cell here in Newgate.

They clattered down the stairs and into the tiny chapel where the ordinary, Horace Cotton, was waiting, red-faced and unctuous. Cotton relished his role of resident chaplain; he enjoyed haranguing soon-to-be-dead prisoners with lengthy sermons full of fire and brimstone. No doubt he was being paid handsomely for this evening's work.

Benedict halted in front of the altar—little more than a table covered in a white cloth and two candles—and raised his manacled wrists to Knollys. The jailer sniffed but clearly realized he'd have to unchain him if they were to proceed. He gave Ben a sour, warning look as the irons slipped off, just daring him to try something. Ben shot him a cocky, challenging sneer in return.

How to put a stop to this farce? He had no cash to bribe his way out. A chronic lack of funds was precisely why he'd been working for Bow Street since his return from France, chasing thief-taker's rewards.

Could he write the wrong name on the register, to invalidate the marriage? Probably not. Both Knollys and Cotton knew him as Ben Wylde. Ex-Rifle brigade, penniless, cynical veteran of Waterloo. It wasn't his full name, of course, but it would probably be enough to satisfy the law.

Announcing that his brother happened to be the Earl of Morcott would certainly make matters interesting, but thanks to their father's profligacy, the estate was mortgaged to the hilt. John had even less money than Benedict.

The unpleasant sensation that he'd been neatly backed into a corner made Benedict's neck prickle, as if a French sniper had him in his sights. Still, he'd survived worse. He was a master at getting out of scrapes. Even if he was forced to marry this mystery harridan, there were always alternatives. An annulment, for one.

"Might I at least have the name of the lady to whom I'm about to be joined in holy matrimony?" he drawled.

The manservant scowled at the ironic edge to his tone, but the woman laid a silencing hand on his arm and stepped around him.

"You can indeed, sir." In one smooth movement, she pulled the hood from her head and faced him squarely. "My name is Georgiana Caversteed."

Benedict cursed in every language he knew.

CHAPTER 3.

GEORGIANA CAVERSTEED? What devil's trick was this?

He knew the name, but he'd never seen the face—until now. God's teeth, every man in London knew the name. The chit was so rich, she might as well have her own bank. She could have her pick of any man in England. What in God's name was she doing in Newgate looking for a husband?

Benedict barely remembered not to bow—an automatic response to being introduced to a lady of quality—and racked his brains to recall what he knew of her family. A cit's daughter. Her father had been in shipping, a merchant, rich as Croesus. He'd died and left the family a fortune.

The younger sister was said to be the beauty of the family, but she must indeed be goddess, because Georgiana Caversteed was strikingly lovely. Her arresting, heart-shaped face held a small straight nose and eyes which, in the candlelight, appeared to be dark grey, the color of wet slate. Her brows were full, her lashes long, and her mouth was soft and a fraction too wide.

A swift heat spread throughout his body, and his heart began to pound.

She regarded him steadily as he made his assessment, neither dipping her head nor coyly fluttering her lashes. Benedict's interest kicked up a notch at her directness, and a twitch in his breeches reminded him with unpleasantly bad timing of his enforced abstinence. This was neither the time nor the place to do anything about that.

They'd never met in the ton. She must have come to town after he'd left for the peninsula three years ago, which would make her around twenty-four. Most women would be considered on the shelf at that age, unmarried after so many social seasons, but with the near-irresistible lure of her fortune and with those dazzling looks, Georgiana Caversteed could be eighty-four and someone would still want her.

And yet here she was.

Benedict kept his expression bland, even as he tried to breathe normally. What on earth had made her take such drastic action? Was the chit daft in the head? He couldn't imagine any situation desperate enough to warrant getting leg-shackled to a man like him.

She moistened her lips with the tip of her tongue—which sent another shot of heat straight to his gut—and fixed him with an imperious glare. "What is your name, sir?" She took a step closer, almost in challenge, in defiance of his unchained hands and undoubtedly menacing demeanor.

He quelled a spurt of admiration for her courage, even if it was ill-advised. His inhaled breath caught a subtle whiff of her perfume. It made his knees weak. He'd forgotten the intoxicating scent of woman and skin. For one foolish moment, he imagined pulling her close and pressing his nose into her hair, just filling his lungs with the divine scent of her. He wanted to drink in her smell. He wanted to see if those lips really were as soft as they looked.

He took an involuntary step toward her but stopped at the low growl of warning from her manservant. Sanity prevailed, and he just remembered to stay in the role of rough smuggler they all expected of him.

"My name? Ben Wylde. At your service."

HIS VOICE WAS A DEEP RASP, rough from lack of use, and Georgie's stomach did an odd little flip. She needed to take command here, like Father on board one of his ships, but the man facing her was huge, hairy, and thoroughly intimidating.

When she'd glanced around Knollys's rotund form and into the gloomy cell, her first impression of the prisoner had been astonishment at his sheer size. He'd seemed to fill the entire space, all broad shoulders, wide chest, and long legs. She'd been expecting some poor, ragged, cowering scrap of humanity. Not this strapping, unapologetically male creature.

She'd studied his shaggy, overlong hair and splendid proportions from the back as they'd traipsed down the corridor. He stood a good head taller than Knollys, and unlike the jailer's waddling shuffle, this man walked with a long, confident stride, straight-backed and chin high, as if he owned the prison and were simply taking a tour for his pleasure.

Now, in the chapel, she finally saw his face—the parts that weren't covered with a dark bristle of beard—and her skin prickled as she allowed her eyes to rove over him. She pretended she was inspecting a horse or a piece of furniture. Something large and impersonal.

His dark hair was matted and hung around his face almost to his chin. It was hard to tell what color it would be when it was clean. A small wisp of straw stuck out from one side, just above his ear, and she resisted a bizarre feminine urge to reach up and remove it. Dark beard hid the shape of his jaw, but the candle-light caught his slanted cheekbones and cast shadows in the hollows beneath. The skin that she could see—a straight slash of nose, cheeks, and forehead—was unfashionably tanned and emphasized his deep brown eyes.

She'd stepped as close to him as she dared; no doubt he'd smell like a cesspool if she got any nearer, but even so, she was aware of an uncomfortable curl of . . . what? Reluctant attraction? Repelled fascination?

The top of her head only came up to his chin, and his size was, paradoxically, both threatening and reassuring. He was large enough to lean on; she was certain if she raised her hand to his chest, he would be solid and warm. Unmovable. Her heart hammered in alarm. He was huge and unwashed, and yet her body reacted to him in the most disconcerting manner.

His stare was uncomfortably intense. She dropped her eyes, breaking the odd frisson between them, and took a small step backward.

His lawn shirt, open at the neck, was so thin it was almost transparent. His muscled chest and arms were clearly visible through the grimy fabric. His breeches were a nondescript brown, snug at the seams, and delineated the hard ridges of muscles of his lean thighs with unnerving clarity.

Georgie frowned. This was a man in the prime of life. It seemed wrong that he'd been caged like an animal. He exuded such a piratical air of command that she could easily imagine him on the prow of a ship or pacing in front of a group of soldiers, snapping orders.

She found her voice. "Were you in the military, Mr. Wylde?"

That would certainly explain his splendid physique and air of cocky confidence.

His dark brows twitched in what might have been surprise but could equally have been irritation. "I was."

She waited for more, but he did not elaborate. Clearly Mr.

Wylde was a man of few words. His story was probably like that of thousands of other soldiers who had returned from the wars and found themselves unable to find honest work. She'd seen them in the streets, ragged and begging. It was England's disgrace that men who'd fought so heroically for their country had been reduced to pursuing a life of crime to survive.

Was the fact that he was not a condemned man truly a problem? Her original plan had been to tell Josiah she'd married a sailor who had put to sea. She would have been a widow, of course, but Josiah would never have known that. Her "absent" husband could have sailed the world indefinitely.

If she married this Wylde fellow, she would not immediately become a widow, but the intended result would be the same. Josiah would not be able to force her into marriage and risk committing bigamy.

Georgie narrowed her eyes at the prisoner. They would be bound together until one or the other of them died, and he looked disconcertingly healthy. Providing he didn't take up heavy drinking or catch a nasty tropical disease, he'd probably outlive her. That could cause problems.

Of course, if he continued his ill-advised occupation, then he'd probably succumb to a knife or a bullet sooner rather than later. Men like him always came to a sticky end; he'd only narrowly escaped the gallows this time. She'd probably be a widow in truth soon enough. But how would she hear of his passing if he were halfway across the world? How would she know when she was free?

She tore her eyes away from the rogue's surprisingly tempting lips and fixed Knollys with a hard stare. "Is there really no one else? I mean, he's so . . . so . . ."

Words failed her. Intimidating? Manly?

Unmanageable.

"No, ma'am. But he won't bother you after tonight."

What alternative did she have? She couldn't wait another few weeks. Her near-miss with Josiah had been the last straw. She'd been lucky to escape with an awful, sloppy kiss and not complete ruination. She sighed. "He'll have to do. Pieter, will you explain the terms of the agreement?"

Pieter nodded. "You'll marry Miss Caversteed tonight, Mr. Wylde. In exchange, you'll receive five hundred pounds to do with as you will."

Georgie waited for the prisoner to look suitably impressed. He did not. One dark eyebrow rose slightly, and the corner of his mobile lips curled in a most irritating way.

"Fat lot of good it'll do me in here," he drawled. "Ain't got time to pop to a bank between now and when they chain me to that floating death trap in the morning."

He had a fair point. "Is there someone else to whom we could send the money?"

His lips twitched again as if at some private joke. "Aye. Send it to Mr. Wolff at number ten St. James's. The Tricorn Club. Compliments of Ben Wylde. He'll appreciate it."

Georgie had no idea who this Mr. Wolff was—probably someone to whom this wretch owed a gambling debt—but she nodded and beckoned Pieter over. He took his cue and unfolded the legal document she'd had drawn up. He flattened it on the table next to the ordinary's pen and ink.

"You must sign this, Mr. Wylde. Ye can read?" he added as an afterthought.

Another twitch of those lips. "As if I'd been educated at Cambridge, sir. But give me the highlights."

"It says you renounce all claim to the lady's fortune, except for the five hundred pounds already agreed. You will make no further financial demands upon her in the future."

"Sounds reasonable."

The prisoner made a show of studying the entire document, or at least pretending to read it, then dipped the pen into the ink. Georgie held her breath.

Papa's will had divided his property equally between his wife and two daughters. To Georgie's mother, he'd left the estate in Lincolnshire. To her sister, Juliet, he'd left the London town house. And to Georgie, his eldest, the one who'd learned the business at his knee, he'd left the fleet of ships with which he'd made his fortune, the warehouses full of spices and silk, and the company ledgers.

His trusted man of business, Edmund Shaw, had done an exemplary job as Georgie's financial guardian for the past few years, but in three weeks' time, she would turn twenty-five and come into full possession of her fortune. And according to English law, as soon as she married, all that would instantly become the property of her husband, to do with as he wished.

That husband would not be Josiah.

Despite her mother's protests that it was vulgar and unladylike to concern herself with commerce, in the past five years Georgie had purchased two new ships and almost doubled her profits. She loved the challenge of running her own business, the independence. She was damned if she'd give it over to some blithering idiot like Josiah to drink and gamble away.

Which was precisely why she'd had Edmund draw up this detailed document. It stated that all property and capital that was hers before the marriage remained hers. Her husband would receive only a discretionary allowance. To date, she'd received seven offers of marriage, and each time she'd sent her suitor to see Mr. Shaw. Every one of them had balked at signing—proof, if she'd needed it, that they'd only been after her fortune.

She let out a relieved sigh as the prisoner's pen moved confidently over the paper. Ben Wylde's signature was surprisingly neat. Perhaps he'd been a secretary, or written dispatches in the army? She shook her head. It wasn't her job to wonder about him. He was a means to an end, that was all.

He straightened, and his brown eyes were filled with a twinkle of devilry. "There, now. Just one further question, before we get to the vows, Miss Caversteed. Just what do you intend for a wedding night?"

Want to read more? Check out This Earl Of Mine on:
Amazon
Barnes & Noble
Kobo
Apple iBooks
Google Play

Printed in Great Britain
by Amazon